LISA ALTHER is the bestselling author of the novels, *Kinflicks*, *Original Sins*, *Other Women,* and *Bedrock*. Born in Tennessee, she now lives in Vermont.

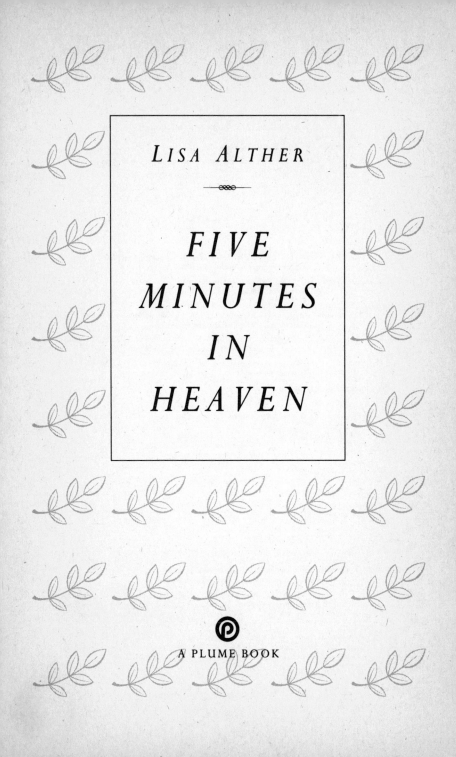

LISA ALTHER

FIVE MINUTES IN HEAVEN

A PLUME BOOK

PLUME
Published by the Penguin Group
Penguin Books USA Inc., 375 Hudson Street, New York, New York 10014, U.S.A.
Penguin Books Ltd, 27 Wrights Lane, London W8 5TZ, England
Penguin Books Australia Ltd, Ringwood, Victoria, Australia
Penguin Books Canada Ltd, 10 Alcorn Avenue, Toronto, Ontario, Canada M4V 3B2
Penguin Books (N.Z.) Ltd, 182–190 Wairau Road, Auckland 10, New Zealand

Penguin Books Ltd, Registered Offices: Harmondsworth, Middlesex, England

Published by Plume, an imprint of Dutton Signet,
a division of Penguin Books USA Inc.
Previously published in a Dutton edition.

First Plume Printing, May, 1996
10 9 8 7 6 5 4 3 2 1

Grateful acknowledgment is made to the following for permission to reprint
from previously published material:

Frank Music Corporation: Excerpt from "Unchained Melody," lyrics by Hy Zaret, music by Alex North.
© 1955 (renewed) Frank Music Corp. All rights reserved.

Gold Hill Music, Inc.: Excerpt from "Love the One You're With" by Stephen Stills. © 1970 Gold Hill Music,
Inc. (ASCAP). All rights administered by this music corporation for the world. All rights reserved
internationally. © secured. Used by permission.

Irving Music, Inc.: Excerpt from "Somebody to Love" by Darby Slick. © 1969 Irving Music, Inc. (BMI).
All rights reserved internationally. © secured. Used by permission.

Satsuma Music and Becky Hobbs Music: Excerpt from "You Wanna Be Loved" by Lewis Anderson and Becky
Hobbs. © 1976 Satsuma Music and Becky Hobbs Music. All rights reserved.

Webster Music Co.: Excerpt from "Twelfth of Never" by Paul F. Webster. © Webster Music Co.
All rights reserved.

 REGISTERED TRADEMARK—MARCA REGISTRADA

The Library of Congress has catalogued the Dutton edition as follows:
Alther, Lisa.
Five minutes in heaven / Lisa Alther.
p.   cm.
ISBN 0-525-93893-1 (hc.)
ISBN 0-452-27613-6 (pbk.)
I. Title.
PS3551.L78F58   1995
813'.54—dc20   94–39252
CIP

Printed in the United States of America

For Jody,
Scout,
and Dill

The only victory in love is flight.
—NAPOLÉON

PROLOGUE

CHAPTER
1

TWO MEN LIFTED A GOAT, hooves wrapped with rope, from the trunk of a blue sedan. As they carried him across the tiled courtyard below, his bearded mouth fell open and he began to pant, eyes rolling wildly.

The French would eat anything that couldn't outrun them, Jude reflected, recalling the weekend market, on rue Mouffetard, near her apartment during her junior year abroad from Vanderbilt. It had featured rows of glistening kidneys, livers, hearts, and tongues in graduated sizes. An entire aviary of birds had hung by their wrung necks, feathered wings limp by their sides. Rabbits still bearing fur had been slit down their bellies and laid open for inspection. But as Simon once said of his fellow Englishmen, no nation that loves animals will ever have a great cuisine.

Jude lit a cigarette and sank into a cushioned wicker chair in the sunlight coming through the glass doors of her sixth-floor walk-up. Still, Paris had a lot going for it. For one thing, it wasn't New York. And having spent the past several months spooning crushed Popsicles into Anna's mouth in her hospital bed at the Roosevelt, she welcomed the change.

It had all begun that night on Simon's deck near Provincetown when the wind shifted to the north, swirling the sand and frothing the surf. Anna had just died. Jude had spent the afternoon pacing the beach, studying how the hue of the sea altered in response to the sky, just as Anna's eyes had altered according to her moods and her surroundings.

When Jude got tired of walking, she scrambled up a dune, scooped out a hollow in the sand, and lay facedown, fitting her frame into its yielding contours as though it were Anna's body. She lay like that for several hours, eyes shut, hands beneath her thighs, listening to the breakers crash, and the foam hiss on the damp sand, and the seagulls shriek, and the dune grasses clash like a knife fight. And remembering the time she and Anna sneaked away from a conference in Boston to race horses down the beach, pounding through the surf, then sliding off their backs to watch from atop a dune as gleaming black whales dove and spouted against the far horizon.

As the sky turned to gore, she wandered home to Simon's tactful chatter and fortifying supper of roast chicken and mashed potatoes. They spread the dishes across the outside table and sat facing the darkening sea. As the tepid night air stirred Simon's black curls, they reminisced about Sandy and his operas, Anna and her poems, the delights of love, and the longing that won't quit when it's taken away.

Then Jasmine arrived, wearing a turban and gold ear hoops, en route to Paris. She strode across the deck, trailed by three young assistants, two women and a man, each dressed in gleaming white trousers and Mondrian tops, as though about to board a yacht at

Cannes. Jasmine was wearing a batik lavalava that made her resemble one of the exquisitely petite stewardesses on Singapore Airlines during Jude's interminable flight to Australia a few months earlier to speak on a panel about feminist editing at the Adelaide Festival.

While Jude subdued her urge to grab a beach towel from the railing and cover up her dingy gray gym shorts and Whale Watch T-shirt, Simon and Jasmine pressed alternate cheeks several times and gazed into each other's eyes as though they had only ten minutes left to live. Jasmine's father had fought with the French Resistance, and Simon's father had been his liaison officer at British intelligence. After the war, their families had visited back and forth across the Channel, and now Simon and Jasmine sold each other translation rights to their respective firms' books. Jude had first met Jasmine with Simon at the Frankfurt Book Fair. Since then, she'd run into her at the American Booksellers Association in Atlanta and the Feminist Book Fair in London and had spoken on a panel with her in Adelaide. She admired Jasmine's accessories, to say nothing of her intelligence and her élan.

Everyone sat down around Simon's glass-topped table to drink the Veuve Clicquot Jasmine had brought and to nibble Godiva chocolates. Alternating between Jasmine's basic English and Jude's and Simon's basic French, they discussed the Frenchwoman's gift for accessorizing, whether it was innate or acquired. Jude described her own bafflement when faced with a scarf. How did Jasmine know what size to pick for which location? Did French mothers give their daughters knot-tying lessons? And what about shoes? Jude had never seen Jasmine wear the same pair twice. Either their color matched or complemented her clothing, or they had some arresting feature like silver heels or straps that crisscrossed her ankles. At that moment, she was wearing golden stack-heeled sandals with thongs between the toes.

"Look at me," demanded Jude, holding up her sandy bare feet with their unpainted toenails. "I'm even underdressed tonight."

"But my dear Jude," said Jasmine, watching her with dark liquid eyes like melted chocolate chips, "you are famous for that. It is your trademark."

Jude blinked. "It is?" Her goal had always been to dress so appropriately as to pass unnoticed.

"Yes, one admires so deeply your indifference to fashion." Jasmine's gaze appeared ingenuous, but her eyes wrinkled slightly at the corners with a certain ironic amusement.

Simon was struggling to hide a smile.

"Thank you," said Jude uncertainly.

The soft sea breeze had mounted to a moaning gale, and the beach towels on the railing were whipping and snapping like flags in a windstorm. They moved inside. As Simon built a fire in his fieldstone fireplace, Jude showed the others through the house, with its walls of glass looking out on the dunes and its giant hand-hewn beams from an old barn in Vermont. The guests seemed a bit embarrassed as they peered into Simon's bathroom with its giant whirlpool tub, reminding Jude that house tours were an American phenomenon.

As Jasmine and her entourage were about to depart in a fog of Eau de Quelquechose for their guest house in Provincetown, she rested her magenta fingertips on Jude's forearm and offered her a job in Paris picking foreign fiction for translation. Jude was too bewildered to reply.

"So what do you think about my going to Paris?" Jude asked Simon as they propped their feet up on the fireplace ledge to commence a postmortem. The orange flames were dancing in Simon's neon-green eyes, converting the irises into small flaring kaleidoscopes.

"Go, Jude," said Simon as he munched a mousse-filled chocolate seashell. "Simon says go. But leave your corpse collection at home. Life is for the living."

This seemed generous of him, since Jude had been living with him and working for him in Manhattan for over a decade. But maybe he was as sick of her grief over Anna as she was.

"What was that nasty crack concerning my wardrobe all about?" she asked.

Simon smiled. "It means she likes you."

Jude gave an astonished laugh.

"If people bore her, she ignores them. When they intrigue her, she provokes them. Like a cat toying with a mouse."

"Charming. And exactly why is it you think I should work foi her?"

"A change of venue would do you good. Some new faces and new neuroses might take your mind off the old ones."

IN ANY CASE, here she was now, trapped in the middle of a Kodachrome postcard, the city spread out below her from the dark highrises of La Défense to the domed Panthéon, the Seine snaking through the center, side-winding past the feet of the Eiffel Tower. Despite her year here during college, she'd never before seen this astonishing view, having passed her days in dusty classrooms on the Left Bank listening to lectures on European history and continental philosophy, and her nights in movie theaters working on her fluency.

In his letters to her mother during the war, which Jude had perused as a child, her father had described seeing this panorama from the square before Sacré Coeur. He had also described being driven by his sergeant through the streets of Pigalle, at the base of the butte where Jude now sat. He had been in the grip of pneumonia, lost and feverish and searching for a hospital. Gaunt women and children clamored around the jeep when his driver stopped to ask for directions. A young woman bared her breast and held it out to them in the icy wind. An urchin perched on the running board and began to scrub their combat boots with a filthy rag. Jude's father handed them all his francs and cigarettes before desperately speeding away.

The sun was hot. Sweat popping out at her hairline, Jude stubbed out her cigarette and threw open the glass doors, shivering in the breeze that was stirring the creamy chestnut blossoms below. She plopped back down in her chair.

On the horizon, the Smokies formed a rolling blue rim notched with kno`` like the knuckles on a fist. Down in the valley, the lazy ocher river drifted toward the mountains, carrying a leafy poplar branch on which perched five cawing crows. Wisps of cloud were floating across the summer sky, furling like breaking waves. Gradually, they assembled themselves into Molly's features, bits of cerulean becoming her irises. She said in her voice that had always been too husky for such a small person, "You may think I'm dead, Jude, but I'm not."

Jude jerked alert. Molly's features were still there, projected against the silver-blue haze above the Bois de Boulogne. Apparently, Jude couldn't escape her, even by crossing the ocean two decades later.

"Fine," snapped Jude. "But where the hell are you?"

As Molly's face evaporated, Jude groped for another cigarette.

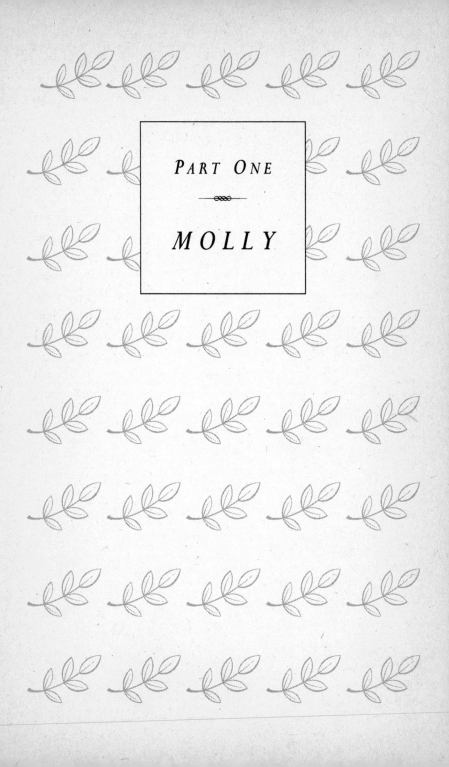

PART ONE

MOLLY

CHAPTER

2

JUDE PEDALED NEXT DOOR on her purple tricycle to inspect the new cellar hole. Careening down the mound of orange clay, training wheels spinning, dark braids lashing like reins on a runaway horse, came a bare-chested girl in shorts. Her bicycle flipped halfway down, hurling her headfirst to the bottom. She jumped up, laughing, chest and cheek streaked with clay like Indian war paint. Righting her bicycle, she stroked its saddle, murmuring, "Easy, boy. It's okay."

"Are you all right?" asked Jude. She had never met another girl who didn't wear a shirt. Her chest was really tan, too, as though she never wore one. Whereas Jude had pale patches from the top her father made her wear at the golf club pool.

"This is my stallion," she replied. "I call him Stormy because he runs like the wind. What's yours called?"

Looking down at her tricycle, Jude said, "I don't know really."

She felt embarrassed that she'd never thought of her tricycle as a horse. She could hear Ace Kilgore barking commands to the Commie Killers in the field across the street. They all rode bicycles, too, making them rear up on their hind wheels to mount curbs. Ace could even balance like that and then twirl around in midair and race off in the opposite direction. Jude was the only kid in the neighborhood who still rode a tricycle. But her father had promised her a bicycle with training wheels for her upcoming birthday.

A blond woman in a sundress covered with flowers the color of tangerine peels appeared from behind the mound, long skirt swaying as she picked her way across the clay in high-heeled white sandals. "My gracious, Molly, what have you done to yourself now?" Taking a flimsy handkerchief with eyelet edges from her white handbag, she dabbed at the clay on Molly's cheek. "Goodness gracious, what am I going to do with my wild child?"

Molly shoved her hand away. "Momma, don't be such a worrywart."

Molly's mother smiled at Jude. "Well, hello there. You must be our new neighbor?"

"What's your name?" asked Molly, leaning over to pick at a scab on her kneecap.

"Jude." A screen door slammed down the block, and Jude could hear ice cubes clinking in glasses on someone's back porch.

"That's a nice name," said Molly's mother. "I'm Mrs. Elkins and this is Molly."

"How do you do, Mrs. Elkins," said Jude, as her father had just taught her.

Molly was watching a white mare's tail flick a far-off mountaintop. The rubber band had broken on one of her braids, which was slowly unplaiting like blacksnakes coming out of hibernation in the spring.

Mrs. Elkins smiled. "Well, my goodness, Jude, aren't you polite, now. I can see you're going to be a good influence on Molly."

Molly's blue eyes narrowed and shifted to gray.

Back home, Jude stood on a chair before the bathroom mirror, wiping at her cheek with a Kleenex and saying in a sugary voice, "Goodness gracious, what am I going to do with my wild child?" Then she pushed the hand away with her other hand, saying, "Oh, Momma, don't be such a worrywart."

"What you doing, Miss Judith?" called Clementine from the kitchen.

"Nothing. Playing." She wondered if Clementine could be persuaded to wipe her cheek with a Kleenex. Probably not. She skipped into the kitchen, where Clementine sat humming "Take Time to Be Holy" and snapping beans for supper. Jude tried to climb onto her aproned lap, but she straightened her legs so that Jude slid down them to the linoleum. She lay there tracing with a finger the grouting between the fake red bricks. "You love me best, don't you, Clementine?"

"I likes you, Miss Judith. But I got childrens all my own what needs me to love them best."

"But so do I."

Clementine had rolled her stockings to just below her knees. A ladder like a tiny cat's cradle ran down one calf and disappeared into her giant white oxford. She said her mother had called her Clementine because of her feet, huge even when she was a baby. Sometimes she sang Jude the song for which she'd been named: "Light she was, and like a fairy/And her shoes were number nine./Wearing boxes without topses,/Sandals were for Clementine."

"You got your daddy to love you best."

"But he doesn't. He loves Momma best. But she doesn't love him best, or else she wouldn't have gone away."

Clementine paused in midsnap to look at Jude stretched out on the linoleum. "Sugar, I done told you that the good Lord took your momma home two years ago."

"But where is she? Where's His house at?"

"In heaven with the angels."

"Well, I wish He'd take me there, too."

"Hush now, honey. That ain't for me and you to say. The good Lord takes us when He wants us and where He wants us."

"How come?" Jude stood up and draped her arm across Clementine's shoulders, one skinny leg straight and the other bent, a flamingo in a red linoleum marsh. Sniffing, she picked up Clementine's familiar scent of furniture polish, snuff, and the vanilla extract she dabbed behind her ears when her husband was about to pick her up.

Clementine glanced at her. "Sugar, go put you on a shirt, why don't you? Little girls wear shirts."

"I don't want to be a girl." With her fingertip, Jude touched a tiny silver curl, like a spring from a broken watch, which was peeking out from beneath the red bandanna Clementine tied around her head like a knitted winter cap.

"But that's what the good Lord made you. It ain't no choice. Just like it ain't no choice if your skin be brown or white."

ONCE JUDE PROVED THAT she could pee standing up, the Commie Killers were forced to accept her as a member, even though she was a girl and the youngest kid in the neighborhood. But fair was fair, and the Commie Killers' mission was to spread justice throughout the land. They consoled themselves with her promise to hide them one at a time in her father's office at her house as he examined patients. You had to lurk outside the door until he went into the bathroom between appointments. Then you slithered across the floor on your belly and slid beneath the huge maroon leather sofa. You could hear him discussing all kinds of interesting things with naked people you later saw walking around town fully clothed. From a certain angle, you could even catch a glimpse of the examining table.

On the day of her initiation, Jude concealed her tricycle in the pine grove by the path to Ace Kilgore's headquarters. Someone dug a cellar hole in the field across the street from Sandy Andrews's house before going bankrupt. Ace and his gang had constructed a network of trenches, bunkers, and tunnels in the abandoned hills of red clay, like an ant colony. Parents tried to prevent their sons from playing with Ace. He threw snowballs with rocks in them at little children. And he tied twine with tin cans on one end to dogs' tails. Once, he and his platoon pushed a junked refrigerator onto the train tracks in the valley, causing the engine to derail. Jude's father said he might get sent to reform school. Every kid in the neighborhood tried to avoid meeting his eyes, which were a dull shoe polish black. If he caught you looking at him, you became the target of an interrogation regarding your secret espionage activities for the Russians.

Nevertheless, every boy in Tidewater Estates sneaked away to Commie Killer meetings except Sandy Andrews, who was a sissy. They made their mothers rip the patches off their fathers' old army uniforms and sew them on their jacket sleeves, and they pinned their fathers' multicolored bars on their chest pockets. Ace had the most because his father had been a hero in the war. Jude made Clementine retrieve her father's olive uniform jacket from the attic. It stank of mothballs, but it sported the requisite bars and patches, which Clementine agreed to stitch onto her jacket if her father gave his permission. Instead, he forbade her to have anything to do with Ace Kilgore.

Jude used to play with the neighborhood girls at Noreen Worth's, but she was tired of diapering dolls with handkerchiefs and rolling around the playhouse floor speaking in tongues. Besides, Noreen, whose father was a Holiness preacher, claimed Jude was a bad

Baptist because at Jude's church people just sat in their pews and kept quiet. She had also played a few times with Clementine's daughters in Riverbend. But all they ever did was jump rope, turning two ropes really fast and chanting things Jude couldn't understand. Whenever Jude tried to jump in, she ended up on the ground, trussed like a calf for branding. She found it hard to believe that these were the children Clementine loved more than herself. So, despite her father's stern injunction, Jude found herself irresistibly drawn to the Commie Killers.

The hideout was dark inside, apart from the light from a white candle stuck in the clay floor. The boys were wearing only Jockey briefs, so Jude hurriedly stripped down to her white cotton panties. Ace passed out several round Quaker Oats boxes and wooden spoons. As some drummed, others danced. Watching from the corner of her eye, Jude copied their writhing, hopping movements, like an Indian war dance. Ace's father's colonel hat with the golden eagle above the brim kept slipping down over his eyes. So excited was Jude finally to be a full-fledged defender of the American Way that she had goose bumps all over her flesh. She thought she could hear a cat yowling from the corner of the cave.

The boys were kneeling in the dirt as Ace leapt from one to another, thrusting his hips against their briefs with sharp jabs while the drummers pounded a syncopated beat. His face was dripping sweat in the candlelight and his licorice eyes gaped like the sockets in the skull on her father's office counter.

Jude got down on her knees, but Ace pushed her over with his foot. "Girls can't do this," he growled in a strange voice. "Men do this."

Then they crouched in a circle around the candle and Ace placed a cherry bomb in his palm. Gravely, he extended it to Jude. She took it. His lieutenant Jerry Crawford, a tall, gawky boy who had smiled shyly at Jude when no one else was looking, carried a cage over from the shadows. Inside was a matted barn cat Jude had seen lurking around the neighborhood. Her eyes were flashing chartreuse. One of her ears had been ripped off during a fight and the tip of her tail bent at a right angle. Several boys put on work gloves, dragged her from the cage, and pinned her against the dirt floor. Jude stroked her forehead with an index finger.

"Don't pet Hiroshima," said Ace. "She's been very bad."

"Why do you call her Hiroshima?" asked Jude.

Ace grinned, white teeth flashing like Chiclets in the shadow cast by the visor of his colonel hat.

"Why has she been bad?"

"She's been stealing my dog's food. But you ask too many questions, little girl. Just shut up and shove that thing up her hole."

Jude looked at the red cherry bomb with the green wick, then at the snarling, struggling cat.

"If you want to be a Commie Killer," said Ace as he struck a match, "you have to do it. And you have to do it now."

As eerie shadows danced on the walls of clay like the flames of Hades, Jude looked at him with horrified comprehension. "No," she whispered. "Don't, Ace. Let her go. Please." She looked to Jerry, who was staring hard at the floor.

"Hurry up! Do it!" ordered the boys as the cat hissed and howled.

Jude scrambled to her feet and ran toward the doorway, clutching the cherry bomb.

"Go bake cookies with that faggot Sandy Andrews!" someone yelled.

"If you tell," called Ace, "we'll hunt you down and do this to you."

Jude stumbled through the maze of trenches, sliding on the slick orange clay. She'd get Clementine. Clementine would make them stop.

She heard a bang. Slipping and falling, she lay for a moment in the sticky mud in her underpants, too stunned to get up.

Pedaling her tricycle fast toward home, she could hardly see the sidewalk through her angry tears. She had saved herself and left the cat to die. She was not a Commie Killer, she was a coward. And if she told, Ace would do that to her next. She couldn't jump rope, and she couldn't speak in tongues. The Commie Killers were not champions of democracy, they were murderers. She would always be alone forever and ever in this horrible place where bullies tortured the weak just for fun. If only she could be safe in heaven with her mother. She stopped pedaling to wipe her wet cheeks with a muddy forearm.

"Don't cry, Jude," said a husky voice beside her. "I'll be your friend."

Jude opened her eyes. Molly was standing there, barefoot, shirtless, smoky eyes troubled, hand on Jude's handlebars.

"You better not," said Jude. "I'm in big trouble. I may be killed."

"I don't care. I'll help you."

As Jude stood in the aisle leading to the altar, the adult choir in their white robes and red cowls were singing "Jesus Loves the Little Children." The dreaded Ace Kilgore was directly in front of her. His brown hair had been furrowed like a plowed field by the teeth of a comb, and he was wearing a red polka-dot necktie. It matched that of his father, who was the usher assigned that morning to lead the children to the Sunday school building.

Ace and his father also had matching black eyes that seemed just to absorb the rainbow light through the stained-glass windows rather than to reflect it as everyone else's eyes did. The other adults tried to avoid Mr. Kilgore's stare just as the kids avoided Ace's. He was always buttonholing Jude's father outside the church, trying to argue about Senator McCarthy. Mr. Kilgore's voice would grow louder and louder and his face more and more red as he described the agents of evil who were infesting the country like vermin.

Spotting Jude in line behind him, Ace leaned back to whisper, "We gonna get you, Goody Two-shoes."

Jude flinched, picturing the cat cowering in the dirt.

Molly, standing beside her, said, "Just shut up, goofball."

Ace looked at her, startled. "Who are *you*?"

"That's for me to know and you to find out."

"Well, we'll get you, too, ugly. And lynch you with those long black braids of yours."

The choir was singing: ". . . red and yellow, black and white, they are precious in His sight. . . ."

"You and what army, cat killer?" asked Molly, whose irises had shifted to a dangerous battle gray.

Ace narrowed his eyes and glared at Jude. "Don't you worry, little lady. The Commie Killers know how to take care of rats, and friends of rats." Grabbing his tie, he pulled it upward, nooselike, mouth lolling open and tongue hanging out.

"Why don't you go eat a vomit sandwich?" suggested Molly as their lines parted before the carpeted steps leading to the altar, on which stood a golden cross with Christ writhing in agony. Jude was impressed by her new friend's courage. No one ever talked like that to the Kilgores.

"MAYBE THERE'S SOME WAY to make a tunnel fall down with the Commie Killers inside it," mused Molly as they sat at a long table coloring pictures of Jesus tending baby lambs.

"I think we should ask Sandy Andrews to help us," said Jude.

"He's a child progeny." She selected a fat ocher crayon for Jesus' hair and beard.

"What's that?"

"He taught himself to read and write when he was four, so they let him skip first and second grade. My dad says he's so smart that they may have to send him away to school. I'm glad I'm not that smart."

"Do you think he'd help girls?"

"Maybe. He doesn't have any friends. He doesn't like to kill things."

"WHY ARE SOME PEOPLE so mean?" Jude asked Clementine, licking chocolate frosting off a beater while the morning sun through the kitchen window turned the red linoleum to orange. When she woke up that morning, her stomach had clenched with dread. The Commie Killers were going to get her. They were going to do to her what they'd done to that cat. Then she remembered her new friend, Molly, who had promised to help her, and she began to feel a faint flicker of hope.

"The good Lord made them that way so the righteous could be tested."

"Like a test at the hospital?"

"Like a test ever day of the year. You gots to be kind to them what treats you cruel." Clementine was spreading the frosting with swirling strokes of her spatula, making chocolate waves.

"How come?"

" 'Cause one fine day they gets ashamed of acting so ugly and they turns to Jesus. And then you wins yourself a golden crown."

Jude studied Clementine, picturing a golden crown atop her red bandanna head cloth. "But what if it's not you they're ugly to? What if they're ugly to something else?"

"What ugliness you seen, Miss Judith?" She paused to study Jude, who was winding her tongue around a beater blade to get at the frosting in back, which was still gritty with sugar.

"Nothing. I'm just wondering."

"A good person will put up with ugliness coming at themselves. But you gots to fight for them what's small and weak." She narrowed her eyes suspiciously at Jude.

To escape her X-ray vision, Jude dropped the beater in the sink and dashed out the kitchen door. Molly was riding Stormy down the sidewalk. She had attached playing cards to the spokes with clothespins to make a whirring sound, and she was wearing sunglasses and a winter cap with earflaps. She landed her airplane on the sidewalk in front of Sandy Andrews's house, elaborate whooshing and sputtering sounds emitting from her mouth.

Sandy was watering the foundation shrubs with a hose. Jude noticed that he was wearing socks and sandals instead of the black high-tops required by the Commie Killers. The shrubs had been clipped into triangles and cubes, like dark green building blocks.

"Hey, Sandy," called Jude from her tricycle, which she'd decided to name Lightning. "This is Molly. She's moved into that new house next door to mine." Molly was hanging her cap by its chin strap from her handlebars.

"Hi," said Sandy, not looking up.

"We're in trouble." Jude dismounted from Lightning. "Will you help us?"

He glanced at her irritably. "How can I say when I don't know what it is?"

"It'd be dangerous for you if we told you."

Sandy put his hand on his skinny hip and said nothing, studying the stream of water from the nozzle, the sun backlighting his blond head and casting a shadow over his face, which was freckled like a permanent case of the measles. He had a cowlick like the thumbprint of a giant to one side of his hair just above his forehead, which gave an interesting lilt to his crew cut.

"Ace might kill you," added Jude.

Sandy looked at her. "That fascist? Just let him try."

"What's a fascist?" asked Molly, tying Stormy to a yew branch by the fringe on his handgrips.

"Never mind. Come up in my tree house, where no one can hear us."

Sandy had never before let Jude visit his tree house. It had a retractable stairway that could be locked, and only Sandy knew the combination. It also turned out to have beige carpeting, a shelf of the *World Book Encyclopedia*, and a shortwave radio with as many dials and switches as Dr. Frankenstein's laboratory. Sandy said he'd built it from a kit. The walls were papered with postcards bearing the call numbers of ham radio operators he'd talked with all over the world. Half a dozen chessboards with games in progress were set up along one wall. A telephone sat on the rug.

"Come over here," said Sandy. He showed them a telescope on a tripod, pointed out the window. Through it, Jude could see right down into the Commie Killer trenches across the street, a grid of red clay gashes and hillocks stretching the length of the field. When Sandy moved the tripod to another window, she could see Mr. Starnes down in the valley, mowing the alfalfa by the river on his ancient wheezing tractor. He was wearing a battered felt hat low over his ears and was spitting tobacco juice from the corner of his mouth. Downriver, his wife was breaking off blossoms in the tobacco patch, the weathered wooden curing shed behind her. And beyond them stretched the mountains, range after range, separated by deep coves and valleys where creeks were flowing and farmers were mowing and a train mounded high with tree trunks and coal chunks was crawling along like a fat, lazy caterpillar.

"But i can't do it myself," concluded Sandy after explaining his plan to the girls, who were sitting cross-legged on the carpet by the phone. "My mother won't let me out of the house after dark."

"Mine won't, either," said Molly, "but I can sneak out."

Jude's father rarely noticed where she was after dark because he was so busy changing dressings on patients in his office, or counseling them on the phone about their sunburns and ingrown toenails, or writing up their records at his desk, or rushing to the emergency room to stitch up their wounds from knife fights and motorcycle wrecks.

"Maybe you can spend the night at my house," said Molly as they climbed down the tree-house ladder, "so we can sneak out together."

As they stepped onto the lawn, Sandy raised the ladder behind them, like the drawbridge of a castle.

While Jude watched from the kitchen doorway, Mr. Starnes, in faded overalls and clay-caked work boots, got out of a rusted red pickup truck and lifted a burlap-wrapped ham from the back. Jude grimaced. Clementine would take slices off it and soak them in water to get the salt out, and Jude and her father would have to eat it with grits and biscuits for the rest of their lives. Mrs. Starnes, wearing a floral housedress and leather oxfords with thin, white socks, carried a foil-wrapped cake. Since Clementine had already gone home to Riverbend for the night, Jude went out on the back porch to greet them.

"My dad's on the phone right now. He'll be out presently."

"My gracious, Jude, haven't you grown up, now!" said Mrs. Starnes. Her hairdo looked as though she'd removed her rollers and forgotten to comb out the hair.

"Yessum."

"I declare, if you don't look just like your daddy," said Mr. Starnes, propping one boot against the bottom porch step.

Jude frowned, preferring to look like her mother, since her father was nearly bald. Mr. Starnes's boot smelled of manure.

"Where's your shirt at tonight, honey?" asked Mrs. Starnes.

Jude shrugged, crossing her arms over her scrawny chest. "It's too hot."

"I'll bet you a dime you won't run around without no shirt in a few years here," chuckled Mr. Starnes. His eyes were as washed-out as his overalls, like clear cat's-eye marbles.

It had rained at the end of the afternoon, forked tongues of lightning striking the distant mountaintops as though the sky were a lake swarming with angry cottonmouths. Then, as the sun shone through a gap in the banks of black clouds, a rainbow had appeared, arcing across the river right down into Mr. Starnes's tobacco shed. At Sunday school, the preacher said a rainbow was God's proof that, even after trying to drown everybody for being so wicked, He forgave them. Sometimes God acted like a big baby.

But now the sky had cleared and the sun had set, turning the faraway mountains the color of grape jelly. Bullfrogs had started to croak in the reeds along the riverbank and fireflies were flickering like birthday candles among the leafy branches of the sweet gums in the valley below.

"That daddy of yours," said Mrs. Starnes, "we think he's pretty special."

"Yessum," said Jude. Now she'd have to hear about each stitch her father and grandfather had sewn in these people's mutilated bodies, each ancestor whose life they'd saved by operating by lantern light with a carving knife on a kitchen table in a remote mountain cabin during a thunderstorm, after a journey across a swollen creek on horseback in the middle of a midwinter night.

"Yessir," said Mr. Starnes, "I recollect the day my paw lost his arm in the combine. . . ."

Jude's father appeared in the doorway in his usual white dress shirt, open at the throat, sleeves rolled to the elbows. Sighing with relief, Jude picked up the foil cake from the porch floor. "Thank you, Mrs. Starnes. My daddy and me loves your cakes." Sniffing the foil, she detected caramel frosting, her favorite.

Her father looked at her with a raised eyebrow to indicate that she'd made a grammar mistake. As she carried the cake into the kitchen and cut herself a large slice, she tried to figure out what it was. Shrugging, she went into the back hall, where she'd been playing Ocean Liner, which Molly had taught her that afternoon. They'd pasted numbers on all the doors for cabins. Striding down the hallway munching her cake, she lurched from side to side on her peg leg. A storm was brewing in the nor'west and it was time to batten down the hatches, whatever they might be. She steadied herself with her free hand against the cases that held her father's arrowhead collection. On his days off, they drove the jeep down into the valley and dug up the moist black silt by the river. As they sifted the soil, he told her about the people who had lived in the valley long ago—the Mound Builders, the Hopewells, the Copena, the Cherokees, each tribe replacing the previous one, all the way back to the dawn of time, when the valley had formed the floor of an inland ocean full of bizarre sea creatures. When the ocean dried up, the Great Buzzard swooped down from heaven to scoop out the mountain coves with its wing tips.

The arrowheads and grinding stones had been made by the Nunnehi, the Cherokee Immortals, Jude's ancestors who lived underneath the mountains and at the bottom of the river and who came to help their descendants when they were in trouble. In autumn, when the whining winds from the north whirled the leaves off the trees, you could sometimes hear them murmuring to one another in the Wildwoods. And in the summer when you cast your line into the river for fish, if it got snagged, you knew the Nunnehi had grabbed it just to remind you that they were always there. And sometimes when the water was really calm and the breeze stirred tiny corduroy ripples across its surface, you could catch a glimpse of the roofs of their houses on the river floor.

As the Starnes's truck pulled away, Jude's father took her sticky hand to lead her into the den, unaware that the swells were running high and their ship was about to capsize. "My daddy and *I love* your cakes," he said. After turning on the radio, he sank into his brown leather armchair. John Cameron Swayze was talking about soldiers being brainwashed by the Communists in Korea. "Oh, Lord," her father said with a sigh. "Poor, suffering humanity."

"Why do they always bring us those awful hams?" asked Jude.

"That's how they're paying me for Mr. Starnes's appendectomy."

"Money would be nicer." She stroked the back of his chair. The leather was crazed with age cracks like the inside of an ice cube.

"No doubt. But they don't have any. Besides, some people consider country ham a delicacy."

"Not me."

"Yes, I know." He smiled.

"Daddy, why are some people so mean?" Jude straddled the arm of his chair, facing the back. It was her new horse, named Wild Child. The other arm was Molly's, which she'd named Blaze. That afternoon, they had been lassoing Molly's boxer, Sidney, in midgallop with pieces of Clementine's clothesline. Time after time, they played

"Git Along, Little Dogie" on the record player—until Clementine marched in and turned it off, announcing, "Miss Judith, if I hear 'yippy tie yay, tie yo' one more time, I gonna bust all your daddy's furniture into firewood and chase y'all round the backyard with a carving knife." Impressed, the girls had switched to Ocean Liner.

"Well, I guess they're mean because they're unhappy."

"But you're unhappy, and you're not mean."

He looked at her. "What makes you think I'm unhappy, baby?"

"Because you miss Momma."

He frowned and lowered his head. "That's true. But I used to be happy when she was here. Maybe that's the difference. People who've never been happy are mean. The rest of us are just sad."

She could smell his aftershave lotion, like cinnamon toast. Leaning over, she licked his cheek. The stiff hairs prickled her tongue and the cinnamon lotion tasted disappointingly bitter, canceling out the sweetness of the caramel frosting.

"Don't, Jude," he said, frowning and wiping his cheek with his hand. "That tickles."

Wrinkling her nose, Jude tried to scrub the terrible taste off her tongue with the back of her hand. Then Wild Child reared, hurling her off his back and into her father's lap. Leaning her head against his chest, she shoved a thumb into her mouth and felt his heart thudding against her cheek like a frog's throat.

"Baby, don't suck your thumb, please. It'll push your front teeth out. You'll look like Bugs Bunny."

Jude giggled.

"Don't you think you should wear a shirt?" he asked. "You're getting to be a big girl now." He patted her pale smooth belly.

"I don't want to be a girl."

"How come?"

"Girls are too boring."

"So you want to be a boy?"

"No. Boys are too scary."

"Well, what do you want to be, then?"

"I want to be in heaven with my momma."

He said nothing. When Jude looked up, his eyes were wet and red.

"I have a friend," offered Jude. "She lives in the new house next door. She's named Molly. She's going to be in the second grade. She doesn't like shirts, either."

"That's good, baby. I'm glad there's someone in the neighborhood now who's closer to your own age. I don't want you playing with Ace Kilgore and those other big boys. They're too rough. Promise me you'll stay away from them?"

Jude said nothing for a long moment. She didn't like to lie. But she wasn't really lying, since she now meant to stay as far away from them as she could. "I promise," she finally said. "Can I spend the night at Molly's house sometime?" She twisted around in the chair until she was reclining in the crook of his arm.

"Sure. If it's okay with her parents." He was gazing at a photo on the end table—of Jude's mother in a low-cut gown, standing inside a wine bottle.

"Why's she inside that bottle?"

"She wasn't really. It's trick photography. It was an ad for a winery."

"She was pretty, wasn't she?"

"She was the most beautiful woman I've ever seen." He was looking at the far corner of the ceiling, where Clementine's dust mop had missed a spiderweb. "I was an intern in New York. I first saw her surrounded by photographers on a corner near Central Park. She was wearing this big old picture hat the wind kept trying to blow off.

I just stood there staring at her until she got annoyed and asked them to make me leave.''

Mr. Starnes had said Jude looked like her father. Did that mean she wasn't beautiful like her mother? ''Why did she have to die?''

''Well, I came back home from the war in France, and we were very happy to be together again. So we decided to give you a baby brother. But your mother's brain started bleeding. She became unconscious and the baby died in her stomach. And then she died.''

''But I didn't even want a baby brother.''

MOLLY'S MOTHER INSISTED THAT Molly say her prayers, even though Jude was there, so the three of them knelt by Molly's bedside, beneath the pink dotted swiss canopy, as Molly recited her blessing list, which included her bicycle, Stormy, and her dog, Sidney. She concluded, ''And God bless my new pal, Jude, and keep her safe from harm. Amen.''

''Do you want to say your prayers now?'' Mrs. Elkins asked Jude.

''I don't have any.''

''But you need prayers, Jude. It's easy. Just try.''

So Jude mumbled, ''God bless my dad, and Clementine. And Grandma. And my momma in heaven. And Mrs. Elkins. And God bless my new pal, Molly, and keep her safe. But not Ace Kilgore. Amen.''

Mrs. Elkins looked at Jude questioningly as she smoothed her blond pageboy with one hand. But then she just stood up and folded back the bedspread. ''Good night, sleep tight, and don't let those old mosquitoes bite!'' she called as she closed the door.

Molly and Jude scrambled up on the bed. Each grabbed a pillow. Every time Sidney tried to crawl onto the mattress, they beat him back with the pillows. The bed was a raft, adrift on an ocean full of ravenous sharks with flashing white teeth. Sidney crouched down on his front paws, cropped tail wagging frantically. He began to bark.

"Oh, shut up, Sidney," muttered Molly, dropping her pillow. "Sharks don't bark." She collapsed with a bounce on the mangled sheets.

Sidney crept up the bed and slithered between Molly and Jude, where he lay panting dolefully in time to the pulsing locusts outside. Molly's father had started snoring down the hall, like a monster growling in a cave. He looked like a monster, too, with dark, curly hair all over his arms and eyebrows that stuck straight out like the bristles of a toothbrush. Molly said he drove around to farms buying cowhides that got cut up and turned into belts at the tannery Sandy Andrews's father owned.

Molly went downstairs to the kitchen, wearing only her shorty pajama bottoms. When she returned, carrying two bowls, she paused for a moment, framed by the doorway, bare chest tanned and smooth except for two pink nipples like cinnamon valentine hearts. Her black hair, which Jude had never seen unbraided before, was floating around her face the way Jude's mother's hair did in a photo on Jude's bedside table. In that photo, she held Jude's chubby cheek against her own on Jude's first birthday. She had a white rose in her hair, perfect white teeth, and pale dreamy eyes.

"Why are you staring at me like that?" asked Molly when she reached the bed and handed Jude a bowl of raspberry sherbet.

"I didn't realize you were beautiful," replied Jude.

"I am not," said Molly, eyes blazing in the faint glow coming through the window from the streetlight. "If you want to be my friend, take it back right now."

Crossing her fingers, Jude said, "Okay, I take it back."

Leaning against the quilted headboard, they licked the tart sherbet off their spoons in a strained silence.

"Do you like God?" Jude finally asked.

"Sure. He's okay." Molly offered her spoon to Sidney, who daintily poked at the sherbet with his large pink tongue.

"I don't."

"How come?"

"He took my mother to His house. She wants to come back home now, but He won't let her."

Molly set her bowl on the bed for Sidney to finish. "Well, I guess I don't like Him anymore, either, then."

Jude decided that Molly was her new best friend.

Once the lights were off in all the houses down the street, they pulled on their shorts and tiptoed down the carpeted stairs and out the front door. The locusts were so loud that they seemed to be gathered inside Jude's head. Swarms of fireflies were making the star-specked night sky sparkle like a black diamond. Jude and Molly trotted across the straw-strewn lawn, the dew chilly on their bare feet, Sidney at their heels.

At Sandy's house, they found the hose coiled behind the foundation shrubs as Sandy had promised. Dragging it across the street, they stuck the nozzle into a Commie Killer trench. Then they recrossed the street and turned on the faucet that protruded from the foundation bricks.

Crouched behind the geometrical yews, ducking a circling mosquito, Jude asked, "Why do you think Ace is so mean?"

"Momma says people are mean because they get up on the wrong side of bed in the morning," said Molly, arm draped across the panting Sidney.

Jude broke a piece off the tall triangular bush beside her and sniffed it. It smelled like the golden liquid Clementine mopped the kitchen linoleum with. She held it out for Molly to sniff. A hoot owl started calling in the Wildwoods.

Every time sleep threatened, one poked the other with an elbow and they gazed blearily at the constellations scrolling past overhead. Jude pointed out the Pleiades and told about how the Cherokees used to make would-be braves count the number of stars in the cluster. They discussed the difficulties of needing glasses before glasses had been invented. Then Molly explained that stars were actually light shining through holes in the night sky. Behind the black, everything was white.

"Maybe that's where your mother is," said Molly. "Behind the sky."

"Is that really true?" Jude asked. "Or did you make it up?"

"I can't remember."

At the first hint of dove gray in the eastern sky, as a pale silver sliver of crescent moon arced above the headstones in the cemetery on the hilltop, they turned off the faucet and dragged the hose into Sandy's parents' toolshed.

"VERY FUNNY," SAID ACE as the two girls pedaled past the abandoned construction site the next morning, purple circles under their eyes like bruises.

"What?" asked Molly.

"That." Ace pointed to the sea of orange mud where the Commie Killer headquarters had been.

"What happened?" asked Molly, blinking her baby blue eyes.

Jude chewed the inside of her lower lip to keep from grinning.

"You tell me, pukeface."

"Did it rain again last night?" asked Jude.

"Tell your parents to start saving for your funerals," said Ace, gazing at them through his opaque black eyes like Sergeant Friday on "Dragnet."

———————

Jude pedaled lightning to her grandmother's large white brick house on the next block to welcome her home from her trip to Savannah for a Daughters of the Confederacy convention. "I told your granddaddy," she once explained to Jude, "if he expected me to leave behind my beautiful colonial Virginia, he'd have to build me a new dwelling place. I wasn't gonna live out my life in his hillbilly shack." After constructing his bride's neo-Georgian mansion and leasing the farmland in the valley to Mr. Starnes, Jude's grandfather sold off the rest of his family farm for house lots and a golf course. Her grandmother named the resulting development Tidewater Estates. Jude and her father now lived in the "hillbilly shack," a rambling house of chinked logs built by Jude's great-grandfather, a half-Cherokee herb doctor.

Jude remembered removing the knitted mitt from her grandfather's three wood so that he could tee up in his backyard and drive his golf ball across the river to the first green of the golf course, whose fairways scaled the foothills like a grassy roller-coaster track. Then he descended the cliff to the river's edge, put his golf bag in a boat, and rowed across the water to continue his game. Having been a left-handed bush league baseball pitcher before his conversion to medicine, he had a golf swing that was the envy of the county.

Following her husband's death the previous year, Jude's grandmother circled the globe twice on the *Queen Elizabeth*, sending Jude postcards and dolls from each country. Jude steamed the stamps off the cards and saved them in an album. And she removed the elaborate national costumes from the dolls to amputate limbs and extract organs. Then she stitched the incisions with needles Clementine threaded for her, as she had watched her father do when she went with him on house calls to hill farms.

Jude mounted the brick steps, white columns on either hand. Standing on tiptoe, she lifted the knocker hanging from the teeth of a huge golden lion head. A row of shiny cars waited by the curb, so her grandmother was probably having a club meeting. She went to one almost every day she was off the high seas—bridge club, garden club, Junior League, Bible study group, DAR. What Jude liked best about her grandmother was how glad she always seemed to see Jude. If you interrupted most adults when they were with other adults, they looked at you as though you were a skunk wandering in from the woods.

An unfamiliar young woman in a starched white uniform and ruffled black apron answered the door. "I reckon you be Miss Judith?" Her front teeth were gapped like a derelict picket fence.

Jude nodded. Her grandmother always hired farm girls from the part of Virginia where she herself had grown up. Her father had been chief of staff at the Confederate Veterans' Home on the outskirts of Richmond. They had lived on her mother's family farm on the Rappahannock River near Fredericksburg, which had supposedly been a land grant to her forebears from King James I for their agreeing to leave England. Jude's grandfather, descending like the Troll King from the misty mountains to the west, had done his residency at the Veterans' Home, wooing and winning the boss's daughter in the process.

"Your grandmaw, she's having her a Virginia Club meeting this morning," the girl said. Accustomed to chopping tobacco and herding cows on hillside pastures, the maids usually found Jude's grandmother's recipe for gracious living as incomprehensible as Jude did. They rarely lasted longer than a few months.

Through the hall archway, Jude could see women in pastel summer suits and flowered hats seated around card tables covered with embroidered linen cloths, eating chicken à la king from flaky pastry shells with her grandmother's Francis I forks, which had silver fruit all over the handles. Her grandmother always insisted this silverware would be Jude's when she died, but Jude didn't even know how to cook. When she grew up, she planned to go for dinner every night to the Wiggly Piglet Barbecue Pit on the Knoxville Highway, where waitresses in short shorts, cowboy boots and hats, and lariat-string ties took your order at your car window.

Sandy Andrews's mother was saying, "But you know, I think I like Tennessee almost as much as I do Virginia."

Jude's grandmother answered, "Yes, but I believe you get a better class of people in Virginia, don't you, Mavis?"

Fortunately, Jude's grandmother had insisted that Jude's father drive her mother across the state line to a Virginia hospital when she went into labor with Jude—so Jude would be able to attend these meetings when she grew up.

Her grandmother spotted Jude in the doorway. "Why, hey there, darling!" She stood up and strode over on spike heels so high that she looked like a toe dancer. Her silk suit was the color of a robin's egg, and the skirt just barely covered her kneecaps. Her hair was also blue, and at her throat was the pearl necklace she wanted Jude to have when she died. In the center were big creamy-pink pearls separated by tiny knots, and the pearls got smaller and smaller toward the ends. The necklace was very pretty, but Jude wished her grand-mother wouldn't always talk about dying. When she bought a silver Cadillac in the spring, she'd said to Jude, "This will be the last car I'll ever buy on God's green earth." (Apparently, she thought she might buy another in heaven.) And each time Jude saw her now, she said, "Honey, this may be the last time you ever see me alive, so take a good long look."

"Evelyn, go get my little Virginia granddaughter a Popsicle," said her grandmother. As Evelyn headed toward the kitchen, she whis-pered, "Honey, where's your shirt at today? Virginia girls always wear shirts."

Evelyn returned, thrusting a cardboard box of Popsicles at Jude.

Her grandmother said, "Now, Evelyn, I've taught you better than that. Remember, you're in high society now."

Evelyn stomped back to the kitchen and returned with a monogrammed silver tray holding several Popsicles.

Jude took a cherry one, saying, "Thank you, ma'am."

Her grandmother murmured, "Darling, you don't need to say 'ma'am' to the servants."

LICKING HER RED POPSICLE, Jude pedaled to the cemetery at the end of the block. She wished her grandmother would stay home more often. When she was gone, Jude tried to avoid going past her big, empty house because it made her feel sad and lonely. What if one day it really was the last time Jude saw her alive, as had already happened with her mother and her grandfather?

Walking across the field to the wrought-iron gate, Jude stooped to pick clover blossoms, until she had two bouquets. To one side were the graves of soldiers killed in the War Between the States and of pioneer mothers who had died having babies. Sometimes their babies were buried beside them with toy headstones. Some of the graves had sunk in the middle when the wooden coffins rotted, and several stones had broken off or fallen over.

Jude placed a bouquet by her grandfather's headstone, a shiny, red granite obelisque that read: "A savior in life, with his Savior in death." He had had kind hazel eyes behind thick lenses in wire-frame glasses that perched like a giant insect on his aquiline nose, funny earlobes that hung down like a bloodhound's jowls, and a cute little double chin that puffed out like a bullfrog's throat when he laughed. Her grandmother said he had spent hours holding Jude over his head playing Flying Baby while Jude's father operated on soldiers in the belly of a troop ship in the mid-Atlantic, with torpedos plowing past and alarms screaming overhead.

Jude remembered sitting on his lap on his screened back porch, watching the Holston drift toward the Smokies. He told stories in his soft mountain drawl about cutting off men's arms and legs in a big tent by a river in Belgium. About a pit like a buried silo, full of German prisoners. About climbing down into it on a ladder, with a big red cross on his chest so they wouldn't hurt him. About a muddy field honeycombed with foxholes, where dead trees poked up like broken toothpicks. About tangles of rusted barbed wire that looked like a blackberry patch in the autumn. About men in metal helmets hanging from the wire, screaming while huge birds swooped down to tear at their wounds with sharp beaks and claws.

Jude's grandmother had come out of the house to ask, "Charles, do you really think it's a good idea to tell this child your horrible war stories?"

He looked up at her through his thick lenses. "She needs to know what she's up against. I wish I had known. All the soldiers at your daddy's hospital told me what an honor it had been to lose their limbs for the South. So I thought I was going to march in a uniform and be a hero."

"Jude's a girl, dear, not a boy."

"She's a human being. We're all in this mess together. That's the only thing that makes it bearable."

For a moment, he looked as if he was going to cry. Jude's grandmother reached for his hand, as small and supple as a woman's, with which he had hurled an unhittable curveball, with which he could chip and putt like a professional golfer, with which he could operate by feel in otherwise-inaccessible sites. As she stroked and kissed it, he began to look less miserable. Then she returned to the kitchen to work on her file box of secret family recipes, which had gotten her elected president of the Virginia Club. She claimed the South Carolina

Club had nothing to equal her Brunswick stew, which she'd adapted to modern times by replacing the squirrel meat with beef.

"Did you ever shoot people?" Jude asked her grandfather, standing up in his lap and patting his cheeks with both hands to cheer him up.

"No. My job was to patch up the ones who got shot, so they could go back to their trenches and kill some more Germans."

"But why?" asked Jude. She studied one of his cheeks carefully. Tiny hairs were sticking out of it like dark blue splinters. She wondered if they hurt him.

Her grandfather shrugged. "Most people are scared as treed coons, and scared people turn nasty."

"Scared of what?"

"Scared of living. Scared of loving. Scared of losing. Scared of dying. Scared."

"Are you scared?"

"Sometimes."

"Not me. I'll never be scared," said Jude, not yet having met Ace Kilgore.

"Not if I can help it, honey," he murmured, kissing her frown lines.

SQUATTING BY HER MOTHER'S GRAVE, Jude placed the second bouquet on the edge of her stone, a simple rectangle of cream-colored marble with forked green veins that branched across it like lightning. Her inscription read: "At Rest at Last in the Arms of the Lord." One day her mother was in the kitchen at home, baking butterscotch brownies and wearing a bulging apron covered with pink roses. The next day she was asleep in a white hospital bed and wouldn't wake up, even when Jude sang "Rise, Shine, Give God His Glory" right in her ear. And the day after that, she was here in this mound, being kept warm by a blanket of beautiful white flowers that smelled like her favorite perfume. And Jude's grandmother from New York City was weeping silently by the grave with a dead fox draped around her neck. It had tiny claws and glittery orange eyes. Her husband, Jude's other grandfather, who wore a gangster hat low over his eyes, kept wiping the orange clay off his shiny black shoes with a white handkerchief.

In a low voice, Jude began to tell her mother about Ace and the cat. When she got to the cherry bomb, she heard rustling among the dried milkweeds left over from winter. Looking up, she saw the Commie Killers in army fatigues and face masks, crawling on knees and elbows like evil insects, rifles cradled in their arms.

Jumping up, she looked all around.

"So," said Ace, leaping to his feet and aiming his rifle at her, "I guess we better show you what happens to little girls who talk too much." His father's colonel hat slipped down over his eyes.

Jude ran toward the sidewalk. Someone tackled her. They dragged her, kicking and biting, to a sunken grave. Pushing her into it, some held her down while others piled fallen tombstones across the mouth of the hole.

"A perfect fit!" announced Ace. "See you around, kid, as the line said to the circle." And the Commie Killers vanished.

Jude could hear a lone cicada droning like a chain saw from a nearby walnut tree. Six weeks until the first frost, Mr. Starnes always said. She pushed at the stones above her head, but they wouldn't budge. She tried to figure out how much clay lay between herself and the skeleton below. What if it reached up and dragged her down into the earth in its bony arms? Maybe if she stayed perfectly still, it wouldn't realize she was there.

She was so scared that she could hardly breathe. What if the stones came crashing down and smashed her into a human pancake?

She wished her grandfather would help her, as he had promised, but he was lying on the other side of the graveyard, probably just as scared as she was.

She paused in her panic to wonder if the tiny blue hairs on his cheeks would have kept growing so that he now had a long beard, and dagger fingernails like Dracula, and toenails that would one day sprout from his grave like blanched asparagus spears.

What if a nest of black widow spiders had been disturbed when the Commie Killers picked up the broken headstones? What if the black widows were crawling all over the stones just above her head? What if they didn't realize that she wasn't the one who had wrecked their home? She sank as far down in the grave as she could. But then she remembered the skeleton below and tried to twist sideways out of its grasp.

She lay there in the dark, eyes closed, breathing as little as possible. At Sunday school, the preacher was always talking about how great nature was because it displayed God's handiwork. But what about black widow spiders? What about copperheads? What about leeches and mosquitoes and bats and ticks and wasps? What about Ace Kilgore?

Gradually, her body relaxed into the contours of the sunken grave. Ace was right: She fit like Cinderella's foot in the glass slipper. This was what it was like to be dead, and it wasn't so bad. If she stayed like this long enough, she *would* be dead and she could join her mother in heaven and never have to see Ace Kilgore again.

Billowy white clouds were drifting like spinnakered sailing ships across an indigo sea of summer sky. Beautiful smiling women in white bathrobes were reclining on them, waving as they passed. One woman with curly black hair and full red lips looked exactly like Jude's mother.

"Wait!" called Jude. "Take me with you!"

But they seemed not to hear.

A dog began snuffling and yelping up above. Jude kept her eyes tightly shut, struggling to return to her mother.

"Jude, are you okay?" called Molly through an opening between the broken headstones. Sidney was beside her, whimpering and flailing frantically at the stones with his paws.

"I guess so.

"Don't worry. We'll get you out," said Sandy, freckled face looming in the window of light. "It's just a question of leverage."

THEY SAT IN SANDY'S tree house drinking grape soda through straws that bent like gooseneck lamps. The Commie Killers, shirtless in the hot afternoon sun, were redigging trenches across the street beneath a Confederate battle flag that hung limply from a pole stuck in the mud. The phone rang.

Answering it, Sandy said, "Oh, hi, Nicolai." He reached for a notebook. "Let's see, what do I have for you today? Oh, yes, queen to king's bishop four. Okay. Talk to you soon."

"Moscow," he explained, running his hand over his cowlick in a futile attempt to smooth it down. "Right, so first of all, Jude, don't ever play alone again. If Molly hadn't seen your tricycle, you'd still be in that grave. I can't spend all day at my telescope watching out for you two. I'm in the middle of some very important chess matches. Why don't you play with Noreen next door?"

"She's a girl," said Molly.

"We're not really girls," said Jude. "We just look like it."

NOREEN AGREED TO LET Jude and Molly be her sons if Sandy would be her husband.

"Okay," said Sandy, standing outside the shed attached to No-reen's parents' garage, "but I'm the kind of father who spends all day at the office. And my office is my tree house. And only my sons are allowed to visit.''

"But pioneer fathers don't go to the office,'' said Noreen from the doorway. Her dark naturally curly hair was parted on one side, and a red plastic barrette shaped like a bow held it back from her face on the other side. The frames of her glasses matched her barrette.

"They go hunting, don't they?'' asked Sandy, walking toward his yard. "Pretend I've been eaten by bears. Pretend you're a widow.''

"You're no fun,'' said Noreen.

"Sorry about that.''

"Well, all right, come in, Jude and Molly.'' Noreen stepped aside. "Sit down. We're having supper.'' Supper consisted of dried clay patties served on wild grape leaves atop an orange crate.

Noreen's "daughters'' were a puling bunch in flared shorts with matching halter tops. Red plastic barrettes shaped their hair into bizarre lumps and mounds, as though their skulls were deformed. Most dandled dolls, nursing and burping them as they ate, and discussing their infant antics in wearying detail.

"Sister Serena, would you please read our Bible lesson for today?'' asked Noreen.

Serena handed her bundled doll to the girl beside her, then picked up a Bible and opened it at its marker. "In my Father's house are many mansions,'' she read haltingly in a high-pitched voice. "If it were not so, I would have told you. I go to prepare a place for you. And if I go and prepare a place for you, I will come again, and receive you unto myself; that where I am, there ye may be also.''

"Halleluia! Praise the Lord!'' shrieked Noreen, keeling over into spasms on the floor.

Jude watched as the other girls set aside their dolls and writhed on the floor, babbling in something that sounded like double pig Latin.

So it was true? "Where I am, there ye may be also." Her mother was going to come get her and take her to God's house. Everyone said her grandmother lived in a mansion. If heaven had many mansions, would it be a development like Tidewater Estates?

Whoops erupted outside. Through the playhouse window, Jude could see the Commie Killers war dancing with feather bracelets at their wrists and ankles. Ace appeared in the doorway in a chicken-feather headdress, a dish towel belted around his bony hips. His face and chest were painted with lipstick lightning bolts. The girls stopped rolling on the floor and began to wail. Holding up his hands for silence, he pointed at Molly and Jude. "We wantum those two shirtless ones. You squaws havum nothing to fear."

"No! Don't take my sons!" Noreen leapt to her feet and shielded them behind her back.

Ace shoved her aside, and his warriors dragged Jude and Molly into the yard. Ropes knotted around their throats and wrists, they were led toward the Wildwoods.

"I'm telling!" screamed Noreen. "Momma!"

"Hush, darling," called her mother from the screened porch, where the Missionary Society was meeting. "Momma's praying."

"Sandy!" Noreen yelled toward the tree house. "Your sons have been captured by the savages!"

"YOU'D BETTER LET US GO," said Molly, wrists and ankles bound to saplings so her body formed an X. Her ribs looked like a xylophone. "My uncle's a state trooper."

"So what?" said Ace, who was flicking the blade of his jackknife with his thumb. "So's mine."

"What are you going to do to us?" asked Jude, bound nearby. She kept picturing that red-and-green cherry bomb. On top of it all, she felt guilty: Molly wouldn't be in this fix except for her. Silently, she summoned the Nunnehi, the Cherokee Immortals, who her father had said would emerge from beneath the mountains and under the river to help you if you were in trouble. But no one showed up.

"We haven't decided yet, ma'am. We may play crucifixion. Or we may leave y'all here as supper for the mosquitoes." After closing his knife and fastening it to his belt, he walked up to Molly and glared right into her eyes with his dead black ones. "Are you now or have you ever been an agent for any foreign power?" he demanded.

"Excuse me?" said Molly, screwing up her face with contempt.

"So you won't talk?"

"Talk about what?"

Slowly, he extracted a chicken feather from his warbonnet. Smiling, he stroked Molly's armpit with it.

"Please don't, Ace," pleaded Molly in a wimpy voice Jude had never before heard from her. "I'm ticklish." She began to struggle against her ropes.

Delighted, Ace continued. The other warriors plucked feathers from their bracelets and joined in on both girls' armpits.

Jude caught on quickly, and she and Molly writhed and grimaced, screaming for mercy as loudly as possible.

Jude was standing on the porch steps before her mother's mansion in heaven, white columns on either hand. Her mother was in the doorway in a low-cut emerald evening gown, smiling, arms outspread, wavy black hair stirring in the breeze.

"Momma, is it really you?" asked Jude.

A siren whined up the hill from town. The boys, feathers frozen, looked at one another.

"I told you my uncle would get you," gasped Molly.

"Holy crow!" whispered Ace, seeing two flat-brimmed hats skimming along above the bushes. The Commie Killers took off through the undergrowth, feathers of torture spiraling to the forest floor.

BY THE CURB IN FRONT of Sandy's house was a khaki-and-forest-green highway patrol car, red light flashing on its roof. Molly's uncle Clarence, holster on his hip, black boots to his knees, opened the back door for Sandy.

"Wait a minute, Uncle Clarence," called Molly. "What are y'all doing?"

"Arresting him, sweetheart." He closed the door. Sandy looked through the window at Molly and Jude and shrugged helplessly.

"But Sandy saved us. You should arrest Ace Kilgore instead."

"We come up here in the first place to pick up Sandy," said Uncle Clarence as he circled the car to the driver's door, "and he told us about y'all. But this son of a gun here tapped into the phone line. He's been calling free all over the world for pert near two year now. He owes the phone company two thousand dollars, plus fines. Your young friend here is in real big trouble, missy."

ON JUDE'S FIRST DAY OF SCHOOL, Molly, a second grader, walked her along the busy highway past the sign with the winged red horse in front of the Texaco station. As they approached the redbrick school building, which resembled the state mental hospital across town, with wire mesh in the window glass and a chain-link fence around the playground, Molly assured her that Noreen's report of a spanking machine in the principal's office was untrue.

"They always say that to frighten the first graders."

In the tiled hallway outside her classroom door, Jude saw several children crying in the arms of distraught mothers, clutching their skirts, clinging to their legs, begging to be taken home, like the pictures at Sunday school of sinners in hell pleading with the Lord for salvation.

Struggling not to be a crybaby, Jude opened the door and

marched into the room. She sat down at the desk pointed out by the teacher, whose chin when she smiled almost touched her nose, like the witch in *Hansel and Gretel*. A piece of manila paper and a box of new crayons with sharp tips sat on her blond wooden desktop, so Jude began to draw a puffy white cloud floating in a blue sky, with a woman in a white bathrobe standing on it, smiling with bright red lips. She made the hair yellow so no one would know it was her mother. As she colored, she began to feel less miserable. She liked the oily smell of the new crayons, the rough texture of the paper against her fingertips, and the bright colors she could spread in any pattern she liked.

"That's very nice, Jude," said the witch, bending over her picture, smelling like flowers that had been left in a vase too long.

"Thank you."

"Is it an angel?" She rested a bony hand on Jude's shoulder.

"Sort of." Jude would never reveal that the angel was her mother. There was no telling what a witch might do with that information.

"So how do you like first grade?" asked Molly in the cafeteria at lunchtime. She had sneaked away from the second-grade table to eat the peanut-butter-and-banana sandwich from her Donald Duck lunch box with Jude.

"All right." Jude took the wax paper off a stack of Oreos Clementine had packed for her. "Except my teacher was making fun of how this boy was holding his pencil, so he threw it at her. And then she spanked him in the cloakroom." Jude separated an Oreo to lick off the sugary white filling. "School is really scary, isn't it?"

"Yeah. But girls hardly ever get in trouble," said Molly. "Just boys, 'cause they always say what they think. They don't understand that nobody cares."

After lunch, Jude and Molly stood beside the high fence around the playground, the only girls in blue jeans, holding hands and watching the Commie Killers play softball. After the Commie Killers' run-in with Uncle Clarence, Jude's father had hired a bulldozer to destroy their trenches. So when they passed Jude on the sidewalk now, they called her "Public Enemy Number One."

Noreen's gang was in a grassy corner, hurting one another's feelings, then making up via networks of earnest intermediaries. Spotting Jude and Molly, Noreen sauntered over in her plaid dress, which had a black patent-leather belt to match her Mary Janes. Her stomach bulged out beneath the belt like a beach ball.

"Why do you spend all your time with that baby first grader?" she asked Molly.

"Because she's my friend." She let go of Jude's hand.

"When you get sick of her, you can come play with us."

"I'm not going to get sick of her, Noreen."

Jude was grinding a pebble into the dirt with the toe of her oxford. She glanced at Molly, aware of her sacrifice in being best friends with a first grader. Even though Molly's voice was calm, her eyes were icy cold.

"You two look like boys in those blue jeans," said Noreen. "Wouldn't your mothers buy you new dresses for the first day of school?"

There was a horrified silence as Noreen remembered that Jude's mother was dead. She whirled around and stalked away, dust coating her glossy Mary Janes.

"Look. There's Sandy." Touching Jude's shoulder, Molly pointed across the playground. He was sitting with his back to the brick wall of the building, playing chess against himself on a tiny portable set. The teacher on duty, a hunched old woman in a navy blue Brooklyn Dodgers cap, was standing over him gesticulating wildly. Sandy folded up his chess set and slipped it into his shorts pocket. Teacher hobbling at his heels, he marched to the softball diamond.

When the Commie Killers saw him coming, they groaned as though they had stomachaches. One yelled, "Oh, no, here comes the convict!" Although Jude's father, who had gone to high school with the president of the phone company, had gotten Sandy excused from the wiretap charges, the Commie Killers wouldn't let him put his criminal past behind him.

The teacher handed him a glove and directed him to right field. He stood there with one hand on his hip, the other holding out the leather glove like a skillet waiting for a flapjack. When Ace hit a fly ball, Sandy's expression as he watched it arc and fall in his direction was one of pure terror. He missed it, and Ace converted his error into a grand-slam home run.

During the next inning, Sandy walked up to the plate, optimistically hefting a black Louisville Slugger. Ace motioned the outfield closer, yelling, "Easy out!" Which it unfortunately was.

After school, Jude and Molly stood toe-to-toe at the crack in the sidewalk marking the boundary between their yards. Each crossed her arms and placed her hands on the other's shoulders. For a long time, they looked into each other's eyes. Jude could see herself and the maple tree behind her reflected in Molly's irises. The bright blue disks were scored with lines, like miniature blueberry pies sliced into a hundred pieces. Around each pupil was a tiny translucent golden ring like a butter rum Life Saver after you'd sucked it for a long time. Gazing into the black pupils, Jude felt suddenly dizzy, as though she were spiraling down the funnel of a whirlpool.

They smiled gravely and patted each other's shoulders, chanting in unison, "Best friend. Buddy of mine. Pal of pals."

After changing from school jeans to play jeans, Jude sat at Molly's kitchen table, spinning a marble around the lazy Susan, pretending it was a Las Vegas roulette wheel. Molly had been mixing them cocktails from several liquids they both liked to smell—vanilla extract, Pine Sol, cherry cough syrup. But each had tasted worse than the last. Now Molly was telling a story her teacher had read that afternoon about an orphan boy who was raised by wolves and had never learned to speak. He was discovered by hunters and taken to live in a cottage on the edge of the forest.

Molly and Jude spent the rest of the afternoon prowling through Molly's house. Their vocabulary consisted of hand gestures and facial expressions. In the bathroom, Jude seized a comb and displayed it to a mystified Molly, who manipulated it in various ways, trying to discover its function.

"What are you two up to now?" asked Molly's aproned mother, lounging in the doorway in her neat blond pageboy, arms folded across her stomach. Startled, the girls stared at her with wide-open eyes.

"What's going on?" She gave a perplexed laugh. They dashed from the bathroom to seek shelter behind the sofa in the knotty pine den, which enclosed them much as the wolves' lair had.

Jude was so enchanted with this game that she continued it at supper that night, marveling over the unknown delicacies served her on a round disk by a black creature in a white uniform with a red scarf wound around her head. It was wonderful to be handed food after a lifetime of chasing moles in the forest.

"So how was your first day of school?" asked a large, pale, hairless one at the head of the gleaming wooden table.

Jude gazed at him as she ate with a bizarre silver twig, unable to comprehend the howls coming from his mouth.

"What's wrong, baby? Cat got your tongue?"

The dark one led Jude up some steps to a pool of water and removed her soiled fur. Jude dipped her toe into the pool. The water was hot! She had known only icy forest ponds and streams. She climbed in. How delicious to float in the warm liquid while the friendly black one rubbed a small slippery stone that smelled like dried rose petals across her coat.

"How you like school, Miss Judith?"

Jude looked quickly at the dark one, whose mouth was making strange sounds.

"You ain't telling, huh?"

"WHAT A NICE DOG," said Mrs. Murdoch as she strolled down the aisle and peered at the picture Jude had just drawn. "I think we need to hang this one on our bulletin board up front, Jude."

"It's not a dog," said Jude, not looking up. "It's a wolf." The wolf was sitting in its cave in the forest, sniffing the morning air.

"Speak up, young lady. I can't hear you."

"I said it's not a dog; it's a wolf."

"A wolf? What an idea! Why is it a wolf?"

" 'Cause I like wolves. I think they're nice." Jude finally looked up. Mrs. Murdoch's bright red lipstick covered an area much larger than her actual lips, and her eyebrows had been plucked out and redrawn as crooked black arches. She looked like a messy clown.

Mrs. Murdoch laughed, chin nearly touching her nose. "You may like wolves, young lady, but they are definitely *not* nice. They are vicious wild animals. Think about the wolf in *Little Red Riding Hood* for just a moment."

Jude said nothing. She was thinking about the boy who got spanked in the cloakroom.

"Well, Jude?"

"Yessum."

"So you agree that wolves are vicious wild animals?"

"Yessum."

"Now, we would not want a vicious wild animal on our bulletin board, would we? Because it would scare us all half to death and give us bad dreams at night. But your wolf could just as well be a dog, couldn't it? And then we could hang it up and look at it without fear."

"Yessum."

"So you can practice your letters by writing D-O-G here along the bottom."

"Yessum," said Jude miserably, printing D-O-G beneath her wolf. Maybe she wouldn't be an artist when she grew up after all.

Mrs. Murdoch sat down at her portable organ in the front of the room and began furiously pumping the foot pedals. "Rise, children!" she shrieked, gesturing upward with her palms. "And lift up your voices to the Lord!"

"BABY, I HAVE TO GO back to the hospital after supper," said Jude's father as he laid a slice of Mrs. Starnes's German chocolate cake on a dessert plate painted with grape clusters and cantaloupe slices. He passed it to Jude. "To work on some reports. Molly's mother said you could spend the night there. Would you mind?" He picked up his fork and studied it.

Jude inspected his lowered face, which was turning bright red beneath his five o'clock shadow as he flicked and stroked his fork prongs. Why was he so embarrassed? He often went back to the hospital after supper if Clementine could stay late. It was no big deal. "Sure. That's fine, Dad."

The next morning, Jude and Molly raced down the hall from Molly's bedroom and into the bathroom to brush their teeth before school. Molly's father was standing in front of the sink shaving. He was entirely covered with curly black hair, except for his white buttocks and a pale little slug that nestled in a mat of fur between his legs.

Finally, Molly asked, "Daddy, what's that?"

Nicking his chin with the razor, he looked down at Molly's pointing finger. Clutching the slug with his free hand while the shaving cream on his chin turned pink, he said, "It's my penis, and I never want to hear you say that word again!"

Molly and Jude crept from the bathroom, teeth unbrushed, and gathered their books from Molly's room in silence, exchanging wolf-speak signs with their fingers that said, He's covered with fur. Can he be a brother?

JUDE'S GRANDMOTHER WAS SERVING garlic grits from a silver casserole dish on her Sheraton sideboard. She was using a pitted serving spoon that her own grandmother had buried in the backyard at the family farm near Fredericksburg to prevent its being stolen by the Yankees. Unable to remember where she'd buried her cache, Jude's great-great-grandmother spent the rest of her life making her yardmen excavate the property. The week after they finally found it, she died.

"A little girl belongs in dresses at school, Daniel," her grandmother was saying, "not blue jeans. It's the talk of the town."

"Don't you find it sad, Momma," said Jude's father, loosening his striped silk Sunday tie, "that this town has nothing better to talk about than my daughter's blue jeans?"

"Don't get smart with me, Daniel. You may be a big man down at the hospital, but you're still my son." She handed him a plate piled high with fried chicken, grits, shelly beans, and a salad of molded cherry Jell-O and shredded carrots topped with a mayonnaise rosette.

He buttered and ate a Parker House roll while his mother continued her critique of Jude's wardrobe.

Jude, whose skirt was hiked halfway up her thighs as she sat with her feet hooked behind her front chair legs, fixed her gaze on the glass goddess in the middle of the table. Baby's breath and pastel snapdragons were sprouting from her head. She clutched a bow and wore a quiver of arrows on her back. A pack of dogs was leaping up around her legs, which were laced with thongs from her sandals.

"Thank you, Momma," said her father. "I'm sure you're right."

Jude glanced at him, scratching her neck, which was itching from her scalloped lace collar. Often he agreed with his mother to her face, then ignored her behind her back. Hopefully, this was one of those times.

Satisfied, her grandmother resumed her account of the siege of Fredericksburg, told to her as a girl by a legless soldier at the Confederate Veterans' Home: "As the Yankees crossed the Rappahannock, Lieutenant Stevens hid behind a stone wall to shoot at them. All of a sudden, he saw a baby girl toddling down the street chasing a rolling shell casing, with bullets whistling all around her. He ran out and grabbed her and carried her down a side street, where he came to a young woman in a dirty ripped dress who was sitting on a pile of rubble."

"Ma'am," he said, "is this here your little girl?"

She and the child reached out for each other. "Sir," she said, "my cow's been shot. It's lying in that shed over yonder. You can go butcher it and take the meat if you want to."

"Thank you, ma'am," he said, "but the Yankees is coming fast, and I surely would be honored if you'd come along with me right now."

"Why, thank you, sir," she said, taking his outstretched hand with a coy smile, as though he'd just asked her to dance. "I don't mind if I do."

As he led her up the street, a shell exploded beside them. He woke up to find a starving hog licking the stumps where his legs used to be. The mother and her baby were lying dead beside him. Down the hill, he could see Yankee soldiers dressed in gowns stolen from the town houses. They were drinking fine French wines from the bottle and waltzing with one another around a bonfire of Chippendale chairs.

"There was no way in the world," Jude's grandmother concluded, "for our fine colonial cavaliers to prevail over that race of barbarians."

It was her favorite story. Although it was a good one, Jude had heard it a hundred times.

"And another thing, Daniel," her grandmother said as she ladled milk gravy over her fried chicken.

He looked up, the green beans on his fork slowly dripping fatback. "Yes, Momma?"

"This poor child has no mother. And the way you're behaving, running around with that floozy from intensive care at all hours of the night, now she has no father, either. It's not going unnoticed around town that Jude is practically living at the Elkins's while you cavort in back alleys with your concubine."

"Yes, Momma," he said, chewing his beans. "I'm sure you're right."

"What's a floozy?" asked Jude, studying the wallpaper over the sideboard, which featured a white columned mansion surrounded by women in hoop skirts and sunbonnets. This was what her mother's mansion in heaven looked like. One day soon, she was going to come take Jude there. It wasn't true that she had no mother. Just because no one else saw her didn't mean she wasn't real. "What's cavort?"

"Momma, tell us about Provence, why don't you?" said her father.

"Provence? Oh, Provence was lovely. You know, I believe I like Provence almost as much as I do Virginia. Except for all that funny food. And that strange language nobody understands except the French."

Her father laughed, running his hand over his bald spot. "I declare, Momma, you're the only person I ever saw who travels the world searching for Virginia. Why don't you just go to Virginia in the first place?"

She sighed and patted her red lips with her linen napkin. "Well, you know, Virginia's not what it used to be. Once, before that dreadful war, it was a gracious land of rolling pastures, where sleek cattle grazed and blackbirds sang. . . ."

"May I please be excused?" asked Jude, laying her napkin on the damask tablecloth, desperate not to hear again about the joys of plantation living.

"WHAT'S A FLOOZY?" Jude asked Clementine on her way out the door to school the next morning.

Clementine paused as she mopped the redbrick kitchen linoleum with the golden liquid that smelled so good and tasted so terrible. "Where you heard that word, Miss Judith?"

"My grandma said my daddy's running around with a floozy."

Clementine grinned, leaning on her mop handle. "That a fact? Good for him."

"What's a floozy?"

"A floozy is . . . um, a woman who likes to have some fun." She tucked a coil of springy hair beneath the edge of her head cloth.

"But what about my momma in heaven?"

"Sugar, be glad if your daddy's found him a new woman friend. He be a good man, and he been so lonely for so long. It don't mean he love your momma less. Fact is, I'd say he got him a graveyard love for your momma.''

"What's that?"

"A graveyard love be a love that lasts till you both be dead and buried in the graveyard. Like what I expect you got with Miss Molly. A graveyard love don't never end, no matter what.''

```
┌─────────────────────────┐
│                         │
│      CHAPTER            │
│                         │
│        4               │
│                         │
└─────────────────────────┘
```

JUDE WAS OPERATING atop the desk in her bedroom on a doll her grandmother had just brought her from India. She had removed and set aside the red-and-gold silk sari. Now she was carefully snipping open the cloth belly with scissors. Reaching into the aperture, she extracted the wad of stuffing that was the dead baby. Once the baby was out, she hoped the mother could be saved.

After sewing up the incision with red thread, Jude discovered that her patient had stopped breathing. Turning her over, she administered artificial respiration, repeatedly pressing her back and lifting her elbows. But she still refused to breathe.

Jude had never lost a patient before. Feeling her throat tighten so that she could hardly swallow, she stumbled down the carpeted hallway and into her father's bedroom, which was painted lime green and had a gold quilted bedspread and velvet drapes. She searched the floor of his closet for a shoe box, intending to dig a grave in the backyard and make a headstone from a brick. Finally, she found a coffin, but unfortunately it was full of letters.

Carrying the box into her room, Jude plopped down on her bed and examined the French stamps on some of the envelopes, which featured the head of a woman statue with wavy stone hair. The letters were between her mother and father while he was away at the war. She removed one from an envelope that had an American eagle stamp. The paper was light blue, and the handwriting was small and squiggly. Right in the middle of the page, Jude spotted her own name.

Being in the top reading group now that she was in second grade, Jude used her father's dictionary to decipher the paragraph containing her name: "Your mother and I rode the train to our nation's capital last week. One afternoon we visited the National Cathedral. While we were looking up at the beautiful stained-glass window, we discovered that Jude, whom I was carrying on my hip, was blowing out all the votive candles in the rack beside us. Darling, I have my hands full with this marvelous child of ours! How I despise this awful war, which has taken so many men away from the wives and children who need them. . . ."

The letter paper smelled like her mother's favorite perfume. Closing her eyes, Jude remembered sitting on the pale green carpet in her parents' bedroom watching her mother get dressed for parties. She'd let Jude fasten the lacy tops of her silk stockings to her garter belt. Jude had been fascinated by the way the little padded buttons slid into the wire hooks. Then her mother would ask her to arrange the crooked seams down the backs of her legs into straight lines. After pulling on her dress, her mother would take the cut-glass vial of Narcissus perfume off her dressing table and dab her wrists and throat and behind her ears with the stopper. Jude would hold out her own wrist for a dab. After her parents' departure, she would lie in bed with her wrist to her nose, breathing in the sweet floral fragrance of her beautiful vanished mother.

Jude held the letter to her nose and took a deep whiff, gazing at the photo on her nightstand of her mother smiling into the camera, holding Jude's cheek to her own, black hair waving around her face like seaweed around a drowning swimmer.

Jude remembered the poor dead doll she'd left lying on the operating table. She got up and cradled it for a moment in her arms. Then she hurled it into the back of her closet and slammed the door.

Hiding the shoe box under her bed, Jude worked on the letters whenever the coast was clear. One evening, Clementine asked as she carried corn bread in from the kitchen, "Miss Judith, what you be doing alone in your room all the time, honey? You ought to be outdoors playing with the other children."

"Nothing. Reading. Thinking."

"I guess we're raising an intellectual here, Clementine," said her father as he cut the meat loaf. He still wore pale green scrub clothes from the hospital and looked very handsome with the candlelight reflecting off the ever-larger bald patch on his head.

"What's an 'interlectual'?" asked Jude, swinging her legs in her chair, pretending she was pumping really high in a swing.

He laughed. "An intellectual is someone who knows what the word *intellectual* means."

"I don't want to be one anyway," said Jude with dignity. "I want to be a medical missionary. Either that or a person who makes little girls' shoes that aren't silly."

"Same difference," said her father. "One heals souls and the other heels soles." He practically fell into his plate laughing.

Jude liked seeing him so happy all of a sudden. But it bothered her that he never stared anymore at the photo of her mother in the wine bottle when they sat together in his brown leather chair listening to John Cameron Swayze. Her mother was talking in her letters about how much she missed him, but here he was cavorting in back alleys with a floozy. It just wasn't right.

"I don't get it." Jude looked to Clementine for clues to her father's hilarity.

Clementine shrugged and limped toward the kitchen in her huge white shoes. Apparently, her arthritis was acting up, which meant rain was coming soon.

Her father sighed. "I wish there *were* some intellectuals around this place," he said, passing her the corn-bread squares, "to appreciate my bons mots."

"Ain't nobody here but us chickens," drawled Clementine from the doorway. It was the punch line from a joke they all loved.

As Jude and Clementine giggled, her father shook his head.

JUDE AND MOLLY CLIMBED into Jude's father's army-surplus jeep. When Jude was younger, he used to wrap her in a blanket and let her sleep on the backseat while he paid house calls back in the hills. If she woke up, she'd sneak over to the lighted windows, through which she might see tall, thin mountain people with gaunt faces and hollow eyes. Sometimes she'd watch her father lance boils or stitch wounds by lantern light.

Her father drove them across the pasture behind her grandmother's house and down through the Wildwoods, the olive hood bobbing and the power lift clanking on the back. The mountains lay spread out below them, a lumpy crazy quilt of rust and mauve and mustard and dark green.

As they sifted the dark loam along the riverbank in the slanting golden rays of the setting sun, Jude's father told Molly the story about his grandfather's mother, Abigail Westlake, whose forebears had lived in bark lodges by the river for centuries, fishing the slow-drifting waters and hunting the steep slopes of the Wildwoods. Later they put up a log cabin, growing corn and grazing cattle on the rich bottomland. By Abigail's time, they had built a plank house, brought slaves from Charleston, converted to Christianity, learned English, and begun wearing white people's clothing. Abigail's brother married a missionary from Baltimore.

One day, white soldiers came with rifles to round them up and march them off to a reservation in Oklahoma. When her brother tried to escape, a soldier shot him in the head. Coming home from gathering herbs, Abigail watched this from the Wildwoods, then hid in a cave while an unfamiliar white family moved into her family's house.

After several days, a neighboring farmer found her, nearly dead from cold and hunger and fear, and carried her back to his cabin on the ridge. He himself had recently arrived in America, having been evicted from his croft in the Scottish Highlands. He confronted the new family in her house and ordered them to leave. After they obligingly moved out, they burned her house to the ground. Jude's father pointed out the cellar hole, which was now overgrown with a tangle of Virginia creeper. An early frost had turned the leaves the scarlet of spilt blood.

Abigail learned from relatives who had survived the forced westward trek that her parents and sisters had died of typhoid in the Ozarks. As she lay in bed week after week trying to recover her will to live, she told the farmer about the dances in this valley when she was a child, at which warriors carrying red-and-black clubs painted their faces vermilion and circled their eyes with scarlet and black. About her cousins, who came down on horses from the deep mountain coves wearing deerskin leggings and embroidered hunting shirts and red-and-blue turbans, to watch the violent all-day ball games on the playing field downriver. About the shamen, who raked the ballplayers in their loincloths with turkey-quill combs to grid their flesh with blood for good luck. About the prophets who had recently begun painting their faces black and proclaiming the end of the Cherokee people.

The farmer told her about having his hut in the Highlands burned down around him in the middle of a winter night because he refused to leave to make way for a herd of sheep. About his wife and baby, who died as he dragged them from the fire. About being forced onto a ship in Ullapool with his young son, bound for no one knew where. About being dumped at Cape Fear on the Carolina coast and wandering across the Smokies in search of an unoccupied spot where he could farm in peace. About the recent Cherokee raid on his cattle, during which his son had disappeared.

Having loss in common, if nothing else, the two fell in love and married. Their son, Jude's great-grandfather, grew up learning from his mother which parts of which plants to use for which ailments. When he became a man, people arrived at his new log house from all over the region for his remedies. During the War Between the States, he patched up soldiers brought to him by both sides, but he refused to join either, having also learned from his mother a certain skepticism about the projects of white men, whatever their proclaimed creed.

Jude looked up from her digging to study her father. He had a big crooked nose just like her grandfather—just like the Indian on a buffalo nickel. And his cheekbones were so broad that his mahogany eyes seemed to be peering out from inside a cave. People always said Jude's eyes were just like his. While he talked, the valley came alive, with painted warriors paddling canoes up the river and shooting deer with arrows in the Wildwoods. With teams of men in loincloths catching balls in the nets of woven squirrel skin at the ends of their long wooden spoons. With bayoneted soldiers herding little children like cattle. With blazing houses and screaming people.

But when her father stopped talking, it all vanished and everything fell silent, except for the whirring of grasshoppers in the with-ered alfalfa and the cawing of a crow from the top of a sycamore.

Her father scraped soil from a pointed shard of rock and handed it to Jude. She and Molly looked at it. It was shiny black with a vein of white down the center and pointed wings at the top for tying it to an arrow shaft.

"Hang on to that," her father said. "Some ancient cousin of yours probably made it."

Jude kept inspecting the chipped edges of the arrowhead with her fingertips. It seemed strange that all that was left were these bits of rock, herself and her father, and her father's stories, told to him by his grandfather, who was told them by his mother. At school, they played a game called Gossip in which everyone sat in a circle and one person whispered something in the ear of the next, who whispered it to the next, and so on. By the time it had gone around the circle, it was completely wrong or stupid.

They drove up to the Wiggly Piglet, which featured an outline of Porky Pig in flashing neon, with a slogan beneath that read: "Our pigs are dying for you to eat." A high-school girl in a cowboy hat and boots arrived to take their order of pulled-pork sandwiches and peanut-butter milk shakes. As the girl strutted away, Molly reported that she had had goose bumps on her thighs below her short shorts.

After the waitress returned, carrying their order on an aluminum tray that she attached to their car window, Jude asked her father, "Why did the soldiers want to march Abigail Westlake's family to Oklahoma?"

"The white settlers wanted their land," said her father, handing out the wrapped sandwiches. "That soil along the river is very rich from centuries of flooding."

"But that's not right, just to take it like that."

He smiled faintly as he unwrapped his barbecue and poured extra sauce from a tiny paper cup onto the coleslaw atop his pork. "No, it isn't. But the Cherokees were sitting ducks. They believed that land belonged to everyone. It never occurred to them that it could be taken away."

"But you said they owned slaves?"

"Yes."

"Negro people like Clementine, who had to do all the work for free?" A speaker attached to the restaurant roof was blaring Hank Williams singing "I Can't Help It If I'm Still in Love with You."

"Yes."

"But that's not right, either," said Jude. The barbecue sauce was so spicy that her nose was starting to run.

"No, it's wrong. Very wrong."

Jude sat beside Molly on the backseat, sucking her milk shake through a straw, trying to figure out how the same people could be right and wrong, both at the same time. She glanced at Molly.

"When your grandfather told you those stories, did it make you sad?" Jude asked, watching the cowgirl write down the orders of three boys in ducktails who were sitting in a convertible with an elevated rear end and an elaborate chrome tailpipe. PARTY DOLL was painted on the fender. She and Molly had already decided to be waitresses here when they grew up, so that they could wear the cowgirl outfits.

"Yes. It made me sad to know that people would treat each other that way. It still does."

"Why do they?" asked Jude, determined to get this settled once and for all.

"Ah, the question of the ages." He wadded up his wrapper and napkin and stuffed them into the paper bag.

"But what's the answer?"

"Jude," he said, "I'm afraid you may be one of those people who spend their lives searching for that answer."

"But what is it?" Jude was starting to feel frantic, as though this was a joke that everyone knew the punch line to but herself.

"Well, I don't know exactly, baby." He turned around to look at her in the light from the flashing neon pig. "The Cherokees used to say that beneath different appearances, all creatures are merely manifestations of the Great Spirit. So that those who harm others unnecessarily disturb the balance of the universe and therefore harm themselves. But many people nowadays seem to feel separate and superior, so it doesn't bother them so much to hurt others."

"Which do you believe?" Molly asked.

"You don't need to believe or not believe something once you experience it."

Jude and Molly looked at him blankly.

"That means I agree with the Cherokees," he said.

Jude and Molly looked at each other. Jude thought that if anyone hurt Molly, she, too, would feel the pain. But if someone hurt Ace Kilgore, she'd feel glad. So which category did she fit into?

Your daddy's so sweet, Molly gesticulated in wolfspeak as he carried their trash to the can and handed their tray to the goose-bumped cowgirl. Jude felt proud of him.

Since her parents were out of town, Molly spent that night at Jude's house, and she taught Jude a game she'd just invented called Pecan. Jude lay on top of Molly, stomach-to-stomach, chest-to-chest, nose-to-nose. They looked cross-eyed into each other's eyes. Then Molly began to giggle. Jude could feel Molly's chest and stomach trembling and heaving beneath her own, so she started giggling, too. Soon it was impossible to tell who was and wasn't giggling.

Molly grabbed Jude's wrists and forced her over onto her side. Then she scrambled to her knees and sat astride Jude's chest, pinning her arms above her head. Breathing heavily, she look down at Jude with triumph, eyes so fierce that they were almost purple. "I could pin you like this with one hand tied behind my back," she announced in her husky voice.

"Probably," said Jude. But she hadn't been fighting back very hard because she had been too interested to find out what Molly would do next.

Before they fell asleep, they agreed that Pecan was such a good game that they should play it a lot, taking turns lying on top.

THROUGH THE BARE BRANCHES across the cave mouth Jude watched the river wind through the valley, a slithering brown snake. Holsteins stood to their knees in the water, patches of black spread across their barreled backs like continents on a globe. A hawk, fringed wing tips fluttering, swooped and dipped and floated on a column of air that was spiraling up from the valley floor. The Smokies rippled like blue sand dunes to the edge of the earth. Wispy puffs of smoke rose up from the mountain coves, where farmers were curing their tobacco.

A dozen yards below, Ace Kilgore was yelling commands to the patrolling Commie Killers, unaware of Molly and Jude overhead. Jude's father had shown them this cave, high up on a cliff, concealed by a thick tangle of mountain laurel, where Abigail Westlake had hidden while soldiers down below marched her family off to their deaths in the Ozarks. Jude and Molly were sitting on a cushion of pine needles, quiet as hunted game, playing Trail of Tears. They had even persuaded Sidney to halt his amiable panting.

Although she tried her best to stay out of Ace's way, Jude often stole glances at him on the playground or in the lunchroom or around the neighborhood. If she and Molly were wolf boys trying to pass unnoticed on the fringes of the forest, Ace was a wolf boy who had refused to come in from the wild. He was completely untamed, frightening but also admirable.

The Commie Killers swept down the cliff face on their mission of national security. Jerry Crawford, Ace's best friend, brought up the rear. He was much taller than Ace, but he always hunched over in an attempt to be the same height. A couple of the others, twins with sleek dark hair whom Jude and Molly called the "Panther Twins," were stronger and faster than Ace. But they always trailed around after him like docile guard dogs, executing his nefarious orders without a flicker of hesitation.

As their shouts faded, Jude extracted Girl Scout cookies and strawberry sodas from her knapsack. She handed Molly a candy cigarette, lighting it for her with an imaginary match. Cigarette dangling from her lips, Molly dealt hands for Over the Moon. Setting aside their soda bottles, they began drawing, exchanging and discarding in an arcane pattern understood only by themselves, since they had invented this game in which low cards were worth more than high ones. Sucking their cigarettes, they cheered and giggled and cursed.

When the game ended, they used the cards to outline the floor plan of the cabin they were going to build on the ridge overhead when they grew up. It would be filled with books and records, and there would be a separate room for drawing and painting. Outside would be a stable for their dogs and horses, with a fenced-in paddock. Their jobs at the Wiggly Piglet would pay for it all.

Jude inspected the floor plan that stretched across the pine needles. "What's that room for?" she asked, pointing.

"I just added it," said Molly. "It's for our babies. We can each have one."

Jude looked at her. "Oh, no, you don't. Not me."

"But it would be fun."

"Babies kill you."

"Not always they don't."

"Molly, I don't want you to die. Promise me you won't have a baby."

"Okay. Relax, Jude. It was just an idea."

Stomach knotted, Jude looked out the cave mouth as a huge, puffy white cloud drifted past like a giant cotton ball. Her mother was reclining on it, dressed in a skirted bathing suit, a white rose in her black hair.

"Is something wrong?" asked Molly.

Jude had told no one about sometimes seeing her mother. Everyone said she was dead. But Molly was her best friend. They told each other everything. "It's my mother."

Molly glanced around the cave. "Where?"

"Out there. See that cloud?"

Molly looked out the cave mouth. "Yeah, it does look kind of like a woman."

"No, I mean my mother is there, riding on that cloud. Lying on that thing that looks like a throne. Wearing a bathing suit. Now she's waving at us."

Molly stared at the cloud for a long time. "I don't see her, Jude," she finally said.

"You don't?" Jude blinked her eyes several times and then looked back at the cloud. Her mother was still there, tossing her a kiss.

"No. But I believe you, Jude. I believe she's really there."

But Molly's frown lines didn't go away, even after they returned to Over the Moon.

Finally, Jude rested her handful of cards on the pine needles. "What's wrong?" she asked, worried that Molly might be wondering if she really wanted to be best friends with someone who saw ghosts.

"Nothing."

Jude shrugged. "It's okay if you don't want to tell."

After a long strained silence broken only by Sidney's panting, Molly said, "Noreen passed a note around class today saying that you're my boyfriend."

"What? That's the dumbest thing I ever heard of."

"And during recess this afternoon, she and all her creepy little friends started singing, 'Molly and Jude, sitting in a tree, K-I-S-S-I-N-G. . . .' "

"But I don't even know how to kiss," said Jude, outraged.

"You don't?"

"Why would I?"

"I'll teach you," offered Molly.

Jude looked at her quickly. "How do you know?"

"I watch my parents—in the living room at night, when they think I'm asleep. I sneak halfway down the stairs and look through the banister." Laying aside her cards, she put the back of her hand to her mouth and opened her lips as though about to take a bite out of it. Then she pressed her lips hard against her hand and closed her eyes, twisting her hand and head in opposite directions.

"Okay. Try it," she said to Jude.

Jude copied her, sucking the back of her own hand with feigned fervor.

"Good," said Molly. "Now try this." She clutched the hand she was kissing with her other hand and turned her mouth aside to murmur, "Oh, my darling, I love you so much."

"Oh, my darling, I love you so much," Jude murmured to her hand, trying to imagine Molly's mother, who was as fragile as a flower, doing such a disgusting thing with Molly's father, who was covered like a bear with coarse, black hair and spoke in a voice that was almost a growl.

"There. You've got it," Molly said with satisfaction.

"But why can't Noreen just leave us alone?" demanded Jude,

letting her adorable hand collapse into her lap. "We've never done anything to her."

"Momma says she wouldn't tease us if she didn't like us."

They considered this bit of adult wisdom for a long time. It sounded far-fetched.

"What do you think we should do?" Jude lay back on the slick, fragrant pine needles, hands behind her head.

"You may have to prove to her that you're a girl."

"How?"

"If you show her you haven't got one of those dumb penises, she'll know you aren't a boy. And if you aren't a boy, then you can't be my boyfriend."

Jude giggled. "Maybe it would be better just to spend less time together."

"We can't let anyone come between us," said Molly.

"Nobody could ever do that."

They glanced at each other doubtfully.

"No," said Molly.

"But if we ignore each other at school," insisted Jude, "they'll think we don't like each other anymore, and then they'll leave us alone."

"We could still meet here every day after school," said Molly, looking relieved.

"Yeah. We're safe here. Nobody could ever find us."

After finishing her homework that night, Jude put on her pajamas and pulled the shoe box out from under her bed. Extracting one of her mother's letters, she climbed under the covers and decoded another paragraph: "This afternoon on your parents' lawn, while I was watching your father drive his golf ball across the river, Jude got a cardboard box from the garage and hung a dish towel over an upright stick inside it. When I asked her what she was doing, she explained that she was making a boat so she could sail down the river and across the sea to visit her daddy in France. Our child is the light of my life in these dark days, darling. Thank you for her, and for our nights of love that brought her into being.''

Smiling, Jude reread this several times. She had been the light of her mother's life. Wrapped in this new knowledge as though in her mother's arms, she sniffed the perfume emanating from the letter and caressed the back of her hand with her lips and remembered her mother leaning down in her long sleek mink coat to press her bright red lips against Jude's cheek as she lay in bed. If she woke up before her parents got home and smelled the smoke from the baby-sitter's cigarettes in the living room, she would get up and look in the mirror and touch the red lips imprinted on her cheek and know that everything would soon be fine again.

The next day, Jude was playing Red Rover with the other second graders when she spotted Molly helping Noreen mat down the tall grass in the far corner of the playground to form a warren of interconnected rooms. Noreen appeared to be the mother bunny and Molly the father. The other girls were apparently baby bunnies, because they were hopping through the grassy chambers sucking their thumbs and wiggling their noses.

Jude caught Molly's eye and glared at her. Molly gestured in wolfspeak when Noreen wasn't looking: Don't worry. You'll always be my best friend. I will never play Pecan with Noreen.

Meanwhile, Oscar, who had been kept back two years and was twice as large as the other second graders, had identified Mary, the frail girl who was holding Jude's hand, as the weak link in his opponents' line. He charged the two of them with bulging eyes and flaring nostrils. As Jude fell to the ground and was trampled beneath his pounding feet, she simply switched off the playground, like changing stations on the radio.

And there was her mother, dressed in her long mink coat, standing in the doorway of her mansion in heaven, arms outspread for Jude.

"How have you been, light of my life?" she asked.

Jude set her alarm for the middle of the night. Tiptoeing into her father's room, she stood by his bedside listening to his soft steady snoring. She felt guilty waking him up when he worked so hard, but it had to be done.

"Daddy?" she whispered.

He sat straight up from a deep sleep, well trained from his years of people pounding on the back door in the middle of the night, bearing the bloody victims of family feuds up in the mountain coves.

"I've been throwing up," she announced in her most pitiful voice. It was only a small lie, because she'd felt like throwing up ever since she saw Molly playing Father Bunny with Noreen.

He reached over to feel her cheeks and forehead with a cool hand. Then he got up, took her back to her own room, tucked her in, and laid a towel along her bedside with instructions to call him if it happened again.

The next morning, he came into her room in his navy-blue corduroy robe and thrust a thermometer into her mouth before going to the bathroom to shave. While he was gone, she held the thermometer against the bulb in the lamp on her nightstand. Then she furiously scrubbed her wool blanket back and forth across her chest and arms until a rash appeared.

When her father returned, dressed in a white shirt and smelling like cinnamon toast, he read the thermometer in the lamplight, placed a damp hand on her forehead, poked her rash with his fingertips, and told her to spend the day in bed.

Jude ended up spending the entire week in bed, eating meals

Clementine brought her on a tray and listening to Arthur Godfrey on the radio while Clementine ironed by her bedside. Her father ransacked the hospital library trying to diagnose her mysterious rash and fever. Molly came over every afternoon after school, bearing candy or cookies she'd saved from her lunch box or bought with her allowance at the drugstore on the highway.

"So how's Noreen?" Jude asked each afternoon.

Each afternoon, Molly averted her eyes and answered, "She's all right."

After Molly left, Jude would take out her mother's letter in which she called Jude the light of her life and sniff its fragrance and remember stroking her mother's calves with her hands as she straightened the seams down the backs of her silky stockings.

On Friday afternoon, Molly's reply to Jude's stubborn question was, "Noreen and I had a fight. We aren't speaking anymore."

To her father's relief, Jude was out of bed and back on her feet for the weekend.

MOLLY AND JUDE, KNAPSACKS on their backs, were weaving through the tangled maze of rock ledges and mountain laurel in the Wildwoods the afternoon following Jude's abrupt recovery from her unidentified disease. They had agreed it might be a good idea to play Pecan when they reached their cave, to make up after their week of estrangement. But when they arrived beneath the limestone outcropping, they found hacked, withering laurel branches strewn around the leafy forest floor. And printed across the pale gray rock face in red paint was DEATH TO ALL BOY-GIRLS!

Inside the cave, their playing cards, torn and twisted, were scattered across the pine needles. And in the middle of the floor, cold and stiff, a necklace of blood around its throat, lay a baby rabbit. Molly and Jude glanced at each other.

"I think we need to talk to Sandy," whispered Jude, groping for Molly's hand.

Molly extracted her hand to say in wolfspeak, Let's get out of here. They may be hiding somewhere, watching us.

Sandy lowered the ladder to his tree house, and they clambered up it as though pursued by enraged yellow jackets. Some maniac was screaming opera from a record player in the corner. A large, black typewriter sat on a low table. Stacks of paper lay everywhere.

"I'm writing a novel," said Sandy, fair hair as scrambled as though he'd combed it with an eggbeater. "It's about alienation on the playground. It's a metaphor for life."

"What's alienation?" asked Molly as they sat down cross-legged on the carpet.

"What's a metaphor?" asked Jude.

"Oh, never mind," Sandy said with a sigh. "What's up?"

"We're in trouble," said Jude.

"As usual." Sandy smiled tightly. "Now what?"

"I'm sure you've heard the rumors at school," said Molly. "That Jude is my boyfriend?"

He nodded. "The solution is simple. I've been wanting to tell you, but you haven't asked."

"What?" they asked in unison.

"Wear dresses and Mary Janes."

They looked at each other.

"It's the only way." Sandy pointed to the socks and sandals on his feet. "I wear these at home, but I wear high-tops at school. I play softball even though I prefer chess. If you look the way they look and do the things they do, they'll leave you alone. You can be yourself in private. Play their game, but know it's a game. Pretend you're double agents. Like on 'I Led Three Lives.' That's the theme of my novel:

the gap between appearance and reality. It's called *The Naked and the Clothed.*"

"It might work," said Molly, studying Jude. She started giggling.

"What?" asked Jude.

"You in those stupid Mary Janes!" Molly began rolling around the carpet, laughing. Sandy and Jude joined her, the tree house rocking on its branches.

After they calmed down and were lying on the floor gasping for breath, Molly said, "Sandy, you're a genius."

"So they say."

That night in bed, Jude read another of her mother's paragraphs under her sheets with a flashlight. This secrecy was unnecessary, since her father let her stay up as late as she liked. But public school was taking effect: She was starting to enjoy the rush of terror at possible discovery by a punitive authority figure.

"Darling, Jude wakes up crying in the night, and nothing will console her but to bring her into bed with me. Sometimes as I doze, I almost imagine it's you there beside me. But when I open my eyes, I see it's only Jude. She's an amusing little creature, but it's you I need, my precious love, in the way only you can provide. You are everything to me. . . ."

Ripping this letter into tiny pieces, Jude carried them into the bathroom and flushed them down the toilet. Then she stuffed the shoe box into the back of her closet and placed her dead doll patient on top of it. It didn't really matter if her mother hadn't loved her best, because she and Molly would wear Mary Janes and spend the rest of their lives together in their cabin on the clifftop.

CHAPTER

5

ACE BRAKED HIS BICYCLE in front of Jude and Molly one afternoon as they were walking home from the grade school up the
hill from the highway. He was wearing chinos, with a bicycle clip on
one leg, a pinstriped oxford cloth shirt, and spotless white bucks, and
he reeked of Old Spice. There was a faint shadow on his upper lip,
and his chestnut hair was pomaded into a rigid flattop. Smiling so his
braces glinted in the weak autumn sunlight, he said in a cracking voice,
"Hey, ladies. How you doing today?"

"Fine, thank you," said Jude, glancing at him suspiciously over
her books, which she was clutching to her chest with both arms. He
had the same dull, dark wounded eyes, but everything else about him
seemed different now that he was in junior high. She and Molly had
heard that the Commie Killers were taking ballroom dancing lessons
at the Youth Center in case the graduates of Miss Melrose's Charm

Class invited them to be their escorts for the Virginia Club Colonial Cotillion. The notion of a room full of those gorillas waltzing in tuxedos with matching plaid cummerbunds and bow ties had reduced them to hysterics more than once.

"Mighty pretty day," he suggested.

As they walked, Jude noticed that the hand with which he was pushing his bicycle had nails chewed down to the quicks.

"Not bad," said Molly, eying this pleasant young Rotarian with curiosity.

Ever since Jude and Molly had started wearing skirts to school three years earlier, they had eaten lunch in the cafeteria and hung out together on the playground every day without being harassed by Noreen and Ace and their mobs. And after school, they donned blue jeans and raced their new horses down through the Wildwoods and along the river. Jude didn't really mind that her father had married his nurse from intensive care and moved her into their house, because Jude now spent most nights at Molly's, curled up with her and Sidney beneath the dotted swiss canopy like puppies in a litter. The only thing that bothered her about this arrangement was that she sometimes woke up in the middle of the night, to hear Molly's parents arguing in their bedroom. Occasionally, there were thuds, as though someone was throwing something. And then Molly's mother would start crying. But Molly always seemed to sleep right through it.

"Say, ladies," said Ace, running his hand up the front of his new scrub-brush hairdo, "Mill Valley has challenged Tidewater Estates to a football game. But we've only got eight players. Any chance you two would play?"

Molly and Jude glanced at each other. It might be a trick. Although the ancient wounds had healed, the scars remained to remind them.

"We need a full team if we're going to stand a chance." He

smiled at them smoothly, and Jude realized that he could have a fruitful career ahead of him as a horse trader.

"That's still just ten," said Molly, leaning over to straighten one of the white bobby socks that was sagging below her crinolined poodle skirt.

"Can you think of anybody else?"

"How about Sandy?" asked Jude.

Ace smiled with polite incredulity. "Sandy? Sandy Andrews? Sandy Andrews on a football field?"

"I played catch with him last year," said Jude. "He was working on his aerodynamics project for the county science fair. And believe me, Sandy knows how to throw a football."

"If Sandy doesn't play, we don't either," announced Molly.

Ace sighed with a sweet, long-suffering smile, a new facial expression in his rather limited repertoire. "All right. But you all ask him. He's not too crazy about me."

"I wonder if this is a good idea," mused Jude as Ace rode off down the hill. "Clementine always says that leopards don't change their spots without a whole lot of scrubbing."

"But he seems pretty scrubbed," said Molly. "We may as well give him a chance. If he's too obnoxious, we'll just quit the team."

ON THE FIELD ONCE pocked with their trenches, the former Commie Killers watched with amazement as Sandy repeatedly sailed the football over the heads of the enclosing tacklers and into Jude's or Molly's outstretched arms. Impressed, Ace promoted him to quarterback and Jude and Molly to ends.

Then they divided into two opposing lines. Crouching for drills like three-legged pit bulls, they collided time after time at a signal from Ace. The tenth time, Ace locked shoulder pads with Molly. Grinning at her with clenched teeth, he butted her backward down the field while she grimaced fiercely and struggled to dig her cleats into the turf and break his advance.

During the tackling drill that followed, Ace kept hurling himself through the air at Molly, bringing her crashing to the ground beneath him. Once, he continued to lie immobile on her like a sack of concrete, smiling up at Jude as Molly writhed and twisted beneath him.

"Get off me, you big lug!" Molly yelled.

Jude felt her hands clench into fists as she stood there watching. Apparently, the new, improved Ace Kilgore still had a few of his old tricks up his sleeve.

Laughing indulgently, he allowed Molly to push him aside.

"Drop dead, creep," she snarled as she struggled to her feet, face flushed and helmet askew.

Jude leaned over and asked her in a low voice, "Are you okay?"

"Of course I'm okay," she snapped, glaring at Ace as she straightened her helmet.

CLOUDS WERE SCUDDING LIKE hockey pucks across the bright blue sky. Noreen's crew wore red-and-white corduroy skirts, saddle shoes, and junior-high letter sweaters. Most sported jaunty ponytails.

"Girls?" the Mill Valley Butchers exclaimed when they dismounted from their bicycles and spotted Molly's black braids hanging down from her shiny red helmet.

"I know that ole girl," said one, pointing at Jude in her red jersey and padded khaki knickers. "She ain't nothing but a fifth grader."

"The Commandos got fifth-grade girls on their team! Oh, man!" They slapped one another's helmets with hilarity.

"You won't be laughing by the time this is over," snarled Ace from behind his plastic face guard.

"Better face it, rich boy," sneered Joe Sneed, "your ass is grass."

Joe's older brother Clyde, a former football star at the high school, home on leave from the marines, had come along as referee. The boys on both teams kept glancing at him as he stood there straight as a linesman's stake in his severe blond brush cut. He'd survived boot camp at Paris Island and killed Commies in Korea.

The Butchers won the coin toss, and Joe effortlessly returned the Commandos' kickoff for a touchdown, striding like a Louisville pacer through the scarlet maple leaves that were swirling like flocks of migrating cardinals across the plateau from the Wildwoods.

"Sorry, guys," Joe muttered to the Butchers as they trotted back up the field, shoulder pads jouncing like saddles. "I shoulda knowed this would be a waste of time."

For a while, Sandy strolled around the backfield in his cleats, hands on his hips, studying the Butchers and holding up a wet finger to assess the breeze. Jude and Molly fled to the sidelines each time the ball was snapped, while the Butchers ground the Commando line into the clay and massacred the ballcarrier. The afternoon gave every evidence of being a long and bloody one, and Jude couldn't imagine why she and Molly had given up cantering their horses along the river in order to be ripped to pieces by a gang of surly hoodlums.

Finally, Sandy announced in the huddle, "Okay, I'm ready."

Jerry Crawford centered the ball to Sandy. The Commando line turned suddenly impregnable, giving Sandy the leisure to fake a lateral and two handoffs to Ace and the Panther Twins so convincingly that the Butchers chased them down the field before realizing that Sandy still held the ball. Jude and Molly, meanwhile, were darting around midfield, causing the pursuing Butchers to collide with one another like enemy tanks. Sandy sailed a perfect spiral pass to Jude, who grabbed it out of the air and dashed untouched across the goal line.

Noreen's cheering squad went wild, prancing and twirling and turning cartwheels. They shook their red-and-white pompoms and thrust out their arms and legs in intricately choreographed patterns. Then they shouted in unison, with the same fervor they used to devote to speaking in tongues: "Hidy, hey, hidy, hoe! Iddley, widdley, waddley, woe! Our Commandos are the best! Better, better than the rest!"

The Butchers slunk home to the mill village after their defeat, and Molly invited the Commandos and the cheerleaders to her basement to celebrate their first victory with Cokes and butterscotch brownies.

"I have an idea," said Noreen as she drained the last of her Coke and brandished the green bottle like a fairy godmother's wand. "Let's play Spin the Bottle!"

The boys in their football uniforms eyed one another, grinning nervously and blushing behind their newly sprouted acne. Then they eyed the cheerleaders, who were draped decoratively around the steel jack posts that held up the ceiling.

"Good idea," said Ace, grabbing the bottle from Noreen. "Me first. Y'all girls get in a circle here."

Molly and Jude sat down cross-legged on the black-speckled linoleum as though before a campfire. Noreen and the other cheerleaders sank to their knees, tucked their feet beneath their hips, and braced their palms against the floor behind them so that their chests puffed out like robins in the spring. Ace stepped into the center of the circle, squatted, and twirled the bottle on the linoleum. It spun more and more slowly before finally stopping on Molly. She and Jude exchanged glances.

"Nobody has to play who doesn't want to," announced Jude.

"Fair's fair," said Molly. She stood up and disappeared in her football uniform behind the furnace with Ace.

Jude watched Jerry spin the bottle, praying it wouldn't land on her, wondering what was going on in the shadows behind the furnace. Would Molly really kiss their ancient enemy? Would she moan and sigh the way she had in third grade when she kissed the back of her own hand?

Jude watched in silent misery as the bottle inched to a halt. It was pointing at Noreen. She jumped up with a squeal, kicking back her saddle shoes in a coy pep-squad hop. As she and Jerry headed for the furnace, Ace and Molly emerged. Molly was blushing. She didn't look at Jude. But Ace did, grinning, his braces glinting in the light from the overhead bulb, which Molly had encased in a red-and-gold Japanese lantern.

Sandy's spin landed on Jude.

"She's too young," said Molly quickly. "She's just a fifth grader."

"She's only a year younger than I am," said Sandy. "I just skipped two grades, is all. Come on, Jude." He held out his hand.

In the dark beneath the cobwebbed heating ducts, Sandy whispered, "Thank God I got you."

"I'll say," whispered Jude. "Do we really have to do this?"

"We might as well get it over with."

As they tried to embrace, their arms collided and tangled. Then they bumped noses and began to giggle. Finally, Sandy managed to plant a peck on her mouth before they both doubled over with silent agonized hilarity.

Afterward, Jude and Molly changed from their football uniforms and walked to the pasture behind Jude's grandmother's house, where they kept their horses. Jude's father had bought them from a friend of Mr. Starnes who trained Tennessee walking horses for shows. These two geldings hadn't made the grade, but they were wonderful for riding because they were so happy no longer to have their hooves weighted for the ring that they seemed to dance on air as they ran. Tennessee walkers originally being bred for plantation owners to ride while surveying their fields, these two could cover miles without tiring, in a running walk as comfortable as rocking in a rocking chair. Although they had elaborate names and pedigrees, Jude called hers Flame because of a flaring white mark down his forehead, and Molly called hers Pal because he was a palomino, with a ghostly pale mane and tail.

On weekends, Jude and Molly rode downriver through pastures of bluegrass and timothy and fescue, past fields planted with tobacco and corn. Through bottomland studded with cottonwood, maple, sycamore, and sweet gum, their branches draped with lianas of wild grape that stirred in the breezes down the valley like serpents writhing in a jungle. After a picnic in the sun by the river, they headed back home along ridges thickly forested with oak and hickory and ash. In the fall, juicy orange persimmons fell into their laps as they passed beneath the overladen branches. And in the spring, dogwoods and redbuds starred the dark brooding woods with bursts of pink and purple and white, like fireworks that didn't fade.

That afternoon after Spin the Bottle, they cantered through Mr. Starnes's alfalfa field, alongside the low-leaning willows by the river. As Sidney leapt and barked beside her, Molly veered Pal toward the shore. Jumping the lip of the bank, Pal plunged into the water, throwing up a spray that glistened orange in the setting sun like sparks shooting from a fire.

Once Molly was thoroughly soaked, she headed Pal back toward dry land. He arced time after time up the rutted clay rise like a salmon leaping upstream. Molly threw her head back and laughed, dark wavy hair fanning out around her face, thighs gripping Pal's straining shoulders, fist maneuvering the rope she'd run through his halter for reins. For a moment, Jude couldn't catch her breath. Molly looked like the goddess on her grandmother's glass vase, the one with the bow on her back and the dogs leaping at her knees.

When Molly reached level ground, she dug her heels into Pal's flanks and lay down along his neck. He broke into a gallop, flying hooves hurling up clods of earth. As his cream-colored mane floated up and mixed with her dark hair, Molly glanced tauntingly back over her shoulder at Jude. Jude leaned forward and Flame shot off across the field after Pal like a land missile. Jude could see each muscle of Molly's back tensing and straining beneath the wet clinging fabric of her pale-blue work shirt.

When Jude and Molly finally slid off Pal and Flame in the stand of giant oaks on the cliff above their cave, the horses were covered with patches of white lather and dark sweat. The girls collapsed on a bed of leathery mauve leaves, laughing and gasping as their horses snorted and stamped and wheezed. In the tops of the huge old trees swayed globes of mistletoe the size of medicine balls.

After catching their breath, Molly and Jude propped themselves up on their elbows so they could watch the indigo mountains below, wave after wave of crenellated ridges like ripples on the sea, all being swallowed up by a maw of vermilion sunset. Jude could smell Molly's sweat and the rotting oak mold beneath the two of them, where a million earthworms were munching away. Molly's breath was stirring Jude's hair and tickling her ear. Suddenly, she recalled Ace's smug smile when he came out from behind the furnace and Molly's averted eyes.

"Do you still want to build a cabin up here when we grow up?" she asked Molly.

Molly turned her head to look at Jude. "Sure. Don't you?"

"Yes. But we haven't discussed it in a long time."

"What else would we do?" Molly reached out her little finger and interlocked it with Jude's.

"That kissing stuff was pretty dumb, wasn't it?" said Jude, relieved.

Molly didn't reply.

Jude's skin prickled with anxiety. "Wasn't it?"

"Yeah," Molly finally agreed. "Count on Noreen to dream up an ordeal like that."

"Sandy and I couldn't figure out what to do with our arms."

"You couldn't? Here. I'll show you."

Jumping up, she grabbed Jude's hand, pulled her to her feet, and arranged Jude's arms around her body. Beneath her fingertips, Jude could feel the damp cotton of Molly's shirt and the firm muscles of her back. Then Molly placed her arms around Jude, one hand holding a shoulder and the other Jude's waist.

"See? Simple." Smiling with just her eyes, she moved closer and kissed Jude firmly on the mouth.

As Molly's chest pressed against her own, Jude experienced an alarming sensation. It was sweet and nauseating, both at once, like eating too much fudge. Her teeth were set on edge and a shudder shook her limbs.

"What's wrong?" asked Molly.

Opening her eyes, Jude found herself staring directly into Molly's, which at that moment matched the blue of her shirt. "I don't know," she said. Shifting her hand down Molly's back, she discovered a piece of elastic stretching between Molly's shoulder blades. "What's this?"

"It's my new bra," said Molly, dropping her arms and stepping back.

"Why are you wearing a bra?" Mothers wore bras. Teachers wore bras. Marilyn Monroe wore a bra. But not kids.

"To support my breasts."

"But you don't even have any."

"I do so." Molly smiled.

"Where? Let me see." Jude reached out and undid her top button.

"Jude." Blushing, Molly turned away to rebutton her shirt.

"Sorry," said Jude, watching Molly uneasily.

The next afternoon while Molly was at the dentist, Jude walked through the revolving doors into Fine's Department Store on the main street of town. Glancing all around to make sure no one was watching, she sneaked into the lingerie department. All around her loomed beige plastic female torsos, severed at the waists, some headless or armless, others contorted into grotesque postures with their severed stumps of arms extended as though for a bloody embrace. Each sported a different type of brassiere or slip.

Clenching her molars for courage, Jude walked into their midst as though into an enchanted forest in which interlopers were chopped up and turned into bra-bearing statues. Reaching out to the nearest rack, she grabbed the first box she came to. After counting out her savings on the glass countertop, she shoved it at the gum-chewing salesgirl and fled.

Back in her bedroom, Jude threw off her flannel shirt and poked at the pale flesh surrounding her small pink nipples. It seemed no different from usual. But Molly always knew the right thing to do before Jude did. Inspecting the cardboard box, Jude read that the bra was size 36C. Removing the white cotton contraption from the cardboard box, she tried to figure out which strap went where. It was as confusing as when she was first learning to bridle Flame. Finally, she got the thing fastened and went over to look in the mirror on her closet door. The stitched fabric cups billowed atop her chest like luffing sails. Smiling proudly, she put her shirt back on and buttoned it. Then she turned sideways to the mirror to observe her new womanly contour.

AFTER EVERY FOOTBALL GAME, there was a celebratory session of Spin the Bottle in Molly's basement. Eventually, Jude had kissed each reformed Commie Killer at least once. These former marauders were so courteous and pleasant, even Ace Kilgore himself, that she was forced to admit that people could change. But try as she did to position her hands and mouth correctly, she felt very little except impatience as the boys pressed their lips against hers and ran their hands over the elastic that hung loosely between her shoulder blades. So she pretended that she was an orphan raised by wolves, participating in the rites of these strange creatures on the edge of the forest only to be polite.

One afternoon in early winter, Noreen announced that Spin the Bottle had become boring. Everyone nodded in agreement except Sandy, Molly, and Jude, who were wary of what she might propose instead. Her new game was called Five Minutes in Heaven. Each girl's name would be written on a slip of paper. Each boy would draw a folded slip. Then he and the girl he'd picked would be locked in the closet together for five minutes to "let nature take its course." Since there were nine couples that day, Noreen calculated that a complete cycle would require forty-five minutes. But several participants had to be home for supper before that, so she suggested locking up three couples at a time, one in the closet, one behind the furnace, and one in the outside stairwell, thus trimming game time to fifteen minutes. Those who ate supper late could play a second round if they wanted.

Jude watched with mounting dread as Noreen wrote out the

girls' names, tore the paper into strips, and folded them. She noticed that Noreen marked her own slip with a tiny *X* when she thought no one was looking, catching Jerry Crawford's eye as she did so. Then she mixed up the slips in the basket that had held the chocolate chip cookies. The first three boys selected one. Jerry unfolded his and gave Jude a look full of meaning. Noreen, meanwhile, looked at him with dismay. Then she glared evilly at Jude through her pointy new white cat-eye glasses.

Walking over to Jude, Jerry seized her hand and led her to the closet to which he'd been assigned. Within was an athlete's paradise —a croquet set, a kickball, fishing gear, a couple of rifles, a bicycle pump, a saddle and bridle, golf clubs and cleats, some deflated plastic beach toys. A badminton net was hanging off the upper shelf. Jerry closed the door, and he and Jude stood there in the dark, Jude wondering what they could possibly find to do with each other for the five minutes that stretched before them like the sands of the Sahara.

As Jerry leaned over to kiss her, his head became tangled in the badminton net. Struggling to free himself, he pulled the net off the shelf, along with several rackets and birdies. Jude also became entangled, and they spent their first two minutes in heaven trying to extract themselves. Finally, Jerry got them out by ripping the net to pieces.

Free at last, he put his arms around her and fitted his lips to hers. She could feel a fine stubble on his upper lip as he rubbed it against her own. Then he pushed his slimy tongue between her lips and into her mouth. She tried to push it back out again with her own tongue. This seemed to encourage him. Breathing faster, he started moving his tongue in and out like a striking snake. Jude turned her head aside, worried that she might throw up. Jerry put his hands on her waist, pulled her hips against his own, buried his stubbly face in the angle between her throat and shoulder, and began sucking her neck like a crazed vampire. She could feel some strange bulge in his football pants. It pressed against her belly like a concealed handgun.

The door flew open. Noreen was standing there looking deeply annoyed. "Time's up!" she announced like a teacher monitoring an IQ test. "Next!"

"So what did you think of Five Minutes in Heaven?" asked Molly after everyone had left. She grabbed the broom and began to sweep up the cookie crumbs on the linoleum.

"Not much." Jude was fitting the Coke bottles into the cardboard six-pack carriers, inspecting the bottom of each for its town of origin. So far, St. Louis was the farthest away.

"You didn't like it?"

"Did you?"

"It was okay."

Jude reflected that Molly's partner had been Sandy. No wonder she hadn't minded. Sandy always performed the minimum that he could get away with in these dumb games. "Jerry kept sticking his tongue into my mouth. It was disgusting."

Molly stopped sweeping to look at her. "You don't like Frenching?"

"What?"

"French kissing, it's called."

"You mean there's a name for it? I thought he'd made it up."

"You just need some practice. Here, let me show you."

Dropping the broom, she walked across the linoleum toward Jude. Jude watched her approach in her red football jersey, feeling strange. Was Molly really going to do that to her? With Molly, it might not be quite so revolting.

Extending the fingers of one hand, Molly placed her thumb beneath her index finger to form an opening. Wetting her lips with her tongue, she held this opening to her mouth. As Jude watched, she licked and caressed the aperture with her lips and tongue.

"Try it," she said.

Jude obeyed, looking at Molly as she did so, fascinated by the unexpected talents of this friend she thought she knew so well.

"I bet you'll like it better next time," said Molly, squeezing her upper arm.

Jude studied Molly, who was bending over to pick up the broom. With a stab of alarm, she wondered where Molly had learned to French kiss.

WHEN MRS. ELKINS ARRIVED in Molly's bedroom to say good night one evening, she was clutching a pink book called *New Life Abounding: A Guide to Christian Marriage.* Perching on the bedside beneath the dotted swiss canopy, she gazed at Sidney, who was panting amiably, filling the room with his sour dog-food breath.

"Girls, there's something we need to talk about," she said anxiously.

Jude and Molly, who were lying under the covers in their pajamas, looked at her with alarm.

"I suppose y'all have been wondering about babies and all like that?"

The girls glanced at each other.

"All right, so here's what happens," she gasped. "The daddy puts his pee-pee in the mommy's wee-wee, and a baby grows in her stomach. Oh, here, read it for yourselves." She thrust the pink book at them. Hyperventilating, she raced from the room.

Astonished by the concept that Mr. Elkins's tiny, pale pee-pee could somehow enter Mrs. Elkins's never-seen wee-wee, Molly and Jude spent several hours giggling nervously over the diagrams of this unlikely procedure. Molly pointed out haltingly that French kissing was merely this unappetizing act performed with the tongue. They gazed at each other with horror as they realized that each had done this with various boys. Did this mean that they weren't "virgins," which the book said it was very important still to be when you gave yourself to your new husband on your wedding night?

As she slipped into an exhausted sleep toward midnight, Jude finally understood that her father had killed her mother with one of those strange lumps that lurked like hand grenades in the pants of the new, improved Commie Killers.

CHAPTER

6

JUDE'S GRANDMOTHER looked up from soaking her baking-powder biscuit in redeye gravy to say, "Daniel, you're raising this child like a boy. Football, and horses without saddles, and jeeps in the pasture. And all this arrowhead nonsense. You may have gone to school in New York City, but you're every bit as much of a savage as your father was. I declare, I'm shocked to my core!"

"Yes, Momma. I'm sure you're right."

Jude realized that her father couldn't have cared less. He was beaming at his wife, whose belly was swelling with new life. Aunt Audrey's carrot-colored bouffant framed a foxlike face with small, pointed features. She was upset that Jude couldn't call her Mother. But each time Jude had tried, her throat had closed up, leaving her gasping like an asthmatic. Calling her Aunt Audrey was their compromise. Jude was trying to like her, but they had nothing in common except Jude's father. So Jude was polite to Aunt Audrey for his sake, and Aunt Audrey was polite to her for the same reason. Her father maintained she'd gained a mother, but she felt she'd lost a father instead.

"At least I wear shirts now," mumbled Jude.

"I beg your pardon?" barked her blue-haired grandmother. "Speak up, young lady."

"Nothing, ma'am."

"At the rate you're going, my dear, you'll never qualify for the Virginia Club Colonial Cotillion. And I refuse to ask them to lower their standards for you simply because I'm president." She returned the ladle to the silver gravy boat with finality.

Jude managed not to say that the only thing she wanted right now was to get this gruesome meal over with so she could go riding with Molly. Now that Molly was in junior high and Jude still in grade school, they saw each other only after school and on weekends. The Wildwoods were suddenly abloom and the alfalfa in the valley was greening up. The air had turned soft and steamy, and the soil would squelch under the horses' hooves when Pal and Flame loped along the riverbank in shafts of sunlight through the chartreuse willows.

Aunt Audrey said, "Yes, Jude, and you've got to think about how you're going to catch yourself a man when you get older." She plucked complacently at her bulging smock of rose linen.

Jude looked at her. If she wanted a man, she could always steal someone's father. Aunt Audrey was always making little jokes no one else thought were funny. It was pathetic.

That evening as Jude lay on her bed reading her assignment for Bible study class on the meaning of the lions in the story of Daniel, her grandmother phoned to say that Jude and Molly were enrolled in Miss Melrose's Charm Class at Fine's Department Store.

Jude held the phone receiver away from her ear and stared at it.

"They'll teach y'all how to dress and walk and sit," her grandmother promised.

"But I can already do that, Grandma."

"Not properly. Not like a young Virginia belle."

THE PROPER WAY TO WALK required placing one foot directly in front of the other as though crossing a tightrope, hips swaying side to side as ballast. Math texts balanced on their heads, Molly, Jude, Noreen, and several other apprentice charmers swayed along behind Miss Melrose (whose shiny false eyelashes and switchblade fingernails were all about an inch long) through the shoe department, down the escalator, past the waxworks of writhing plastic amputees in the lingerie department, and into the makeup department, which reeked of competing colognes.

"Now, girls," said Miss Melrose from behind the glass counter as she picked up a cotton ball and a bottle of caramel-colored liquid that looked like a urine sample, "at this particular moment in time, y'all's lovely little ingenue faces aren't anything but nasty old cell cemeteries."

Using the moistened cotton, she demonstrated on Noreen's oily forehead how to defoliate and moisturize these cemeteries. Then she promised to unveil the mysteries of eyeliner at the next session. Their homework assignment was to memorize the first ten silverware patterns in their *Learning to Be a Lady* handbook. She warned that they would be tested on this.

"Now y'all don't forget to bring you some high-heeled shoes next time," she called as they exited through the revolving door to the street, "and we'll practice our walk some more."

"Oh, please," muttered Jude as she and Molly headed home in the soft spring twilight, up the main street past the display windows at the five-and-dime. Jude felt acutely conscious of the incorrectness of her everyday gait, an ambling shuffle, faintly pigeon-toed. But Ace maintained that the fastest sprinters were always pigeon-toed, and it was true that Jude could outrun everyone else on the football team.

Molly was silent, which was making Jude uneasy. She had seemed alarmingly attentive during the skin-toning demonstration. The next thing you knew, she'd be wearing false eyelashes and a piecrust of makeup, just like Miss Melrose.

"I have something to tell you," said Molly as they passed their redbrick church, its white spire topped by a copper cross tarnished to the blue-green of bread mold. "I hope it won't hurt your feelings."

"What, for God's sake?"

"I'm having a party in my basement Friday night."

"A slumber party?"

"A boy-girl party. A Dirty Shag party."

"But you don't know how to shag."

"Yes, I do, Jude. They have sock hops at junior high during lunch break. To raise money for different charities."

"Well, I guess you could teach me to shag by this weekend."

"Jude," she said in a low, guilty voice, "it's just for junior high kids." She was staring at the sidewalk.

"Okay," Jude finally said. "So I'll just see you Saturday morning. We'll watch 'Fury' together. And maybe go riding. Or look for arrowheads in the afternoon with my dad."

"Great," said Molly. "You know you're my best friend. Nothing can ever change that."

"Yes, I know that."

They had reached the crack in the sidewalk between their two yards. For old times' sake, laughing, they put their hands on each other's shoulders, glanced into each other's eyes, and chanted in unison, "Best friend. Buddy of mine. Pal of pals." Molly seemed relieved to have made her confession, and Jude vowed always to help her feel free to do what she wanted.

Following supper and homework, Jude and Molly stood side by side in their shorty pajamas before the mirror in Molly's bathroom, setting their hair on rollers as big as frozen orange-juice cans. Then they encased the rollers in stretchy silver lamé hair nets that made them look like spacemen. Climbing into Molly's bed, they tried to discover a comfortable sleeping position that wouldn't result in stiff necks in the morning.

Finally settled on her side with Molly's chest against her back, Jude tried to relax, despite the fact that her ear was touching her shoulder. Molly twitched her legs irritably several times. Sighing, she sat up.

"What's wrong?" asked Jude, rolling over to look up at her in the glow coming through the window from the streetlight.

Molly reached under the covers and stroked one of Jude's calves. "Your legs. They tickle when we sleep like that. Couldn't you shave them?"

"I guess I could," said Jude. "I never thought about it." She ran her hand along one of Molly's calves. It was silky-smooth.

Molly rested her pumpkin head against the quilted headboard. "Jude," she said, "you know, it's not that easy for someone in junior high school to be best friends with a sixth grader."

Jude sat up and looked over at her. "I know it must be hard," she said, recalling her rash vow that afternoon to help Molly do as she wanted. "Do you want to see less of me?"

Molly said nothing for a long time.

God, Molly, don't leave me, Jude screamed silently. But she gritted her teeth and revealed nothing, as though bluffing during Over the Moon.

"No," Molly finally said. "But do please think about shaving your legs." She scooted to the far side of the bed and pulled the covers up to her chin.

Jude lay in the dark listening to the soft, steady whoosh of Molly's breathing. She could smell the floral cologne Molly had started splashing on her limbs after baths. She wanted to reach across the expanse of sheet and stroke Molly's hair. Or roll on top of her and lie nose-to-nose with their limbs aligned, giggling in unison and gazing into each other's crossed eyes. But they weren't children anymore.

Sidney yelped and snuffled in his sleep on his cushion in the corner. Baby frogs were peeping down by the river, and a coonhound was baying from some distant moonstruck cove.

Finally drifting off to sleep, Jude dreamed fitfully of losing her pocketbook, and being late for school, and having a flat tire on her bicycle, and having her teeth fall out in her hand at a party. Abruptly, she woke up. Molly's father was growling down the hall, followed by the high-pitched wail of her mother. Why couldn't they just be nice to each other and keep quiet? They were supposed to be the parents. Grabbing a tissue from the nightstand, Jude tore it up, plugged each ear with a wad, and tried to ignore their incomprehensible misery.

Toward dawn, she descended into an exhausted stupor.

She and Molly were lying on a raft in the river under a hot spring sun, floating past drooping willows that were mustard with new shoots. The raft rocked slowly in the current. Cawing crows were wheeling overhead. Sunbeams were flickering like hummingbird wings, back and forth across their flesh.

While the raft bobbed, the water began to flow faster and faster. She and Molly rolled toward each other and fitted their bodies together, interlocking their thighs and enfolding each other in their arms. As they were swept along down the river, their mouths met. They began to caress each other's lips with their tongues.

The current raced more and more swiftly, as though about to carry them over a waterfall. The rutted red banks rushed past on either side. And then a towering wall of water rolled down the river and raised the raft high up toward the sky, swirling it into the air like an autumn leaf on a whirlwind. And Jude felt a sweet, haunting pain pulsing through her body, as though she were being stung to death by a swarm of bees injecting her veins with honey.

And then the whole world burst apart like fireworks. Bits of Molly's and her flesh flew off into the churning river and roiling sky. And they were no longer Molly or Jude. They were each other and everything. The mountains and the trees and the birds singing in the swaying branches. The river and the pastures and the cows grazing on the lush grasses. They all formed a whole. They always had and they always would, but she had lacked until now the eyes to see it.

Waking up in the scarlet rays of the rising sun, Jude discovered that she and Molly were completely wrapped up in each other's arms and legs in the middle of the bed, breasts pressed together. Molly's eyes fluttered open and she stared blankly into Jude's, only inches away, as though unable to remember who she was or who Jude was. Slowly, the blankness faded and was replaced by consternation. Hurriedly, she untangled her limbs and scooted to the far side of the bed.

Glancing around bemusedly, Jude discovered that their giant curlers had been yanked out and hurled around the room and that their hairdos for that day were in ruins.

At school, Jude sat through her classes in a daze, constantly reviewing what had happened between Molly and herself. It comforted her to know that Molly was sitting in study hall at the junior high school just then, also trying to figure out what it meant.

She watched a gray squirrel on a branch of the oak tree outside her classroom window. It sat on its haunches munching an apple core retrieved from the trash basket. Its fluffy, twitching tail was draped along its spine like a Mohawk haircut. As she watched, Jude thought maybe she finally understood what her father had always tried to explain to her. Beneath their different appearances, she and that squirrel were animated by the same force. It was the force that had joined Molly and her together last night. The Cherokees called it the Great Spirit, and Clementine called it graveyard love.

JUDE CRAWLED ACROSS THE LAWN to Molly's house, trying to pretend that she was an orphan raised by wolves who had just emerged from the forest. She was actually nothing more than a common Peeping Tom. But Aunt Audrey and her father were at the hospital having their baby, so no one would miss her. She lay in the shrubbery, looking through a basement window. Molly was dancing with Ace to "The Twelfth of Never." Ace had her arm twisted behind his back in a reverse hammerlock. Molly's hair was teased into dark cascades around her face. Eyes closed, she rested her cheek against his thick neck. Jude realized that Molly actually had the hips they'd been encouraged to sway at Charm Class.

Then there was a power failure and the lights went out. But the song continued: "Hold me close. Never let me go. . . ." So apparently it wasn't a power failure.

Yet the lights stayed out until Jude heard Mrs. Elkins's voice on the steps: ". . . and I insist that these lights stay on, Molly. If I have to tell you one more time, there'll be no more parties in this basement, young lady."

When the lights came back on, Jude could see Molly standing apart from Ace, who was wiping his mouth with the back of his hand. Molly's lips looked swollen. But how could she be kissing Ace Kilgore tonight after what had gone on between them last night on the raft?

Sidney came sniffing up to Jude's prostrate body. Whimpering, he lay down beside her, resting his chin on her shoulder. Jude draped her arm across his back. They watched Molly knead Ace's muscled shoulder with one hand while they resumed dancing, and Jude tried to figure out how to switch the lights off so that Mrs. Elkins would ban future parties. Closing her eyes, she willed the whole scene to vanish by the time she opened them.

Her mother was riding a puffy white cloud, a large picture hat clamped to her head with one hand. Smiling, she waved with the fingers of her free hand. Jude watched, worried to see her again after so many years, because her mother usually appeared whenever Jude was in for a bad time.

WHEN JUDE ENTERED MOLLY'S back door the next morning, Molly was sitting at the kitchen table eating a bowl of Cheerios. She had purple circles under her eyes, and so did Jude. Jude had lain awake all night trying to decide what to do about Molly's betrayal.

Plopping down in the chair beside her, Jude asked, "So how was your party?"

"Fine, thank you," said Molly without looking up. She tilted her bowl to spoon out the remaining milk.

"Was it any fun?"

"Yes, thank you." Still Molly wouldn't look her at her. And she seemed annoyed. Could she have seen Jude spying on her? Jude had believed that Molly should be free to do as she wanted, but that was at a time when she thought that what Molly wanted was to be with her.

Pulling herself together, Jude asked, "So do you want to go riding this morning, or what?"

"I'm afraid I can't." Molly leaned back in her chair, balancing on the rear legs like a circus tumbler. "It's one of Those Days."

"Which days?"

"I have cramps."

"Did you eat too fast?"

"No, I mean I have The Curse." Molly tossed her wavy black hair off her forehead with the back of one hand.

"The what?"

"My period. You know, like we read about in that pink book my mother gave us last year."

"You're kidding?"

"No."

"Since when?"

"Since yesterday."

"So you can have babies now?"

"Yes, I guess so," said Molly. She sounded vaguely pleased.

"Molly, for God's sake, be careful." Jude grabbed her forearm. "Babies can kill you."

"Your Aunt Audrey just had one, and she's still alive."

"She was just lucky."

"Honestly, Jude," said Molly, irritably wrenching her arm out of Jude's grip. "Grow up."

Jude looked at her angrily. "Fine," she snapped. "Have a baby. Die in childbirth. Get buried in the cemetery with all the other dead mothers. That's where you'll end up anyway if you get involved with Ace Kilgore."

Molly glanced at her guiltily. "What does Ace have to do with this?"

Jude said nothing for a long time, trying to decide whether to confess to what she'd witnessed through the basement window. "Noreen told me you have a crush on him," she finally murmured.

"What business is it of yours?"

Jude was stunned by Molly's contemptuous tone of voice, stunned that she didn't deny the crush, and stunned that she could even ask such a question. "How could it *not* be my business?" she asked in a low voice.

"What do you mean?" asked Molly, averting her eyes.

"After the other night . . . You know . . ."

"I don't know what you're talking about." Molly returned her chair legs to the floor, stood up, and carried her bowl to the sink.

Jude watched her in disbelief, feeling desperately lonely. The most important experience of her life to date had been just a dream. And the indestructible bond it had established between Molly and herself existed only in her own imagination.

"SO IF YOU KEEP your knees together tight, girls, and smile up at your date while you swing your legs under the dashboard, you can get into any sports car, no matter how small, without displaying all your worldly treasures." Miss Melrose was demonstrating her technique in her desk chair as she talked. The Charm Class was assiduously copying her movements, even though none of the boys they knew could drive.

As Jude secured her worldly treasures beneath her imaginary dashboard, she noticed that Molly had painted her fingernails pink. Now that Jude was in junior high, she, too, shaved her armpits as well as her legs. And she put on lipstick, eyeliner, and mascara every morning. Thanks to Miss Melrose, she knew never to wear white shoes before Easter or after Labor Day and not to make chicken salad with dark meat. But Molly was always one step ahead.

Except in the classroom. Despite her efforts to score poorly on the placement exams, Jude had been assigned to a special seminar, along with the nerds who played slide-rule games in the lunchroom while all the cool kids did the Dirty Shag in the gymnasium to raise money for cerebral palsy. Jude had also been elected seventh-grade representative to the student council, which was dominated by classmates who were Episcopalian and Presbyterian and who lived in the big, fancy houses of the Yankee mill executives along Poplar Bluff.

But Molly never even congratulated her on her student council victory. And if Jude tried to explain some of the ideas she was learning about in the seminar, Molly would just shrug and say, "Afraid you've lost me again, brainchild."

Some afternoons after school now, instead of racing Flame through the Wildwoods, Jude sat with Sandy in his upstairs bedroom discussing the big bang theory and natural selection and relativity. Out the window, they watched Noreen coaching Molly in Noreen's backyard for the upcoming cheerleader tryouts. Sometimes their lyrics reached Jude and Sandy through the open windows:

> "Well, down my leg and up my spine!
> We've got a team that's mighty fine!"

She and Sandy would pause in their discussion of Hegel's dialectic to giggle. Then Jude would frown at herself, feeling disloyal.

As they strolled home from Charm Class through the twilight, allowing their kilted hips to sway with every step, Jude said, "My dad said he'd teach us to drive the jeep down that hill behind the cemetery on Saturday afternoon."

"Oh, Jude, I'm afraid I can't."

"But it would be really neat to be able to drive, wouldn't it?"

"I'm afraid I'm tied up on Saturday afternoon."

"Doing what?"

"Jude, I'm not your slave. You don't need to know my every move."

"Sorry."

They walked in silence past yards full of tulips. Ever since Jude had realized that her experience on the raft with Molly had been just a dream, she hadn't known how to behave with her. It seemed impossible to recapture the unselfconscious accord of their childhood, but no guidelines for their distressing new separateness had emerged. So they often experienced awkward silences or irritated outbursts, followed by frantic attempts to backpedal to the harmony they used to take so effortlessly for granted.

"I like the white tulips best, don't you?" Molly finally said.

"Me, too," said Jude, accepting the apology.

"Actually, I'm going to the lake with Ace Saturday afternoon. To ride in his father's motorboat." She was trying to sound casual.

Jude glanced at her. Molly and Ace often danced together at the noontime sock hops. And although Molly never admitted it, Jude suspected that they talked on the phone a lot at night. Occasionally, the three of them sat together on the bleachers at lunch to watch intramural basketball. Ace and Molly weren't going steady, and they never went out on dates, but Jude could tell that Molly was sometimes preoccupied with him.

"But why Ace?" she finally asked, genuinely curious. "I just don't get it. Have you forgotten how mean he was to us?"

"There's a really sweet side to him that you've never seen, Jude. He may act tough, but inside he's just a sad, scared little boy." She was smiling fondly, as though describing the antics of her dog.

"Please spare me the details."

"Besides, there are reasons why he was so mean."

"Such as?"

"His father isn't a nice man."

"His father is the best lawyer in town. My dad says he was a big hero in the war."

"I can't say any more."

Jude studied her from the corner of her eye. "We've never had secrets, Molly." They were passing more tulips. Jude decided she hated them, especially the white ones.

"I promised Ace."

"So Ace is more important to you now than I am?"

"No, of course not, Jude. But he needs me. I think I can help him."

Reaching the crack in the sidewalk marking the boundary between their yards, they turned to face each other. Molly's shirt collar was peeping out from beneath her sweater. On it, Jude spotted a tiny dagger made from a straight pin, a piece of red plastic cord, and some multicolored beads the size of BBs. Noreen had started this fad, which had swept the halls of the junior high school. She and the other cheerleaders made sets consisting of a miniature dagger and sword. The boys bought them, and the cheerleaders donated the money to muscular dystrophy. The boys wore them crossed on their collars until they wanted to go steady, at which point they gave their girlfriends their daggers.

"What's that?" asked Jude, pointing at Molly's dagger as though at a scorpion.

Molly started, then looked quickly away. "Ace asked me to wear it today."

Jude said nothing for a long time. She was losing this battle, but she was damned if she'd make it easy for either of them. "What about me?"

"But Jude, you're a girl," said Molly gently. "You're my best friend, but Ace is my boyfriend. Why don't you get a boyfriend, too?

Then we can double-date to the movies. What about Jerry Crawford? Ace says he really likes you.''

''What about our cabin?'' Jude asked doggedly. She didn't want Jerry Crawford. She wanted Molly.

''What cabin?''

''The cabin we were going to build on the ridge above the cave. With the paddock for Flame and Pal.''

''But we were just kids then, Jude. It was like playing house.'' She was gazing at Jude with loving concern.

Jude felt the bottom drop out of her stomach, like a trapdoor to hell. She had known she was losing, but she hadn't realized that she'd already lost.

''Please don't do this, Molly.''

Molly laughed weakly. ''But I'm not doing anything.''

As Jude walked up her sidewalk, she reflected that if she had one of those weird things growing between her legs, like Molly's father or the boys behind the furnace, she'd be able to slow-dance with Molly and go steady with her and all the things she had started wanting since entering junior high. Jude had no choice but to build their cabin alone, without Molly, who would be living somewhere else with Ace Kilgore and their mutant babies.

Aunt Audrey was upstairs talking to her new baby, Daniel junior, who was cooing and gurgling. Jude went into the kitchen and cut herself a piece of Mrs. Starnes's latest cake—chocolate fudge with buttercream frosting. Carrying her plate into the living room, she sat down in the brown leather chair whose arms she and Molly used to ride, lassoing Sidney with Clementine's clothesline. Reaching over to the end table, she opened the drawer and extracted the framed photo of her mother in the wine bottle, setting it up on the table. Her father always put it in the drawer now, explaining that it upset Aunt Audrey. And Jude always removed it, not explaining that it upset *her* to have

Aunt Audrey sleeping in the very bed in which her father gave her mother the baby that had killed her.

Yet the birth of Aunt Audrey's two babies hadn't killed *her*, so Jude was having to reexamine her assumptions. And she had to confess that she adored her little half brothers, with their toothless grins and tiny twitching digits and intense navy-blue gazes. Munching her cake, she stared at the photo of her beautiful mother, trapped in a bottle like an exotic flower. She wondered whether her mother had felt the same fierce devotion for her that Aunt Audrey seemed to feel for her babies. She thought probably so, judging by the look on her face as she held Jude's cheek to her own in the photo by Jude's bedside.

IN A TENT LIKE the circus big top, pitched in the middle of the county fairground on the outskirts of town, a visiting evangelist with a vanilla pompadour and a smile that wouldn't quit was enjoining the Baptist Youth from throughout the area to swear forever to forgo dancing, drinking, card playing, swearing, and the "illicit pleasures of the flesh." Jude watched from her folding chair beside Jerry Crawford as Molly and Ace joined the throng moving down the center aisle toward the front platform to be born again. She was appalled by the ease with which Molly was making a vow she'd never keep, loving Over the Moon as she did. Ace was evidently turning her into a liar. She'd been behaving very oddly since becoming pinned to him. Her blue eyes had lost their luster, and she walked like a robot, as though hypnotized by an evil wizard.

The new recruits for salvation gathered behind the glad-handing preacher, facing the audience. Meeting Molly's eyes, Jude gestured in wolfspeak, What the hell are you doing?

Molly looked away, smiling proudly up at Ace. The perpetually grinning agent of the Lord extended his arms as though walking a tightrope and invoked the Lord's blessing on "these the future leaders of our great Chrush-chen nation," who had pledged henceforth to lead new lives "swept clean by the push broom of Christ!"

Afterward, the Baptist Youth from Jude's church piled into their hay-filled delivery truck. As it rumbled down the road toward town, someone began singing "Jacob's Ladder."

Jerry leaned down, searching for Jude's lips in the dark. His Dentyne-fresh breath was warm on her cheek. Jude turned her head aside and feigned a deep commitment to getting the alto harmony just right on "If you love Him, why not serve Him?" Jerry sighed and rummaged through the hay for her hand, which he pinned beneath his own like copulating starfish.

In the middle of "This Little Light of Mine," everyone began waving flashlights around the truck. In the sweeping beams, Jude spotted Ace and Molly buried in hay in the rear corner, bodies pressed together, mouths gasping like dying fish. Apparently, they had decided to ignore the strictures against the illicit pleasures of the flesh.

Molly glanced up for a moment and her glazed eyes met Jude's. They gazed at each other for a long moment, and Jude thought that her heart was going to shatter into a thousand jagged shards right there on the blanket of hay. Eyes still interlocked with Molly's, Jude turned her head toward Jerry's and finally opened her lips to his. Through angry eyes, she watched Molly watch her as she drew Jerry's tongue into her mouth and placed his rough crustacean hand on her newly swelling breast.

As they walked home from school beneath the flying red Texaco horse, Molly announced that she and Ace had registered together for a Baptist Youth retreat in the Virginia mountains the next weekend. Although she urged Jude to sign up with Jerry, Jude had by now accepted her waterloo. She had been trying to save Molly from Ace, but she had finally understood that Molly didn't want to be saved.

Since she no longer had anything to lose, Jude said, "I wouldn't even go to heaven if I knew Ace Kilgore would be there."

Molly's blue eyes flared liquid ice. "Ace may not be very nice sometimes," she snapped, "but at least he's not boring."

"Meaning I bore you?" Jude clenched her jaws to keep from crying.

"No, you don't bore me," said Molly, retreating hastily. "It's just that sometimes I feel a little bit suffocated with you, Jude. It's like you want us to build a cabin on the ridge and stay children forever."

"Well, you won't have to worry about Ace Kilgore's suffocating you," muttered Jude, "because he'll probably be in prison soon."

"You and I are the ones who are in danger of prison," she said, staring at the sidewalk.

"What's that supposed to mean?"

"Some of the things we've done—they're just not right."

"Like what?"

"Oh, you know." Molly gazed across the street. "Playing Pecan. All that stuff."

"What was wrong with it?" It hadn't felt wrong at the time. It had felt right—for both of them. Now Molly, in addition to destroying their future, was rewriting their past.

"Two girls aren't supposed to do that together."

"Who says?" asked Jude weakly.

"God does," replied Molly with serene conviction. "The Bible says that a virtuous woman should be a crown to her husband."

Jude stopped walking and turned to look at her. "Since when have you cared what the Bible says?"

"Since I accepted God as my Lord and Master at that revival." She looked at Jude with defiance, blue eyes gone stone gray.

As Jude looked back, she felt her jaw fall open. Taking on God as well as Ace Kilgore was clearly hopeless. "But, Molly, I love you," she said softly, accepting defeat.

For a moment, Molly looked confused, her present self warring with a more ancient one. "Maybe I love you, too, Jude," she finally replied in a choked voice. "But not like that."

"Like what?" asked Jude with sudden urgency. She watched Molly closely.

Molly said nothing for a long time, staring hard at a cluster of red ants dragging a dead wasp along the pavement. "Not like that night on the raft."

THE SATURDAY AFTERNOON of the Baptist Youth retreat, Jude's father came into the kitchen to ask, "Do you and Molly want to go drive the jeep with me?"

Jude was lying facedown on the fake-brick kitchen linoleum. "Molly's gone."

He stood over her and looked down. "Oh?"

"She's in Virginia on a retreat."

"Didn't you want to go, too?"

"No." Jude had spent the past several days swinging violently between elation and despair. The dream about Molly and herself on the raft hadn't been a dream after all. Or if it had been, Molly had dreamed it, too. Together, they had experienced something profound. After loving each other for nearly a decade, they had set aside the boundaries that normally separated two people. They had merged with each other and with all creation. No one and nothing could ever take that knowledge away from Jude. But Molly wanted to. First she pretended it hadn't happened. Now she insisted it wasn't important.

That afternoon, Jude had forced herself to face the fact that Molly loved Ace *because* he was so awful. She liked the idea of saving a sinner, taming a wild beast, reforming an outlaw. Since he was a bad boy, she could feel like a good girl. Unless Jude could have a personality transplant and become even more wicked than Ace, there was absolutely nothing she could do to compete.

That night in the living room, Aunt Audrey passed Danny to Jude to hold as they all chuckled over the antics of Sid Caesar on "Your Show of Shows." Danny was cuddly and sweet-smelling in his flannel Dr. Denton's. Holding him upright, Jude let him tread her lap, his chubby legs churning as he pretended to walk. Then he reached out with his tiny, perfect fingers to grab her lower lip. Clutching it, he stared into her eyes with his open, trusting, quizzical gaze. He was so uncomplicated and innocent and vulnerable, loving to seize and examine anything within reach, loving to have any area of his soft velvet skin stroked by anyone anytime. How did an enchanting creature like this turn into an Ace Kilgore? Jude wondered.

Her father was holding Sam, his older son, on his lap. Sam also wore flannel Dr. Denton's. He was squirming as Jude remembered squirming, climbing all around the puffy leather armchair, experimenting to find the most comfortable position in relation to his father's large frame. Then he played hide-and-seek with Jude, believing that if he covered his eyes so that he couldn't see her, she couldn't see him, either. Her father laughed at this until his face turned scarlet. Jude was glad to see him so happy.

Molly was happy, too, with someone besides Jude. But Jude wasn't a lonely motherless child anymore. She was first in her class and in line to be secretary of the student council. The president, a ninth grader from Pittsburgh who lived on Poplar Bluff, had invited her to a party at his house the following weekend. She had a life apart from Molly and her father, just as they did from her.

The phone rang. Her father answered. His cheerful face contorted. "I'll be right down," he said in a voice turned suddenly terrible.

He stood for a moment with his hand on the receiver before facing Jude. "Baby, Molly's been in a car wreck. I have to go to the emergency room."

Aunt Audrey put her hands to her face but said nothing.

Jude looked up from her armchair. "Can I come, too?"

"Maybe you'd better not."

"It's bad?"

"It's real bad."

"I'm coming."

Jude sat in the waiting room with Molly's parents as people in rust-stained white rushed in and out. Ace's parents were there, too. Jude kept looking at Mr. Kilgore in his khakis and sports shirt, trying to figure out why he wasn't a nice man. Apart from his dull black eyes, he looked like every other father in town. Other parents Jude didn't know were also there.

Seven Baptist Youth had been riding in a car driven by a high-school junior. Ace had taunted him to go faster on the winding mountain road, yelling encouragement as the speedometer needle climbed higher and higher. He cheered as it reached fifty, then sixty, then seventy. Molly, who was sitting on Ace's lap beside an open back window, began yelling at the driver to slow down. The other girls screamed and wept.

The car missed a curve, skidded off the shoulder, and rolled down a steep embankment. Molly was thrown partway out the window on the first roll. On the second roll, the car landed on top of her.

Molly's mother was holding Jude's hand and crying softly. Molly's father was pacing the room. *Jude was on an ice floe at the South Pole, floating silently on a frozen silver sea.*

Ace came out on crutches, explaining to his mother, "So I tried to hold on to her. I tried to pull her back in. I had her around the waist. But then we were upside down and I lost her. . . ." He looked at Jude and stopped talking. She looked back at him. He swung out the door between his parents.

Hours later, Molly was rolled out on a stretcher. Her dark, wavy hair had been shaved off, and careful catgut stitches snaked across her skull like lacing on a softball. Her face was black and purple. One arm was in a cast. Plastic tubing from her nose and hand attached to bags of liquid on a rack being pushed by a nurse.

Jude's father appeared in green scrub clothes stained with Molly's blood.

"Is she going to be okay?" asked Jude. Adults died, not kids.

"I've done everything I can." But his maroon eyes were squinty, as though seeking refuge in the caverns formed by his high cheekbones.

Jude, her father, and the Elkinses followed the stretcher to a small room and watched orderlies transfer the body to a narrow white bed. Jude's father routinely saved lives, or so people all over town told her. He'd save Molly.

"Go home and have a rest," said Molly's mother, stroking Molly's inert arm.

"Good idea," said Jude's father. "I'm beat. We'll be back soon."

While her father showered and changed, Jude put some things into a paper bag—*Mademoiselle* and *Seventeen* to read to Molly once she was awake; nail polish so she could paint Molly's nails, which had gotten chipped during the wreck; a piece of Mrs. Starnes's orange-blossom cake, Molly's favorite, wrapped in foil.

Leaving the house to wait for her father in the car, Jude discovered Sidney sitting by the back door. She squatted down and patted him. Looking up, she saw Molly standing under the mulberry tree by the garage.

"Oh, you're back already?" said Jude, standing up. Sidney stood up, too, staring at Molly and whimpering.

As Jude walked toward her, she realized it wasn't Molly after all. It was just a shadow cast by the moon through the mulberry branches. But Sidney was still staring at the shadow, trembling all over.

WHEN JUDE AND HER father got back to the hospital, Molly was dead.

JUDE REFUSED TO GO to the funeral. She didn't want to hear Noreen keening by the grave as though over a lost football game. And she didn't want to meet Ace Kilgore's gaze. She lay on her bed eating raspberry sherbet and wondering if she'd gone on that retreat whether Molly would be lying beside her right now. Molly had once saved her from the Commie Killers, but she had not saved Molly.

She heard Sidney howling outside. Inviting him in, she let him lie on her bed and listlessly lick sherbet from her spoon.

She was gazing across a vast, empty snowfield that glistened under a merciless sun. She looked into the electric blue overhead for a cloud to carry her mother, but the sky was empty.

Out the window, Sandy and her father, dressed in suits and ties, were returning from the cemetery alongside Aunt Audrey, who was carrying Danny zipped into a padded powder-blue snowsuit. Their breath was frosty. Her father came into the house and up to her room. He sat down on the bed and patted Sidney.

"I don't know what to say, Jude. Just that I know how awful you feel right now. The years roll by and life goes on and new people come along. But some people can never ever be replaced."

Jude kept eating her sherbet. If he had just died in the war in

France, her mother would still be alive. Besides, he was a quack. He
hadn't saved Molly.

Sometime later, Sandy appeared in her doorway, still dressed in
his suit and tie. "I'm really sorry, Jude."

"Thanks."

"You'll always have your memories of Molly. No one can ever
take those away."

Jude looked at him. "That may be all I ever had."

"What do you mean?"

"Do you think dreams are real?"

He shrugged. "I've read they're wish fulfillment. Or just random
firings of neurons at rest."

"I thought Molly and I loved each other, but maybe I made the
whole thing up."

"No, Jude. Molly loved you."

"Then why did she stop?"

"She didn't stop. But I think she got scared."

"Scared of what?"

"Scared of being different. Scared of losing herself in you. Molly
wasn't as strong as you are."

Jude frowned. It didn't make sense. Molly was older. She had
usually been the leader. And Jude didn't feel strong. She felt like
crawling under her bed and never coming out.

He patted her awkwardly on the shoulder, and when she thought
to look up again, he was gone.

That night she went down to her father's office and found an
Ace bandage. Removing her shirt and bra, she bound her new breasts
so tightly that they ached. Then she let Sidney outside to pee and got
some more raspberry sherbet.

When Clementine arrived the next morning, Jude and Sidney

were lying on her bed surrounded by sticky bowls of melted sherbet, even though it was a school day.

"Sugar, I'm just so sorry," said Clementine.

"If Molly and I have a graveyard love, I guess we're halfway home," said Jude.

"You'll feel better by and by, I promise you."

Clementine stroked her back. Feeling the Ace bandage, she unbuttoned Jude's shirt and looked down at her tightly wrapped chest and the angry chafed flesh around the edges. "What you done to yourself, Miss Judith?"

"I don't want to be a woman," she said. "You become a woman, you love a man, and it destroys you."

"O Sweet Jesus, my poor lost lamb," murmured Clementine, taking Jude into her arms, rocking her and humming a gospel tune about Christ gathering His flock into the fold at twilight.

JUDE RODE HER BIKE into town. With her allowance, she bought a red-clay pot of white tulips. Holding it in one arm, she pedaled past her grandmother's huge white house. She'd just received a card from the Great Wall saying: "The Chinese are so polite and gracious, very much like Virginians."

Entering the cemetery, Jude walked over to the hillock of fresh clay that now encased Molly's bruised and broken body. As she set the clay pot among the withering wreaths from the service, Jude realized that to do anything at all, even to buy these flimsy flowers that would shrivel in the evening chill, was unnecessary. She and Molly had been dead to each other for nearly a year now.

"Best friend. Buddy of mine. Pal of pals," she murmured to the red-clay mound before turning away to ride back home, down the tunnel of arcing elms whose leprous limbs were coated with hoarfrost.

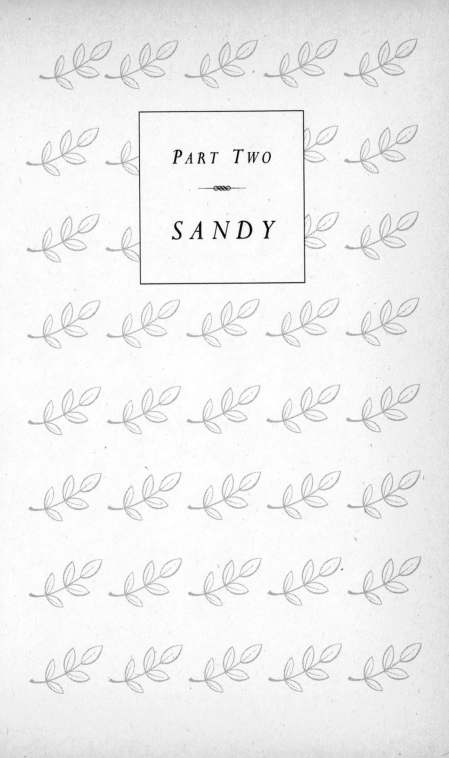

PART TWO

SANDY

CHAPTER

8

"OH, MY," said Sandy as he opened the door of his Riverside Drive apartment and discovered Jude in her cream blazer, navy-blue A-line skirt, and tassled loafers. "A coed." He smiled whimsically. "Fancy that."

"And a hippie," said Jude, studying his octagonal granny glasses, bleached overalls, and the strawberry blond hair that curled like maple shavings around his shirt collar.

The focal point of the living room being an electric heater, they sat down before its orange glow in decrepit Danish-modern armchairs whose cushions were extruding foam. Not having seen each other for eight years, they had little to talk about except a past Sandy had repudiated, having refused to return home since leaving for college. They glanced at each other uneasily.

"Tea!" said Sandy. "Whenever the English are at a loss for words, they make tea. I'll make us some tea, shall I?"

"We're not British."

"No, but I worked at the National Opera in London when I was draft dodging, so I learned the drill."

As Sandy filled a kettle in the tiny kitchen and took tea bags from a canister on the counter, Jude studied his back. He'd filled out since high school, like a colt turning into a horse. He had a convex chest now and arms braided with muscles. The rumor around town was that, after dropping out of RPI, he'd been classified 4-F because of asthma. Most young men Jude had known at Vanderbilt were in ROTC, awaiting their chance to defend democracy in the Delta. When it came to fight or flight, Jude's ancestors had usually picked the latter, so her sympathies were with Sandy. If any one of her forebears had died a hero on some distant battlefield, disrupting the evolving chain of DNA, she wouldn't have been here.

Where would she have been instead? she wondered as she stood up and strolled across the battered parquet floor to peer out one window into an air shaft, then out another to the murky Hudson with the roller coaster of Palisades Amusement Park scalloping the far shore. A hallway with several doors off it led from the living room, the walls of which were papered with colorful posters announcing operas at the Met—FIDELIO and DER FLIEGENDE HOLLANDER and THE LOVE FOR THREE ORANGES.

The door to the outside hallway opened, and in walked a lanky young man with black curls and a drooping mustache. He wore a cracked, brown leather motorcycle jacket with a fur collar and a navy-blue Greek fisherman's cap. Studying Jude with the greenest eyes she'd ever seen outside of the cat kingdom, he said in a British accent, "Sandy's mate from childhood, I presume?"

"That's right. Jude."

"I'm Simon. One of Sandy's roommates."

"How many are there?"

"Four of us at the moment, I believe." He finally smiled, as though from duty. "Please. Make yourself comfortable, if that's possible in these collapsing chairs."

Both sat. Jude fiddled with a button on her blazer. Simon inspected the blue braid on the cap in his hands. Finally Jude asked, "How do you know Sandy?"

"We met at a bar in London."

"You're English?" The kettle in the kitchen began to whistle like Sandy's father's tannery back home at high noon.

"Yes."

"From London?"

"Yes."

"Have you been in the U.S. long?"

"A year."

"What's your job?"

"I'm a book editor."

Southern men were usually off and running with their autobiographies by now. Charm Class hadn't prepared Jude for the English. Fortunately, Sandy arrived with the tea. "Ah, Simon. I see you've met Jude."

"Yes. She's been interviewing me. The way you Americans always do."

Jude glanced at him. She was merely trying to be polite.

Sandy looked at him quizzically while setting the tea tray on a low table before the electric heater. "I'll be mother, shall I?" he said, attempting a British accent. He sat down, picked up a crockery pitcher, and splashed milk into each mug.

"So, Jude, why are you in New York?" Simon looked up from his cap with a sudden seizure of manners.

"I'm a Ph.D. candidate at Columbia. I just got my master's from Vanderbilt."

"What are you studying?"

"History."

"Where are you living?"

"On West Sixty-Seventh Street, near Central Park. With my grandparents—my mother's parents."

Sandy handed them each a mug, then held out a jar of honey while Jude spooned some into her tea.

"How do you like it?"

"Fine, so far. But I've just arrived."

Simon tossed down his tea and stood up. "I'll leave you two to reminisce over steamy nights in the slave quarters. I've got to change and go out. Lovely to meet you, Jude."

They watched him stride on long legs across the ratty maroon carpet, which smelled of mold.

"It's good to see you again, Sandy," said Jude as Simon vanished down the dark hallway. "Growing up appears to agree with you."

"And with you. Did you drive all the Sig Eps at Vandy to despair?"

Jude smiled. "I didn't date much, actually."

"Twenty-three and never been kissed?"

"As near as makes no difference."

After Molly's death, Jude had refused even to talk to Jerry Crawford for several months, hanging up each time he phoned and sidestepping him in the corridors at school. He reminded her too much of his best friend, Ace Kilgore. Maybe Ace hadn't killed Molly with his own hands, but he had certainly played a role in her death, like some evil incubus.

Finally, Jude agreed to go to the movies with Jerry one night, and on her doorstep afterward, he insisted on reclaiming the yardage he'd already gained, running his hands under her sweater and pushing his tongue through her lips. She realized she'd actually missed him, especially the animal comfort of a warm body against her own. She relaxed against his chest and tentatively caressed with her fingertips the ridges of muscle that formed the valley down his spine.

That night, she first dreamed of Molly—skull scalped and stitched with catgut, tubes snaking from her nostrils, face purple like a smashed plum. *"Listen to me, Jude,"* she insisted. *"Don't let this happen to you."* Ever since, whenever Jude had felt stirrings of desire for someone, Molly had appeared in this Medusa mode, mouthing warnings.

At Vanderbilt, Jude had been pinned for three years to a KA named Bradley Caldwell, a fair-haired Ashley Wilkes type whose parents owned an antebellum mansion in Natchez that was always included on the spring garden-club tours. When Jude visited, they housed her in a remodeled slave cabin. Bradley always treated her with a respect bordering on reverence, which even Molly didn't seem to find alarming. He wanted to marry a virgin, and he wanted that virgin to be Jude. So their definition of virginity had become as complex as a Catholic priest's definition of celibacy.

But the strain of being Bradley's beloved had finally become too great. Jude had called the whole thing off and caught the next train to New York. Bradley, however, who was working at a bank in Charlotte, was currently threatening to arrange a transfer to New York.

"They must be blind, is all I can say," said Sandy, sipping his tea.

"Thank you, Sandy. You may have rejected the South, but you're stuck with the gallantry."

"Don't worry. We'll find you a gallant Yankee."

"Isn't that an oxymoron? Everyone seems so rushed and rude up here."

"Oh, there are a few gallants left. But they're mostly from Tennessee. Speaking of gallant young men, whatever happened to Ace Kilgore?"

"He joined the marines. He's in Vietnam right now."

"So he finally gets to kill some Commies. Apparently, there is a God."

"Jerry Crawford is in his platoon. They're fighting side by side, like Achilles and Patroclus."

Sandy grinned.

"Did you hear that Jerry married Noreen after high school? She's head of the Welcome Wagon now."

Sandy started laughing.

The outside door hurtled open again, and a woman in knee-high mahogany boots with spike heels clattered into the room like a show horse. Her jeans were so tight that she must have needed a shoehorn to fit them over her buttocks. Her hennaed hair was shaved on one side of her head and chin length on the other.

"Mona, meet Jude," said Sandy, jumping to his feet like a good southern boy.

"Enchanted," she said distractedly, extending to Jude a clammy hand with sharp plum nails before vanishing down the hallway.

"Who's Mona?" asked Jude as Sandy sank back into his chair.

"One of my roommates. She does makeup at the Met."

"Tell me about the others."

"Simon, you met. Then there's Earl, who's a dancer from Cincinnati. And Tony, who's a set carpenter at the Met."

"Do you all eat meals together?"

"Hardly ever. Everyone's so busy and on different schedules. But sometimes we have group parties or holiday feasts. It's a nice mix of independence and companionship. Besides, it's all any of us can afford right now. How's your dad, by the way?"

"He's fine. After you left, my grandmother died of a heart attack—on a cruise of the South Sea Islands. They had to store her in the freezer until they reached land."

"My mother told me. I'm really sorry. She was a great lady."

"Thanks." They sat in silence for a moment, remembering the elegant old woman in her silk suits and spike heels, with her own unique version of the War Between the States, in which the South lost not because it had no gunpowder factories at secession but because the Yankees were not true gentlemen. Jude finally owned her Francis I silverware and her graduated pink pearls, but it definitely wasn't a fair swap.

"So we moved into her house," Jude said. "Dad and Audrey have four children now."

"That must be weird for you."

"He's happy, so I'm glad for him."

"It's your old friend Sandy here, Jude. You don't have to be so careful." He set his teacup on the tray and lay back in his chair with his legs extended.

"Well, I guess I did resent Audrey's trying to take my mother's place. But since Dad had her, it was easier on me when I left for Vanderbilt. What about you, Sandy?"

"What about me?" He clasped his hands behind his curly blond head, elbows out.

"What do you do for fun around here? Do you have a girlfriend, for example?"

He blushed just as he used to as a boy, crimson rising like the gauge on a thermometer from his throat, up his freckled face, and across his forehead. It was nice to know some things never changed.

"I'm too busy working."

"At the Met?"

He nodded. "I'm a stage manager. I know that sounds like a big deal, but there are dozens of us."

"How did you get from astrophysics at RPI to opera?"

"Physics was too pure for me. I like some meat on my bones."

"Were your parents upset when you dropped out of RPI?"

"Not really. You know they dote on me. Besides, the opera is an honorable institution."

"I wouldn't know. I've never been." She drained the last of her tea, which had cooled to lukewarm and was thick and sweet with honey.

"I'll take you one night."

"Okay, but I should remind you of how much I despised 'The Firestone Hour' on television when we were kids."

He laughed. "You'll like it. Trust me. Opera is almost as surreal as reality itself."

"SO WHAT DID YOU do today, dear?" asked Jude's maternal grandmother as she served something that looked like bean stew from a gray pottery bowl painted with dark blue cornflowers.

"I went to visit a boy I grew up with who lives on Riverside Drive now. I hadn't seen him in eight years, and he's turned into a man. It was quite a shock."

"Then you understand how it is for us to see you," murmured her grandfather as he poured some red wine into her glass. Wine at their table seemed to flow as freely as iced tea back home.

Jude glanced back and forth between the grandparents she'd known mostly through Christmas and birthday cards and presents— her grandfather, tall and distinguished-looking, with a full head of silver hair and piercing raisin eyes; her grandmother, in gold pince-nez, with an elaborate bun of salt-and-pepper hair that sat on her head like a puffy cushion. A couple of times, they'd stopped off to see her en route to Florida vacations, and they'd often invited her to visit them, but she'd never accepted before. She had the impression her father and they didn't like one another. When they had picked her up at Grand Central with their driver the previous night, she had told them in the car en route to their apartment that her father sent his love (which wasn't true). They had merely thanked her, without inquiring about him.

Jude glanced around the dining room, with its walnut wainscoting and leaded glass windows and cabinet doors, determined to locate a subject for conversation. All they had in common was a woman who had died nearly two decades earlier, but her name hadn't yet been spoken. "How long have you lived here?" she asked her grandfather, who was carefully unfolding his linen napkin and placing it in his lap.

"Let's see, we bought this place after I got back from the war," he said. "In 1919, I suppose. Nearly fifty years ago. All the buildings on this block were built at the turn of the century by a group of Europeans who wanted a neighborhood. Some Alsatian friends of my father's got us involved. We used to call this street New York's Alsatian ghetto. I guess you could say we were an early commune." He smiled at her in the candlelight, but his dark eyes looked remote and unhappy. He was still wearing the three-piece pinstriped suit she'd seen him in early that morning as he departed with his uniformed driver for his office on Wall Street, where he negotiated international grain deals.

"So my mother grew up here?" asked Jude, risking the unmentionable.

Her grandfather grimaced, as though with heartburn.

Her grandmother nodded. "Her bedroom was the one you're staying in now."

"Where did she go to school?" Jude continued mercilessly. She'd picked Columbia for her Ph.D. and agreed to stay with her grandparents partly because she wanted to get to know them and, through them, her mother. None of this would happen if she pussy-footed around the topic as she always had with her father. Her father was all wrapped up in his new family now. Her mother had no one except Jude to bear her memory into the future. Therefore, Jude needed to remember what her memories of her were. Jude had gone to Paris her junior year at Vanderbilt with some vague notion of learning about her mother, whose parents were mostly French by origin. Many of the women she'd passed in the streets had had her mother's diminutive build and dark beauty. But she'd returned home with only an increased sense of her mother's absence.

"She went to a private school on the East Side. Your grandfather dropped her off every morning on the way to his office and our driver picked her up—until she was old enough to walk across the park with her friends."

"What was she like?"

Jude's grandmother glanced at her husband, but he was concentrating on his stew. Then she surveyed the room as though searching for an escape hatch. She drew a deep breath and exhaled it. Then she looked at Jude helplessly, as though asking to be let off the hook.

"She was very . . . definite," she finally replied. "She knew what she wanted, and nothing could dissuade her from having it."

Jude's grandfather didn't show by so much as a twitch whether or not he agreed. They sat for a while in silence, Jude uncertain of whether her grandmother's description was meant to be approving or not. One of the things Jude's mother had insisted on having was Jude's father. She poked at her stew—of beans, bacon, sausage, and pork in a tomato sauce. It was pleasant not to be eating country ham and corn bread. "This is delicious," she finally said. "What is it?"

"Cassoulet," her grandfather replied. "From *southern* France. To help you feel at home." He smiled.

"Please," said Jude with a laugh. "I'm so sick of southern food, I could scream—fried chicken and corn bread, barbecue and biscuits. It's a wonder I can still digest at all."

As the maid removed the dessert plates, Jude's grandmother stood up and walked over to a dark, glossy armoire. Pointing out some wooden pegs, she explained to Jude how her Huguenot forebears had collapsed the chest to carry it with them when they fled France in the seventeenth century. She was genealogist for the National Huguenot Society, and Jude gathered that she spent most of her time poring over passenger lists of ships that had left European ports after the revocation of the Edict of Nantes.

Extracting a fat, ivory-colored candle from the armoire, Jude's grandmother set it on the dining table and lit it with a taper from the silver candelabra. "Today is St. Bartholomew's Day," she explained.

"Good God, Rose," muttered her grandfather, "we've got company." Tossing his napkin on the table, he pushed back his chair.

"My dear," said Jude's grandmother, "your lack of interest doesn't alter the fact that on this day in 1572 your ancestors butchered mine."

"But not enough of them, darling, because here you are." He glanced at Jude with a faint smile.

"You can mock me all you like, Christophe. It won't bring back the hundred thousand that your forebears slaughtered like cattle in an abattoir."

"A hundred thousand is a mere drop in the bucket, my love," he said, rising to his feet, silver mane reflecting the candlelight. "A hundred *million* have died from man-made violence in the twentieth century."

"But not at the hands of the very people who had invited them to a wedding of their own kinsman."

"Stalin killed twenty million of his own people. So did Mao."

Jude studied her genteelly embattled grandparents, who seemed envigorated by this ancient religious enmity as they hadn't been by her mention of their lost daughter. Her suave grandfather was tossing off grim statistics of disaster as though dealing with so many sacks of grain.

"Go away, Christophe," her grandmother said, "before I add you to the body count."

Laughing, he exited.

But Jude stayed, to be polite, and listened to her grandmother's account, which sounded as ritualistic as an Icelandic saga. Howling Catholic mobs burst into Huguenot homes in Paris, stabbing the occupants, shooting them, hurling them from high windows to the pavement below. They tossed babies screaming for their murdered parents into the Seine to drown. Carts piled high with corpses left pathways of blood that led to a Louvre courtyard, where flies swarmed around stacks of mutilated bodies that lay festering under a hot summer sun. Giggling ladies from court inspected the genitals of a dead man suspected of impotence.

As she listened, Jude studied a medallion at her grandmother's throat—a Maltese cross, with fleurs-de-lis in each corner. A tiny golden dove in downward flight was hanging from the bottom arm. Her grandmother, in her billowy bun and gold pince-nez, had seemed so reticent discussing her daughter earlier in the evening but was now describing with relish the rivers of France—so clogged with bloated corpses that people refused to eat fish for months afterward —and the wolves that crept down out of the forests to feast on the bodies that washed ashore. Jude settled comfortably into her side chair and sipped her wine, feeling at home already in the heart of New York City.

Following her recitative, Jude's grandmother blew out the candles, kissed Jude good night, and vanished up the stairs and into her bedroom, separate from that of her husband. Jude went into the paneled den and turned on the television. Unable to find anything of interest, she switched it off. Studying the walls, she noticed Audubon prints, but no photos, no school diplomas, nothing that would testify to her mother's existence.

She strolled into the living room, which was two stories high and had dark walnut paneling and beams. At the second-floor level, there was a balcony off which the bedrooms opened. Wandering around the shadowy room, she tried to imagine the games her mother must have played there as a child. In the dim lamplight, she noticed that the wine-colored Oriental carpet had a paisley pattern like footprints. Carefully fitting her feet into the protozoan outlines, she walked across it splayfooted. Then she turned around and jumped back across it in the opposite direction, alternating feet, sometimes landing on both, playing hopscotch.

Reaching the leaded glass windows along one wall, she studied the window seat, which was cushioned with burgundy velvet. Upon lifting the lid, she discovered an empty space within. Climbing into it, she lay down, lowered the lid, and pretended she was in a coffin. She remembered lying like this in the sunken grave back home, trapped by the Commie Killers. For a few moments, it seemed easier to continue lying there while her grandparents ransacked the apartment in search of her than to emerge and have to set up an entirely new life.

As she climbed back out of the window seat, her grandmother's voice overhead said, "That's exactly what your mother used to do."

Looking up, Jude saw her standing in the shadows on the balcony. "Sorry, Grandma. I was just poking around."

"No need to apologize, my dear. Our home is your home now."

But Jude detected a note of tightly controlled agitation in her voice.

—

JUDE WRAPPED HER ARMS around Molly's waist as the car fishtailed crazily. Then it plunged down a cliff and began to roll. As Jude clung to her, Molly was slowly dragged out the window. Sweat broke out on Jude's forehead as she struggled to pull Molly back inside. Losing her grip, she clawed frantically at the sticky red-clay bank outside. . . .

". . . I've hungered for your touch a long lonely time," wailed the Righteous Brothers from the clock radio. "Time goes by so slowly, and time can do so much. . . ."

Jude opened one eye and saw the gold wallpaper striped with Prussian blue in her new bedroom at her grandparents' apartment. The buzzer on the alarm went off.

Shutting it off, she scooted up to lean against the headboard of the mahogany sleigh bed in which her mother had slept as a girl. She blotted the sweat off her forehead with her pajama sleeve and tried to calm her jagged breathing.

Just as Molly used to insist that stars were actually tears in the night sky through which the light behind it streamed, so Jude had concluded that everyday reality was just a period of each day allotted for attending to the needs of the body so it could continue to host the dreams that constituted the *real* reality. Some nights, she relived this car wreck that never ended. Other nights, she lay trapped by the Commie Killers in a sunken grave, Molly's skeletal arms dragging her down into the center of the earth.

But sometimes she and Molly sat in their cave playing Over the Moon, as the indigo Smokies outside the cave mouth vanished and reappeared in swirling autumn mists. Or they galloped their horses beside the churning river, as mauve clouds collided overhead and cast dark racing shadows on the valley floor. Or they lay in each other's arms on a raft in the ocher river, rocking with the current, while dancing rays of summer sun licked their flesh like a thousand tiny tongues.

The buzzer on her alarm went off again. She had to go to Columbia to register for fall courses. Lying still, she listened to the city come to life around her, like a curtain lifting on a stage set. At dawn back home, lone roosters crowed one by one until the sun popped up from behind the mountains and the bird chorus commenced its concerto to daybreak. Here, a solitary siren first broke the silence, followed by a car horn, then the whirring of a truck digesting garbage in the street below. Then more sirens, the roar of a bus, schoolchildren shrieking, a helicopter pucking overhead, dogs barking on their way to Central Park. Finally, the urban oratorio at full blast.

WAITING IN THE CAVERNOUS GYM in a line of history students who also wanted the seminar on the French Revolution, Jude inspected her new classmates, a scruffy bunch in their jeans and overalls, T-shirts and work shirts, paratrooper boots and basketball shoes, especially in contrast to the cashmered coeds and tweedy fraternity boys at Vanderbilt. Several exuded the musky odor of sweat mixed with marijuana smoke. A sorority sister at Vanderbilt, whose boyfriend played Dobro in a country-and-western band, used to sneak the joints he gave her into the Kappa house, where Jude lived. They smoked them sitting on the gabled roof. The effect on Jude had always been negligible, although a few times the antics of the birds in flight over the campus had seemed more engaging than usual.

She started thinking about her grandmother's version of the St. Bartholomew's Day Massacre the previous night—the marriage turned massacre, the wolves feasting on the bloated corpses. Like the evening news, everything Jude had studied in her career as a history major had focused on wars, assassinations, famines, and epidemics. No doubt

the guillotine would be the star of this seminar on the French Revolution. But surely sometime, somewhere, people had merely tilled the
soil and harvested their crops, year after year, until they died quietly
in their own beds, bored to death, surrounded by those who loved
them.

SANDY HAD PLACED A STRAIGHT-BACK chair amid a rigging of
ropes and pulleys behind the maroon velvet curtains, from which Jude
could see most of the stage. He was sitting at a switchboard behind
her, watching the stage on a TV screen and following the music in a
bound score. He wore headphones with an attached mouthpiece
through which he was receiving reports and issuing instructions to
technicians stationed all around the hall.

Jude, meanwhile, was bewildered by the plot. The young Count
Octavian, played by a woman, was lying in bed singing sweet nothings
to the *Marschallin*, whose husband was out of town. While the count
disguised himself as a chambermaid so as to conceal their affair from
the *Marschallin*'s approaching cousin, the *Marschallin* sang an aria be-
moaning her knowledge that the count would eventually leave her for
someone younger and more beautiful. Then the cousin, a man, became
enamored of the young count-turned-chambermaid.

At intermission, Jude remained in her chair, watching as the huge
platform carrying a Viennese drawing room rolled out from the wings,
escorted by a team of muscled young men in T-shirts and blue jeans,
with pouched leather carpenter belts around their hips and pirate-style
bandannas around their heads. One with a brown ponytail and a gold
hoop through his earlobe was Sandy's roommate Tony.

During the last act, Jude tiptoed to the switchboard and stood
behind Sandy, watching him turn the pages of his score. The *Marschallin*, aware that her young count had indeed fallen in love with a woman
his own age, was struggling with herself to let him go. Finally giving

him her hand to kiss for one last time, she swept bravely from the room.

Inexplicably, Jude found herself wanting to stroke Sandy's blond hair where it curled up around his collar. She touched a curl with her fingertip. Sandy turned his head, catching a glimpse of her finger as she withdrew it. Raising his eyes to hers, he smiled.

Walking back to Jude's grandparents' apartment through the cool night air, Sandy and Jude savored the sudden silence, broken only by an occasional passing car or a siren down Broadway. Sandy began humming the *Marschallin*'s aria during which she realized that the count would leave her.

"That was really beautiful," said Jude.

Sandy began singing it softly in German.

"What do the words mean?"

He thought for a moment. " 'With a light heart and a light hand, we must hold and take, hold and let go. If not, life will punish us and God will have no pity.' Something like that."

"Do you know German?"

Sandy nodded.

"What else?"

"Just the opera languages—Italian, French, a little Spanish."

"And East Tennesseean."

He smiled. "Yes, and British. From Simon."

They walked for a couple of blocks in companionable silence, pursued, overtaken, and abandoned by their own shadows as they passed through the patches of illumination laid down by the street-lights.

Finally, Sandy said, "Late at night, these side streets by the park are almost as quiet as Tidewater Estates."

"We might just as well never have left."

"That's the *only* similarity."

"Why did you never come back home, by the way?"

"Why would I go back? I was miserable down there. And after Molly died, even you turned into a zombie."

"I turned into a zombie?"

"Suddenly, you were perfect in every way. Those Villager shirt-waists you used to wear, pressed as carefully as altar cloths. Student council secretary. Baptist Youth Group. Hospital volunteer. Citizenship award. First in your class. Endlessly baby-sitting your siblings. And when I'd look in your eyes, there was no one home."

Jude studied her tassled loafers as they moved along the sidewalk through some tattered leaves that were giving off the dusty scent she would always associate with the Wildwoods in autumn, where wisps of smoke from fires in the farmers' curing sheds had drifted past like morning mist.

"There's still no one home, if you ask me."

Jude said nothing, amazed to learn that she'd projected such torpor when her heart had felt like Pompeii during the lava flow. After Molly died, she'd spent her free time racing Flame along the river, howling into the wind. She'd slide off him on the ridge where she and Molly had planned to build their cabin and pound the carpet of rotting leaves with her fists.

"I guess I'm just a faithful kind of gal," she murmured.

Sandy shrugged. "I used to envy you and Molly. You were like twin space aliens. When you were playing, you'd move in concert, without words, like birds in flight. But you've paid a very high price."

"I'm all right."

"So you say. But I knew you before, and I see you now."

"I'm not a child anymore."

"Yes, you are. You're off in Never-Never Land with Molly Pan."

Jude looked at him quickly. This was the closest anyone had ever come to guessing about her vivid night life with Molly. It felt threatening, even if it was only Sandy doing the guessing.

"I remember you at the Colonial Cotillion spring break of my senior year at Exeter, waltzing in your hoop skirt and satin heels, with kid gloves to your biceps and that ridiculous Marie Antoinette hairdo. You looked like a Stepford wife."

"You were supposed to be busy waltzing with Kitty Fairchild."

"But I was watching you. I always watched you, Jude. Around the neighborhood from the telescope in my tree house. You worried me. Your mother dead. Your father working all the time. Your grandmother off on her trips. Clementine struggling to raise you in addition to her own kids. The Commie Killers torturing you. I wanted to protect you, but I didn't know how."

"But you did, Sandy. You were wonderful. You were like my older brother."

"When Molly came along, I was relieved to have reinforcements. But I was also jealous. Because I thought of myself as more than just your big brother."

Jude looked at him, surprised. "Why did you never tell me?"

"What was the point? First there was Molly. Then that goon from the football team—Jerry. You two were like Beauty and the Beast."

Jude smiled, remembering Jerry's hard, muscled body and matching brain. But his brain was the organ that had interested her least.

Beneath the doorway to her grandparents' building, which was decorated with stone oak leaves, acorns, and squirrels, Sandy leaned over and kissed her cheek. Then he walked away fast.

As Jude undressed and hung her clothes in the closet, she thought about the kiss, as awkward as their first attempt beneath the heating ducts in Molly's basement during Spin the Bottle. Basically, Sandy had said he loved her. She loved him, too—as a brother, as a friend. Seeing him now was bringing it all back—his kindness and courage on her behalf. She felt at home with him as with no one else. Because of their shared childhood. Because they knew each other's families. Because he'd known Molly. Because he'd known *her* when she was with Molly.

She realized she was humming the *Marschallin*'s aria. "With a light heart and a light hand, we must hold and take, hold and let go. If not, life will punish us and God will have no pity." She had held on tightly to Molly. She was still holding on tightly. But if you could take love lightly, was what you were feeling love? Or was it just indifference?

Still, Molly was dead, and Jude was only twenty-three years old. Sometimes she envied the abandon with which her peers dated and dumped one another and hopped in and out of bed, foot soldiers for the sexual revolution. Maybe she and Sandy could go out some and see if anything more exotic developed. He'd said he didn't have a girlfriend. And he was attractive, sweet, smart, fun. Besides, if Bradley arrived from Charlotte as threatened, it would be helpful to have a new boyfriend already in place to stave off his adoration. What he adored wasn't her complicated and contradictory self, in any case. It was some ideal of purity that existed only within his addled antebellum brain.

Climbing into her mother's sleigh bed, she switched out the light.

As she drifted off to sleep, Molly was there waiting for her, tubes snaking from her nostrils, bloodshot blue eyes flaring.

"Forget about it, Jude!" she screamed as they raced their horses along the river. "You belong to me. Besides, Sandy is going to hurt you."

"Sandy wouldn't hurt a flea. You know that."

"Everyone ends up hurting each other. It's the law of the jungle."

"Nobody could ever hurt me as much as you did, Molly."

"It wasn't on purpose."

"You could have fooled me."

Molly lowered her head, hair writhing around her contused face like snarled blacksnakes. *"So Sandy is your revenge for Ace Kilgore?"*

"No, Sandy is my chance for a normal life."

CHAPTER

9

"AS SMOKE IS DRIVEN AWAY, so drive them away," the black-cassocked priest chanted in French.

"As wax melts before the fire," responded the congregation, "so let the wicked perish at the presence of God."

These were the same psalms, reflected Jude as she stood beside her grandmother before a carved oak pew, that had sustained the Huguenot guerrillas in the eighteenth century in their caves in the Cévennes as the Sun King's troops chased them down like wild game.

Behind the priest was an altar covered with a white cloth, on which sat two silver vases of white lilies and two white candles in plain silver holders. The wall in back of the altar was of opaque leaded glass. Right in the center was a Huguenot cross with a descending dove, identical to the one at her grandmother's throat, in indigo, ruby, and gold stained glass.

The tiny church with its polished oak beams was the epitome of austere good taste, as was the service. And the parishioners were dressed accordingly, as though for the funeral of a Fortune 500 executive. Over half a million of their ancestors had been tortured, butchered, and exiled simply because they didn't want to clutter up their altars with crucifixes. This had been especially unfortunate for France because it left behind only those citizens whose idea of beauty was Versailles. Jude felt unworthy of such forebears. If someone had so much as mentioned thumbscrews to her, she'd have let them put anything they wanted on her altar.

Around the walls near the ceiling hung the coats of arms of Huguenot families who had escaped the two centuries of slaughter to settle in New York City—Cresson, Robert, Runyon, Bayard, Jay, Maupin, Delancey, Perrin, three dozen others. The Sauvage coat of arms of Jude's ancestors featured four golden manticores—human heads, lion bodies, and dragon tails—on a scarlet background. There was no motto. Jude decided it should have been: "When in doubt, get the hell out."

Jude pondered all the torment these people had endured to worship as they pleased, whereas she had always spent a lot of time trying to get out of going to church at all. Earlier that morning, she had wanted to stay in bed with her memories of Molly instead of crossing Central Park in the cold January air to listen to French that she couldn't always understand. She had come along only from a wish to be amiable to her grandmother and to chat some more about her mother in the absence of her grandfather. Her grandmother had gradually become more forthcoming and now seemed even to enjoy reminiscing about her daughter, but Jude's grandfather still preferred to suffer in silence.

On the walk over, beneath trees iced silver in the night, Jude asked, "Did my mother used to come to this church with you?"

"Sometimes. Especially when she was too young to refuse."

"Could she speak French?"

"Enough to follow the service. Your grandfather and I spoke it at home with our Alsatian neighbors. And she had a tutor."

The pale winter sun hung suspended above the apartment buildings along Fifth Avenue like a blob of luminescent sugar cookie dough.

"Frankly," her grandmother admitted in a strained voice, "your mother was never very enthusiastic about her Huguenot heritage. All she wanted was to buy beautiful clothes and go out on dates. Of course, that's what you're supposed to want when you're young. But she made her father very unhappy by insisting on being a model."

"Why?"

"He thought it was tawdry. He wanted her to go to Barnard and become a classics professor. He'd groomed her for this all her life, helping her with her homework and hiring tutors. But that wasn't who she was. In any case, he had also always encouraged her to look beautiful. He gave her all the money she wanted for clothes and makeup and hairdos. He even advised her himself on the art of flirtation and seduction."

Jude glanced at her as she fell silent. She sounded jealous of her daughter's relationship to her husband. The idea of a daughter being more important to a father than his wife was a novel one for Jude.

"Thank you for at least pretending to be interested in my Huguenots," she added.

Interrupting Jude's protest, she said, "No, I know that this is something one gets interested in when one is older and is trying to figure out the point of it all. Young people are content to follow the dictates of their hormones."

"Don't forget, I'm a history major," said Jude. Although she didn't say it, it also seemed possible that her hormones were less insistent than those of her peers. How else could she have endured Bradley's regime for reestablishing her lost virginity?

"So you are," said her grandmother, who then proceeded to drill her on the ten Presidents of Huguenot descent, the famous writers, the Revolutionary War heros, the abolitionists and pioneers and suffragettes. And Jude had to admit that it was an impressive list. Apparently, there was nothing like terror to turn out high achievers.

As Jude stood to sing the recessional, she counted up the generations of her mother's family on her fingers as though saying a rosary. She realized that only two of her grandmother's thirty-two thrice-great-grandparents had been Huguenot. Several had been Dutch, for instance. Yet these distant Huguenots were the grit around which her grandmother's pearl of selfhood had coalesced. Similarly, only one of Jude's father's eight great-grandparents had been Cherokee. Yet to hear him tell it, you'd have thought he'd grown up in a tepee chipping arrowheads. They had both grabbed hold of only one thread of their DNA, clinging to it like a lifeline in a typhoon. Like Jude's Tidewater grandmother, both mourned some lost golden age. They all lived in a dream, a mythical time long since past.

But Jude knew she'd been doing the same thing, freeze-drying Molly in her memory. And she had decided it was time to recover from this crippling family malady. So she had accepted Sandy's invitation to move into a room in his Riverside Drive apartment. Molly was livid. Every night for weeks, she'd performed her Medusa act. Until Jude had finally realized that, like the Wizard of Oz, Molly was all bluster.

Walking home past the jammed skating rink, her grandmother's gloved hand holding her arm, Jude said, "By the way, Grandma, I've been thinking maybe it's time for me to move out."

Her grandmother looked up at her quickly. "I hope you're not unhappy with us, my dear."

"Not at all. You've been wonderful to me. But I guess I'd like my own place. After all, I'm twenty-four years old."

They walked on in silence alongside the Sheep Meadow, the huge apartment buildings of Central Park West stacked before them like a child's blocks under the sullen winter sky.

"I know it must have been lonely for you. Your grandfather and I aren't very much fun."

Jude smiled. "I feel very comfortable with *you*, Grandma. But I'm afraid I haven't really gotten to know Grandpa yet."

All she'd succeeded in eliciting from him were the facts: His father and four brothers had fled Alsace in 1870 to avoid fighting in the German army against the French. Having owned a gristmill in a country town, they opened another mill when they reached upstate New York. Jude's grandfather had parlayed his boyhood experience with the grain trade into a successful career on the commodities exchange.

"Well," said her grandmother as they passed some horse-drawn carriages waiting in front of the Tavern on the Green, "you may not realize it, but you remind us of your mother. Your grandfather was devastated when she moved south with your father. Frankly, I think he was half in love with her himself. He avoids you because it's painful for him to remember her. I'm very sorry. I know that you need to hear whatever he could tell you about her right now. But he just can't do it. I'm sure it would be wonderful for him if he could. It has been for me."

"Why do I remind him of her?" Jude asked. "Do I look like her?"

"You're taller, of course, but your faces are similar. Though you have your father's eyes. Her eyes were blue. I'd say you're a blend of the two."

Jude smiled. Her father had always denied any resemblance. "Why doesn't Grandpa like my father?"

Her face clouded. "It's not that he doesn't like him. We just didn't consider him appropriate for your mother."

"Why not?"

She laughed uneasily. "Well, let's just say that we were snobs. Your father was from Appalachia. He was part Cherokee. We wished him well, but we didn't want him in our family. I'm ashamed to admit that your grandfather used to refer to him as 'the hillbilly.'"

Jude smiled, thinking about the reality of her father's life—his mother's huge white house and voyages around the world, his medical degree from Cornell. L'il Abner he was not.

"Also, your father was absolutely relentless in his pursuit of your mother, practically camping out on our doorstep and trailing her around the city whenever she went out. Your grandfather felt that he didn't leave your mother any choice in the matter. After she married him, your grandfather wouldn't have anything to do with her, although I continued to see her while they were still living in New York and to write her in Tennessee.

"But once you were born, your grandfather agreed to visit on our way to Florida. When your father went to France during the war, your grandfather invited your mother to move back home with you until his return. But your mother refused, which estranged them once again. And then she died, and it was too late for another reconciliation. It's a sad and silly story. We were wrong. After all, we had struggled similarly with our own parents because I was Protestant and your grandfather was Catholic. Every generation seems to fight its own battles and then lapse into complacent bigotry." She sighed. "By the way, have you talked to your father about living alone?"

"I wasn't thinking of living alone. There's an extra room in my friend Sandy's apartment. It's closer to Columbia, too."

"You want to live with a man?" Her hand tightened on Jude's arm.

"It's one of those huge old places on Riverside Drive. He has four other roommates. One is a woman. Dad says since it's Sandy, it's okay. I've known him since we were babies. He's like my brother."

For the past several months, she'd seen a lot of Sandy. There seemed nothing they couldn't say to each other. Often they lay like a long-married couple on his mattress on the floor, watching old movies on television in their sock feet. Or else he studied opera scores while she marked up her history texts with yellow Magic Marker. Occasionally, they fell asleep side by side, but Jude always had to dash out into the night to take a taxi back to her grandparents so they wouldn't worry. If her room was just down the hall, life would be much simpler.

As Jude hung their coats in the hall closet, her grandmother said, "Before you leave, though, Jude, I want to give you something." She vanished into the dining room, returning with a flask about a foot high that had lion-head handles. On it was painted a scene in m⁻ _y blues and golds of Atalanta, the unvanquished, stooping to pick up a golden ball just dropped by her competitor Melanion. He was sprinting past her, backed by trees and mountains. A hovering cherub, holding the victor's laurel wreath, appeared to be trying to persuade Atalanta not to be duped by these silly golden balls into losing her first race.

"I gave this to your mother," her grandmother said, handing it carefully to Jude, "but she never liked it. She didn't even take it to Tennessee. It was made by one of our Huguenot ancestors in Nevers, just before they fled France at the end of the seventeenth century. It's almost a museum piece, so take good care of it. It was given to me by _my_ grandmother. It seems to be true that interest in these things alternates generations."

"I love it, Grandma. Thank you."

"Thank *you*, as I said, my dear, for being interested. I had thought my poor Huguenots would end with me and be forgotten. The dead depend on the living to carry on their memory."

"So I gather," said Jude a bit grimly.

Her grandfather came out of his study and looked down from the balcony. "What's going on?"

"Jude is leaving us, I'm afraid, dear."

"So soon? Where to?" Jude was pleased to note that he sounded distressed.

"To a room in her friend Sandy's apartment."

"Ah, a young man. Then I know there is nothing I can say to persuade her to stay."

"No."

Jude felt strange being discussed in the third person, as though she'd already left. "But I'll be only twenty blocks away, Grandpa. I'll stop by all the time. You'll never get rid of me." She felt guilty, however, as though she'd relentlessly extracted from them what she needed and was now moving on.

"I hope not," her grandfather replied in a fatigued voice. He turned around and shuffled back toward his study, shoulders bowed, an unhappy old man who had never recovered from losing the daughter he'd loved too much. This was the dark side to graveyard love. The *Marschallin* might be right after all: Maybe the proper conduct of life required the ability to let go of love when the time came.

JUDE SAT IN HER CHAIR behind the curtains, watching Samson, draped in chains, strangle a snotty Philistine prince in front of a pagan temple while a golden idol spewed flames in the background. As Delilah awaited Samson in her bedchamber, Jude sneaked over to Sandy at his switchboard, resting her hand on his shoulder while he turned the pages of his score and spoke quietly into his mouthpiece.

Samson finally arrived, wearing a leather tunic that revealed his hairy barrel chest and tree-trunk legs.

Delilah began weaving around him in a transparent peignoir, singing in French, ". . . my heart opens to your voice as a flower to the dawn. . . . Respond to my tenderness; fill me with ecstasy. . . ."

Falling to his knees and burying his face in her silky gown, Samson joined in with his deep baritone: ". . . the blossom trembles in the gentle breeze. So does my heart tremble, longing for your voice. . . ."

Glancing down at Sandy, Jude saw that he was mouthing Delilah's lines. And tears had flooded his eyes behind his octagonal glasses. Suddenly, Jude understood his fascination with opera. The plots often embodied this perennial dream of tenderness taming savagery. And even when deceit and blood lust won out, the murdered actors stood up afterward for their curtain calls. On the playground back home, the Commie Killers had tormented Sandy for preferring chess and opera to football and rock 'n' roll. He had endured it all without protest. But on stage at the opera, the Commie Killers were vanquished. She absently stroked his blond curls with her hand.

Looking up, he reached for her hand and knitted his fingers with hers. A jolt shot up Jude's arm, so powerful that her hand shook. Sandy's sweetness moved her as no other man ever had. And because of it, Jude was beginning to want to give him everything. It wasn't that she was looking for the intensity of her experience with Molly that night on the raft. Although it remained vivid in her memory, the way a flashbulb leaves its imprint on a piece of unexposed film, she had written it off to unstable adolescent hormones. All she wanted now was some cozy companionship and physical affection with someone she cared about.

After the pagan temple had crashed down around everyone's shoulders, the painted cardboard blocks swinging from invisible ropes inches above the singers' heads, the curtain descended and the crowd erupted into bravos as though at a bullfight.

On the walk back to the apartment, Jude and Sandy murmured a few appreciative words about the performance before falling silent. And unlike their usual silences, this one was uncomfortable. Something was waiting to be said, but neither was willing to take the risk of saying it.

Entering the apartment, they found the living room empty of people. But some beer bottles, an ashtray full of cigarette butts, and a cardboard pizza box sat on the carpet by the armchairs. The odor of marijuana smoke and pizza filled the air. The only thing Jude really missed about her grandparents' apartment was their French cook. In a matter of months, she'd moved from ham hocks to cassoulet to Chinese takeout, and she was suffering from gastronomic culture shock.

Sandy and she walked down the shadowy hallway to their bedrooms. Outside Jude's door, they paused. Jude tried to decide whether to invite him in. It should be simple, something both had no doubt done before with other people. Yet neither made a move. Not only had the hand-holding during *Samson and Delilah* not broken the ice, but it seemed as well to have introduced some new awkwardness that Jude couldn't fathom. Finally, Sandy leaned down and pecked her cheek. "Sleep tight," he said as he turned to walk to his own door, tennis shoes squeaking on the wood floor.

Lying in bed, Jude could hear Mona next door, thrashing and gasping with her latest lover. Once they really got going, the bedsprings began to shriek like an entire pen of pigs being slaughtered. This often recurred sporadically throughout the night. Jude was awed by Mona's stamina. In the morning, she sometimes ran into the men in the bathroom, standing bare-chested in unzipped jeans, gazing at themselves in the mirror, eyes fatigued, faces gray and haggard, as though trying to figure out what disaster had just befallen them. Mona didn't usually appear until noon, wandering down the hall in a hot-pink chenille robe, lips chapped and swollen but smiling, mascara smudged around her eye sockets. Humming tunes like "The Impossible Dream," "My Way," and "I Gotta Be Me," she mixed ghastly concoctions in the blender that involved raw eggs and brewer's yeast, no doubt the source of her potency.

Jude wrapped the pillow around her head, but she could still hear the bedsprings pounding like a printing press. She wondered whether she should just get up and go to Sandy in his bed. She was pretty sure he wouldn't send her away. But they were both Southerners: He was the man; therefore, he was supposed to do the pursuing. Sliding a hand between her legs, she gripped it tightly with her thighs and directed all her mental energies toward him, willing him to appear by her bedside.

The next thing she knew, it was morning and she was late for class. Jumping up and throwing on her jeans and turtleneck, she raced down the hallway and into the living room. Earl, who danced in chorus lines for Broadway shows, had one heel propped on the windowsill, head resting on his knee. Dressed in a sweat suit, he looked like a soft sculpture. "Morning, Earl," she called as she hurried past. But he was so shy that there was no reply.

In the kitchen, Sandy was sitting at the table with half a dozen cereal boxes before him. When he was a boy, his mother insisted on buying only one box at a time, finishing it before buying the next. Now that he was on his own, Sandy bought a dozen different brands at once and sampled several every morning. It seemed a harmless-enough form of rebellion, when his peers were dumping blood on draft records at recruitment centers all across town.

He looked up at her and smiled. "Morning, Jude. Sleep well?"

"Yes, thanks. And you?"

Gazing at her with a perplexed frown, he said, "Not so great."

"No?"

"No." He lowered his eyes.

"I'm late," she said, grabbing a glass and pouring some orange juice.

"There's a good movie tonight at ten," he called as she tossed down the juice and dashed out the door. "Don't be late."

JUDE AND SANDY LAY on his bed drinking red wine, eating pretzels, and watching the movie. A man and a woman, married to other people, had met by chance in a train station and fallen in love. It was what Sandy and Simon called a "chick flick," in contrast to "dick flicks," which involved car chases, war, and violent crime.

Jude could tell that Sandy wasn't really paying attention, and neither was she. They had carefully avoided touching all evening. And they were now lying with the width of a sidewalk between them, arms crossed over their chests like funerary statues.

Sandy set his empty glass and the wadded pretzel bag on the rug beside the mattress, so Jude put her glass down, too. Both stared straight ahead at the TV screen while the couple struggled endlessly with their guilt toward their spouses over their platonic love for each other.

Sandy uncrossed his arms and stretched them awkwardly alongside his body, fists clenched, the muscles of his lower arms flexing and unflexing like a pulsing heart. As Jude watched from the corner of her eye, his hand unclenched, stirred, and crept a few inches into the no-man's-land between them. So Jude uncrossed her arms, too, and placed them on the bed beside her.

The couple had arranged to be alone together in a friend's apartment to consummate their love. As they fell into each other's arms, the friend arrived home early from work.

Jude scratched her head, then let that hand fall a foot away from her side. Sandy put his hand to his mouth to cover a yawn and returned it to the mattress within inches of Jude's hand.

Anguished, the couple parted in the train station where they'd first met, the man en route to South Africa with his family so he and the woman need never encounter each other again. Sandy's hand twitched where it lay, seeming to want to take Jude's but not daring to. She had watched it so carefully that she was sure its pattern of branching veins, like a turquoise road map, was now etched indelibly into her gray matter.

"Well," murmured Sandy as the credits rolled, "they always say the only love that lasts is unrequited love."

"Who does?" asked Jude irritably. There was a time for caution and a time for getting the show on the road. What was he waiting for?

The door flew open, and in strode Simon in his brown leather jacket and Greek fisherman's cap. Sandy shoved his hand under his thigh, like a crab scuttling away from a squid.

"Hope I'm not interrupting?" asked Simon, taking off his jacket and cap and dropping them on the floor.

He studied the *tableau vivant* on the bed for a long moment. "Now that you're living here, Jude, we should fill you in on the drill: I read Sandy a bedtime story every night."

Crawling up the mattress, he settled himself between them. Then he extracted a newspaper clipping from his pocket and read about a Japanese fisherman who put his wife in a net and dragged her behind his boat as shark bait.

Jude and Sandy smiled politely.

Simon read a second clipping concerning an Australian cyclist who had been attacked by a 350-pound ostrich, which she had managed to strangle with her bare hands.

Sandy lay there in silence while Jude tried to figure out what was going on.

"I was riding the IRT at rush hour this afternoon," Sandy said, "and this guy in a leather cap who was crushed up against me whispered in my ear, 'Drop dead, faggot.'"

"And what did you say?" asked Simon, studying him with interest.

"Nothing."

"Why would he say that?" asked Jude. All her life, people had been calling poor Sandy a faggot. She'd spent a lot of time defending his honor in high school.

Simon turned his stunning green eyes on Jude, saying, "Go on, mate. Tell her."

Sandy said nothing.

Jude leaned forward to look at him. His face was the color of a cooked lobster.

"I guess you don't need to," she said, rolling off the bed. "Sweet dreams, boys." She closed the door behind her.

Jude lay in bed, struggling to sleep so that she wouldn't have to feel so stupid. So the rumors about Sandy in high school had been true. And she had been the only one naïve enough not to believe them. And he had played on her naïveté, urging her to move in, leading her to think that a romance was possible between them. But why? Probably so that he could have the cover of respectability.

As she wept into her pillow in the dark, Mona's bed began to squeak rhythmically. Mona started to gasp in spasms. It was like a jazz ensemble. Soon the man would add his grunts to the improvisation, and then Mona would alternate her gasps with shrieks and moans.

Jude rolled over and pounded on the wall with her fist. "For God's sake, shut up!" she screamed.

The squeaking ceased abruptly and there was a long silence. Finally, it started up again, slowly and tentatively at first but rapidly gaining confidence and momentum. Jude decided to move back to her grandparents' in the morning.

JUDE WAS WRAPPING HER Atalanta flask in a sweatshirt when someone knocked at her door.

"Come in," she said glumly.

The door opened, and Sandy stood there in his bleached overalls, face and neck bright red, bangs splayed out around his cowlick as though he'd been standing in the funnel of a tornado. "Jude, I guess we need to talk," he said.

"What's there to say?" She placed the flask in her suitcase.

"Well, that I'm sorry, for one thing."

She stopped packing to give him a look. "I thought we could tell each other anything. So why didn't you tell me this?"

"I guess I was afraid you'd be appalled. And I can see that I was right."

"I'm not exactly appalled."

"What are you, then?"

"Confused, I suppose. What was that Dance of the Mating Hands all about?"

He grimaced. "I guess I hoped something might work out between us."

"And where would that have left Simon?" she asked angrily.

"All I know is what I felt. And feel. Life outside of Tidewater Estates can sometimes be complicated."

"Your life certainly seems to be," snapped Jude. She turned her back on him to stare out the window at the Ferris wheel in the amusement park across the river. She'd miss this madcap view of roller coasters and sailing yachts and garish sunsets.

"Please try to understand, Jude. Simon is my Molly. But that doesn't prevent me from loving you as well."

"So who does that make me? Ace Kilgore?" As she turned back around to study his earnest scarlet face, she softened. What he'd said was true. A current of connection that was almost palpable flowed between them. She had felt this with no one else but Molly. If it wasn't love, what was it? All the hours and days spent with Jerry and Bradley and a couple of others, in bed and out, talking and laughing and fooling around—that had been something else, often very pleasant, occasionally exciting, sometimes boring or annoying, but not love.

"There are different kinds of love," Sandy said, looking at the floor, "and different ways of expressing them. We can find a way, Jude. Please don't go. You and I have never been normal. Why should we start now?"

Jude smiled at his logic. Perhaps she could model herself after the *Marschallin*, who had vowed to love her count enough so that she could love even his love for someone else. It seemed a superhuman feat, but Jude knew from her years with Molly that real love involved more than just generating friction between various body parts, as though human beings were nothing more than cicadas droning in the waning summer dusk. And real love, if you found it, seemed the only thing that mattered. The rest was just passing the time until death claimed you.

Removing the flask from her suitcase, she unwrapped it and returned it to its spot on her windowsill. "Okay," she said.

Sandy grinned.

```
┌─────────────────────────────┐
│                             │
│         CHAPTER             │
│                             │
│           1 0               │
│                             │
│                             │
└─────────────────────────────┘
```

ONE WALL OF THE PENTHOUSE was glass, and through it Jude
could see the lights of lower Manhattan spread out below her
like a carpet of glowworms. A Marlboro man, a state trooper, and a
tutued ballerina with thick ankles were passing a joint beside tubs of
blue-gray junipers on the balcony.

The living room was packed. Sandy, wearing a white-net strapless
gown with a hoop skirt, a black bouffant wig, and elbow-length gloves,
was Scarlett O'Hara. Simon, in a Confederate army uniform, with a
sword in a silver scabbard and black boots to his knees, was Ashley
Wilkes. They planned to trade costumes the next Halloween.

Jude was wearing a swirling baby-blue chiffon Loretta Young
hostess gown, a merry widow with Kotex stuffed into the too-ample
cups, stiletto heels, rhinestone jewelry, white gloves, and a blond
Dolly Parton wig. And she had on more makeup than an embalmed

corpse. Wiggling her way to the doorway of the cleared-out dining room, she watched the dancers writhing shoulder-to-shoulder, drinks sloshing, heads ducking the swaying crystal chandelier, elbows pumping like pistons.

Jude felt something cold and wet between her shoulder blades. A deep voice whispered in her ear, "I'd like to crawl up under that skirt, darling, and suck that stiff piece of meat between your legs."

Jude turned her head and met the glazed gray eyes of Mae West. They scrutinized hers, turning suddenly bewildered. "Wait a minute," he said. "You're not a man."

"Sorry," said Jude.

Removing his glass from between her shoulders, he flounced off with a toss of his blond fall.

Jude felt guilty even being at the party, since she was straight. "Don't worry," Sandy had said as she made him up in the bathroom at home. "There are always a few hets at these things, trying to 'pass.' Besides, maybe you'll meet a nice woman." He grinned with his cherry red lips.

"I'm afraid I'm not that kind of girl," she said, carefully dotting a beauty spot on his cheek with her eyeliner.

"And what kind of girl are you, my dear?" asked Simon, leaning in the bathroom doorway, twirling his waxed mustache tip like Simon Legree. (Jude had just read that Harriet Beecher Stowe's model for Simon Legree had been a Huguenot. She was trying to decide whether to break the bad news to her grandmother.)

"A fag hag, apparently," said Jude, rubbing rouge into Sandy's cheekbone.

Her struggle to love Sandy enough to love even his love for Simon had consumed quite a few months. She had watched with misery as the two tumbled and tussled on Sandy's bed, cuddling and cosseting each other. And she couldn't help thinking that if only her anatomy had been male, she could have been in Simon's place. She didn't covet a penis per se, but she wouldn't have minded having one in order to have access to those who did covet them.

Some nights after Jude had gone to bed, Simon and Sandy departed for their sublife of bars, bathhouses, piers on the Hudson, and seedy movie theaters. Occasionally, it involved costumes, such as Sandy's yellow hard hat and grease monkey coveralls and Simon's fringed chaps and leather vest. And it often involved drugs with nicknames Jude couldn't keep straight, poppers and angel dust and black beauties, which they traded with their friends like marbles or baseball cards. Sometimes Jude heard them come crawling home in the dawn like mauled tomcats. This bad-boy act was a facet to Sandy that she'd never seen before. It seemed to clash with the daylight choirboy she knew so well.

"So how's it going, Jude?" yelled Sandy over the Jefferson Airplane, putting his arm around her and hauling her to his side so that his hoop skirt lurched upward, revealing lace garters and knobby knees.

Arranging the blond corkscrew curls around her face, Jude said, "This guy in drag got annoyed with me because I'm not a man. I'm getting confused." She was also getting drunk. The room was beginning to sway along with the dancers.

As Sandy was swept away by a tide of revelers, Joan of Arc appeared before Jude, wearing chain mail, dark tights, and shiny metal shin guards. All Jude could see of the face behind the visored helmet were the eyes, which were lapis lazuli in the shadows, just like Molly's. For a moment, she couldn't remember if she was awake or asleep. Her heart lurched unsteadily.

"Molly?" she said.

"Excuse me?" said Joan of Arc.

"Sorry. I thought you were someone else."

"I *am* someone else," she said, eyes crinkling with amusement. Jude laughed.

As the stunning blue eyes probed hers, Jude felt her flesh prickle.

"You make a beautiful woman," murmured Joan of Arc, one hand holding a staff with an attached blue banner studded with white fleurs-de-lis.

"I *am* a woman," said Jude.

"Obviously. And a most attractive one, too."

Joan was dragged off by a crowd of revelers pressing toward the dance floor, where the Jefferson Airplane were shouting, "Don't you want somebody to love? Don't you need somebody to love? Wouldn't you love somebody to love? You've got to find somebody to love! . . ."

William, the host, loomed in front of Jude. He was dressed as a Roman senator, in a white toga with a wreath on his head. A labor lawyer by day, he was pale and pudgy, like a pregnant ghost. His lover, Sid, was dressed as a gladiator, in some crossed leather straps, sandals, and a pouch for his genitals. But since he was a stevedore, he had the build to carry it off.

"Having fun, my pet?" asked William, repositioning his wreath.

"It's a wonderful party, William. Who's the woman dressed as Joan of Arc, by the way?"

He wrinkled his shiny bulbous nose. "Her name is Anna Olsen. She's a poet and a teacher. But forget about her, Jude. She's bad news."

"I wasn't thinking of her like that."

"No, certainly not," said William sternly. "I forgot. Our divine Jude is most regrettably het-ero-sex-ual." He enunciated each syllable with deep, mocking respect.

"Why is she bad news?" demanded Jude, smiling tolerantly.

William drifted away toward the plate-glass window like a blowfish in an overpopulated aquarium. Jude called after him, "William, why is she bad news?"

SANDY, SIMON, AND JUDE stumbled up the sidewalk, raincoats over their costumes. No taxi would stop for them because they looked both demented and drunk. So they were trudging north from the Village en route to Riverside Drive. Sandy and Jude had removed the spike heels from their blistered feet and were limping along in tattered stockings. Sandy's skirt was dragging the dirty sidewalk like a flaccid peacock tail. Jude was walking in the middle, arms linked through theirs, still a bit shaken by mistaking Joan of Arc for Molly. Was Molly now going to start invading her waking hours as well?

"Sandy, you look like Scarlett in the turnip patch after the burning of Atlanta," she observed.

"I know. And my hair—I can't do a thing with it." He yanked off his black wig and tossed it into a trash basket.

Giggling, they passed some young men who were standing by the entrance to the Port Authority. One in a leather cap and motorcycle boots called to Sandy, "Come over here, faggot. Give me a blow job, will you, darling?" His friends laughed and punched his tattooed biceps.

The man followed them up the sidewalk, stroking the crotch of his tight jeans and murmuring, "I got something here I could shove between those pretty red lips of yours." His friends ambled along behind him, making obscene sucking sounds.

Jude tightened her grip on Simon's trembling arm to prevent him from turning around and saying something that would get them all killed.

The men finally got bored and went away.

"I always get bussed at the bus," Sandy said with a sigh.

"Very funny," growled Simon.

"I suppose we asked for that," said Sandy. "Swishing around the streets in these getups."

"I thought this was the land of the free?" said Simon.

"Free if you're normal. Perverts must pay. You know what? I'm pretty sure that's the same guy who called me a faggot on the IRT the other day. They both had leather caps and blind right eyes."

"Bloody hell," said Simon.

A taxi finally stopped for them, and they rode back to the apartment in silence, Sandy's net skirt filling the backseat like foam in a beer mug.

Outside Sandy's room, Jude kissed them both on the cheek and headed down the hall.

"Jude," called Sandy.

She stopped and looked back at him. His face was scarlet beneath his smudged makeup.

"We'd love for you to stay with us tonight if you want to."

Simon nodded, hand absently stroking his filigreed sword handle.

Jude looked back and forth between them, Scarlett O'Hara and Ashley Wilkes in the wake of Sherman's March to the Sea. After the hatred she had just witnessed in the street, it would be reassuring to reassert the power of love.

"Uh, could you do that? I mean . . . I thought . . . aren't you . . ."

"We have both been known to make exceptions for irresistibly lovely women," murmured Simon, smiling gently beneath his drooping mustache, neon eyes glowing in the shadowy hallway.

Jude was astonished to find herself seriously considering the idea. She'd come a long way since the Virginia Club Colonial Cotillion.

"I'm afraid it would be too kinky for a simple Huguenot girl from Tennessee," she finally concluded. "But thank you for the sweet invitation."

"Just say the word if you change your mind," said Sandy. He looked relieved.

"We would have fun," Simon assured her.

Jude smiled. "I'll let you know, boys." Chiffon skirt swirling, she swept down the hallway, élan restored.

Lying in bed, she became intrigued by the mechanics of it all—how to keep track of two penises in various stages of tumescence. One was complicated enough. She would probably feel as frantic as someone in a straitjacket with a case of poison ivy. But it certainly seemed the most interesting way to resolve their triangle.

She fell asleep for a while. When she woke up, she found that she had in fact changed her mind. She got out of bed, slipped on her robe, and tiptoed down the hallway to Sandy's door. Placing her ear against it, she heard nothing. Either they'd gone out or they were asleep. She had no idea what time it was. Maybe she could just crawl in between them and see what happened. After all, they had issued her a standing invitation.

Slowly she turned the handle and opened the door. Across the room, she saw them, naked in the moonlight through the window. Sandy was bent over, legs planted well apart, gripping the windowsill with his hands and his teeth. Simon, standing behind him, grasped Sandy's hips with both hands. He was rocking back and forth against him, murmuring things Jude couldn't distinguish, while Sandy gasped and moaned and gnawed the windowsill.

Seeing the light from the cracked door fall across Sandy's back, Simon froze. He looked back at her—and it wasn't Simon. For a moment, Jude thought it was the young man with the blind eye from the bus station. But then she wasn't sure.

Sucking air through clenched teeth, Sandy snarled in a voice like the growl of a cornered beast, "Jesus Christ, Jude, get the fuck out of here!"

Backing into the hallway, Jude closed the door and leaned against the wall, mortified and afraid—and aroused. Shivering violently, she returned to her room and climbed back into bed, where she lay perfectly still, breathing heavily.

SANDY AND JUDE WERE STROLLING down Columbus Avenue inspecting the Roosevelt, where her father had been an intern. For several years, he had ridden the yelping ambulances into alleys where no one sane would venture on foot. The hospital was looking seedy, with newspapers and fast-food wrappers blown up in sodden heaps against the redbrick walls. Across Fifty-eighth Street was a Renaissance Revival apartment building from the turn of the century, with arched windows, and designs formed by blue-and-gold tiles inlaid among the red bricks. The windows were boarded up, and antiwar graffiti was spray-painted across the plywood—peace symbols and YANKS OUT OF NAM and MAKE LOVE NOT WAR. A sign on the door announced that the building was slated for demolition.

"My parents lived on the fifth floor of that building after they got married," said Jude as a sharp wind off the Hudson came swirling down the street. She and Sandy were being very careful with each other this morning, keeping things light and polite, as though by not acknowledging the events of the previous night they'd dissolve.

"It's sad to see a noble old place like that on its last legs," said Sandy. "When you think about all the lives that were lived in there. The joy and the sorrow those walls must have absorbed."

"My God," said Jude, "I just realized: I must have been conceived in there. When they headed south, my mother was pregnant with me."

"Ha!" said Sandy. "So you're actually a Yankee!"

"Thank God my Virginia grandmother isn't around to hear this."

"Imagine that," said Sandy, wrapping his arms around himself for warmth. "You've returned to the site of your inception. Like a salmon swimming upstream to her primordial spawning grounds."

"Let's not get carried away," suggested Jude. "Where do you think you were conceived?" They headed back uptown to meet Jude's grandparents for brunch at Café des Artistes.

"Right there in Tidewater Estates, I imagine. On a Saturday morning in midwinter. Saturday mornings were the only time they ever did it, as far as I could tell. My father would hand me a bowl of Cheerios and lock me in the playroom with my erector set. They didn't appear until lunchtime, and they remained in a haze of well-being for the rest of the weekend. I always waited until Saturday afternoon to ask for things they might object to."

"But maybe they were on a vacation somewhere more exotic?"

"Not bloody likely. Even their vacations were humdrum. Gatlinburg or Ruby Falls or Rock City."

"So where did all your evil genius come from?" asked Jude.

"Someone somewhere along the line must have cut loose with a hired hand."

"By the way," said Jude, unable to endure this charade any longer, "I'm sorry about last night."

Sandy blushed violently. "I'm sorry I was . . . otherwise engaged. Please try me again sometime."

Jude said nothing for a while. Finally, she replied, "I don't think so, Sandy. You're out of my league."

"So I gather you're shocked?"

"Who was he?"

"Who knows?"

"Where was Simon?"

"Who knows?"

"Do you really think this is wise?"

"Wisdom has nothing to do with it," said Sandy curtly.

"Clearly."

The truth was, Jude realized as Sandy opened the restaurant door for her, that she was afraid of him now, as though he were the carrier of some dark, brute force brought home from the docks, about which she knew little and wanted to know less. And the knowledge that a succession of strangers apparently wandered around their apartment in the middle of the night left her very uneasy. But it was, after all, Sandy's apartment. And she was unable to deny that the sight of him and the stranger grappling in the moonlight had excited her.

"WE USED TO BRING your mother here for Sunday lunch," Jude's grandfather said to Jude as he trimmed the fat off his sirloin. "In the days before that dreadful word *brunch* was ever invented."

Naked nymphets were cavorting on the walls all around them, behind forests of healthy indoor plants.

"I remember Jude's mother pretty well," said Sandy as he ripped apart a piece of baguette. "She used to give me a butterscotch candy whenever she saw me on the sidewalk in Tidewater Estates. So I started going over there all the time. She asked me to teach Jude to ride her new tricycle. Jude's legs were so short that her feet kept slipping off and spinning the pedals. And she thought that was so neat that she couldn't be bothered to try anything else."

Everyone laughed.

"Once she caught on, though," Sandy added, "she was a demon. She'd race down the block toward the highway before anyone realized she was gone. Her mother used to bribe me with candies to keep up with her."

"And here I thought you just liked me," said Jude. She hadn't seen him in a jacket and tie since he was at Exeter. He looked deceptively respectable.

"I must have, because I kept at it even after your mother died."

"Well, Jude tells us you are like a brother to her," said Jude's grandmother in her navy wool suit, Huguenot cross at her throat. "That makes you our grandson, and I want you to know that you will always be welcome in our home."

"Thank you very much," said Sandy. "I'm honored."

Jude studied her honorary brother as he bewitched her grandparents. If only Sandy weren't who he was, she and he would have made the perfect couple. But he was who he was, whoever that might be, and he would never be hers. The time had come to find a lover she could actually have, Jude had concluded, one who approximated the man she'd imagined Sandy to be. She'd been thinking about offering the position to Craig, a fellow Ph.D. candidate with whom she often discussed the Franco-Prussian War over cups of coffee at the West End Bar. Recently, he'd begun to touch her forearm as they talked and to press her knee with his beneath the table. He was too thin and he reeked of sandalwood incense, but otherwise he filled the bill.

"I remember the day Jude's father came home from the war," Sandy was saying.

Jude looked at her grandfather, who was listening to Sandy with attention. He seemed to have relaxed around the subject of Jude's mother. Maybe hearing Jude and her grandmother discuss her so much had desensitized him.

"The whole town went down to the train station and waved little American flags on sticks. The high school band was playing this god-awful mess that was supposed to be 'Stars and Stripes Forever.' Jude's mother was carrying Jude on her hip. Her father climbed off the train in his uniform, and I thought he was the most handsome man

I'd ever seen. Jude, who hadn't seen him since she was an infant, took one look at him, smiled coyly, reached out her arms, and cooed, 'Daddy!' And everybody laughed and cheered.''

Jude watched her grandparents smile sadly as the busboy removed their plates.

"He was always a fine-looking man," agreed her grandfather.

Jude and her grandmother glanced at him, then at each other.

"Tall and lean and broad-shouldered," continued her grandfather. "With that copper skin and those mink-brown eyes."

Jude's grandmother shot her an astonished smile.

"I imagine y'all don't remember meeting me at the funeral," said Sandy, "but I remember you. Because you were the first Yankees I'd ever seen, and I was disappointed that you looked so normal."

"What were you expecting?" asked Jude's grandfather. "Horns and cloven feet?"

"Something like that," said Sandy. "But the only sinister thing about you was the dead fox around your wife's neck."

"I remember that fox," said Jude. "It had beady orange eyes."

"But I'm not even a Yankee," said her grandfather. "My family was in Alsace during your civil war."

Sandy smiled. "To Southerners, every American who isn't a Southerner is a Yankee."

By the time Jude and Sandy left her grandparents beneath the Tiffany light above their doorway, Sandy had promised them a free box at the opera. Jude's grandmother had written down his address so she could put him on the mailing list for the National Huguenot Society's newsletter, and her grandfather had noted his phone number so he could call him for a game of squash at the New York Athletic Club.

"My God, what a love feast," said Jude as they walked down 67th Street beneath the bare trees.

"Can I help it if I'm irresistible?" asked Sandy.

"Probably," said Jude. "But don't stop. It's so charming. Wait just a minute—you don't even know how to play squash."

Sandy grinned. "No. But I like locker rooms."

"With my *grandfather*?"

"He's very attractive, with all that steel-gray hair and that gun-slinger jaw."

"You're sick," said Jude.

"I thought you said I was charming?"

"You're both. That's what makes you so dangerous." She was only half-kidding. How would she ever be able to integrate his daylight and moonlight selves?

"I like being perceived as dangerous," he admitted. "I was always such a Boy Scout back home."

"Well, you seem to be making up for lost time," murmured Jude.

Sandy glanced at her. "And you don't like it?"

"Not much," Jude replied hesitantly, appalled by the excitement she still felt when she pictured the faceless stranger thrusting into him.

"Well, let's see if I can defend myself to you, Jude. For years and years, I tried to be a good boy. For instance, I never touched you, however much I might have wanted to. You would have been shocked, but I don't think you'd have turned me down."

Jude thought for a moment, then shook her head no. "Maybe I wish you had, Sandy," she said, wondering if she had returned his love for her at that time whether his desire for men would have emerged nonetheless. Probably.

"Well, maybe I wish that, too. But I didn't. Instead, I bottled up my libido for years and years. When I got to London and started going to gay bars, I met hundreds of former Eagle Scouts just like myself. And we gave each other what we'd been doing without for

all those years. Without having to say I love you, or to ask each other
to go steady, or even to know each other's names. It was dangerous
and mysterious and exciting. And it still is.''

Jude reached over for his hand. Knitting fingers, they walked
along Broadway in silence. What would happen, Jude wondered, if
they should ever both want each other at the same time?

''But surely this is something you understand, Jude?''

''Why do you say that?''

''Well, you were always a bit of a Girl Scout back home yourself.
You must have had to confront your own shadow side by now—the
part of you that longs for your dutiful everyday self to be obliterated
by some all-consuming passion?''

Jude looked at him mutely, not knowing the answer to such an
alarming question. Her everyday self had been obliterated only once
—that night on the raft with Molly. And it had been overwhelming.
But she didn't expect it to happen ever again. And she couldn't have
said that she wanted it to.

LATER THAT WEEK AFTER a study session at the Columbia library,
Jude and Craig ran the gauntlet of antiwar protesters who, waving
Chippendale chair legs, defended the captured administration building.
Back at Jude's apartment, she sneaked him down the hallway and into
her bedroom. The night that ensued was uninspired, since it was
sparked by only lukewarm affection and respect. But Jude made as
much noise as possible within the bounds of credibility, as retaliation
against Mona and Sandy.

In the sunny kitchen the next morning, Sandy's face was grim.
He practically bumped chests with Craig, like rival seals. Taking the
hint, Craig departed quickly.

''You could have at least been civil,'' Jude said to Sandy after
letting Craig out the door.

"I don't have to be civil to any old scum you happen to drag in off the street," he snapped, grabbing several cereal boxes from the shelf.

"What about the scum *you* drag home? Besides, Craig's not scum. He's very sweet and bright." She hacked off a slice of bread and thrust it into the toaster.

"What would your father say?" He grabbed a bowl and slammed it down on the table.

Jude laughed incredulously. "Sandy, snap out of it."

"Out of what?"

"I think you're jealous." She studied him with gratified amusement.

"Oh, sure. Right. A gay man jealous of a straight woman."

"What's your problem then?" The toast popped up. She buttered it and spread it with raspberry jam.

He said nothing for a long time, pouring and mixing several cereals, hurling flakes around the room. Then he smiled sheepishly. "My problem is that I'm jealous."

"There. That's better," said Jude, patting his shoulder.

"Don't ever do that to me again," he said, looking up at her through bloodshot eyes.

"I'll do whatever I please." She headed out the door, carrying her toast.

"Yes, I know," he said, sadly munching his flakes. "You always have."

SIMON AND JUDE WERE SITTING propped up on Sandy's bed splitting a pepperoni pizza from a cardboard box and drinking V-8 juice. They'd tried to wait for Sandy, but hunger had won out. Scattered across the spread were pages from a manuscript Simon was editing on the Freedom Riders, mixed up with a rough draft of Jude's dissertation proposal. She'd decided to write about the perennial French phenomenon of a small group that defined itself as the "saving remnant," which everyone else then tried to murder as painfully as possible, using as case studies the Cathars, the Huguenots, the Jacobins, and the Resistance. Her delighted grandmother had been stuffing information down her throat like a mother bird feeding worms to her fledgling.

She had just interviewed a French friend of her grandfather's, who had fought with the Resistance after a Jewish shopkeeper in his village in the Alps had been crucified upside down by the SS, his mouth packed with cow manure. The man described partisans from his village mining a tunnel through the mountains with explosives to slow down the German advance. The plot was betrayed by a local farmer, and all the conspirators who were caught were forced to march into the tunnel themselves, where they were buried alive by their own trap.

As usual, Jude was actually trying to figure out the difference between people like Ace Kilgore, whose goal in life was to harm and destroy, and those like her father and grandfather and Sandy, who tried instead to defend and heal. She had concluded that it had something to do with Ace's eyes, two dead, black holes that neither reflected light from without nor projected it from within. Since he himself was cut off from the light, he was wounded and vengeful and determined to spread his contagion of rage, like some kind of spiritual rabies. It gratified him to plunge others into darkness, to prove that it was more powerful than the light that had shunned him.

But the real mystery was why ordinary people like Jerry Crawford and the Panther Twins had followed him into this void. Once while they were dating, she'd asked Jerry what he saw in Ace. He replied, "He's so strong. He's not afraid of anything." But Jude had come to suspect since that Ace was actually afraid of everything. His was the fake strength that reverted to violence under pressure.

Meanwhile, she had been delivering a discourse to an uninterested Simon on V-8 juice—why it had tasted awful to her as a child but was now delicious. Simon kept interrupting to discuss Marmite on toast. The evening news was playing on the television at the foot of the bed, the commentary a soft murmur as an American soldier incinerated a peasant hut with a flamethrower.

The phone rang. Groping for it on the floor, Simon picked up the receiver, listened, then said in his most winning voice, "Speaking!"

Holding out the receiver, he studied it and shrugged. "Funny. He hung up."

"Who was it?" asked Jude.

"Some guy asking to speak to the lady of the house."

As Jude laughed, Sandy walked through the door from the hallway, looking grim.

"Hard day at the office, dear?" called Simon from the bed.

"Hard day in the subway," he said.

"What happened?" asked Jude, alarmed by his voice, which sounded numb.

"It's not important."

"You can't come in here looking and sounding like Marilyn Monroe after her suicide and not tell us why," said Simon. He bounced off the bed and padded in his sweat socks over to Sandy. As Simon put his arms around him, Sandy started to cry angrily. Simon led him to the bed, and they sat down on the edge.

"Sorry," said Sandy, blotting his tears on the sleeve of his work shirt.

"What's wrong, love?" asked Simon, stroking the red-blond hair out of Sandy's eyes.

"When I got off the IRT just now, that same guy who harassed us at the Port Authority last Halloween, the one with the leather cap and the blind eye, was getting off with three of his friends. We were alone in the tunnel to the stairway, and he said, 'Well, well, if it isn't our friendly neighborhood homo searching for an asshole to fuck.' I turned around and gave him a look, and he said, 'And he isn't going to find one, either, because he's so fuckin' ugly.' And one of the others said, 'Maybe we should just put him out of his fuckin' fairy misery and kick his fuckin' faggot brains in.' I'd been working back-stage all day during the dress rehearsal for *Aida*, and I was so tired and so scared that I just opened my mouth and hit a high C. It bounced back and forth off those tile walls. They looked at me as though I was a crackpot and ran up the steps as fast as they could."

Sandy smiled weakly, waiting for them to laugh, but they didn't. "I just feel so helpless."

"Bloody hell, Sandy, please be careful," said Simon.

"What can I do?" he asked softly.

"What about telling the police?" asked Jude. Her eyes strayed to his windowsill, on which she could see the indentations of his teeth. Could a taste for danger, like a pact with Satan, actually attract it in ways you hadn't bargained on? She wanted to protect him as he had her, but how?

The two men laughed bitterly.

"They probably *are* the police," said Sandy.

"Walk," said Jude. "Take a bus. A taxi even. It's cheaper than a funeral."

"SO THE COPS TRIED to herd them into a paddy wagon," Sid was saying to the dozen people sitting around the cluttered dining table in Sandy's apartment, "and they refused. Those motherfucking queens staged a riot like those fascist pigs had never dreamed of in their worst nightmares. Bopping them with their handbags. Stabbing them with their nails. Stomping them with their spike heels. Falsetto screams. And then a bunch of dykes and motorcycle dudes joined in, throwing bottles and swinging bike chains and hefting tire irons. And soon the whole damn block was in chaos. So the cops shoved their badass nightsticks back into their holsters and split."

Everyone erupted into cheers, except Mona, who looked deeply bored to be in a roomful of men who never looked twice at her.

"Out of the closets and into the streets!" yelled Simon, standing up and raising his beer bottle in a toast.

Jude clicked her wineglass against Sandy's. He was smiling ironically at Simon's sudden ascent to the barricades.

"No more Mr. Nice Guy!" cried Earl, which was practically the first thing Jude had ever heard him say.

"Oh, gracious, watch out, homophobes!" said William. "Earl is on a rampage!"

Earl leapt up from his chair and began to whirl around the room in his sweatpants in a graceful frenzy, like something out of *Le Sacre du Printemps.*

Sandy handed Jude the joint that was circling the table. She drew on it and passed it to Tony in his pirate head scarf. Exhaling, she whispered to Sandy, "I don't know why I bother. This stuff has never worked for me."

Getting up, Sandy stood behind Jude and began to massage her scalp as they watched Earl's war dance, which the others were accompanying by clashing together their dirty cutlery. Tony was striking the empty and half-empty wine bottles with his knife, creating a discordant melody. Eventually, like the Pied Piper, Earl led everyone but Sandy and Jude in a bunny-hopping conga line out the door, en route to the carnival that had filled the Village streets ever since the riot.

Jude, meanwhile, was going out of her mind as Sandy continued to knead her scalp and her neck. Her only wish was that he never stop. He began to run his fingers around the folds of her ears and in and out of the passageways. Abruptly, she turned her head to one side and sucked his index finger into her mouth. He drew a sharp breath.

Jude pushed up from her chair. She turned and they faced each other, startled and afraid. They moved into each other's arms like horseshoe magnets. Their mouths joined.

Eventually, Jude turned her head aside to gasp, "We'd better wait for Simon."

"I don't want to wait anymore, Jude," Sandy said. "I've been waiting for you since I was a boy."

Jude just stood there, paralyzed by the ethics of the situation, feeling Sandy's erection against her abdomen.

"Please, Jude. Just once and never again. It will get it out of our systems."

"Or infect us like a wasting disease." Her breathing was turning jagged.

Smiling down at her whimsically, he said, "You always did think too much, brainchild."

At the sound of Molly's nickname for her, pronounced in the identical soft mountain drawl, she let him lead her down the hallway to his room.

"I WAS WRONG," she murmured to Sandy later as they lay among the tangled clothing that littered his bed and carpet. A breeze through the open window was drying their sweat and chilling them.

"What about?" He reached for her shirt and draped it languidly over her chest and abdomen.

"I'm crazy about you as a bad boy."

He smiled lazily as a boat horn blared on the river. "In matters such as these, there's no bad or good. Only love and the courage to live it. Or not.''

''DON'T WORRY ABOUT IT, JUDE. It's cool,'' said Simon the next evening as they sat in the breeze wafting through Sandy's window, sharing a joint and watching pleasure craft glide down the Hudson in the twilight. ''Just as long as I get equal time one of these days.''

''It could happen,'' she said, studying her friendly rival with his dark curls and his Fu Manchu mustache. Since the stated goal of their generation was to ''smash monogamy,'' he had no choice but to appear blasé. But he seemed really not to mind. Yet if he knew what had gone on between Sandy and herself the previous evening, he would have minded a great deal. It hadn't been that conditioned reflex you could have alone or with anyone else, of spasming muscles pumping blood through swollen tissue. It had been another order of experience altogether, parallel to that night with Molly on the raft, but even more moving, if that was possible, because they had both been wide awake and unafraid and unashamed. Afterward, they had cried—from astonishment to have shared such an unlooked-for moment. From sorrow that it was over and might never recur. What she couldn't tell Simon was that she now had no wish to give him equal time or even to share Sandy with him anymore. The only person she wanted was Sandy, as soon as possible, as often as possible, for as long as possible.

Even so, she wished she hadn't drunk all that wine and smoked all that dope, so she could have avoided such delirium. Because she and Sandy and Simon were now headed down some gloomy labyrinth in which at least one of them would lose the way. Probably herself, since, as Clementine used to say, leopards didn't change their spots. Especially if they were happy leopards. Why hadn't she left well enough alone?

Sandy looked as tense and miserable as Jude felt when he arrived in the doorway and spotted her and Simon sitting together by the window. From a car radio in the street below, Janis Joplin was begging someone to take, and break, a piece of her heart.

Simon looked up at Sandy through shrewd green eyes. "Don't worry, mate. I know you love her. I love her, too. These things happen. They'll happen again. Maybe for me next time, if I get lucky."

"It's not that," said Sandy, walking in and sitting down on his mattress. He propped his elbows on his knees and buried his face in his hands.

"What's wrong, Sandy?" demanded Simon.

Sandy drew a deep breath, then exhaled. "I was standing on the subway platform just now. It was rush hour, so it was really crowded. That guy with the blind eye turned up right beside me. As he pushed past me, he snarled, 'Out of my way, queer boy.'

"I don't know what came over me, but all of a sudden I just couldn't take it anymore. So I said in a really loud voice, 'This man is a fascist!' I stood on tiptoe and pointed him out as he dodged through the crowd, trying to get away. 'He follows me around threatening me and calling me names!' I yelled.

"Most of the people ignored me, but a few looked at me sympathetically or studied him as he fought his way to the exit. On the steps, he turned around and looked at me as though I were a cockroach he was about to squash."

WHEN SANDY DIDN'T COME HOME from work the next night, Simon phoned all the hospitals in the city, finally locating him in intensive care at the Roosevelt. Someone had found him unconscious in an alley near the Port Authority.

Jude walked into his hospital room. He was tucked tightly into a narrow white bed, his face black and purple, tubes snaking from his nostril and hand. As he gasped for air, she noticed that several of his teeth were missing.

Sitting down beside him, she laid her head on his bedside and closed her eyes. People in serious accidents reported having their lives flash before their eyes. But at that moment, Jude experienced just such a retrospective of Sandy's life. Like a slide show, she saw him as a fair-haired little boy in socks and sandals. She saw him in his tree house, writing his novel, his cowlicked hair scrambled like a rat's nest. And playing chess by the brick wall on the playground at school. And throwing passes to her halfway down the football field as boys twice his size closed in on him. Sandy in a tweed jacket chattering charmingly to her grandparents, and sitting at his switchboard at the opera, overseeing dozens of workers and technicians. Sandy lying beneath her, eyes closed, languorous smile playing across his lips, hands stroking her buttocks as she braced her fists against the wall and moved up and down on him, slowly, slowly, trembling and sweating, struggling to make a finite moment last forever.

She could feel him ebbing away. She reached over and grabbed his hand to try to make him stay, but it was limp and dry and cold.

The next night while Jude ate a grim and silent dinner with Sandy's parents, who had just arrived from Tennessee, Sandy died from a blood clot to his brain while Simon dozed in the chair by his bed.

When Jude and Simon reached home after midnight, Simon followed her to her room. "Please may I stay with you tonight?" he asked.

They lay in each other's arms on her bed. Periodically, Simon cried while Jude stroked his back and blotted his tears with the sheet. She knew this drill by heart. First came the numbness, the way the stump of a newly severed limb didn't bleed. Then the fury, when you lashed out at anyone who got in your way. And finally the memories that wouldn't quit. But maybe expecting the joy of communion without the pain of its loss was like wanting to eat candy without getting cavities.

Toward dawn, Simon said in a hoarse voice, "You were the last person he made love to. I turned him down the other night. I guess I was punishing him for you. I said it was okay. But it wasn't. His tricks were one thing. Sexual encounters with men he'd never see again. But he really loved you. Eventually, he'd have left me for you."

"No, Simon. It was nothing. We were drunk. Stoned. It should never have happened. I'm sorry it did," she lied.

"Don't apologize. It was inevitable. He loved you, Jude, all his life."

"But not as much as he did you. You were the soul mate he'd always wanted and never found."

Their mouths abruptly undertook an urgent exploration of each other's faces and necks. Jude could taste the salt of Simon's tears. As he entered her, their bodies shuddered, fumbled for a rhythm, and finally moved together. And since each was fantasizing that the other was Sandy, for a moment it seemed he really was there, hovering over them, blessing their clumsy union with his whimsical smile.

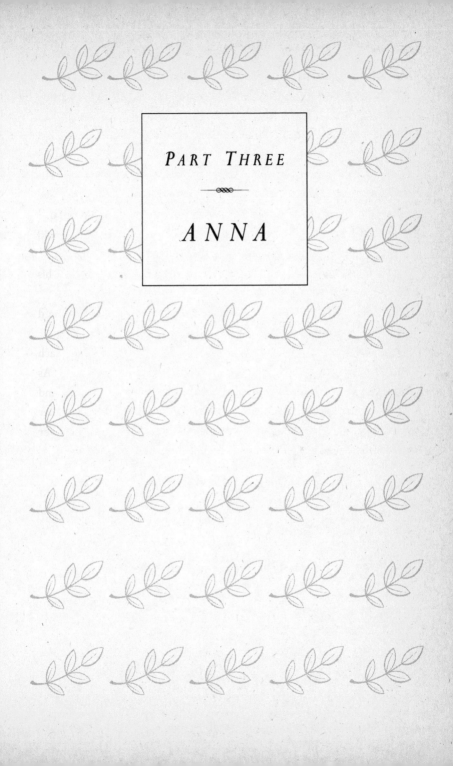

PART THREE

ANNA

CHAPTER

1 1

A WOMAN IN A LONG, burgundy wool overcoat stood in the
doorway of Jude's office, smiling and frowning, both at once.
Jude smiled back from her cluttered desk. She felt she should know
the woman but was unable to place her. She sported a glossy, dark,
flapper hairdo and mauve lipstick.

The woman snapped her fingers. "Dolly Parton!"

Jude smiled politely. "Excuse me?"

"That Halloween party a few years ago. You were Dolly Parton.
And I was Joan of Arc."

The eyes. Now Jude remembered the eyes, which had been shad-
owed by the visor of her helmet as she stood before Jude in her chain
mail and shin guards. At the moment, the eyes were sapphire blue
against cheeks flushed from the cold, and they were framed by dark
crescent eyebrows and long lashes.

"I'm Anna Olsen. Simon sent me. I just ran into him on his way out. He said maybe you'd have a minute to listen to my book idea."

"Come in," said Jude, standing up to clear a stack of manuscripts and page proofs off her tweed love seat. "How do you know Simon?"

"I don't very well. We have some mutual friends—the men who gave that party." She perched on the edge of the love seat.

"William and Sid?" Jude returned to her swivel chair.

Anna nodded.

"You have quite a memory," said Jude. She herself did not, however, because something was nibbling away at the edge of her awareness, something disturbing William had said that she couldn't quite recall.

"For memorable events, I do." She unbuttoned her coat, revealing a large wool scarf in shades of blue and purple.

Jude looked at her with a half smile, having just remembered Anna's telling her that night that she made a beautiful woman. She was quite the flirt. Too bad she was barking up a dead tree. "So what's your book idea?"

Anna, a poet, taught creative-writing workshops in the city high schools. She was proposing an anthology of pieces by her students, who represented more than a dozen nationalities. She was intrigued by the ways in which they adapted their cultural inheritances to the American mainstream, or failed to. America wasn't a melting pot, she maintained; it was a stockpot, full of intact lumps.

Jude nodded, hands clasped before her chin. It was what America was supposed to be all about—a haven for those who needed a fresh start, freed from ancient traditions and taboos, yet no doubt bearers of them nonetheless.

"I'll talk to Simon," said Jude, having difficulty removing her eyes from Anna's, which were now turquoise in the zebra shafts of

light through the slatted blinds, like deep seawater penetrated by sunbeams. "It sounds like an interesting idea. Leave me your number and
I'll give you a call."

"I'll call *you*," Anna said quickly. "When would be good?"

"Early next week?"

After seeing Anna to the elevator by the reception desk, Jude
returned to her office and sat back down at her desk, swiveling her
chair around to watch the woman at her keyboard in the glass building
across the street. When the blinds were up, they sometimes waved
to each other like next-door neighbors. Jude admired her wardrobe
—a seemingly endless parade of tailored suits and silk blouses such as
Jude aspired to once she could afford them.

Simon had hired Jude as his assistant when she dropped out of
Columbia. After Sandy's death, everything seemed pointless, especially
the study of history. She no longer wished to know about the idiotic
atrocities committed by the human race since the dawn of time. So
she'd been mindlessly typing and filing, fielding phone calls and visitors, and ransacking reviews for favorable quotes to use in ads. She
planned to remain an assistant forever. But Anna's book idea interested
her.

She kept thinking about Anna's eyes, how similar they were to
Molly's—the same shifting shades of blue, like a mood ring. The same
way of narrowing with skepticism and sparkling with amusement. They
were Molly's eyes in a different face. Anna's physique, however, was
tall and slender.

Turning back to her desk, Jude typed a memo to Simon rec-
ommending Anna's project. Clipping it to her outline and samples,
she took the package next door and laid it on his black Formica tabletop, on which sat several dozen paperweights—a bronze penis with
a happy-face head, an Empire State Building with a removable King
Kong. Jude selected what Simon claimed was the varnished hoof of

Secretariat to secure her memo. Also on the tabletop sat a photo of
Sandy in a silver frame. He was smiling into the camera, wearing a
white undershirt that displayed his well-cut biceps and pecs, a grassy
Cape Cod dune looming behind him.

In the years since his death, Jude and Simon had both been on
a tear. Simon roamed the streets at night with a switchblade at the
ready in the pocket of his leather jacket, searching for the young thug
with the blind eye he was convinced had killed Sandy. Despite the
fact that Sandy's missing wallet made robbery the apparent motive.
Often he came home to their apartment bruised and bloodied from
fights he'd picked with bewildered hoodlums. Periodically, Jude removed the switchblade from his pocket and threw it in a trash basket
on her way to work. But he always bought another.

Jude herself had become a bedroom guerrilla, ambushing half a
dozen young men, leading them on, then leaving them high and dry
and humiliated, while they phoned and fumed and leapt from tall
buildings. Occasionally, she and Simon sought relief from their fury
in each other's arms. But apart from the night of Sandy's death, Simon
made it clear that it was just a diversion. "Rearranging the hormones," he called it. And in the morning, he was brisk and distant,
as though they hadn't been lying together panting like marathon run-
ners a few hours earlier. Sometimes Jude wasn't even sure if it had
really happened or if she'd dreamed it. She had never told him about
the intensity of the interchange between Sandy and herself, and she
never would. Simon had referred a few times to "your little fling with
Sandy." It was clear that he needed to think of it as nothing more
than what she and he experienced together—some warmth in the night
with friendly flesh.

But Jude had recently become disgusted with herself as a con-
quistador. She'd realized that she was wounding innocent civilians in

her war of attrition. And she sometimes longed for a comrade-in-arms with whom she could lay down her weapons and find peace. But at other times, she concluded that she was finished with love. It hurt too much. Since she seemed incapable of taking it lightly, her only recourse was to jettison it.

Dreams were currently her sole consolation. During the weeks of numb disbelief following Sandy's death, Molly appeared for the first time since Jude had moved in with him.

"I told you he was going to hurt you," she said, briskly dealing hands for Over the Moon on the pine needles that cushioned the floor of their cave in the Wildwoods.

"Bravo. Right again," said Jude. "I thought I'd gotten rid of you."

"Dream on. You'll never get rid of me, sweetheart. So you might as well learn to listen to me."

"I do listen to you, Molly. I just don't always agree." Jude swept her cards together, picked them up, and fanned them out.

Molly shrugged and threw down the jack of spades. "Falling in love with a fag was probably just your way of staying faithful to me."

"Stop calling Sandy a fag," snapped Jude, tossing down the ten of hearts.

Molly grinned. "Poor little Jude. Forever in love with phantoms."

JUDE'S PHONE BUZZED. It was Simon, asking her to come next door. He was sitting behind his table in his striped dress shirt and Jackson Pollock tie, curly black hair pulled back into a ponytail, studying Jude's memo with his limpid green eyes. "Since you like Anna's idea so much, I think you should handle it." He wound up a green plastic *Tyrannosaurus rex* and they watched it lumber across his desktop on duck feet, red eyes flashing. "It can be your first solo flight. We'll do a small printing and see how it goes."

"Fantastic," said Jude from his doorway. "Thanks, Simon."

Back at her desk, Jude felt frustrated that she couldn't call Anna with the good news. Why had she been so weird about giving out her number?

JUDE MUNCHED A BREAD STICK while Anna fished the olive out of her second martini with her plastic swizzle stick. She was wearing a suit of very fine wool in a subtle plaid of mauve and forest green with some gold lines through it. Looped loosely around her throat was a scarf that repeated the mauve and gold in bold swirls.

"I can give you the names of some agents if you want," said Jude like a policewoman reciting her rights to a detainee. The waiter, who wore a tux even though it was only lunchtime, set their chicken Marengo before them with a flourish, then poured Pouilly-Fuissé into their glasses.

The decor of the midtown restaurant, which Simon maintained was run by gangsters, centered around the apricot of the marble walls and floors. She and Anna were sitting side by side on a cushioned banquette, looking out across the nearly empty room. On their table was an exotic lily with a mauve and yellow center that harmonized with Anna's suit. This was Jude's first expense-account lunch, and she had decided that she didn't want it to be her last.

"That won't be necessary," said Anna. "I trust you to treat me fairly."

"Thank you," said Jude. "I'll try not to betray your trust." As she cut her chicken, she suddenly recalled what William had said— that Anna was bad news. She looked up from her plate. Anna met her gaze with smiling cool-blue eyes. She certainly didn't look like bad news.

As they sipped their cappuccinos, Jude went over the various clauses in the contract. Afterward, on the sidewalk outside, while the irate drivers of a line of taxis honked and swore at a vacant double-parked delivery truck, Anna and Jude agreed to meet every other Wednesday afternoon after Anna's writing workshop at Julia Richmond High School.

"So how did it go, Jude?" called Simon as Jude passed his door.

She paused in his doorway. He was sprawled on his carpet in his sock feet, eating a sandwich. "A struggling writer could have eaten for a month on what that lunch cost," she replied.

"True," he said, looking up. "But think about it: A writer gets to sit home all day in Levis, telling himself amusing stories. Whereas we have to get dressed up, and ride the subway downtown, and hassle with printers and page proofs. We do all the dirty work, and they get interviewed by Dick Cavett. So we deserve a nice lunch from time to time."

Jude smiled. "Very feeble."

"Struggle is good for writers," insisted Simon. "If their lives are miserable, they have more of an incentive to create a fantasy world."

Jude laughed.

"Anna is very attractive, isn't she?"

"Is she? I didn't notice."

Simon smiled.

"What?"

"Oh, nothing," he said, biting into his corned beef.

"William once told me she was bad news. Why, do you think?"

"William has very little use for women. Especially sexy ones."

"You find Anna sexy?"

"Don't you?"

"I wouldn't know. I'm not that kind of girl."

"Neither am I," said Simon, "but I know it when I see it."

"I'M AFRAID IT'S TOO ABSTRACT," Anna was saying about one student poem.

She and Jude were walking across Central Park to the West Side as the wan winter sun sank behind the luxury apartment buildings along Central Park West. The black tree branches were making curlicue patterns like wrought ironwork against the darkening sky. The paths were mostly deserted, except for a few solitary dog walkers hunched against the cold. But Jude was so engaged by the conversation that she wasn't feeling the cold. "That may be the whole point," she said. "He's from Martinique. His culture is French, and French culture tends toward abstraction."

"I think it's just bad poetry," said Anna, who was wearing a tall mink Cossack hat. Her glossy hair framed her face like the wing tips of a raven.

"Bad, good—those categories are culture-bound. Americans are practical people, so we prefer concreteness."

"You're no help." Anna laughed, squeezing Jude's upper arm with a gloved hand. "I thought you were supposed to give me some answers, not raise more questions."

"But this one is crucial," insisted Jude. "Do we include pieces we think are good or pieces that would be regarded as good within the students' cultures of origin? And if the latter, how do we determine which those are? Because to do the former is a form of cultural imperialism." The problems Anna's project posed mirrored those within Jude's own head, where the conflicting claims of a dozen different groups clamored for primacy—Yankee and southern, Baptist and Huguenot and Catholic, Dutch and Alsatian and French, Cherokee and Scottish and English. Sometimes she envied the simple ethnic clarity of the Hitler Youth.

Emerging from the park, they strolled down Jude's grandparents' block past the Café des Artistes. This part of New York had come to feel as familiar as Tidewater Estates to Jude by now. She had walked its sidewalks almost every day for six years—through dirty slush and sodden leaves, beneath trees feathered chartreuse with bursting buds, or bare and blasted by icy winds. She often dropped by to see her grandparents when they weren't at the retirement house they'd bought on Captiva. Her friends and colleagues lived all around her.

Jude's mother had once walked these sidewalks herself, ridden horses along the paths in the park, and posed for photographers on benches and street corners. She had fallen in love with Jude's father in the cafés and restaurants and made love to him in his tiny apartment across from the Roosevelt. Jude could imagine her shock when she found herself stranded on that plateau in Tennessee, surrounded by mile after mile of forested mountain peaks and coves. By the time she was Jude's age, she was buried in a grave of sticky red clay atop that same plateau. In some odd way, Jude felt she was living out the unfinished portion of her mother's life, making the opposite choices —not marrying, not having a baby, not going back to the South, pursuing a career, sidestepping romantic commitments.

Upon reaching Broadway, Anna and Jude went into a diner that was tiled in black and white and trimmed with stainless steel. They perused the glass case that held the cakes and pies, then sat down at a table topped with black-flecked granite. After ordering tea and scones from a woman in a starched white cap that looked as though it belonged on a Victorian nurse, Anna pulled a piece of paper from her handbag and read the poem in question, which rhymed *beauty* with *duty* and *truth* with *youth*.

Jude buried her face in her hands. "I'm afraid you're right. It's just bad poetry."

"But to him, it's good. He's very proud of it. I hate my job."

"I hate mine, too. At the office, I read the manuscripts that come in unsolicited. The slush pile, it's called. I know that each one is *War and Peace* to the person who wrote it. But many of them are frankly unreadable."

"Maybe we should call this whole thing off," said Anna. "Clearly we're too tenderhearted."

"Fine," said Jude, "if you'd like to pay back your advance."

"Oh, well, I guess I'm not that tenderhearted."

As they parted on the sidewalk, Anna leaned forward to kiss Jude good-bye just as Jude extended her hand for a shake. Both stepped back. Then Jude leaned forward for a kiss, into Anna's outstretched hand. Laughing, they came together for a hug. Then they held each other at arm's length and exchanged a smile. Anna's eyes were almost indigo in the rapidly descending dusk. Jude was surprised to discover that she and Anna were the same height, a rare event for someone as tall as she.

Jude watched Anna for a moment as she strode south in her long burgundy overcoat and mink Cossack hat, looking like a guard at the Kremlin. Then Jude turned around and headed uptown toward home.

This soon became a ritual. Anna came to Jude's office building from Julia Richmond and waited in the lobby for Jude to descend with her usual satchel of manuscripts and galleys. They crossed the park, the air warming and softening with the arrival of spring. As the weeks passed, magnolia, crab apple, apple, and Japanese cherry trees, one after another, extruded their fragrant blossoms and then shed them on the pavement. While the two women walked, Anna recited in a mesmeric alto voice the poems she was considering for the book, and

Jude commented on them. At the Broadway diner, they drank tea, ate pastries, and debated possible book titles involving melting pots and rainbows. Then they embraced gingerly and each headed home.

Although they discussed the book in all its aspects—content, format, jacket, title, publicity—they rarely discussed their personal lives. Jude had managed to piece together that Anna had grown up in Chicago with a Swedish Lutheran father and an Italian mother who was devoutly Catholic. Thus, she shared Jude's cultural cacophony, which was probably why she was interested in editing such a book. She'd come to New York to do her doctorate in comparative literature at NYU, writing her dissertation on the French Symbolist poets. Now she taught workshops and wrote poetry. And she lived somewhere downtown. With whom, if anyone, Jude had no idea. There was no wedding band on her left hand. And Jude had first encountered her in a roomful of homosexuals. Occasionally, Jude recalled William's warning that Anna was bad news. But she had concluded that there was some private rancor between them. Once she knew Anna well enough, she'd ask her.

Simon was so impressed by the unprecedented diligence Jude was bringing to Anna's book that he hired a new assistant and began giving Jude manuscripts of history books to edit. At first, she insisted that the deadly antics of the human race no longer interested her. But Simon doubled her salary and persuaded her to benefit the firm with her academic training.

One afternoon in early fall, shortly before the manuscript was scheduled to go to press, Jude and Anna sat sipping iced coffee in "their" café on Broadway. "I'll miss these meetings, Jude," said Anna. "They've been lots of fun."

Jude stirred more sugar into her coffee in silence. It hadn't really occurred to her that they wouldn't go on seeing each other. In Tennessee, only death interrupted a relationship, if that. But it was true that she was Anna's editor, not her friend. Once the book was finished, there would be no basis for further contact.

"Could we still meet for a walk now and then?" asked Anna. She seemed agitated.

"Definitely," said Jude.

"Good. I wasn't sure if this was just another book to you." Anna broke their gaze to glance out the window at a young man passing by wearing a Comanche headdress and little else.

"I like you, Anna, as an author and as a person."

Anna returned her eyes to Jude's. "I like you, too. You know what intrigues me most about you?"

"What?" Jude realized this was the most intimate conversation they'd ever had.

"Your transparency. With you, what one sees is what one gets."

Jude shrugged. "Isn't that usually the case?"

Anna smiled sardonically. "In my experience, most people are a house of mirrors."

As Jude walked uptown, she tried to decide whether it was a compliment to be called transparent. Its opposite, opaque, implied mystery and subtlety. Transparency suggested naïveté. Was it corny to be naïve, or did it indicate authenticity and integrity?

A couple of weeks later, Anna didn't show up outside the entrance to Jude's building at the usual hour. Jude paced the marble lobby for a long time before heading home, surprised to notice how disappointed she was.

That night, she and Simon split some Chinese takeout in front of the electric heater in their dingy living room. After Sandy's death, as normal attrition claimed their roommates, they hadn't bothered to replace them, lacking the energy. Besides, they could afford not to have roommates now. So she and Simon lived alone in the echoing apartment with its constant reminders of Sandy. The same battered Danish-modern armchairs that had been there the day Jude first visited were still the only furniture in the living room. One night, Simon, in a seizure of grief, had started ripping the opera posters off the walls. Since he hadn't completed the job, they were still hanging there in tattered strips that flapped in the breezes off the river.

"One of these days we should fix this place up," said Simon, opening a white cardboard container of moo goo gai pan. "Paint and paper it. Buy some new rugs and furniture. Now that we're high-powered publishing executives."

"Good idea," said Jude. "It does look like the day after Woodstock in here. By the way, do you have Anna Olsen's phone number?"

"I don't really know her." He paused with his chopsticks in midair, dribbling rice onto his plate. "I've just seen her a few times at William and Sid's."

"Alone?"

He grinned, green eyes flashing. "Sandy would be so proud."

"What?" she asked irritably.

"What's it to you, darling, whether she was alone or not?"

"I need to reach her about her book, but for some reason, she's never given me her number. That's all, okay?"

"Yes. Alone." He was struggling not to smile. "All alone. Utterly alone. Gloriously alone."

Flouncing down the hallway to her bedroom to escape Simon's lurid implications, Jude turned in at Sandy's room, closing the door behind her. In the moonlight shining through the window, she surveyed the TV on which they'd watched so many chick flicks. And the phone on the rug that would never again ring for him. And the closet with its door ajar, in which a few deserted shirts swayed in the current of air under the door. And the stripped mattress on the floor, on which she and Sandy had experienced together something remarkable that still eluded her capacity for definition.

Standing there on other nights, Jude had sometimes pretended that she could feel Sandy's presence. But it wasn't true. This was an empty room with dust balls in the corner. Molly occasionally turned up in her dreams. But Sandy had vanished without a trace, leaving behind only Simon's and her memories of him, which they served up to each other from time to time like soggy leftovers from some distant bacchanal.

Anna called Jude the next morning at work to apologize for standing her up and to say that she couldn't see her until the following week.

"But I have a new title idea and I need your opinion," said Jude, doodling a mountain range across her notepad. Which, she abruptly realized, looked like the profile of a naked woman lying on her back, knees in the air.

"Okay, shoot."

"But I have to show you some roughs for a new jacket, if you like the new title," said Jude, suddenly desperate to see her, and startled by the desperation. "We don't have much time. They were about to print the jacket when I stopped them."

"I'll meet you at that café at seven."

When Anna appeared in the doorway in a belted khaki trench coat, she was wearing sunglasses, even though it was almost dusk. Sitting down, she removed the coat but not the glasses.

"Greta Garbo, I presume," said Jude, reaching for them. She wanted to see those eyes.

Anna jerked her head aside. "I'm having trouble with my vision. My doctor told me to wear these."

Jude watched her own reflection in the dark lenses as she told

Anna about her new Baptist-bred title, *Precious in His Sight*. Anna thought she preferred it to their previous choice. While studying the sketches for a new jacket, she swept off the glasses to see them better. One of her eyes, ringed with royal purple flesh, was thickly powdered and nearly swollen shut, as though she'd been stung by several bees. Realizing what she'd done, she touched it self-consciously with her fingertips, explaining, "I ran into a cupboard door."

Jude studied her, saying nothing. "Is there some way I can help?" she finally asked.

"You do help, Jude. Much more than you realize."

"I'd like to strangle whoever did this to you." Jude reached across to touch the swelling with her fingertips.

Anna laughed weakly, taking Jude's hand in both hers and holding it on the tabletop. "You'd better not. He's much bigger than you."

"Who is?"

"My husband."

Jude looked at her. "I didn't realize you were married." She glanced down at Anna's hand. It was still ringless.

"It hasn't been a real marriage for years. We just stay together for our children." She squeezed Jude's hand, then released it. Jude removed it to her lap. It lay there on her thigh, tingling.

Jude's head fell forward, so her chin rested on her chest. She gazed at her napoleon, which was oozing custard. "Children?" she murmured.

"Two, a boy and a girl. They're at prep school."

Jude looked up from her pastry to Anna's face. That probably meant Anna was over forty. At least a dozen years between them. Practically a different generation. She studied Anna's swollen eye. "Why do you stay with him if he treats you like this?"

"He didn't mean to."

"They never do," said Jude. "But is that any excuse?"

"He has many other nice qualities."

"I'm sure even Hitler had his moments," replied Jude.

"Besides, I provoked him. He gets very jealous. Yesterday, he got jealous over you, as a matter of fact. That's why I stood you up."

"Over me? Why?"

Anna lowered her head as though consulting her tea leaves for guidance. "Well," she said slowly, "I guess he feels we spend a lot of time together. And maybe I've mentioned your name a few too many times."

"But is it a crime to have a new friend?"

Anna looked up, eyes clouded with anxiety. "Not if she remains just a friend."

"So what's the problem then?" Jude glanced nervously around the diner, all the occupants of which seemed to be eavesdropping on Anna and herself.

Anna smiled brightly. "There is no problem." She scribbled a number on her paper napkin and handed it to Jude. "It's best to call me in late afternoon," she said, "before Jim gets home."

As Jude walked north toward Riverside Drive, her brain was as chaotic as the stock exchange after the crash. She kept picturing Anna's swollen face. She wanted to protect her from this man, whoever he was. But he was her husband. And he was jealous of Jude? Was this why William felt Anna was bad news? She was too passive to extract herself from an abusive marriage? But Jude had been seeing her for months, and this was the first time she'd noticed any bruises. Maybe it would be best just to back off and give it all a rest. But, oh God, those eyes that shifted like the waters of the sea, from cerulean to indigo to turquoise. Having watched them all these months, how could she give them up?

When Jude woke up the next morning, she discovered a feeling of dread in the pit of her stomach. As she gazed past her Atalanta

flask to the drifting gray waters of the Hudson, she remembered Anna's bruised eye and her own wish to protect her. But Jude wasn't a
home-breaker. And Anna was her author. It was unprofessional to get
involved in her private life. She would make a point of not phoning.
And if Anna phoned her, she vowed to keep it brief and focused on
the book, in compliance with her family motto: "When in doubt, get
the hell out."

Simon appeared in her office doorway toward lunchtime that day,
carrying a disheveled manuscript. "Here. A present." Giving her his
most winning smile, he plopped it on her desk.

Picking up the first few pages, Jude skimmed them. It was a
scholarly history of lesbianism from the Middle Ages to the present.
Looking up, she said, "Please don't do this to me, Simon."

"Do what?"

"I've got too much on my plate right now as it is," she
temporized.

"But you're the only one who can edit it, Jude. You're a history
Ph.D. manqué. Besides, everyone else is about to go to St. Thomas
for the sales conference." He backed out of her office, grinning.

That night, Jude sat by her phone for a long time, the new
manuscript lying unread on her bed, inspecting the number Anna had
scribbled on the paper napkin. It had four 4s in it. Four was Jude's
favorite number.

Finally forcing herself to start the manuscript, she read into the
night about women who lived alone being burned as witches. About
women being tortured and hanged for dressing as men. About women
being stoned for refusing to marry. About women killing their female
lovers to prevent them from marrying men. The manuscript needed
a lot of work. The stilted language made the horrors sound almost
bland, and each page was half-filled with arcane footnotes. She scribbled suggestions to the author all over the pages.

The next day at work, Jude jumped each time her phone rang. When she answered and discovered that it wasn't Anna, she became irritated and snapped at whoever it was. And when she hung up, she wracked her brain for some detail about the anthology that required Anna's opinion. She was worried about her. She wanted to be sure she was okay. But the manuscript was already at the printer's and everything was regrettably under control. And besides, she had taken a vow to let Anna resolve her marital masochism alone.

Jude walked home up Columbus Avenue, looking into shop windows, wondering whether she should buy a new fall outfit. Anna rarely wore the same clothes twice. Whereas Jude usually paid very little attention to her own appearance. But it might be nice to give Anna something fresh to look at when they next met.

Beside a display window in which she'd been studying shoes, Jude spotted a doorway she'd never noticed before. It opened on a staircase that led, according to a small hand-printed sign, to: MADAME TOUSSAINT, VOODOO SPELLS AND TAROT READINGS. On a whim, Jude climbed the dirty linoleum-covered steps. At the first landing was a battered steel door with a buzzer beside it. A card underneath read: MADAME TOUSSAINT. Jude buzzed. The door buzzed back and Jude pushed it open.

She was assaulted by the scent of patchouli oil. The walls and ceiling of the room were draped with gold-patterned Indian bedspreads that billowed like spinnakers in the draft from the door. Soft music sounding like reggae Gregorian chants floated down from two speakers near the ceiling. Large cushions covered in Prussian blue velvet lay on the floor around a brass tray on bamboo legs.

The strands of colored beads in the far doorway parted, and the largest black woman Jude had ever seen squeezed through the door frame. She was wearing an African-print muumuu and matching pillbox headgear in shades of orange and brown. Extending her hand, she murmured, "Welcome. I am Madame Toussaint. How may I help you this afternoon?"

Jude studied the face. The eyes were surrounded by so much flesh that they seemed to be squinting. Chins were stacked one atop another like the overlapping ranges of the Smokies. "I'd like a reading," Jude said, astonished at herself.

Madame Toussaint gestured to a cushion by the tray. Jude plopped down, sending up a cloud of dust. Madame Toussaint sank down on her cushion with a grace Jude would have thought impossible in someone so large. Watching Jude with her tiny bright eyes, she shuffled the cards, an ordinary deck with DELTA AIRLINES printed on their backs. Jude cut them. The woman dealt some out on the brass tray. Then she studied them for a long time, occasionally glancing at Jude, while voices from the speakers near the ceiling chanted softly about rivers flowing red with the blood of white oppressors.

Finally, Madame Toussaint closed her eyes and started talking in a listless monotone. About money and success that were headed Jude's way. About the spirits of departed loved ones who were whispering messages for Jude into Madame Toussaint's ear. About a past life as a courtesan on Atlantis, where Jude had been faithless in love, for which she was now doing atonement. Jude listened with growing indignation. Clearly this was a scam.

"A new love is moving toward you very fast," Madame Toussaint intoned, rocking rhythmically with her eyes closed. "With someone older than yourself. Someone who is troubled. Someone you can help. Someone who will help you."

Jude had snapped to rigid attention.

"This relationship will be deep and lasting and very important for both women," continued Madame Toussaint.

Jude shuddered. "Women?" she echoed faintly.

Madame Toussaint nodded slowly, still rocking. "A water sign. A creative person. An artist of some sort."

Anna was a poet and a Pisces.

Who was this storefront charlatan? Jude jumped up.

Madame Toussaint opened her eyes and watched calmly as Jude fluttered around the room. After her panic had subsided a bit, Madame Toussaint murmured, "Twenty dollars, please."

Reaching into her shoulder bag, Jude thrust a bill at her and headed for the doorway.

As Jude gripped the doorknob like an activated hand grenade, Madame Toussaint added for free, "There are worse things in this world than a woman who loves you."

Jude rushed out the door and down the steps. In the street, she discovered that she had a four-aspirin headache.

SINCE SIMON AND ALL the top brass had departed for the sales conference in St. Thomas, Jude decided to stay at her apartment the next day so she could edit without interruption the manuscript on the history of lesbianism. She asked her assistant to forward her phone calls. Then she assembled the manuscript, some pencils, and a cup of coffee on the low table in the living room. She put some records on the turntable to drown out the din from Riverside Drive. Then she sat down and went to work on the turgid prose, crossing out and rewriting all morning long. She found a certain satisfaction in locating the nugget of meaning hidden in the dross of a paragraph and restating it in one succinct sentence.

Also included with the text were some photographs of the handful of famous lesbians from the past who had managed not to be murdered or incarcerated in loony bins. One featured two women in Victorian gowns with pinched waists and bustles. They had their arms around each other and were gazing into each other's eyes with unmasked adoration. As she studied them, Jude wondered if she and Molly had been lesbians. They had loved each other deeply, and both were female. They had explored each other's bodies to a certain extent and had experienced some sort of orgasm together that night on the raft. But labeling their interaction so clinically robbed it of its wonder. In any case, Jude had been with half a dozen men since. So did that make her bisexual? But she had never loved a man and a woman both at once. And none of the men had engaged her as Molly had, not even Sandy. Although he might have if he'd lived. But she and Molly had shared years of peace and passion, whereas she and Sandy had just begun. Most people she knew didn't fit into these pigeonholes anyway.

Jude realized that the last song on the last record in the stack was repeating time after time. Sipping her cold coffee, she concentrated on the lyrics:

Every night you sit and watch the TV screen,
And the life you live is only in your dreams.
But I think I know what it is on your mind.
Yes, I think I know what you're thinking 'bout all the time.
You want to be loved.
You want to know somebody somewhere cares. . . .

Lying back in her chair, she listened to these lines again and again, debating their accuracy vis-à-vis herself. She had been convinced that she *didn't* want to be loved anymore.

Abruptly, she recalled Anna's remark that her husband didn't mind if Anna had a new friend so long as "she remains just a friend." Jude realized she'd been deliberately obtuse during that conversation. Anna had raised a topic that they needed to deal with, yet Jude had sidestepped it. Sitting up, she switched off the record player, picked up the phone, and dialed Anna's number.

After a dozen rings, Jude hung up. Jumping up, she grabbed her jacket and left the apartment. Taking the bus through the park to the East Side, she walked downtown until she came to Julia Richmond High. Going into a coffee shop across the street, she sat at a table by the plate-glass window and ordered a grilled cheese sandwich. She didn't even like grilled cheese sandwiches, but they were Anna's favorite. As she chewed the greasy cardboard bread, she watched the school doorway. It wasn't Anna's usual day there, but who knew? In any case, Jude had no idea where downtown she lived, so this was her only chance of finding her.

After waiting for an hour and a half, nursing a cup of coffee under the scowl of the gum-chewing waitress, Jude went out into the street. Striding to the park, she followed the route back to the West Side that she and Anna usually took, discussing with Anna in her head how they should defuse the attraction that was undeniably building between them.

Upon reaching Columbus Avenue, Jude ducked into a bookshop. Going directly to the poetry section, she extracted from the shelves volumes by Rimbaud, Baudelaire, and Mallarmé. Anna had written her thesis on them, but Jude could remember very little from her poetry course at the Sorbonne. She wanted to reread them so she could discuss them intelligently with Anna. Their exchanges about literature and history were the most crucial part of their relationship. Maybe if they emphasized them more, the physical attraction would simply wither away from lack of encouragement.

As she headed toward the cash register, she spotted a rack of magazines. On it sat a road atlas. Picking it up, she looked up Illinois. Locating the inset showing the streets of Chicago, she studied it closely. She'd never been to Chicago, so she tried to imagine the tall

apartment buildings along Lake Michigan and the quaint ethnic neigh-
borhoods inland that Anna had once described to her. This was Anna's
hometown. She wondered what street she had lived on, what games
she and her friends had played, where she'd gone to school, whether
she'd had a pet. She'd have to ask her when she next saw her. Which
would be in eleven days now, she calculated on her fingers.

Returning the atlas to its shelf, Jude noticed a stack of *Vogues*.
Grabbing one, she added it to her pile of poetry books, hoping it
might give her some ideas for the new outfit she wanted to assemble
in time for this next meeting with Anna.

En route to her apartment, Jude turned in at her local liquor
store and bought a bottle of Pouilly-Fuissé. This was the wine Anna
had suggested for the chicken Marengo at their first lunch together.
Jude recalled that she herself had drunk only one glass, trying to keep
her wits about her for the discussion of the book contract. Anna had
polished off the rest of the bottle alone. Jude admired her gusto. She
ate pastries and grilled cheese sandwiches and washed them down with
wine or beer or Irish coffee. Jude wondered whether she might have
a thyroid condition, because she stayed so slim.

Plopping down in the armchair before the coffee table, the manuscript lying in stacks all across the carpet, Jude opened the wine and
poured herself a glass. Sipping it, she read Baudelaire out loud, de-
spairing over her French accent, which had gone to hell in her years
since Paris.

When the bottle was half empty, Jude came to a poem entitled
"*Femmes Damnées*." "Have we then committed such a strange act?"
Hippolyta demanded of her lover, Delphine. "Explain if you can my
turmoil and my terror. I shiver with fear when you call me 'my angel.'
But I feel my mouth drawn to yours."

Jude paused to finish the wine in her glass and refill it. "Far
from the living, condemned wanderers, prowl through the wastelands

like wolves,'' suggested Baudelaire to the distressed women. ''Fashion your own destiny, muddled souls. And flee the divine spark that you carry within you.''

Drawing a deep breath, Jude let the book fall into her lap. She couldn't detect within herself the shame she was apparently supposed to feel over her love for Molly. She personally had no problem with prowling wastelands like a wolf. She liked wastelands. After all, she'd grown up in one. She'd also grown up regarding herself as a wolf child on the fringes of the forest, longing for her wilderness home. Sometimes her thimbleful of Cherokee blood came in handy.

Heart thudding, she grabbed the phone off the floor and dialed Anna, sitting there in terror as the phone rang time after time.

''Hello?'' said a pleasant male voice.

''Is Anna there?''

''Who is this?'' The voice had turned gruff and suspicious.

Jude hesitated, wondering whether she should just hang up. ''Allison,'' she ad-libbed.

''Allison who?''

''Allison Marks.''

''I guess we haven't met.''

''I work with Anna at Julia Richmond.''

''Well, she isn't here right now. Shall I have her call you back?''

''Never mind. It's not urgent. I'll see her next week at school.''

Jude slammed down the receiver and lay back in her chair, rattled to have made first contact with the enemy, annoyed to have resorted to a pseudonym. She reached over and turned on the record player to the song from that morning. Time after time, she listened to the soppy lines, heart beginning to feel like a piece of wrung-out laundry: ''You want to be loved. You want to know somebody somewhere cares. . . .'' Reaching for the bottle of Pouilly-Fuissé, she guzzled the remaining two inches, while the frenzied singer wailed about wanting to know that somebody somewhere cares.

WHEN JUDE WOKE UP toward noon the next day, she found herself sprawled in the armchair in the living room, her manuscript scattered all around the room. She felt as though someone had buried a hatchet in her forehead, and her mouth tasted as though she'd gargled with old zinnia water. Standing up, she felt nauseous. Not having eaten anything since the grilled cheese sandwich, she went into the kitchen, picked the mold off some stale bread, and toasted the slices. After three cups of black coffee and two aspirin, she showered and changed her clothes. Then she returned to the living room and tackled the manuscript anew, struggling all afternoon to pare down the footnotes that threatened like a cancer to eclipse the text.

As the sun sank behind the high-rises of Fort Lee, Jude took a tea break. Picking up *Vogue*, she carefully studied the latest fashions draped on the contorted frames of the mutant models. Then she came to the horoscopes. Hers read: "Planetary forces are conspiring right now, Arians, to shake up the stability you've so painstakingly constructed for yourself. The more you fight your need for transformation, the stronger it will grow, like the monster in a fairy tale. So accept the inevitable, and be grateful for the new wisdom it will bring you."

Frowning, she read Anna's forecast: "New seas await you, Pisces. If you plunge in, you will locate the treasures of the deep. But if you wish safety, then remain on the shore."

Jude let the magazine flutter to the carpet like a shot duck. Leaning her head against the chair back, she speculated on whether Anna wanted treasures or safety. And if she should decide to plunge in, would she change her mind and climb back out again as Molly had done, leaving Jude to flounder alone?

Jude realized she was starving and there was nothing in the kitchen, so she threw on her blazer and headed out the door. When she reached Broadway, she bought a hot dog from a street vendor. Leaving a Hansel and Gretel trail of oozing mustard and catsup, she headed south. With all these planetary forces ganging up on them, maybe she'd run into Anna if she wandered around the Village.

Stalking the four miles in record time, Jude paced the narrow, winding streets one after another, watching brave women holding hands, watching women alone as they eyed her eying them. But always she was on the lookout for Anna's tall, slender frame and her glossy black cap of hair.

Passing a movie theater, she noticed a placard planted on the sidewalk out front, bearing an enlarged review from the *Times*. She discovered that the movie inside, called *Dark Desire*, concerned a love affair between two women. The review was a rave, and a show was about to start.

Sitting in the dark with her head in her hands, Jude tried to get a grip. She didn't believe in planetary forces or hypothyroidal psychics or astrological mumbo jumbo. She didn't even believe in love anymore, and certainly not love with a married mother. So what was happening to her?

The plot concerned a university teacher named Deirdre who was in love with a younger student named Karen. Flattered, Karen also fell in love with her. Unfortunately, Karen was married and had three children. After about two minutes of excitement and happiness, the problems began. Karen's children failed at school, and cried themselves to sleep at night, and were rejected by their playmates, and became pyromaniacs and shoplifters. Karen's husband, Jason, a prince among men, who did the dishes after meals and took his own clothes to the cleaners, demanded a divorce. He remarried an adorable doormat who was a gourmet cook and who liked to fall to her knees and give him blow jobs whenever he walked through the door. They sued Karen for custody of the basket-case children. Karen, meanwhile, had had to drop out of college to support herself as a laundromat attendant. Deirdre, weary of hanging around all the time with a grumpy laundromat attendant, deserted her for a woman in silver full leathers who raced a Harley around London for an express message service. In the end, Karen hanged herself in Deirdre's bedroom, above the bed on which they'd first so blissfully made love.

Stumbling out into the street, Jude wandered along it searching for a taxi, profoundly demoralized to see the direction in which she and Anna were headed if they didn't do something fast. Maybe she should ask Simon for a transfer to the London office? She could vanish without leaving a forwarding address. In the short run, they'd suffer, but they'd be spared even greater future suffering.

Looking up, Jude saw flashing above her head like a UFO some neon palm trees and the words: THE OASIS. The sign hung above the doorway into a bar. Through the front window, she spotted a mural that featured camels and sand dunes and shapely veiled figures with clay jugs on their heads. The room was packed with women. Two were kissing on the mouth in a corner.

What the hell, decided Jude, if the gods needed for her to be a lesbian, at least let it be with a woman who wasn't someone else's wife. She marched through the door like John Wayne into a saloon infested with desperadoes. All across the room, heads turned to inspect her. Bellying up to the bar, she ordered a glass of white wine, feeling her stomach turn queasy in protest. After a few sips, she summoned the courage to glance around at the other women. The one standing beside her met her gaze with a smile. She had a lean face with high cheekbones and a pointed chin. Tiny silver Scottie dogs hung like Monopoly pieces from her earlobes.

"I like your jacket," she said, nodding at Jude's blazer, a loose-weave plaid in shades of gray and blue.

"Thanks," said Jude. She sipped her wine, elbow propped casually on the bar. "Do you come here often?"

"Every now and then. And you?"

"From time to time."

"I think it's really the nicest women's club in New York. It's cozy. More like a neighborhood pub. Less like a meat market."

Jude nodded as though she, too, were a jaded habituée of the lesbian meat markets of New York. They sipped their drinks. The other woman was drinking scotch. Her flannel shirt was a Macdonald plaid.

"Would you like to sit down?" asked the woman. "I see a table over there in the corner."

They sat. The woman introduced herself, explaining that her nickname was Scottie because she raised Scotties in Bayonne, New Jersey. Each bought the other a drink. A couple of times, they gyrated to the throbbing disco music. The second time, they stayed on the floor for a slow dance. Scottie was as tall as Anna, and their bodies fit together well as they swayed to the languid beat, each with an upper thigh stroking the other's pubic area.

When they sat back down, Scottie said, "Jude, there's something I want to ask you." She looked off across the room. "I hope I'm not out of line."

"Go ahead," said Jude, heart beating fast. This was it. It wasn't love, but it would take her mind off Anna and safeguard Anna's marriage.

"No, never mind," said Scottie, suddenly embarrassed.

"Please. I want you to."

"I can't," mumbled Scottie.

"But that's why I'm here."

"Huh?"

"Just tell me."

"Okay. Here goes." Scottie took a deep breath. "I was wondering if you'd be willing to make a donation to my fund for breeding my championship bitch to last year's Best in Show at Westminster?"

Sighing with relief, Jude handed her a twenty and headed home.

SIMON RETURNED FROM ST. THOMAS the next afternoon with a stunning tan, a new straw hat, and a planter's punch hangover. "You look like shit," he informed her when he found her guzzling Pouilly-Fuissé in the living room while an hysteric on the record player shrieked about wanting to be loved. A manuscript was strewn around the floor. "What's wrong?"

"This damn book you assigned me," she snarled. "It's a fucking mess."

"Sorry I asked," he said, heading down the hallway with his suitcase. "I need a nap."

After a few minutes, Jude trailed him to his room. He'd lowered the shades, dropped his Hawaiian shirt on the floor, and crawled under the covers. Jude stepped out of her jeans, threw off her T-shirt, and climbed in beside him. His back was turned, but she could tell by his breathing that he was only pretending to be asleep. "Pretty please, Simon?"

"I'm sorry, Jude, but I'm hung over."

She reached across his back and began to touch him in ways he usually found irresistible. "I've got a headache," he whimpered like a frigid wife.

"Look, we both know you use me shamelessly whenever you don't have the time or energy to find a man. So now it's my turn."

"Do I have to?"

"Yes," she said, gratified to have produced a halfhearted hard-on.

He rolled on top of her without enthusiasm. "I'm not the one you should be fucking."

"Just shut up," she snapped, a hand on each of his hips, pulling him into herself.

When he finally collapsed in a sweaty heap, she moaned, "God, Simon, don't stop yet."

"Get a goddamn dildo," he snarled. As he rolled off her, he said, "Call the woman, Jude."

"Who?"

"For God's sake, stop acting like you've never been around the block!"

"What if her husband answers?"

"Tell him you're in love with his wife."

"I'm not in love with her," Jude insisted.

"Tell him you want to rip off all her clothes and do unspeakable things to her body."

"You're no help."

"God helps those who help themselves."

"Obviously I'm no lesbian," she said reasonably. "Considering what I've just been doing with you."

"Give me a break. Go see a therapist. I need to sleep."

Jude jumped up, grabbed her clothes, and stalked back to her own room. Sitting down on her bed, shivering from the chill, she picked up the receiver and dialed the first five digits of Anna's number, finger lingering hopefully over her lucky 4s. Then she slammed it down and returned naked to the living room to polish off the Pouilly-Fuissé.

———

As Jude walked into her office the next morning, the phone on her desk was ringing. She lunged for it as though for the brass ring on a merry-go-round.

"All right, I give up," said Anna's alto voice. "You win. When can I see you?"

"How about right now?" asked Jude, elated, watching her resolutions for a sane and happy life fly out the window.

"This is not a good idea," said Jude as they strolled through Central Park, a warm breeze swirling cherry blossoms all around them like fluffy pink eiderdown.

"I agree," said Anna.

"I don't want this in my life," said Jude, feeling happier than she had in years.

"Nor do I. So how do we stop it?"

They halted and turned to face each other. Jude studied Anna's eye. The swelling had subsided and her bruise was fading to the turquoise of her irises. "Tell me about your husband," she requested. "That might help."

Anna put her arm around Jude, and they resumed walking. "We have so little time," she said, "and I don't want to spend it talking about him. Or my children. They have nothing to do with you and me. They're my responsibility, and I'll deal with them. But you're my escape from all that. I don't need to be your lover, but I want you as my friend."

"You already have my friendship. You know that."

"And the other?" she asked without looking at Jude.

Jude hesitated, struggling. "I love you, Anna. But not like that." She remembered Molly's saying these same words to her.

Anna's face fell. "Well, never mind," she said. "The one who is able to set limits loves less. But I accept that. I just want to spend time with you, Jude, in whatever way is possible."

"Maybe the one who sets limits loves more," said Jude. "Maybe she doesn't want to endanger something that has become absolutely vital to her happiness."

Anna's smile was like the sun coming out from behind a cloud. "Why would developing a new facet to our relationship doom it? It could very well deepen it."

Jude remained silent. She had just understood that because of her losses, she had learned to equate love with longing. But what if the longing should cease and the love should bring fulfillment instead?

JUDE PROWLED HER LIVING ROOM, which she and Simon had refurbished with ivory grass cloth on the walls, tweed sofas and arm-chairs, and thick plum-colored wall-to-wall carpeting. Having so care-fully preserved all traces of Sandy, Simon now wanted them completely obliterated. Manic from a new love affair of his own, he had also bought a house on Cape Cod, where he was spending the weekend with a lawyer named Marvin, who was as brunette as Sandy had been blond.

Anna was supposed to be arriving at any moment to discuss yet again why their love had to remain platonic. This had been going on for several weeks, to Simon's sardonic amusement. He referred to their maneuverings as the Dyke Dramarama. But for him, sex was about as complicated as blowing his nose—and about as meaningful.

There were, after all, many issues to consider: Anna's husband and children. The age difference. The fact that Anna could lose her teaching job. The fact that they could both be murdered in the street, as Sandy had been, as women had been throughout history. And Jude had additional fears she hadn't yet voiced. Anna had acknowledged being with other women. Would she be disappointed by Jude's in-experience? Hopefully Anna could lead, but could Jude follow? Most of all, though, Jude was terrified. Her mother, Molly, and Sandy had died. What if loving Anna meant losing her as well?

Anna walked in and kissed the air beside Jude's cheek. Jude helped her out of her new royal-purple silk windbreaker and hung it in the closet. Both had been investing small fortunes in new clothes and personal grooming, providing each other with a kind of visual potlach.

Sinking into Simon's new couch in a tight skirt that rode halfway up her thighs, Anna said, "So, Jude, what compelling new reason do you have tonight for why we should keep our hands to ourselves?"

She sounded irritated. In the beginning, Jude's compunctions had touched her, but she seemed to be getting fed up. At their most recent session at the café on Broadway, Jude had explained that she was determined to make this startling new love of theirs last, even if preserving it required them to renounce it. Anna had studied her with disbelief before standing up and marching out the door. But she returned a few minutes later to inform Jude that she was seriously psychotic.

Jude sank down beside her on the new couch and handed her a piece of paper listing the sales figures for *Precious in His Sight*.

"Very nice," said Anna, handing it back. "But so what?"

"Simon wants us to make it an annual thing, with contests and awards and scholarships."

Anna smiled. "But that's fabulous!"

Jude went into the kitchen and returned with a chilled bottle of champagne. They toasted their new series.

"But what does this have to do with our personal relationship?" asked Anna as she sipped her champagne, legs carefully crossed so that Jude could see her finely turned ankle, exquisitely fitting Italian shoe, and the seam up the back of her dark silk stocking that led into the shadowy realm between her legs. Jude's fingers twitched, longing to straighten the seam.

"Well, once the book came out, I was no longer your editor, so we were free to pursue whatever connection we wanted. But now I'm back to being your editor. And it would be unethical for me to have an affair with an author. Like a lawyer romancing a client."

"That's too bad." Anna sighed. "Because I've just written you an incredibly romantic poem. I guess I'll have to read it to someone else." She studied her carefully trimmed nails.

"What's it called?"

"Leda and the Swan Song."

"All right, let's hear it," said Jude with a half smile.

She removed a piece of paper from her handbag and began reading. The early stanzas acknowledged the chagrin of past loves lost. The middle ones dwelt on the delights of new love, despite an awareness that it must one day fade.

In closing, Anna looked up right at Jude and recited from memory:

> *I'll touch you so gently tonight, my friend,*
> *That you'll scarcely recall all that gall*
> *You'll cry as before, but this time for joy,*
> *In the red through the window at dawn.*
>
> *Stay with me tonight.*
> *Hand me your pain.*
> *Look in my eyes.*
> *Let love live again.*

They sat there in silence, each stroking with her eyes the planes and hollows of the other's face.

Jude set her champagne glass on Simon's antique oak end table. Leaning over, she placed a hand on either side of Anna's head and looked into her eyes, which were flaring in the lamplight like cool, blue flames. After several prim kisses, their mouths opened, and the debate was concluded. They lay in each other's arms for a long time as desire swept over them in waves, too weak from its pummeling to undertake anything more exotic. Out the window at the foot of the couch, the Ferris wheel across the Hudson was a spinning hoop of sparks.

CHAPTER

1 2

A S THEY STROLLED UP BROADWAY, Anna was telling Jude
about the son of the French poet Stéphane Mallarmé, Anatole,
who had died of rheumatism at age eight after many months of horrible
suffering. Stéphane had struggled to master his grief by writing poems
about the experience.

Anna began to recite in French some of the fragments he'd
composed before admitting defeat: " 'What has sought refuge, your
future in me, becomes my purity throughout life, which I shall not
sully. . . .' "

Anna's French was rhythmical and almost unaccented to Jude's
American ear. She wasn't listening too closely for the meaning because
the sound of the sorrowful words alone was so haunting.

" 'We have learned through you a better part of ourselves,

which often evades us,' " continued Anna, " 'but shall now reside within us. . . .' "

The closer they got to Jude's apartment, the faster they walked, until they were nearly trotting, eager to fall onto Jude's bed and feel the blood course through each other's veins. Anna was the Florence Nightingale of sex. With her, Jude had been experiencing a passion she'd never guessed was possible—hours of long, slow arousal involving every limb, digit, fold, and recess of flesh, until each cell in both bodies was vibrating with a tension that screamed for release.

With Sandy, there had been a searing incandescence from hard, silky, swollen flesh pounding like a pestle into her slippery secret passages. And a thundering through their flesh like the hooves of wild horses as they fought and bucked and reared and plunged. Whereas with Anna, there was rather the faint, salty scent of a sea marsh at dawn. And tongues that delicately teased and tested and tuned, sending ripples of desire radiating outward like dragonflies skimming the surface of a glassy pond. And moist velvet walls that opened and pulsed and clung like bivalves. And the sound of the surf swirling in tiny sucking whirlpools.

It was the difference between galloping across a plain under a white-hot sun at high noon and diving deep beneath the sea. If the French were correct to call orgasm *la petite mort*, Sandy had provided death by auto-da-fé, and Anna, death by drowning. Either seemed worth planning the rest of your life around. But Jude's single episodes with Molly and Sandy had sizzled her like stray bolts of lightning, whereas Anna seemed to be rewiring her circuits for an ongoing supply of high-voltage power. She was a high priestess of passion, approaching lovemaking as a ritual, one that had to be respected and revered, one that could be replicated indefinitely by observing the established rites.

As in any religion, some of the regalia were flowers, candles, incense, and wine. Others were perfume, new sheets, massage oil, and assorted hors d'oeuvres on a tray by the bed. And she liked very slow music that sounded like the spheres revolving in outer space, and icicles shattering on lunar rocks, and winds howling across the tundra. Her variety of holy communion required that all the senses be activated and focused, then fused, and finally obliterated, before the dove of peace could make its descent.

Jude wandered through her workdays in a haze of exhausted arousal, accomplishing almost nothing, waiting for the night. Fortunately, Simon was in a similar coma over Marvin, so he didn't notice. Both mooned around the office, gazing out windows with dumb, dazed grins while their company's sales figures plummeted to new lows. Their coworkers were humoring them, like the parents of children with chicken pox who wait for the fever to break and pray that their own immunity hasn't worn off.

The afternoon after her first session with Anna, Jude had found herself buying out the lingerie shop next door to her office building. Molly and Sandy would have preferred her to be a boy. But in a matter of hours, Anna had erased all that, leaving Jude grateful to be female, and the more female, the better. Anna liked to lie on Jude's bed and watch her remove the silk camisoles and satin teddies—not like a strip show but like an actual flesh-and-blood woman undressing in the flickering shadows cast by the candle flames. She reminded Jude of herself as a little girl when she used to watch her mother dress for parties, worshiping at her altar in a hushed silence, intoxicated by her perfume, which mixed with a strange musky odor that seemed to emanate through her pores from somewhere deep inside her body. Now Jude understood what that exciting, frightening fragrance had been—the scent of a woman in love. It filled the room now when she and Anna were together and permeated the sheets where they had lain. One time, Anna left behind a cashmere sweater, which Jude had decided not to return. On the nights when they weren't together,

Jude buried her face in it while she slept, breathing in the blend of Anna's Opium, her sweat, and that unmistakable scent that proved to Jude beyond any words or deeds that Anna desired her. If that scent should vanish, Jude knew it would be a warning that their passion was languishing.

" 'The ultimate goal,' " recited Anna as the elevator ascended to Jude's apartment, " 'was nothing but to leave life pure. . . . You accomplished this ahead of your time. . . .' "

Unable to wait any longer, Jude forced her knee between Anna's knees and buried her face in Anna's neck, breathing deeply of her Opium. With one hand, she pressed the red stop button.

"Jude," gasped Anna as Jude's other hand slid up her thigh and beneath her skirt, "what if someone's waiting for the elevator?"

"Tough luck," said Jude, watching Anna's gorgeous blue eyes go bleary and flutter shut as her thighs parted and her head fell back against the wall. Jude's role in Anna's religion of love was that of the heretic who defied and flouted the creed. Like the good Catholic girl she had once been, Anna was turned on by transgression.

When they at last reached Jude's floor, Anna was still breathing spasmodically as she straightened out her clothing. The door slid open. Simon and Marvin were standing there looking deeply annoyed. Simon glanced from Jude to Anna. "I think the girls have discovered your elevator stunt, Marvin."

"Aren't these young studs remarkable?" Anna asked him smoothly, patting her black hair into place.

Although he smiled, Jude suddenly suspected that Simon didn't like Anna. She wasn't sure why not. In the beginning, he had egged Jude on. Surely he wasn't jealous, since he had a new love of his own?

"TELL ME SOME MORE POEMS," murmured Jude, lying amid her mangled sheets later that evening. Her entire body felt sated and fatigued, and her mind was glazed and dull, as though Anna's Opium were ether.

Anna began languidly to recite Baudelaire while Jude watched the waters of the Hudson reflect the flickering lights from the amusement park in wavering, golden party streamers. She recalled the similar safe feeling of lying on a mattress of pine needles in the cave back home, watching the sunset reflected in the river and listening to Molly describe their future cabin on the clifftop while dozing mourning doves cooed from their coves in the Wildwoods.

As though echoing her thoughts, Anna murmured, " '*Mais le vert paradis des amours enfantines. / Les courses, les chansons, les baisers, les bouquets, / Les violons vibrant derrière les collines. . . .' "*

"The green paradise of childhood love, the races, the songs, the kisses, the flowers, the violins trembling behind the hills. . . ." Anna's and her raft was this bed, and the Hudson had replaced the Holston. But everything else was the same now as then. The long arc of lonely hours had finally come full circle, and Jude had recreated with Anna the happiness she had once known with Molly, a closeness and contentment she thought she'd lost forever. The green paradise of childhood love was alive again here in this New York City apartment.

"You're crying," murmured Anna, pausing in mid-Baudelaire. "Why are you crying, my love?"

Jude began to sob. She rolled over against Anna's long, lean body and laid her head on her lovely breasts. When she finally calmed down enough to look up through puffy red eyes, she discovered that Anna was watching her, her blue eyes suffused with a tenderness Jude had never before experienced. She shut her own eyes and felt her heart ascend to her throat so that she almost choked from happiness.

"So tell me, sweetheart," said Anna, stroking Jude's hair, "are you crying because you're happy or because you're sad?"

"Both," wailed Jude, starting to cry all over again.

Sitting up to blot her eyes and blow her nose, she told Anna for the first time in any detail about Molly and Sandy and their deaths, about her own loneliness and grief and rage.

After listening for a long time, Anna concluded, "So now, with me, you've been given another chance."

Jude started crying again. She felt as vulnerable as a hermit crab that had left behind its old shell but hadn't yet located a new one.

Anna pulled her back down alongside her own body and held her close, kneading the quivering muscles of her back. After a while, she began softly singing a lullaby of popular songs from her youth— "Sha Boom," "Qué Sera Sera," "Glow, Little Glowworm," "Mr. Sandman," "Three Coins in a Fountain," "Don't Let the Stars Get in Your Eyes."

On and on she sang, each tune worse than the last, until Jude began to laugh, begging her to stop. "What was wrong with you teenagers in the fifties?" she demanded. "Those are the worst songs I've ever heard!"

Anna shrugged. "We were romantics. 'If you can't be with the one you love, love the one you're with.' You call that a love song?"

JUDE WAS LYING ON the living room couch in her sock feet, reading a manuscript about the Knights Templars that Simon had just assigned her. The inquisitors sent by the Pope to examine the London Templars had just returned home to France in disgust, complaining that no one in England knew how to torture properly. Their recommendation was that the English Templars be shipped to France, where torture was state of the art. As usual, Jude was trying to figure out the difference between the torturers and the nontorturers.

The doorbell buzzed. Jude wasn't expecting anyone. Anna was at the opera with Jim, and Simon was on the prowl down in the Village, having thrown over poor, baffled Marvin. Every month or two, he was madly in love with some new man, whom he portrayed as perfect in every regard. A few weeks later, he had evolved a list of irremedial faults that required him to dump the man in question and plunge into a depression, swearing he would never love again. It was his version of graveyard love. No real person could ever measure up to the ideal of Sandy that he carried in his heart, flashing it like a silver sheriff's star at anyone who got too close. Jude understood. It was easier to love the dead. They rarely talked back.

Getting up, she padded to the door in her jeans and turtleneck. Through the peephole, she saw Anna in her sealskin coat, glossy dark hair framing her face.

Opening the door, Jude asked with a delighted smile, "What are you doing here?"

Anna pushed her into the entryway, slammed the door, grabbed her hand, and dragged her into the living room. "Quick!" she said. "I have to meet Jim at the opera in forty minutes."

Accepting the challenge, Jude removed Anna's fur coat, silk dress, and elaborate undergarments like a sailor unrigging a luxury yacht. They rolled around the plum carpet like the Marx brothers in a car chase, Jude fully clothed. Afterward, Jude rerigged her and sent her out the door with something to think about if *La Traviata* turned boring.

Plopping back down on the couch with a smile still on her face, Jude reflected that the only thing that bothered her about this delirious love was that Anna would never spend an entire night. She always rolled out of Jude's arms at some point to throw on her clothes and race home to Jim. But when Jude had complained, Anna replied, "You don't want to be married to me, Jude. Marriage kills off any tenderness you ever felt for someone. I'm older than you and I've had more experience, so you'll just have to take my word for it."

There was plenty Jude had to take her word for, because Anna

was running the show. Most days, she phoned Jude at the office whenever Jim wasn't around. A few times a week, if she had several hours
free, she proposed that they meet—for a walk, a meal, a museum,
or a nap. Anna was determined that Jim know nothing of their liaison
lest he destroy it, as she claimed he had others in her past. Since Jim
kept a professor's unpredictable hours, Jude never knew when Anna
would phone, so she had rearranged her life to be eternally available.
All she did now was work and wait for Anna. She made a point of
rarely being far from a phone for which Anna had the number. And
when she was with Anna, she often glanced at her watch to see how
much time was left before Anna would go away and she'd have to
start waiting again.

Having this affair with Anna was like being an undercover agent.
But sometimes she thought she wouldn't want to bring it out into the
open even if Anna would allow it. All their intrigue, some of it a bit
exaggerated, was exciting. And because Anna always left her hungering
for more, the yearning that Jude had learned as a child to label *love*
was never quenched, so she never found out the answer to her original
question of what might remain after satiation.

When she wasn't with Anna, however, Jude's imagination sometimes went into overdrive. Did Anna still see the women she had
loved before Jude? Did Jude measure up, or did Anna pretend that
Jude was someone else while they were making love? She pictured
Anna at the Oasis Bar in the Village, picking up attractive young dog
trainers from New Jersey, taking them back to her house near Washington Square (which she had never let Jude visit). She imagined Anna
doing to them all the lascivious things Jude knew she was capable of.

But often when her thoughts took this gruesome turn, the doorbell would ring and Anna would be standing there with her arms full
of lilacs. Or Jude's phone would ring during an editorial meeting at
work and Anna would be on the other end, impersonating an obscene

phone caller with a thick Polish accent, describing in lurid detail all the things she planned to do to Jude if Jude could manage to escape to her apartment within the next hour. This had gone on for over two years now, and Jude's only requirement was that it never end.

Simon, however, seemed eager for it to end. He kept proposing business trips he maintained were essential for Jude's career advancement. She always replied that she didn't want to leave town. Finally, he insisted that she go with him to the Frankfurt Book Fair. "Ten thousand publishers from all over the world, Jude. It's the most important publishing event of the year. You need to be there to make contacts for selling the foreign rights to your books. It's not fair to your authors not to go."

"Thanks, but I have all the contacts I want," she said from her desk chair as he lounged in her doorway at work.

"You have contact with me and with Anna. That's it. You'll never become a world-class editor by lying in bed day after day with the same person."

"But I don't want to be a world-class editor," she replied. "All I want is to be Anna's love slave."

Simon laughed, despite his disapproval. "Please say you'll go with me to Germany for a week, Jude. If you do, I'll send you and Anna to the National Conference for the Teachers of English in Boston next month. To promote Anna's handbook."

Jude instantly accepted this bribe. Anna had done a workbook to help secondary school English teachers establish student-poetry contests and anthologies on a local level, as she had done in New York City. If they went to this conference, they could at last spend an entire night together. Two nights, in fact—in a strange hotel room with a king-size bed and room service.

Jude sulked her way through the Frankfurt Book Fair, hanging around her company's stand in the vast exposition hall while Simon

met with a different publisher every half hour. In the evening, they
went to elaborate cocktail parties and dinners with hosts of fascinating
people, but Jude merely waited sullenly for the moment when she
could rush back to her room at the Intercontinental and phone Anna
in New York. Anna went to Jude's apartment at the end of each
afternoon to receive this call. If she didn't answer, it meant she'd
gotten tied up, and then they had to wait another twenty-four hours
for their next hit of sweet nothings. After each call, Jude felt calmed
and soothed, as though Anna's voice had injected her with heroin.

The only thing in Frankfurt that made any impression on Jude,
other than the exorbitant price of phone calls to the United States,
was a publisher from Paris named Jasmine, a friend of Simon's since
childhood, whose father had fought with his during the war. The three
of them dined one night in a brasserie near the train station. Jasmine
was one of those elegant women Jude used to spot in the streets of
Paris, as petite as Jude's mother, but with a presence as formidable
as that of Charles de Gaulle. She was wearing huge, pale rose gem-
stones at her ears and on one finger, as well as a beaten-silver Indian
belt etched with intricate arabesques of fruit and flowers.

Simon ordered the three of them a dark German beer he found
superior. As they sipped it, Jasmine studied Jude so intently with her
dark eyes that Jude felt like bacillus under a microscope. But her eyes
weren't critical, just curious.

Simon and Jasmine exchanged news about their respective families. Then they traded tips about the books being hawked and hyped
at the fair.

"Tell Jasmine about your titles, Jude," Simon instructed.

Jude described Anna's student-poetry anthologies and the new
handbook. Jasmine seemed interested although dubious about whether
such a self-help concept would float in France, given its centralized

educational bureaucracy. Then Jude mentioned her history of the Knights Templars, due to appear the following spring, which seemed to leave Jasmine cold.

"And I edited *Forbidden Fruits*," continued Jude. "It's a scholarly history of lesbianism from the Middle Ages to the present. It came out a year ago, to very good reviews. The paperback rights went for six figures, and so far we've sold rights to Holland, England, Sweden, and Germany."

Jasmine nodded, exhaling a stream of cigarette smoke. "Ah, yes. I have heard good things about it from our scout in New York."

She was still studying Jude carefully. Jude wondered whether she could read from her face that her only real interest in life was making love to another woman. If so, did this disgust her?

"Would you be so kind as to send me a copy?" asked Jasmine. "Though I am not certain such a book would sell in France. We prefer not to categorize our romantic behavior quite so succinctly as the Anglo-Saxons."

Simon laughed and said, "But, Jasmine, many of the events in the book took place in Paris."

"But this is not our fault," she replied. "Repressed Protestants from all over the world flock to Paris to enjoy our supposed sexual license. These are the people you read about, debauching themselves on the Left Bank. But there is no specific word in the French language that means 'to have sex.' We only 'make love.' And true Parisians are the most austere race you will ever encounter. The quality of an interaction is all that interests us, not frequency or quantity."

"Garbage!" snapped Simon.

"But this is true," insisted Jasmine. "Take those pastries as an example."

Simon and Jude looked at the plate of exquisite apricot and marzipan tarts that they'd both been devouring with their coffee. But Jasmine hadn't taken even one. Simon guiltily held out the plate to her.

"But this is my point," she said, fending them off with one hand. "I have been enjoying their scent of apricot and almond, mixed with the odor of the coffee. Mixed also with your aftershave, Simon. And with Jude's marvelous perfume. And with the tobacco of our cigarettes. I enjoy looking at them there, dark orange on the blue plate, topped with ivory slivers of almond. With that pot of yellow and orange narcissus behind them. I have eaten hundreds of similar tarts in my life, so I can taste in my mouth right now the contrast between the acid and the sugar. I feel on my tongue the stickiness of the fruit, the graininess of the marzipan, the crunch of the almonds beneath my teeth. So I have no need to eat one. The experience is complete as it stands."

"But, Jasmine, tarts are made to be eaten," retorted Simon. "That's their function."

"Be my guest," said Jasmine. "But if you eat one, you have destroyed it. And since the hunger for sweetness always returns, why not stop short of destroying the tarts and learn to enjoy instead the hunger that they stimulate."

Simon and Jude looked at each other blankly.

"You know something, Jasmine?" said Simon. "You're a bleeding lunatic. I always suspected it, but now I know for sure."

She laughed, and then she and he exchanged some witty, sophisticated double-talk in which it was impossible for Jude to tell what either was actually saying. Suddenly, Jude found herself wondering if Jasmine didn't perhaps share her taste for women. There had been a certain shrewd candor in her eyes as she so frankly inspected Jude— which you didn't often find in women who were primarily interested in how they might be appearing to whatever men were in the immediate vicinity.

For the first time since she'd gotten involved with Anna, Jude had actually listened to a conversation that didn't directly concern Anna. Nor had she excused herself to go to the ladies' room so she could close her eyes and picture Anna's face and whisper her name. Nor had she once consulted her watch to discover when she could return to the hotel and phone Anna. Realizing this, she felt guilty, as though she'd been somehow unfaithful.

As Jude and Simon strolled back to their hotel through the dark streets strewn with international publishers at play, Jude asked, "Is Jasmine a lesbian?"

"I don't really know. I've wondered the same thing. She has a husband somewhere, but I've never met him."

"As we know, that means nothing."

"I think the French are schizophrenic," confided Simon. "They have a public self and a private self, and there's often an unbreachable chasm between the two. They veil their private selves behind a persiflage of charm and theorizing. But once a Frenchman reveals himself to you, you have a friend for life. In contrast to an American, who's your best friend after twenty minutes and then you never see him again."

"And what about the English?" asked Jude. She was intrigued by the ease with which Simon and his European colleagues spoke in terms of national characteristics.

"We use our famous rapier wit to make sure that no one ever gets close enough to be a friend in the first place."

"But that's not true," said Jude with a laugh. "You're a wonderful friend to me, Simon."

"But I emigrated, didn't I?"

JUDE WAS SITTING DOWN front in the ballroom of a hotel near the Boston Public Gardens, where Anna was delivering a pitch for her

handbook to the assembled high school English teachers. She had
warned Jude that she wasn't going to look at her from the podium
lest she smile or blush. Jude, however, was looking at Anna, who was
wearing the same mauve and forest-green wool suit from their first
lunch. And she was recalling the marvels that lay just beneath that
fabric of fine wool. She pictured Anna naked on the carpet in their
room earlier that morning, hips swiveling lubriciously against Jude's
thigh. And Anna sprawled in an armchair in the morning sun, robe
fallen open, moaning softly like a purring cat, hands gripping Jude's
head, which was buried between her thighs. It amused Jude to think
that many of the teachers who were listening so admiringly to Anna's
excellent presentation would be mortified to know how she'd passed
the hour just prior to coming down here to speak to them on educating
the youth of America. But how many among them, Jude wondered as
she searched their attentive faces, *wouldn't* be mortified?

Jude's company had a stand in the adjoining hall, along with
eighty other publishers. Each featured titles of interest to high school
English teachers. An editor from her firm's textbook division was in
charge of their display. Jude's only responsibility, Simon had informed
her with a tiny, indulgent smile at last week's marketing meeting, was
to keep Anna content. The promotion department had set up interviews for her after lunch and the next morning. Otherwise, they
planned to remain in their room, working on Anna's contentment,
pausing only long enough to tip the waiters from room service.

JUDE WOKE UP THAT NIGHT in the unfamiliar bed and reached
over for Anna. But Anna's side of the bed was cold and empty. She
waited for her to return from the bathroom, but she didn't. "Anna?"
she called. There was no response.

Sitting up, she switched on the light. The clock on the bedside
table read 1:30 A.M. She climbed out of bed and padded into the

bathroom. Still no Anna. Her plaid suit had vanished, but every-thing else remained. Jude paced the room, wondering what to do. She phoned the front desk, but the night clerk had seen no one matching Anna's description. Finally, she started putting on her underwear.

A key scratched around the lock. The door swung open and Anna walked in.

"Where have you been?" asked Jude, sitting on the bedside with a stocking half on.

Anna's expression turned furtive. "I had to find a phone."

"How come?"

"I told Jim I'd call."

"At one in the morning?"

"He stays up late."

"But there's a phone right here." Jude frowned, wondering what Anna had to say to Jim that Jude couldn't hear.

"I didn't want to wake you."

"I wish you had. I've been worried."

"I'm a big girl, Jude. I can take care of myself." She sounded irritated.

Anna undressed in silence. For a moment, Jude wondered whether she'd met some alluring English teacher as she autographed books after her talk and had gone to her room for an assignation. Then she dismissed this as too ridiculous, with herself right there, ready to satisfy Anna's slightest whim. But maybe Anna missed the challenge of someone she wasn't sure she could have.

"Did you really have to call him right in the middle of our time alone together?" murmured Jude, sitting immobile on the bedside as she stared at the print on the wall of Paul Revere racing his horse across Concord Bridge.

"He's my husband, darling. He still has a few rights."

"Yes, but he has you to himself most of the time."

"If we're going to start complaining about the ghosts of loves past, what about that wax museum you carry in your heart? Sandy and Molly and God knows how many others."

"You know perfectly well that my waxworks had a meltdown the night we first made love," said Jude, smiling.

Anna smiled back and said in a softer voice, "Once the children are in college, I'll be all yours, my love." She slid under the covers and reached for Jude. "You already have me in a way that Jim doesn't," she added as she unhooked Jude's bra and slipped the straps off her arms. "I don't make love with him anymore."

As she pulled Jude down beside her, Jude was swept with relief. She'd often wondered about this but had felt she couldn't ask, since she was the new kid on Anna's block. As Jude shuddered with desire and subsided into Anna's embrace, she thought she smelled alcohol. But they had split a bottle of wine with dinner.

As Anna did her final magazine interview in their room the next morning, Jude went to the front desk to settle their account. On the invoice, she noticed a charge for half a dozen drinks in the Ironsides Lounge, where she and Anna had never set foot.

"I'm afraid I've been charged for someone else's drinks," she told the cashier.

He rifled through some slips and handed her a bill dated the previous day and signed by Anna. Shaken, Jude wrote her name on the credit-card slip. Anna must have gone to the lounge last night when Jude couldn't find her. She had signed for six drinks, so someone else must have been with her. But who? And why had she lied about it?

On the way back to the room, Jude tried to decide whether to confront Anna. Did she think Jude wouldn't notice the extra drinks, or had she done it on purpose, as a declaration of independence here in Freedom City?

The reporter had left, and Anna was packing for home. Jude didn't want their last hours together to be spent arguing, so she decided to put her ugly suspicions on ice. She knew Anna loved her. What more did she need to know?

As she packed, sick with misery that their time together was ending, and ending for her on a sour note, Jude had a sudden inspiration. "Listen, Anna," she said urgently, "call Jim and tell him you have to stay for another night . . . to do some interviews in the morning. We'll drive to the Cape. Stay at Simon's house. Rent horses and ride them on the beach."

"It sounds wonderful," she said as she closed and latched her suitcase, "but I've got to get back."

"Please, Anna. Who knows when we'll have another night together?"

Anna finally did as Jude asked, phoning Jim. Listening to her lie so smoothly to him about the importance of tomorrow's fictitious interview, Jude felt suddenly uneasy. If Anna sometimes lied to her, she wouldn't be able to tell the difference any more than Jim could right now.

Later, they settled in at Simon's glass-and-beam house among the dunes. Driving to Provincetown in their rented Cutlass, they bought jeans, sweatshirts, and tennis shoes. Then they went to a stable on the outskirts of town and hired two horses. The horses weren't happy to have their fall vacation interrupted. They plodded resentfully among the grassy dunes toward the beach, snorting and shaking their heads time after time in protest. But once they reached the hard-packed sand by the sea, they caught some of Jude's and Anna's enthusiasm and began prancing through the foam along the water's edge as though tiptoeing across hot coals.

Jude slackened her reins and her horse took off, shooting down the beach like an arrow from a bow, careening through the surf, hooves hurling up a spray of salt water mixed with flying sand. For a moment, she worried that Anna might not be able to handle such speed, since she said she'd learned to ride in a ring at summer camp. But looking back, Jude saw her lying low along her horse's arching neck, a grin on her face.

When the horses finally gave out and slowed to a jouncing trot, Jude headed hers toward the dunes, Anna's following. Sliding off the horses, the women looped their reins around a jagged branch of driftwood. Then they scrambled up a dune and sat down in the sand. As they surveyed the ocean, the horses stamped and whinnied below. On the horizon, several shiny black whales were surfacing and spouting with a sound like an erupting geyser, then diving beneath the waves again.

ANNA AND JUDE WALKED into Simon's kitchen. Anna had been silent and sullen on the ride home from the grocery store, shrugging off Jude's attempts at conversation.

"Is something wrong?" Jude finally asked as they set the bags on the counter.

"I'm just tired," said Anna in a lackluster voice. "All those dumb interviews. I'm not used to being with other people day and night."

"Why don't you sit on the deck with a gin and tonic while I make supper?"

"That would be marvelous. Do you mind?"

"No, that's why I offered. Simon told me that my assignment is to keep you content."

Anna smiled wearily. "Well done, my good and faithful servant."

As she peeled and deveined shrimp in the sink, Jude watched Anna lying in a deck chair, languidly squeezing the slice of lime into her drink. In repose, her face looked its age, as it never did in motion. Her jowls sagged slightly and her cheekbones were becoming more pronounced as the flesh began to fall. There were a couple of folds of loose skin at her throat and a network of fine wrinkles that stretched like a rigging from the outer corners of her eyes. Her ink-black hair had developed a few silver highlights. Recently, she'd had some hot flashes, and her menstrual periods had become as unpredictable as a two-year-old's tantrums. Jude felt she was watching in Anna the unfolding of her own future. The baby fat of youth was being replaced by bones and wrinkles. This was the first time Jude had ever seen her so moody. Since they normally got together by appointment only, each made sure to be at her most charming. They saved their sulks for the lucky men they lived with.

By the time Jude set their supper on the glass-topped table on the deck, Anna had downed three gin and tonics and seemed more cheery. She filled their glasses with Sancerre while Jude served rice and topped it with the shrimp, which she'd sautéed with tomatoes, garlic, sherry, scallions, and parsley.

"Where did you learn to cook so well?" asked Anna after sampling the dish.

"If you can read, you can cook," replied Jude.

"That's not true. I'm a terrible cook. And not from lack of reading. If it hadn't been for Shake 'n Bake, my kids would have been regulars at the soup kitchen around the corner. When we live together, you do the cooking and I'll shop and clean."

"It's a deal," said Jude. "Where shall we live—your place or mine?"

"How about Paris?"

"God, I'd love to live with you in Paris, Anna."

"We will," Anna assured her. "At least for a year. If professors can take sabbaticals, why can't we? We'll have an apartment in Montmartre, overlooking all of Paris. You'll cook me perfect little meals like this one, and I'll devote myself to your sexual fulfillment."

Jude smiled. "You're on. Someday, though, I want to show you the Smokies."

"With pleasure. They sound spectacular."

"They are. Especially if you don't have to live there."

"I thought that was your plan. To build a cabin and stay there forever with Saint Molly?"

"Ah, Molly . . . That's another story. If Molly had lived, you and I would never have met. There I'd be right now, in my Tennessee mountain home."

"Maybe you and I should build that cabin," mused Anna.

Jude grinned. "You'd better wait and see if you like the place first."

Jude passed Anna the salad and refilled their wineglasses, while the surf crashed and the breeze off the ocean toyed with their hair.

"I wish we didn't have to go back," said Jude. "I wish we could stay right here like this forever."

"I doubt if you'd love me if you saw me all the time," said Anna in a strange voice.

"Of course I would."

"I can be very unpleasant. You have no idea."

"I doubt that," said Jude.

"Trust me on this, darling."

STANDING BEFORE THE TEAL DOOR of Anna's tiny town house in a cobblestoned mews near Washington Square, Jude seized Simon's hand so that they would look the part of a young couple about town. She'd had to beg him to come along in the first place. Jim had finally figured out that Anna was having an affair. But he didn't yet know with whom, so Anna wanted to cover her tracks. Simon was appalled by such intrigue, but Jude was prepared to do anything to placate Anna.

Although placating her had become quite a challenge now that Jude was traveling so much. Simon had laid it on the line: He'd stuck his neck out for her by making her an editor when she had no experience. If she didn't work out, it was his head that would roll. Therefore, she had to shake herself out of her stupor of lust and start doing her job. So Jude was now supposed to go each year not only to Frankfurt but also to the ABA, the MLA, and the AHA, depending on what books she had to promote. And twice a year, she went to Los Angeles to peddle film rights.

The end result was that Jude was away from New York now as much as two months a year. And often on weekends, she went to Simon's beach house on the Cape to help entertain authors or publishers from abroad. When she returned from these trips and weekends, Anna was usually sullen and withdrawn, like a child punishing a parent for an absence. This annoyed Jude, because before she started this regimen, Anna had sometimes allowed as much time as such a trip required to elapse between their encounters. It was as though she wanted Jude always on tap, even if she didn't have time to see her.

In any case, Anna was almost always tied up with Jim on weekends. She spent much of the summer with him and her children at their cottage on the Jersey shore, and at Christmas their whole family went skiing in Colorado. Was it possible to have an affair, Jude wondered, with someone you never saw? Or was that precisely why it had lasted so long? As though each relationship had a certain amount of capital you could draw on, and the less you withdrew, the longer it could endure.

Once, when Jude tried to discuss all this, Anna broke down in tears on Jude's couch, saying, "I feel as though you're moving on, Jude. In the beginning, we were in this thing together. My anthology was the first book for both of us. But here I am, still teaching my workshops, while you fly around the world meeting exciting new people."

"No one will ever excite me as much as you do, Anna," Jude replied, taking Anna's hand in both hers.

She laughed bitterly, extracting her hand. "But for how much longer? I'm turning into a boring old failure, but you're a rising star."

Jude sat in silence, recalling various offers Anna had turned down that would have resulted by now in a flourishing career as an educational consultant. Jude had been forced to realize that Anna was actually a bit lazy. Her children were away at school. She had a housekeeper who cleaned and shopped and cooked. She taught two workshops a week and sometimes wrote poetry. What did she do all day? For a brief panicked moment, Jude wondered whether she had another lover. Or two.

"I did it for you," Jude maintained, realizing this wasn't entirely true. She'd done it partly for Simon. "I thought you'd find me more interesting if I was successful. And the extra money I'm earning can finance our year in Paris. Or our cabin in the Smokies."

"Ah, Jude, my love," she murmured, planting a kiss on her mouth. "My eternal touching innocent. You always believe what other people tell you."

"What's that supposed to mean?"

ANNA OPENED HER DOOR. She was wearing gray-green silk hostess pajamas and dangling earrings of silver filigree, like tiny frosted spiderwebs. "How nice to see you both," she said with her most charming smile. "Jim, these are my publishers. Simon and Jude, this is my husband, Jim."

Anna ran her arm through Jim's as he shook hands with them both and murmured a welcome. He looked every inch the suave professor in his tweed jacket with suede elbow patches. His long salt-and-pepper sideburns matched his bushy eyebrows. Jude was shocked to realize that he was her father's age. It was the same old story: He'd been Anna's thesis adviser. They'd fallen in love over Mallarmé. He'd left his wife and children to marry her and produce a second batch of children. The passage of time having banked their fires, he now had affairs with students who seemed younger with each passing term.

Fingering his lapel, Anna said anxiously, "Jim has a new jacket from Scotland. Isn't it handsome? Doesn't he look elegant?"

Jude had never seen Anna so coy.

As he turned to walk away, Jim said under his breath, "Screw you, Anna."

Acting as though she hadn't heard, Anna ushered Jude and Simon into the living room, which was packed with drink-sipping, canapé-munching students and faculty. French doors opened onto an enclosed garden with ivy-drenched walls. The room itself was lined with books. Four plush sofas formed a conversation pit around a huge, square coffee table with an ivory marble top. After fixing a scotch for them both, Anna departed to pass hors d'oeuvres and introduce strangers. Across the room, Jim was holding forth on Rimbaud to a young woman in a miniskirt the size of a dish towel.

Jude watched Simon study Anna in her clinging silk hostess pajamas. She was weaving a bit as she walked. Getting drunk at your own party seemed a bad idea, but the crowd looked so dreary that Jude was downing her drink too quickly, as well.

"You don't like her, do you?" she asked Simon.

"I never said that."

"You don't need to."

He hesitated, then drew a deep breath. "It's not that I don't like her, Jude. I just don't think she's right for you."

"Why not?" asked Jude. Because she had made Jude want to quit her job and spend all day in bed? "In the beginning, you were our biggest fan."

"I asked William about her awhile back. I wish I hadn't, because I haven't been able to decide whether to tell you what he said."

"What, for God's sake?"

"He said her husband has affairs with young women, so Anna does, too. She likes the stimulation of the chase."

"Don't we all?"

"Yes, we do. But it ends there for her. Once the woman is really hooked, Anna dumps her and rushes back home to Jim for solace. And he does the same. Apparently, they've both left corpses scattered all over town. It's the glue that holds them together."

"Well, it's not like that with us," Jude snapped. "Anna loves me. She says she's finally met her match. We're both intelligent and well educated. We adore lovemaking. We have fun together when we go out. She and Jim aren't lovers anymore, and they're going to split once their children are out of school. And then she'll move in with me or get a place nearby. We're going to live in Paris for a while. Maybe build a cabin in the Smokies. You have to understand, Simon —I love Anna more than I've ever loved anyone else in my entire life."

He shook his head, awed to have triggered such a diatribe of devotion. "I hope you're right, Jude. Please forgive me for meddling."

"Of course, I forgive you, Simon. It means you care about me."

"I just don't want to see you demolished again. Sometimes you don't seem to know how to protect yourself."

"In this case I don't need to protect myself."

As Simon wandered off in search of more scotch, Jude thought it over irritably and decided he was mistaken. Although their time together was more limited than in the beginning, she and Anna still ate delicious meals together. They attended concerts and operas and painting exhibitions. At the movies, they sat there stroking each other's palms with their fingertips and then rushed back home to Jude's bed. They exchanged cards and flowers and candy. They saved up their brightest thoughts and funniest jokes. Jude continued to serve as Anna's demon lover, making the rest of her dreary life bearable. And

Anna remained Jude's tour guide through the previously uncharted realms of her own passions.

Whereas Anna and Jim got to argue over picking up the cleaning, the ring around the bathtub, and how much to tip the plumber.

Given the scotch, Simon's remarks, and jet lag, Jude realized she was feeling awful. She was just back from a week in London at a new biennial Feminist Book Fair. As it turned out, the event had had very little to do with books and a lot to do with feminism. Everywhere you looked, some outraged special-interest group was caucusing. The women of color were angry at the white women. The working-class women were angry at the middle-class women. The non-English-speaking women were angry at the Anglophones. The lesbians were angry at the heterosexuals. The heterosexuals were angry at the lesbians. And everybody was angry at men.

The high point of the conference for Jude was her dinner with Jasmine at a carvery on the Strand that featured huge, dripping roasts of ham, beef, lamb, and pork upended on spikes, from which the waiters hacked slabs. A Baptist God might have created just such a place in the hereafter—as punishment for evil vegetarians. Jasmine, who turned out to be a food snob, insisted that the only way to avoid gastronomic catastrophe in England was to stick to such unadorned meat and potatoes.

As they consumed enough animal flesh to have nourished a pride of lions for a week, they discussed the funnels of rage that were swirling like twisters through the conference hall. Jasmine described the rival feminist factions in Paris, one of which had bombed another's printing press and hounded its leader into exile on the Canary Islands. She explained her theory of the dynamics of minority political movements, learned at her father's knee during the French Resistance: External injustices generated anger. When it seemed impossible to right the wrongs, the stalled anger pooled within the oppressed group, causing it to split into warring factions, which then destroyed one another, completing the tyrant's task for him. The only way to avoid this disintegration, Jasmine maintained, was to move beyond the anger, using it to fuel efforts to change specific conditions without allowing yourself to become attached to the results.

Jude wandered up to Anna's second floor, searching for a bathroom whose medicine chest might contain an aspirin. It was odd to be in the house where Anna had lived with Jim and their children for close to two decades. It was a warm and welcoming place, with lots of carpets, cushions, and curtains.

Passing a door that was ajar, Jude glanced in. It was a bedroom. And kneeling on the carpet was Anna, with Jim standing over her.

". . . and I know I'm disgusting," she was moaning. "And I know if I weren't so disgusting, darling, you wouldn't need to sleep with all these other women." She embraced his knees. "I didn't mean to drink so much this time, Jim."

Jim was gazing out the window into the bare branches of a scrawny maple tree in the garden, apparently uninterested.

"Please forgive me," begged Anna.

Jim refused even to look at her.

Anna reached up and began fumbling for his zipper. "I know what you like, darling, and I can do it better than any sophomore you will ever meet."

Still staring out the window, Jim grabbed her wrist. Gradually, he tightened his grip, until she was whimpering. He wrenched her arm sharply to one side so that she fell to the floor.

She lay there crying and gasping, "You hate me, Jim. I know you hate me. I don't blame you. I'm disgusting."

Jude stood there mortified, wanting to rush to the rescue but paralyzed by disbelief. Jim hauled Anna back up to her knees before him and began unbuckling his belt.

Jude ran along the hallway and down the stairs. Grabbing coats from the closet, she dragged a startled Simon into the street.

"What's wrong?" he asked, still carrying his sloshing plastic cup of scotch.

"Nothing."

Simon raised his eyebrows. "Tell me, Jude. Let me help."

"You already have."

"... SO I WAS UPSTAIRS in the bathroom," Anna was saying as she and Jude walked down the street from Jude's office toward the park, "and when I came back down, you and Simon had vanished."

Jude said nothing. There was a bruise around Anna's wrist like a wide purple shackle. It matched the dark circles under Jude's eyes from her past two nights of insomnia. As she lay wide awake in the dark, she kept asking herself if it had been a setup. Not that Anna had planned for Jude to witness this exact scene with Jim, but that she had planned for *something* to happen to shake Jude up. But did she want to shake Jude up in order to end the relationship or in order to revitalize it? Whichever, she had certainly succeeded. Jude was a wreck.

"Is something the matter?" asked Anna.

After a long pause, Jude said, "I thought you didn't make love with Jim anymore."

Anna looked suddenly secretive. "Why do you ask?"

Drawing a deep breath, Jude described what she'd seen. The two stopped and faced one another in the middle of the sidewalk, so the other pedestrians had to detour irritably around them.

"Well, I guess I was pretty drunk," admitted Anna. "But what's a blow job between friends?"

Jude grimaced. Anna wasn't usually so crude. She realized that the blow job wasn't the entire issue. Taking Anna's hand, she stroked the ugly bruise with her fingertips. "Anna, no one should treat you like that. You have to leave him. Or take him to a therapist. Or do *something.*"

Jude was being forced to realize that Anna might be terminally passive. When they were first together, she had said she'd leave Jim when their children were in college. Now her timetable for departure required them to be *out* of college.

Anna gave her a look. "How can I leave him when I have no money?"

For the first time, it occurred to Jude that someone who taught a few workshops and wrote mostly unpublished poetry wasn't self-supporting, even with the royalties from the anthologies. The odd blow job was probably a small price to pay for the clothes and restaurants and concert tickets Anna invested in with such insouciance.

"Move in with Simon and me," said Jude. "I'll help you out. You can look for a job."

"Who'd want to hire a middle-aged mother who can't type?" she asked. "What am I supposed to do? Wait on tables?"

"Why not? It's honest work. More honest than blow jobs for men you no longer love."

"So my hillbilly honey has finally reverted to type. Miss Southern Baptist has never done it with someone she didn't love."

Jude had never heard this sarcastic tone of voice from Anna before. She was appalled. "Yes, of course I have, Anna. That's not the point."

"The green paradise of childhood love, bullshit. It's time you grew up, little girl."

"Anna, don't." Jude felt as though Anna had just socked her in the solar plexus.

"Welcome to the black pit of adult lust, my darling."

Who was this woman? Jude wondered. Certainly not her tender

lover of last week. Studying her contorted red face, Jude noticed that she was swaying as she stood there, like a skyscraper in an earthquake. She was drunk.

A FEW NIGHTS LATER, Anna arrived at Jude's apartment building in a taxi with a couple of cardboard boxes of belongings. She acted as though the ugly scene between them on the sidewalk hadn't happened, so Jude did, too. But every cell in her body was hanging back, watching, fearing a reappearance of Anna's evil twin. She'd been telling herself that if you opened the Pandora's box of passions, they all came out, not just the pleasant ones. But an occasional moment of unpleasantness was worth all the happiness.

Jude stashed the boxes in Sandy's old room, pending a discussion with Simon as to which free room could be Anna's. Elated by this evidence of movement on Anna's part, she let Anna lead her down the hallway to her own bedroom. In the full moon through the window, she began to remove Anna's rayon jumpsuit. And she discovered a dark splotch across her hip and thigh.

Turning on the lamp by the bed, Jude inspected the moist purple contusion with her fingertips.

"I fell in the bathtub," said Anna.

"Please stay here tonight," Jude replied. "Simon and I will go to your house tomorrow and get your stuff."

"I've decided to come live with you, Jude. But not tonight."

"When then?"

"Tomorrow night," she said, turning off the lamp and taking Jude's hand. Sinking onto the mattress, she pulled Jude down beside her. Succumbing, against her better judgment, Jude maneuvered Anna onto her back and began to kiss her breast.

"Bite it," said Anna.

"What?"

"Bite my nipple. Hard."

Jude looked up at her.

"Please."

"But I don't want to hurt you."

Grabbing a handful of Jude's hair, Anna wrenched her head back down to her breast. "I said bite it, goddamn it!"

Seizing Anna's bruised wrist, Jude struggled to free her hair. They wrestled ferociously across the mattress like jungle cats, straining and struggling, crashing against the wall. Anna finally let go of Jude's hair. With her free hand, she reached over and grabbed the Atalanta flask from Jude's windowsill. She hurled it across the room, where it fell to the floor and shattered into a dozen pieces.

"Goddamn you to hell, Anna!" screamed Jude, a flash of fury scrambling her brain. She hauled back her fist to slug her. Then she froze with her hand in midair, teeth bared, muscles shaking and quivering. Anna cringed away and sank back down on the bed.

Scalp throbbing, Jude leapt off the bed, careened across the room, and slammed her fist into the wall. Anna rolled over into a fetal position and began to rock back and forth, whimpering like a wounded animal.

Eyeing the shards of her cherished flask, Jude sat back down on the bedside, breathing heavily. She began to pat Anna's back, trying to calm her as she would have a spooked horse. "I'm sorry, Anna," she murmured. "I didn't mean to yell at you." Leaning over to kiss her shoulder, she discovered that Anna was gnawing her own knee.

"Anna, don't."

Anna looked up, eyes wild. She'd chewed through her skin, like a frenzied vampire queen, and her mouth and knee were dripping blood in the moonlight.

"You've got to get some help," Jude finally said. "Something's gone wrong."

"Mind your own damn business," muttered Anna, rolling off the bed.

"It is my business. Because I love you."

"If you really loved me," said Anna as she fastened her bra and stepped into her jumpsuit, "you'd do what I ask. You don't love me. You love your *idea* of me. You've assigned me a role in this lesbian 'Little House on the Prairie' that goes on inside your head. But it's got nothing to do with what I might want or need. You keep telling me how marvelous I am, but you don't know the first thing about me."

Jude sat in a stunned silence. Could this be true?

Upon reaching the door, Anna turned to say, "Well, we can't sink much lower than this. So I'm going to do you a favor, Jude, and not see you anymore. Please don't try to get in touch with me."

Jude looked up at her incredulously. "Just like that?"

"Just like that." Anna walked out.

Sitting on the edge of her bed, rubbing her bruised hand, Jude relived that endless moment when her fist had been cocked to beat the shit out of Anna. For the first time in her life, she understood the phrase *to see red*. She had seen red, bloodred. And she had nearly reproduced this vision in red by battering Anna to bits right there on the white sheets. She could feel even now the visceral satisfaction it would have brought her to bury her fists time after time in Anna's cowering flesh. Anna was right: Jude couldn't sink much lower than this. After a lifetime of deploring it in others, she had caught a glimpse of her own capacity for violence and of the intoxicating erotic charge it could carry.

As she squatted down and collected the shards of her grand-mother's flask, Jude realized that Anna was right not to stay with someone who had come within a hairsbreadth of beating her up. Yet her departure was actually a sexist act, since she'd stayed for years with a *man* who beat her up. Picturing Anna's mouth dripping blood in the moonlight, Jude felt a certain reluctant comprehension of Jim's behavior. Yes, he sometimes injured her. But apparently if someone else wouldn't do it for her, she'd do it herself. Dazed, Jude tried to analyze the steps by which she'd started out trying not to hurt Anna, only to end up wanting to kill her.

Jude remembered Anna's telling her in the beginning that most people were a house of mirrors. If she'd paid attention then, she could have spared herself a lot of agony. But now she was lost inside the fun house.

Before descending into an exhausted sleep, she vowed to cut her losses. She'd obey Anna and not contact her. If Anna needed someone to punish her for their bouts of illicit pleasure, like the flagellation of depraved medieval monks, it wasn't going to be Jude. Jim could do it.

For the next few days, Jude wandered around the office in a haze of misery, unable to eat or sleep. Several times, she caught Simon watching her with concern. Finally, she went into his office to announce, "You were right about Anna."

He looked up from a pile of papers. "What's happened?"

"She's dumped me without a backward glance."

He grimaced. "I'm sorry. If it's any help, I love you."

"It helps. But not much."

He smiled sadly.

"Simon," ventured Jude, "when you and Sandy used to go down to the docks in your chaps—what was that all about?"

He gave her a look. "What do you think it was all about? Lust."

"Weren't you afraid?"

"My dear child, that's the whole point. The terror of the chase.

The wild beast that may rip you to shreds once you corner him.''

"Well, in the end, that may be what turns Anna on—pain and fear.''

Simon raised his eyebrows. "The difference is that no one on the docks pretends it has anything to do with love.''

"I wonder if there's a workshop I could take to win her back. 'Hurt Your Way to Happiness.' If only I could behave as badly as her husband, she might leave him to be with me.''

Simon didn't smile.

"Yes, I know you tried to warn me," she said. "So did William.''

Upon leaving her office that afternoon, Jude decided to stop by Madame Toussaint's for a sixty-thousand-mile checkup. After all, she had helped lure Jude into this quagmire with Anna in the first place. Maybe she could advise her on how to climb back out again, or at least tell her what was in store for her around the next bend in this enchanting cosmic tunnel of love.

But when she reached the block where Madame Toussaint's lair had been, she couldn't find it. She couldn't even find the doorway or the staircase, much less the little hand-printed sign. She searched up and down five blocks in either direction, along both sides of the street. Then she went into several shops to inquire about a large tarot-reading psychic. But no one had ever heard of Madame Toussaint.

THAT NIGHT, JUDE DISCOVERED that her index finger had a life of its own. Like Lassie to the rescue, it dialed Anna's number, despite feeble protests from her benumbed brain.

Anna answered.

"It's Jude. I have to talk to you.''

"I'm afraid I can't right now. Jim's here." Her voice was calm and pleasant.

"When then?"

"Soon. Don't be so impatient, my darling," she murmured. "We'll have the rest of our lives together in our cabin in the mountains."

Jude held the receiver away from her ear to stare at it. Had she gotten a wrong number?

Jim shouted in the background, "Did you hear me, bitch?"

"Got to go," Anna whispered. "He's angry."

"Get the fuck over here!" he yelled.

"Anna, I'm coming to get you right now," said Jude. "Be ready."

"No, Jude, don't. . . ." Her phone clicked off.

Jude dashed from her building and grabbed a cab to the Village. Instructing the driver to wait at the end of the mews, she ran to Anna's house. When she pounded on the front door, no one came. Trying the handle, she found it unlocked. She pushed the door open and raced in. Like a bloodhound on the trail of an escaped convict, she scurried around the living room and kitchen.

Anna and Jim were sitting on a black leather couch in the den at the back of the house, watching the local news on a television set built into a wall of wooden shelves and cabinets, which were crammed with stereo equipment, books, and objets d'art. Both were holding lowball glasses full of ice cubes and a milky liquid. Anna, who was wearing a scarlet caftan, looked up at Jude through barely focused blue eyes. Her sleek hair stood on end at the crown, like a kiwi bird's head feathers. Jim had risen unsteadily to his feet, his flushed face webbed with broken veins.

"Who the hell are you?" he asked.

"Don't you remember Jude from our party last month, dear?" asked Anna, the perfect hostess. "She's my editor."

"What the fuck are you doing in my house?"

Jude tried to decide. "I've come to take Anna back to my apartment."

"What are you—a nut or something?"

"I've seen her bruises, Jim. I know you beat her up. And it's going to stop."

"What business is it of yours?"

"It's my business because I love Anna," Jude was alarmed to hear herself confess.

Anna dropped her glass, spilling her drink all down the front of her caftan.

"Get out of my house," Jim said calmly, face turning purple.

"Not without Anna. Come on, Anna."

Anna just looked at her with bleary distress, making no move to rise. Jim headed around the corner of the couch toward Jude.

"I'm calling the police," said Jude as she edged toward the doorway.

"Call whomever you like," said Jim, fists clenching. "This is my house and my wife. And you're trespassing on private property."

In the taxi on the way home, Jude felt like a fool. Anna had made no move on her own behalf or in support of Jude. Jude had felt as helpless as she must have as a toddler, trying to rescue her mother from the stranger in the army uniform who everyone claimed was her father. As she had the afternoon she tried to persuade Molly not to go on the Baptist retreat with Ace Kilgore. As she had the night she saw Sandy coupling with the stranger in the moonlight. Why was she always drawn to people who wanted to slow-dance with danger? She was like a moth who flitted around a candle flame while her fellow moths immolated themselves in it.

But danger you could find anywhere. It was kindness when she came across it that lured her like a flame. She remembered standing in her grandfather's backyard as a toddler, holding a large rock above her head, about to drop it on a toad just to see what would happen. As she let it fall, her grandfather appeared from nowhere and caught it in midair. He squatted down and picked up the toad, whose throat was pulsing repulsively. It sat on his palm, ugly eyes bulging.

"Jude," said her grandfather, stroking the horrible warty back with his fingertip, "our job is to protect and provide for other creatures. That's the minimum requirement for being human. It's what the word *love* means. Many people behave like rabid dogs, but that's no reason to join them."

CROSSING THE MARBLE LOBBY of her office building the next afternoon, Jude spotted Anna waiting for her by the door for their usual Wednesday stroll. Baffled, Jude kissed her cheek. As she backed away, she noticed that the whites around Anna's cornflower blue irises were faintly tinged with yellow. There was also a sore on her neck, which she'd powdered and tried to conceal with a dashing white aviator scarf.

"What's this?" asked Jude, touching the sore.

"A spider bite," she said. Her lips were trembling.

All of a sudden, the pieces fell into place for Jude: She'd learned enough from her years with her father to recognize jaundice when she saw it. They walked toward the park in silence, Jude trying to figure out what to do with this new suspicion.

"Is everything okay?" asked Anna anxiously.

Jude looked at her with disbelief. Did she not even remember breaking up with Jude? Or Jude's failed rescue attempt the previous night?

"Anna," she finally replied, "I don't know how to say this, but I'm worried about your drinking."

Anna looked startled, then stealthy.

"I think you're overdoing it."

"If you had a husband who slept with every coed in town, you'd probably overdo it, too. And children who flunk out of every college in the Northeast. And students who expect you to solve the ghastly problems of their decaying cultures and dysfunctional families. And a lover who thinks that life is an episode from 'The Waltons.' Believe me, I have good reason to overdo it."

"Who doesn't have reason?" snapped Jude. "Having reason is no reason."

At Broadway, they headed uptown for Jude's apartment. And Jude was forced to confront the fact that she was as much of a masochist as Anna. Any healthy person would have sent Anna home to her own fate. But by now, Jude's fate seemed irretrievably merged with Anna's.

After making love as tenderly as in the beginning, they held each other and listened to thunder rolling in from the Poconos. Jude knew that no matter what was happening to them, she herself wouldn't be able to end it—even if that was what was best for them both. But it would mean more for her than just the death of their relationship. It would be the death of her dream that happiness with another person was possible in this life.

During their lovemaking, Jude had discovered more "spider bites" on Anna's arms and back, and her abdomen had seemed faintly distended. She made a mental note to phone her father and find out what this meant.

"Anna, I can't bear to lose you," she murmured.

"You're not going to lose me, Jude. You know I love you. I'll never leave you."

As Jude watched rainwater flow in torrents down the window-panes, she tried to figure out which was the real Anna—the snarling beast who ripped apart her own flesh with her bared teeth, or the woman who lay beside her right now, stroking her hair and running her tongue around the folds of her ear and talking about the apartment they'd rent in Montmartre once she divorced Jim.

"You know I'm going to Australia for a few days on Friday?"

Anna sat up abruptly. "How could I know when you don't tell me?"

"I did tell you, Anna. A couple of times."

"No, you didn't," she insisted.

"Well, maybe not," said Jude, deciding it wasn't worth an argument. "But anyway, I am."

"Why?"

"I have to speak on a panel about feminist editing."

"Will that woman be there?"

"Which woman?"

"That French friend of Simon's."

"Jasmine. Yes. She's one of the organizers."

Anna said nothing for a long time. Jude began to feel guilty without having anything to feel guilty about.

"Please don't go," Anna said.

"I'm sorry, my love, but I have to. They're counting on me. But I'll be back before you know I'm gone."

"If you stay here, you could help me move some things into your apartment."

Jude turned her head to look at her. Was this really true, or was it just a ploy?

"What if something terrible happens while you're gone?"

"Jesus, Anna, please don't do this to me," Jude moaned. "You'll be fine for a few days. It'll give you time to see a doctor and find out about these sores. Then when I get back, we can move you into my apartment. Okay?"

"Okay," she finally said.

"Promise me you'll see a doctor while I'm gone."

"I promise."

JUDE AND JASMINE TOOK a local bus to the seaside south of Adelaide as a remedy for their jet lag. As they strolled along the deserted white beach under a searing sun, they discussed ideas for the panel. Would women, free from the pressures of the marketplace, write differently from men? What were these pressures, and how did they distort women's writing? What role did fiction play in challenging or confirming the dominant stereotypes of women in Western culture? Was it possible to run a successful publishing house in a capitalist economy without a hierarchy among the employees and a star system among the authors?

As she and Jasmine wrangled over these issues and others, Jude felt herself becoming more energized than she'd been in months. The deadly struggles with Anna faded from her mind, and she felt her tensed muscles relax and her breath start to flow freely again. They sat down at a green metal table beneath some eucalyptus trees, alongside a roadhouse with a metal roof. As the sun sank into the ocean, they sipped Australian beer and discussed Simon's inability to find a love that lasted longer than three weeks.

"Yet three weeks of pleasure is not nothing," said Jasmine.

Even on safari in the outback, she was impeccable, in spotless white cotton pedal pushers and a loose silk shirt in shades of orange and red that coordinated with the sunset. Under the open shirt, she was wearing a lacy white camisole, and she had a gold herringbone chain at her throat.

"No, but I think he longs for what he had with his friend Sandy. But he'll never find that again, because Sandy was a very unusual person." Jude was studying the ash-gray bark of the trunk tree beside her, which was mottled with impetigolike patches of rust and black. They reminded her of Anna's scabs. She hoped Anna would go to the doctor as she had promised. But often these days, she seemed not to remember what she said from one moment to the next.

"I never met Sandy. But he was also your friend, was he not?" asked Jasmine, watching the golden sea shining like molten ore in the setting sun.

"That's right. We grew up together. He was like a brother to me."

"But more than a brother?"

Jude looked at her quickly. "Simon told you that?"

Jasmine nodded.

"Did he also tell you I've been with a woman for the past several years?"

She nodded again. "Sometimes our dear friend Simon talks too much. I hope you do not mind. Because I am supportive of you in this regard."

Jude blushed. "No, I don't mind. And thanks for your support." But was Jasmine saying that she also loved women? Jude couldn't tell, but she couldn't ask, either. Jasmine's manner discouraged familiarity.

Also speaking on their panel were editors from England, Holland, and Australia. The five women sat at a long table beneath a huge white-canvas tent and discussed women's writing among themselves and with the large and lively audience. Afterward, the panel members dined with the festival officials at an Indian restaurant in downtown Adelaide and everyone agreed that the event had been very successful.

In the hotel lobby, before ascending to their rooms on different floors, Jasmine, who was departing at dawn for Paris, said to Jude, "I must say good-bye to you now. But I will look forward to our next meeting. At the ABA in Atlanta, no?"

"Yes. In May. I look forward to it, too. And meanwhile, take good care of yourself, Jasmine."

Jasmine smiled and gazed into her eyes. Placing her hands firmly on Jude's shoulders, she leaned forward and kissed each of her cheeks in decisive slow motion.

The attentive stewardesses on Jude's endless flight back to the United States on Singapore Airlines the next day had the same fragile build and carefully kempt dark beauty as Jasmine. Unlike Jasmine, though, they seemed submissive and eager to please. Jude realized that what impressed her most about Jasmine was that she was in charge of her own life. She ran a successful publishing company. She traveled around the world. In contrast to Anna, whose lifetime of laziness was coming home to roost, limiting her options in ways that were punishing Jude as well.

She remembered how she and Anna used to debate literature and philosophy and art in their early days together. Anna recited her poems and Jude made suggestions. Anna read the books Jude was editing and they discussed them. But now all they talked about was their next meal. It was as though the intensity of their physical exchanges had extinguished all their more subtle forms of intercourse. She vowed that when she got home she would once again initiate with Anna the kind of conversations she had just enjoyed in Adelaide. Maybe it wasn't too late.

When the plane finally landed in Los Angeles, Jude was disturbed to realize that she'd thought more about Jasmine as she hurtled across the Pacific than she had about Anna. But it was a new experience for her to be able *not* to think about Anna. For years, her first thought upon waking and her last before sleeping had been of Anna. And throughout each day, she had replayed every word that they had exchanged the previous day. Anna's name had echoed continuously through her brain, like a Moslem on a pilgrimage to Mecca chanting, *"La illaha illa Allah."*

Stumbling through the international arrival gate at JFK after thirty-two hours in transit, Jude was astonished to find Anna waiting for her. This was a first. All around them, reunited lovers, relatives, and friends were embracing, so Jude and Anna tried to parody the friendly welcoming hug of long-lost sisters.

"Do you have any idea," Anna whispered in her ear, "how much I want to bury my tongue deep inside you?"

Jude stroked her cheek and gazed into her eyes, but she was thinking that the only thing she wanted deep inside her right then was some hot coffee.

Anna grabbed her bag and led her to the exit door. They waited at the curb for a bus to town. A van from the Hilton pulled up. As Anna climbed aboard with the suitcase, Jude called, "Wait a minute, Anna. This isn't us."

Gesturing frantically for her to get on, Anna whispered, "I've rented us a room for the day."

Jude smiled, but her heart sank. She was exhausted and she had a million things to do. Back at her office and apartment, a hundred phone messages and several days of mail awaited her.

Anna had stopped off at the room on her way to the airport. It was as crammed with yellow tulips as a Dutch wake, and a bottle of sparkling cider was packed in melting ice in the sink. Anna phoned room service and ordered chicken salad and toast points.

All Jude wanted was to sleep. Instead, she drank cider while Anna informed her that she was absolutely right: She used to have a drinking problem. But no longer. She'd sworn off alcohol for good.

"What about the sores?" asked Jude as they sat at the linen-shrouded table rolled in by the waiter from room service. "Did you go to the doctor?"

"He said it was an allergic reaction," said Anna. "To some sleeping pills I was taking."

"And?" Jude eyed her suspiciously, having no idea anymore what was truth and what was fabrication.

"And now that I'm not taking them, the sores will go away."

"That's a relief," said Jude, picking up a piece of toast and tackling the chicken salad, her sixth meal since Hawaii.

"So did you sleep with her?"

"With whom?"

"With Jasmine."

"Of course not. Did you think I would?"

"Yes."

"Did you care?"

"Very much. I've been miserable."

"So now you're relieved?"

"Temporarily."

"Don't worry," said Jude without enough forethought. "She's married."

Anna regarded her ironically. "But that's what turns you on, isn't it? The primal triangle? Stealing Mommy from Daddy?"

Jude paused with the toast point halfway to her mouth. "Is that how you see it?"

"And once you succeed," Anna continued blandly, "Mommy seems very boring."

Jude thought this over. "Maybe so," she finally conceded, not even caring enough to argue. Though she actually thought that her waning interest in Anna had more to do with not knowing from one moment to the next whether she'd be dealing with a tender Madonna or an avenging destroyer. Loving Anna had become like trying to love Kali. Finally, you just gave up.

Anna insisted that they take a bath together, slithering around on each other like minnows in a hatchery. Afterward, she dried Jude with a large, fluffy towel. Then she basted her like a turkey with lotion and massaged her on the bed until she was groaning with fatigue. Stripping off her own robe, Anna lay down beside her. Jude stroked her belly, which seemed even more puffy than before. "What did the doctor say about your bloating?"

"It's menopause," she said. "Water retention. I've put myself on a diet and exercise plan to regain my girlish figure. In a couple of months, you won't recognize me. I want it to be like it used to be for us, Jude."

"So do I."

Lying in the giant bed later that afternoon, nearly delirious with exhaustion, Anna asleep beside her, Jude recalled their first hotel room, at the conference in Boston several years earlier, and her own anxiety at waking up in the middle of the night and finding Anna gone. Something had happened between them since then. Who knew what. The worm had turned. The wind had shifted. Now it was Anna who waited for Jude, Anna who felt anxiety over being left behind.

She had good reason to, Jude reluctantly acknowledged. Their luxurious afternoon in bed had felt to Jude like just another chore, one among many that had to be dealt with upon her return. To generate enough energy for lovemaking, so that they could get this reunion over with and go home, Jude had found herself visualizing that walk along the white sand with Jasmine and their talks that had stimulated so many exciting new ideas. There was a whole world out there, full of people Jude had never met, people with horrible problems that they didn't expect Jude to solve.

Holding the sleeping Anna in her arms, Jude was swept with sadness. Anna was right: Jude was moving on. She would have stayed put if she could have, but she was like a flailing swimmer being carried out to sea on a riptide. She had no plans to leave Anna, but emotionally she was already gone. She thought about Molly with new sympathy, because this time it was Jude who had stopped loving first and who would feel the guilt for the rest of her life. Her throat tight, she kissed Anna's closed eyelids. Anna smiled in her sleep and snuggled closer.

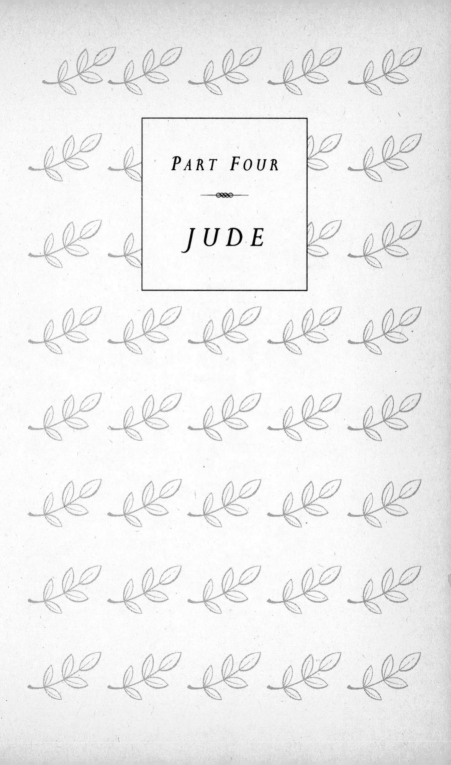

PART FOUR

JUDE

Balancing a glass of champagne, Jude wandered across the closely cropped lawn of Jasmine's seventeenth-century stone town house, wondering how it had escaped being torched during the Revolution. After winding along the tourist-crammed side streets near St. Germain des Prés, she had passed through black iron doors in a high stucco wall and discovered this lawn strewn with wrought-iron furniture and shaded by horse-chestnut trees full of ivory obelisks. Jasmine, who had a spiky new frosted waif hairdo, kissed her on both cheeks. Then she tucked her arm through Jude's to conduct her to the champagne table, where she cast her adrift on a sea of bright Ungaro sails.

Although Jude knew that she was presentable in her raw-silk trousers and coral linen blazer, she had always felt like Godzilla in Paris, possessing as she did the long, lean mountaineer build of her father and his father—in contrast to her urban mother, who had reportedly had wrists the size of a broomstick.

Jasmine was talking to a young woman in a black silk jumpsuit who had draped a silver-studded black leather carbine belt diagonally across her chest. The woman was studying Jude's breasts. Slowly, her kohl-ringed eyes rose up Jude's chest. When their gazes met, the woman smiled faintly, as though to indicate anything was possible. Jude recognized *le regard*, the famous French technique for seducing one another and unnerving visitors. She smiled back, struggling to feel playful despite her chagrin at looming like Gulliver over everyone else on the lawn.

The woman arrived by her side. "You are new here, yes?"

Looking down from her heights, Jude nodded.

"From America?"

The kohl was making the woman's dark eyes look huge and appealing. "From New York."

"On holiday?"

"No, I'm going to work for Jasmine."

"How fortunate for us."

Jude smiled. "Thank you. For me, too."

"I am Martine. I also work for Jasmine."

"Delighted to meet you. I'm Jude."

As Jude sipped her champagne, the woman continued her inspection of Jude. In Tennessee, people wooed with words. Strangers who looked too intently at someone they didn't know were considered either rude or insane. But for the French, the eyes were the initial erogenous zone.

Across the lawn, Jude spotted Jasmine by the champagne table, talking sotto voce with the young man Jude recognized from that night on Simon's deck, when she had first offered Jude a job. Jasmine looked up, right at Jude, and seemed to give her a small nod, as though of encouragement. Was a flirtation with Martine the initiation rite that would usher Jude into Jasmine's inner circle?

Drawing a deep breath, Jude returned her attention to Martine. She hadn't flirted in years. While Anna was alive, she lacked the interest. Now that Anna was dead, she lacked the energy. She wasn't sure she remembered what to do anymore. With an uneasy sideways glance, she studied the small firm breasts that formed the valley down which Martine's carbine belt meandered. She remembered lying with Anna while out the window the lights from Palisades Amusement Park wavered like party streamers on the drifting waters of the Hudson. She remembered cradling Anna's beautiful breast in her palm, its nipple caressing her heart line. . . .

Abruptly, Jude understood that all she wanted at that moment was to go back to her new apartment on the butte of Montmartre, and watch through the curly iron grillwork as the sun set bloodred behind the parkland to the west, and review her final evening with Anna. Not even this attractive woman in her high-fashion carbine belt could erase that image of Anna in her hospital bed, hands bound with gauze so that she couldn't scratch the scabs off her sores.

"What is the matter?" demanded Jasmine as Jude bent over to peck her cheeks and murmur thanks for the party. "You don't like Martine?"

"I like her fine, but I don't feel very well tonight." Jude realized too late that she'd been rude to rush away like that, leaving Martine alone on the lawn in the dusk with swallows swooping through the shadows cast by the giant looming chestnut trees.

"But you are perhaps lonely and would like a lovely companion?"

"She is lovely, but I'm hung up on someone in New York."

"But you would nevertheless like a small adventure when you are away from home?"

"I guess not."

Jasmine shook her head. "I will never understand Americans. But perhaps you will have dinner with me soon and explain yourself?"

Searching for a taxi by the Seine, Jude reflected that if this was *l'amour*, it bore little resemblance to what she knew of love. But then again, that wasn't much.

THE FOLLOWING WEEK, as raindrops bounced off the cobblestones in Jasmine's courtyard, Jude gazed up at the muscled granite torsos of two Greek gods who supported the front balcony on their shoulders. Across the balcony stretched arabesques of wrought iron indistinguishable from real vines, leaves, and grape clusters. She wondered who had first decided to try to make metal look like vines, and why.

"Tonight is my night for recreation," announced Jasmine as she hung Jude's damp raincoat in the closet. "Everyone else is at my house in Picardy. So we can say and do whatever we like."

Jude glanced at her. She had expected a dinner party. But Jasmine was wearing casual trousers and a black T-shirt with shoulder pads, and there was no evidence of other guests. Jasmine steered her by the elbow into a high-ceilinged room filled with Louis-the-something settees and armchairs as maladapted to the human form as the wrought-iron furniture on her lawn the night of her garden party. Wine velvet drapes shut out the dripping twilight, and crusaders in tunics emblazoned with red Maltese crosses glared down from splendidly caparisoned horses in gilt frames on the walls. These crusaders in their fish-scale chain mail and steel skullcaps had Jasmine's hooded eyelids and dark, intense gaze.

Observing Jude's interest, Jasmine nodded at one. "He fought with Simon de Montfort at Minerve in 1210. One hundred and forty Cathars were burned at the stake for heresy."

"Neat," said Jude, noticing that the painted toenails in Jasmine's open-toed, high-heeled mules matched the mauve on her eyelids.

Jasmine inclined her head toward a bottle of Jack Daniel's on the coffee table. "And this is how *your* people pass their time, *n'est-ce pas?*"

Jude smiled. "Yes. How kind of you to help me feel at home."

She poured bourbon and Perrier into two tumblers, adding an ice cube to Jude's. "I believe all Americans like ice?"

Toasting Jude's new job, they sipped the amber liquid. Jude could feel it creeping down her esophagus like a grass fire.

"You are enjoying Paris?"

"Yes, very much. It reminds me a bit of the American South, as a matter of fact."

"Oh? In what way?"

"The overfeminized women. Scarlett O'Hara must have been part French." Jude laughed.

"Why do you laugh?" Jasmine was smiling politely.

"I had a grandmother who compared every foreign country she visited to Virginia. And I just realized I was doing the same."

"You find French women overfeminized?" Jasmine settled back against the wine brocade cushions.

"Compared to American women. But your heritage is courtly love. Ours is survival on the frontier. Your ancestors were fighting boredom. Ours, extinction."

"You are still fighting extinction, no? With all your bombs and missiles."

"And you, boredom, with all your elaborations on daily necessity."

Jasmine said nothing. For a moment, Jude wondered if she'd been rude without realizing it, or whether Jasmine was just reluctant to acknowledge that accessories could be optional. On the coffee table, she noticed a large silver bowl that contained packs of every conceiv-

able brand of cigar and cigarette. "What was the heresy in Minerve?"
she asked.

"*La liberté*," replied Jasmine. "They wanted to rule their own
kingdom."

"We tried that in the South, too. It was a big mistake."

"Southerners should never cross swords with Northerners."

Jude smiled. "Sometimes you leave us no choice. Submit or die,
so we march to our deaths, heads held high."

"Courageous, but not very smart."

"Southerners have never been noted for intelligence. We're simple country people."

"Yes, as simple as a Moorish screen," Jasmine observed with a
wry smile. "Shall we move to the table?"

Two places were set on a blue paisley cloth with enough crystal,
silver, and burnt-sienna bone china for a complete trousseau. As Jasmine exited into the kitchen, Jude studied her fork handle, encrusted
with the omnipresent vines and leaves. She didn't recognize the pattern, despite having memorized all the most popular ones during
Charm Class in junior high.

Jude's own pattern, which she'd selected at age six under the
tutelage of her grandmother, was Francis I, which she'd loved because
it had twenty-eight pieces of fruit on the knife handles. Every Christmas and birthday, she'd received pieces from her grandmother, who
didn't allow herself to die until Jude possessed twelve complete place
settings. Inheriting her grandmother's twelve settings, Jude then
owned twenty-four. Molly's pattern, forced on her by her mother in
the face of her total indifference, had been Burgundy, which was similar to Francis I but without the fruit. After Molly's death, her mother
insisted Jude take Molly's seven and a half settings as a memento.
Jude's thirty-one and a half place settings of unused flatware were now
tarnishing in Simon's attic on Cape Cod, waiting for her to hostess a

banquet. Her father used to say that men struggled to pass on their genes, and women their silverware.

Jasmine returned with two scalloped grapefruit shells mounded high with avocado slices, grapefruit sections, and prawns. She poured white wine into one set of glasses, Evian into another. Jude watched to see which fork she'd use before committing herself. Once upon a time, she'd known them all—the dinner fork, the salad fork, the shrimp fork, the ice cream fork, the lobster fork, the lemon fork, the olive fork, the half-olive fork, the pickle fork, the tomato fork.

"This is marvelous," said Jude, tasting a hint of garlic mayonnaise and feeling a stab of nostalgia for the French cook at her grandparents' apartment when she first moved to New York. "I didn't know you could cook."

"I have a wonderful woman from Corsica who left this meal for us. Tonight is her night off."

Removing the empty grapefruit shells, Jasmine returned with medallions of lamb in a plum sauce that matched her toenails, parsley-flecked new potatoes glistening with butter, and embryonic peas and carrots with a faint scent of mint. She poured some red wine from a bottle that had evidently been breathing on the mahogany Empire sideboard as they sipped their Jack Daniel's.

Raising her crystal goblet, Jasmine gazed into the wine, murmuring, "When one drinks wine in France, one engages all the senses."

Jude nodded politely.

"First, we observe the deep burgundy blood of the grape."

Jude raised her glass and looked down into her grape blood.

Chopping up a cherry Popsicle in a Dixie cup, Anna watching her from the blood-flecked sheets, the whites of her eyes a urine yellow, her lips gray and cracked.

"Jude, I'm not afraid to die," she said, "but I don't want to die alone."

"I will be here," Jude replied numbly. "Wait for me." Looking up from the crushed Popsicle into Anna's weary lapis lazuli eyes that used to dance and sparkle just like Molly's.

Putting her nose into her glass, Jasmine inhaled deeply and held it, as though smoking a joint. Then she exhaled. "Next, we allow the bouquet to ascend our nostrils, to the pleasure center of the brain."

Jude sniffed her wine obligingly, but her pleasure center was unfortunately sealed.

Jasmine took a sip and swirled it around her mouth, studying Jude with her intense crusader eyes. She swallowed. "Then we taste the wine, which of course engages the taste buds. But also the sense of touch, as the wine caresses the tongue and the moist cavities of the mouth."

Meeting her gaze, Jude obediently sipped and rinsed as though at the dentist's. But her senses were unengaged, and she intended to keep them that way.

"Well," said Jude, "that covers four out of five. And how about hearing?"

Lowering her eyes, Jasmine said nothing for a while. "Hearing has been involved all along," she finally replied. "You have been listening to my voice, no?"

"Oh. Yes. Right you are."

Abruptly, Jasmine put down her glass and picked up a knife and fork. They ate in silence.

"And how is your apartment?" Jasmine eventually asked.

"It's fine, thanks. I have a wonderful view of Paris. You'll have to come see."

"I rarely go out. People come to me here." She sounded annoyed. Jude felt anxiety prickle the hairs at the back of her neck. "And your work? Is everyone at the office helping you get started?"

"Yes, everyone's been wonderful."

"You know, if you are going to get along here, you should at least pretend to play." She looked Jude in the eye, but with *la réprimande*, not *le regard*.

"But if you pretend," said Jude, "then you're playing." She

toyed with her ivory knife rest. This was, after all, her new boss, and bosses had to be placated. But she'd spent her years in New York trying to learn to be straightforward. A challenge, since in the South directness had been second only to bad hair on the list of deadly sins.

"Exactly."

"So don't you all ever stop playing?"

"What is the alternative? Boredom, followed by death."

"Childhood is for playing. Then life becomes serious."

"And did you play as a child? *Ah, non.* Children are earnest in all that they do. Only adults can really play, because we have learned that life is a game in any case. One that will soon be over."

"Well, I guess I'm not feeling very playful these days." Jude laid her knife and fork parallel on her plate to indicate that she was finished. But did this gesture symbolize the same thing in France?

"Ah, yes. You have said that you are—how do you say, carrying the torch? And this person in New York does not desire you?"

"She's dead."

"She was your lover?"

"Yes."

"Someone new would perhaps help you to forget her."

"I don't want to forget Anna."

Jasmine studied Jude, then said gently, "But she is dead. And you are not."

Jude looked down at the black geometric pattern across her burnt sienna plate.

"Americans are so sincere." Shaking her head, Jasmine passed Jude the cut-glass salad bowl. "It is touching."

"Well, as corny as it may sound, I'm afraid I can only make love to people I love," Jude muttered, realizing as she served herself some romaine and chopped escarole that this wasn't entirely true.

Jasmine smiled. "But one can love for a single night, no? Or for a week.

A love does not have to endure into the next century in order to be love."

"Children in the South play a kissing game called Five Minutes in Heaven. But once you become an adult, you're supposed to graduate to what we call graveyard love."

"And this is what—your graveyard love?"

"Graveyard love is a love that lasts until both people are dead and buried in the graveyard."

"Oh, I see. As in Shakespeare. 'Love is not love which alters when it alteration finds.' "

Jude nodded, impressed that Jasmine should know the English classics in addition to her own.

Jasmine shook her head. "And they say that Americans are not romantic."

"Who does?"

"I believe Europeans think of Americans as Puritans. Practical and efficient. And somewhat naïve to believe that the world operates like that."

"But graveyard love isn't American; it's southern. The South was settled by broken-down cavaliers, not religious fanatics. It's the Citadel of the Lost Cause."

Jasmine carried out the salad plates, Jude's mostly untouched. She returned with a marble slab holding several cheeses—cubes and wheels and wedges, dark orange, pale yellow, white coated with black pepper or flecked with blue-green. She might have poured another wine or two, but the grape blood was all as one to Jude by now.

"General de Gaulle once asked how he could be expected to govern a nation that made three hundred and forty-six varieties of cheese," said Jasmine.

Jude smiled. "Yes, but they all begin with milk and end with mold. Just like people. So that simplifies things a bit."

Jasmine regarded Jude thoughtfully, opened her mouth, then closed it without saying anything.

The meal concluded with balls of sherbet, passion fruit and citron, in scalloped silver bowls, accompanied by disks of fragile dark chocolate lace.

They moved back to the living room for coffee. The thick, bitter espresso held out the promise of eventual sobriety, followed by terminal insomnia.

"Would you like to smoke?" Jasmine nodded toward the bowl of cigarette packs.

Jude extracted a Dunhill and lit up, sinking back into the cushions. Jasmine picked up an embossed leather album from the coffee table and showed Jude photos of her other houses—an ancient family château in Picardy, a modern glass-and-timber structure on Martinique. Clearly there would be many fringe benefits to Jude's job. If she managed to keep it, given her reluctance to play. At the back of the album were photos of people—one of Jasmine as a teenager, attired in a riding habit, seated on a horse in the middle of a flying change.

"Do you still ride?" asked Jude.

"Not in years."

"I used to ride, too. But I never did dressage. In fact, we never used saddles. We just jumped on and took off."

Jasmine eyed her speculatively, a Hun at the city gates. While returning the album to the coffee table, she scooted closer on the couch, until her thigh barely touched Jude's. A scent close to chrysanthemums mixed with coriander seemed to be emanating from her flesh, ascending Jude's nostrils to waft around the barred portals of her pleasure center.

Sitting by Anna's bedside at the Roosevelt, dabbing with a cotton ball soaked in witch hazel at an oozing sore that wouldn't clot. Anna's seersucker robe had fallen open. The pale breast she had begged Jude to bite was lying there like a poached egg. A nurse entered and unpinned the urine-soaked diaper. The sad, gray, sour-smelling genitals, the matted pubic hair, the sagging belly whose unused muscles had turned to flab . . .

Jude turned her head away from Jasmine to deflect the spicy scent. Jasmine murmured concern that she seemed chilled.

Jude found herself rising to her feet. "I have to go now." The part of her that had once leapt like a brazier with Anna was now frozen solid. Jasmine was right: Jude was chilled. Permanently.

Jasmine looked startled. "But it is early."

"I'm really tired. Also a bit drunk."

"If you would like to stay," she said, "my driver can take you back to Montmartre when he returns from Picardy later tonight."

"Thanks, but I'd better go home and sleep it off."

Jasmine shrugged, looking somewhat pleased. As she retrieved Jude's coat from the closet, Jude suddenly understood that to refuse to play was to play. The only way not to play was to stay, thereby short-circuiting the game. But she didn't love Jasmine. Besides, she was confused. She had thought it was Martine that Jasmine had lined up for her. Or were these overtones of seduction just hospitality as usual in Paris?

"Jasmine?" she murmured. In New York, she could have asked someone outright what was going on. But with Jasmine, she always felt tongue-tied unless they were discussing abstractions.

Jasmine looked at her. Her hooded eyes with their hint of mauve seemed to convey disappointment at Jude's possible change of strategy. Would she have been able to believe that Jude had no strategy?

"I just realized," said Jude, "that in English the word *love* is close to *live*. Whereas in French, *l'amour* is close to *la mort*. What do you think that means?"

Jasmine studied Jude as she held out her coat.

JUDE SAT BY HER OPEN DOORS watching the lights of Paris flicker and sweep and flare like heat lightning on a hot southern night. Some fans were conducting a séance in the shed in Jude's courtyard, trying to summon the shade of Dalida, a famous French singer who had recently committed suicide in her house at the end of the block. Jude could see the flicker of candles and hear voices softly chanting Dalida's greatest hits. Jude's inebriation was turning into a migraine, one sensation Jasmine hadn't included in her catalog of the delights of wine drinking in France.

The phone rang. Picking it up, she heard Simon's BBC voice from New York, where it was late afternoon. He was still at work. Jude pictured him with his long legs stretched out beneath his huge black Formica desk, hands toying with one of his bizarre paperweights.

"So how's it going over there, Jude?"

"Not too bad, thank you. It's fascinating trying to figure out the tastes of the French reading public. But socially, I'm a flop."

"I refuse to believe it."

"Alas, it's true. They're playing Hearts and I'm playing Old Maid."

"I think you should learn to play Hearts again."

"Five minutes in heaven and a lifetime of pain. No, thank you."

"I know how you feel, Jude. But it's the only game in town."

"Some of us learn life's little lessons."

"I do understand. Part of you died with Anna. But you have to plunge back into the swim."

"Why?"

"Because you're a V-eight engine who's sparking on only two cylinders."

"You're mixing your metaphors."

"Stop changing the subject."

"But I'm an editor, Simon. I'm paid to notice these things. Anyway, don't worry. Jasmine is doing her best to provide me with romantic interludes."

"She's just trying to help."

"You've discussed me with her? Is that why she invited me to Paris?"

Simon hesitated. "We spoke about you at the ABA. I'm sorry if you feel betrayed. She cares about you. So do I. We hate seeing you so devastated."

"Simon, you're such a busybody. Maybe I just need to lick my wounds alone in my lair."

"No, I'm with Jasmine on this one, Jude. The City of Light on midsummer night. What could be bad?"

After hanging up, Jude sat counting the bridges over the Seine, along which cars were crawling like lightning bugs on parade. Was Simon right? When Sandy died, Simon lay sobbing in Jude's arms all night long. For months afterward, he wandered New York like the soul of an unburied corpse, losing so much weight that he belted his jeans with an extension cord. Yet now, plump and jolly, he danced in Provincetown bars until dawn with handsome men, each younger and blonder than the last. He claimed he'd become a New Testament scholar, studying Matthew, Mark, Luke, and John at every opportunity.

She switched on the television to a movie featuring two French journalists, a man and a woman, in Naples to cover the drug trial of a mafioso. While threats were made against their lives, they gave each other *le regard* in every bistro in town, even though they were married to each other's cousins back in Paris. Every time one said, "This is impossible," they fell into each other's arms in a sixteenth-century pension and made mad passionate love while hit men lurked in the street below. But whenever one said, "I love you and want to spend the rest of my life with you," both leapt up, packed their bags, and raced out the door in opposite directions. In the end, the woman, a cool blonde who seemed the picture of wholesome propriety, turned out to be in league with the hit men. Dying from a gunshot wound as a result of her betrayal, the male reporter whispered to her with his last breath that he had never loved her so much as he did at that moment.

As the credits rolled, Jude realized that there was much that she didn't yet understand about her reading public.

CHAPTER

1 5

RIBBONS OF SUNLIGHT were weaving through a grid of holes in the white domed ceiling. The round table was crammed with salads, charcuterie, cheeses, baguettes, and bottles of mineral water. Jude was studying Martine, who was insisting to their assembled co-workers that desire by definition implied lack and therefore to consummate it was to destroy it. So appealing when Jude first saw her crossing Jasmine's lawn in her black silk jumpsuit and studded carbine belt, Martine was currently wearing a tiny navy-blue double-breasted pinstriped suit with a scarlet pocket handkerchief and wing-tip shoes.

Cecile, the new editor, who wore red-framed eyeglasses with tinted lenses the size of teacups, replied to Martine that no one truly possessed another. Even the merging during lovemaking was temporary and illusory. The unattainable, of necessity, always remained unattainable. So long as a single breath was left in the body, one was doomed to a desire without fulfillment. Or at least that seemed to be her line. Jude's grasp of French was modest even when someone wasn't speaking as fast as a tobacco auctioneer and with an intensity appropriate to the final stages of labor.

Martine curled her upper lip like Elvis Presley and called Cecile the French equivalent of scumbag of the Western world. If they'd been Southerners, Cecile would have pulled out a handgun and shot Martine at this point. Yet no one but Jude seemed alarmed, including Cecile herself. In fact, they all smiled faintly and ripped off chunks of baguette with renewed appetite, hurling crumbs around the room.

Jude tried to think of something supportive of Cecile to say in her fumbling French, having no idea whether she agreed with her or not. But Cecile was a newcomer, and this episode from the Spanish Inquisition seemed an unacceptable welcome.

Martine began talking about the role of the father in rupturing the mother-child fusion and his introduction of the child into the compensatory realm of the symbolic, in which fantasized images could substitute for the original lost love object. Although it sounded very much like the story of her own life, Jude realized that she had reached the outer limits of her French vocabulary. So she sat back and observed Martine's body language, which involved a stabbing index finger, karate chops with the side of her hand, pursed lips, and elaborate shoulder shrugs.

Simon had always presided over their work lunches in New York with his dry British wit, joking and gossiping and punning, humoring those gauche enough to argue until they stopped it. But the women in this office seemed to have elaborated argument into an art form. Jude was impressed, having herself been trained to be pleasant at any cost. "Smile, girls, smile!" Miss Melrose used to shriek, fluttering her Minnie Mouse eyelashes. "And if you don't feel it, fake it. The only thing a southern woman must never fake is her pearls."

Martine was now slashing and lunging at Cecile like Cyrano de Bergerac over something to do with the role of the Other as a tool for honing self-definition. She seemed to feel that you knew who you were by identifying who you weren't. Her dark eyes were blazing and her head was tossing like a horse on too tight a rein. She was gorgeous, even with a mouth like an Uzi. But she'd been avoiding Jude ever since Jude walked away from her on Jasmine's lawn, leaving rooms when Jude entered and pretending not to see her when they passed in the corridor. Jude wondered if she was supposed to be feeling *le manque*, which in a normal French person would apparently engender *le désir*.

Abruptly, the dispute concluded. Cecile and Martine appeared to have called a truce rather than reaching agreement. Cecile took a tiny mirror from her handbag and carefully applied enough scarlet lipstick to frost a cake. Everyone else lit a cigarette and relaxed into her chair, as though after inspired lovemaking. Martine offered Cecile a Gauloise, gazing into her eyes over the lighter. Cecile was now one of the gang. Jude's colleagues glanced at her, a deaf-mute cowboy Other with whom they were saddled because of some whim of Jasmine's.

"Alors, la première phase . . ." said Martine, exhaling a cloud of blue smoke. And everyone proceeded to deconstruct her argument with Cecile, like the instant replay of a football game.

Stubbing out their cigarettes, they stood up, dusted baguette crumbs off their laps, and headed for their offices, crunching across the carpet of crumbs as though over a plague of locusts. Martine glanced behind her as she exited in her fetching suit. To be sure that Jude was noticing that she wasn't noticing her? Jude did notice, but she found it irritating rather than alluring. Although she was beginning to wonder if the more unpleasant Martine was to her the more it meant that she liked her. Because the French seemed to thrive on contradiction. The oldest bridge in town was called the Pont Neuf.

Entering her office, Jude looked out the window and down an alley to the tumbled stone ruins of the Roman baths, sacked and burned by the barbarians in the third century. History Ph.D. manquée that she was, this city enchanted her. It was a *feuilleté* of superimposed civilizations—Gallic, Roman, Hun, Norman, Frank. Since her job required her to develop an understanding of French culture so that she would know which books to choose for translation, she'd hung a map of Paris the size of a bedspread across one wall. Accustomed to the rectangular blocks of New York City, she initially found a round city disturbing. But in time, she realized that there were thirty-six gates around the circumference. She decided to slice the *feuilleté*, hiking from one gate to its opposite in eighteen diameters, reading her guidebook before whatever landmarks she encountered, stopping at cafés for coffee when she got tired. She'd done this twice already, marking her meandering routes on the giant map with a red felt-tip pen. Each trip requiring a full afternoon, she'd put herself on a regimen of one per week. As a grand finale, she planned to walk the circumference of the city, then the smaller circles within, where previous town walls had stood. In six months' time, this map would resemble a giant red spiderweb.

Upon hearing Jude's plan, Jasmine had cocked her frosted head quizzically and said, "But this is insanity." She was probably right, but at least it was well-organized insanity.

Next door, Jude could hear Martine growling and snapping in a staccato phone conversation. Then a heavy object crashed against her wall. Jude got up and went to her doorway. Martine dashed out, slamming her door so hard that the entire wall shuddered.

The woman across the hall, a pleasant copper-haired secretary named Giselle, was also standing in her doorway, watching Martine careen down the corridor and out the entrance in her pinstriped suit, screaming, *"Merde!"*

Jude looked questioningly at Giselle.

"Her lover left her last month," Giselle explained. "Martine had a nervous breakdown and tried to kill herself. She is still very upset."

Jude returned to her desk feeling apologetic toward Martine. They had both just lost their lovers. No wonder their interactions with each other were so befuddled. She vowed to make more of an effort with her.

Since much of Jude's job involved reading manuscripts at her apartment or meeting with scouts and agents, she came and went as she pleased. As it was a beautiful sunny afternoon, she decided to undertake that week's requisite trek across Paris. This fieldwork was, after all, an important part of her job. So she took the Métro to Porte de Charenton and walked over to Porte de Bercy. From there, she headed up the Seine in the direction of Porte de Champerret, past docks and cranes, with a forest of glass-and-steel high-rises on her right and a jammed highway on her left, a panorama decidedly different from the ancient ruined splendor most people thought of as Paris.

As she walked, Jude pondered the notion of an encounter with the Other as a route to self-definition. It seemed pretty flimsy to know who you were only by knowing who you weren't. What would you do if you were alone in a cave?

Crossing the Pont Sully to Ile St. Louis, Jude strolled down a quiet street lined with elegant seventeenth-century stone town houses. Arriving at an ice cream parlor, she sat down in the sunshine at an outside table and ordered a dish of chocolate chip. As she waited, she read in her guidebook that this island had served as a medieval dueling field. And across the bridge in front of her was the house where Abélard had been castrated for love of Héloïse.

While she ate her ice cream, Jude gazed at Notre Dame, which crouched before her like a giant horned insect with flying-buttress limbs and compound eyes of stained glass. She kept glancing back and forth between the barbed spires straining toward heaven and the grotesque stone gargoyles, half dog and half dragon, that vomited rainwater off the roofs.

After paying her bill, Jude crossed the Pont St. Louis and wandered down the Quai aux Fleurs. As she passed the Tour de l'Horloge, from which a bell signaling the St. Bartholomew's Day Massacre had been rung, she paused to lean on the stone parapet of the Pont au Change, where hundreds of the butchered had been dumped into the Seine to drift downriver past the Louvre, trailing wakes of blood.

Jude arrived at the park at the tip of Ile de la Cité. Caressing couples sprawled on the benches and reclined along the stones shelves that sloped down to the river. Sitting on a green slatted bench, she tilted her head back and closed her eyes, the sunshine warming her face. Thrushes were chattering among the bushes of red roses, which were filling the air with their cloying sweetness. On the far shore, two dreadlocked black men were playing reggae on steel drums, while a *bateau mouche* swarming with camera-clicking tourists plowed the gray waters and doused the torrid lovers lying along the banks. As Jude watched them, she realized that she'd never before felt so lonely as here in this city where she and Anna had planned to commence their life together.

JUDE SANK DOWN in the chair by Anna's bedside and took one of her twitching hands. Earlier that week, Anna had slipped into a coma. Dusk was descending beyond the bouquets along the window ledge. Anna's room at the Roosevelt was on the fifth floor. Directly across the street was the condemned apartment building where Jude's parents had lived during her father's residency, its arched windows boarded up with warped plywood.

Turning from the window, Jude studied Anna's yellow face with its crescent eyebrows and cap of dark hair. She looked as though she was merely asleep and would wake up like Sleeping Beauty if Jude kissed her. Was Anna's collapse actually her fault, Jude wondered, for having ceased to love her? Had she felt Jude's withdrawal and gone on a terminal binge? But to be in such bad shape now, she must have been marinating herself for decades. All those nights when she had rolled out of Jude's arms to go home to Jim, she had actually been going home to her only real love—Smirnoff. But why? What secret pain did she carry inside herself that had to be so brutally anesthetized? What ancient horror was she trying to externalize by remaining with a man who beat her up and by trying to provoke a woman who adored her into doing the same? Jude searched the waxen mask of Anna's face as though it belonged to a stranger.

The door opened and Jim walked in, followed by a middle-aged man and woman Jude had never seen before. The woman had Anna's crescent eyebrows and raven hair. Jim, florid-faced and reeking of alcohol, looked at Jude with a flicker of recognition as she placed Anna's hand on the bedside and stood up.

"Hello," she said. "I'm Jude."

"Yes, I know," he said without enthusiasm. He gestured to the couple. "Stanley and Muriel Rivers. From Chicago. Muriel is Anna's sister." To them, he said, "This is Anna's editor."

Jude gazed at him coolly, wondering whether to wrangle with him over something that was drawing to a close in any case. "And her best friend," she added, feeling childish. But what she wanted to say was, "Listen, asshole, I've experienced aspects to Anna that you don't even know exist."

Grabbing her coat, she murmured, "I was just leaving." She watched Jim closely as he moved to Anna's bedside and looked down at her, swaying unsteadily. His salt-and-pepper hair was scrambled and his bushy sideburns needed a trim. She felt a certain reluctant kinship with him: Anna had been cheating on them both all these years, coupling with a lover with whose charms neither could ever have hoped to compete.

Suddenly, Jim buried his face in his hands and started sobbing. Muriel raced to his side and put her arms around him. As Jude watched, she felt her hands clench into fists, eager to wrap themselves around his throat. Was he upset because now he had no punching bag? He could move right into the role of grieving widower, and no one but Jude would know what a farce it was.

Out in the street, Jude stalked north up Broadway, gripped by rage—rage against Jim, but also rage against Anna and herself. Why had they lived a lie for so many years?

Entering the diner where she and Anna used to discuss Anna's anthology, she sat down at their usual granite-topped table by the window and ordered their usual Earl Grey tea. As she sipped it, she forced herself to confront the complications of what she'd imagined was her green paradise of childhood love revisited—the ways in which she'd blinded herself to Anna's desperate situation. The warning signals she had missed or ignored. Anna's complicity in Jim's cruelty; his, in her drinking; Jude's, in their ghastly marriage. Anna's and Jude's final months together had been like slicing open a fragrant pineapple from the tropics, only to find it dark brown and putrid at the core.

The apartment was dark and empty when Jude reached home. Simon was at his house on the Cape with two Dutch publishers. After hanging up her coat, Jude sat down on the living room couch. She remembered lying on that couch with Anna the first night they ever kissed, after weeks of titillating indecision. Apparently, this was the price you paid for a clandestine affair. When it was over, there was no one to turn to in your grief, no one to burden with all your touching memories. Simon, William, Sid, and a few others were the only ones who knew about Anna and herself. Everyone else regarded Simon and her as a couple, since they lived together. And Jude had arranged her life to exclude other confidants. She worked and spent time with Anna. That was all. She grabbed the phone.

"You sound awful, Jude," Aunt Audrey yelled while children fought in the background. "What's wrong, honey?"

"A friend of mine is very sick. Is my father there?"

When she described Anna's current condition, her father sighed and said, "I wish I could give you some hope, baby, but I can't."

"So she's dying?"

"I'm afraid so. And it's a horrible death. Especially for those who have to watch it."

Jude went completely numb. She felt no anger, no sadness, nothing at all.

"You and Anna are very close, aren't you?"

"Very." This was as near as she'd ever come to acknowledging the relationship to him. She wondered whether he got the picture. He'd met Anna only once, on a trip to New York to show Aunt Audrey and the children the sights. Jude had brought Anna to a chaotic family dinner at Mamma Leone's. Her father and Anna had had a chance to exchange very few words as the baby bopped Danny on the head with an asparagus spear, but Jude noticed them glancing at each other throughout the meal. Afterward, Anna said that she'd been impressed by his combination of kindness and strength. Kind men were often weak and strong men cruel, she said, but he seemed to combine the best qualities of both sexes. "He's what a man is supposed to be." At the time, Jude hadn't thought to wonder why, if Anna knew this, she stayed with a weak, cruel man.

296 LISA ALTHER •

"She seems like a lovely person."

"She is. I love her, Dad."

"Yes, I know," he said. "I'm sorry, baby. Life can be very unfair sometimes."

"Did I tell you she's at the Roosevelt?"

"No kidding."

"Her windows look out at the fifth floor of that apartment building where you and Mother used to live."

"My God," he said. "It's so strange, the way things recycle."

"Which apartment was yours?"

There was a long pause, during which Jude wondered whether he was upset or simply unable to remember. "The fifth, sixth, and seventh windows from the left," he replied in a strained voice. "Please give them my best regards."

A few nights later, Jude was sitting by Anna's bedside holding her hand, which had been bound to a splint with gauze so that she couldn't rip the scabs off her sores. The night nurse had apologetically explained that Anna was very willful about picking her scabs, even while unconscious, and that her wounds would barely clot now. Her sheets became blood-soaked and had to be changed constantly. Jude hated the idea of giving the already overextended nurses more work, but the splints appalled her and she was considering removing them. They reminded her of the metal mittens Victorian parents had put on their children's hands to prevent them from masturbating.

As she debated this issue, Jude studied Anna's face, still remarkably beautiful despite the puffiness and the mustard tint to the skin. It was so familiar. Jude's fingers and tongue must have stroked each ridge and hollow a thousand times.

Her mind finally relinquished its ethical struggle over the splints. Gradually, it quieted and cleared—until it felt like a high mountain lake reflecting the sky. And in that moment, Jude sensed the presence of Anna, as though Anna's heart had suddenly yawned open to receive her and enfold her in an embrace. And Jude knew in that instant that their love for each other hadn't vanished after all. It had just transformed itself, like water evaporating into mist. Apparently, there were detours to union that bypassed the flesh.

As this fugitive taste of connection faded, Jude sat there watching this woman she loved, this woman she now realized she would always love. But if Anna weren't dying, would she have been able to feel this? Jude wondered. Before Anna's collapse, they'd reached a dead end with each other. Was the essential ingredient for a graveyard love the grave?

Later that evening, as Jude sat by Anna's bedside marking a manuscript for the printers, she asked absently, "Would you like a Popsicle, my love?"

"Yes, please."

Jude looked at her. Her eyes were closed. Her body was still. "Anna, can you hear me?"

There was no response.

"If you can hear me, move your hand."

Not a muscle moved, except for Anna's mouth, which pursed to receive the Popsicle, like a newborn's mouth searching for the nipple.

"Anna," said Jude, just in case, "I want you to know that our time together has been the happiest in my life. And although I don't see right now how to go on without you, I don't regret a moment of it."

Anna's hand crept to her breast and used its splint to scrape off a scab. Blood welled up and ran like a freshet down her side, pooling inside her robe and soaking through to the clean white sheets.

"Goddamn it, Anna, stop that!" screamed Jude, grabbing the hand. She burst into tears. "Please talk to me. For one last time before you go."

Anna's eyes remained closed, her lips puckered for more Popsicle.

Jude pictured Sandy, inert in his hospital bed, his teeth shattered. And Molly on her stretcher, head stitched like a softball, face the purple of a smashed plum. And herself at her mother's bedside all those years ago, singing "Rise, Shine, Give God His Glory." When her mother refused to wake up, Jude began yelling the lyrics right into her ear—until her father had to pick her up and carry her into the hallway as she still sobbed that stupid, hopeless hymn.

CHAPTER

16

JASMINE'S OFFICE was furnished very differently from her antiques-crammed, crusader-haunted living quarters several blocks away. The house was dark and muffled, but the office featured gleaming chrome, black leather upholstery, and the latest in office equipment. Jude had been describing an American novel she thought Jasmine should buy, concerning a love affair between two nurses.

"Ordinary women living ordinary lives, women who happen to love each other," said Jude, semireclining before Jasmine's desk in a designer dental chair.

"But it is too long," said Jasmine. "And it would increase a third in translation. And it is too boring—going to work, shopping, cooking dinner, helping children with schoolwork. Our readers are interested in the chase, not the collapse into tedium that follows."

"But that's life."

"Your life perhaps. Because you do not know how to play."

Jude smiled. She hadn't picked a book yet that appealed to Jasmine. She couldn't imagine why Jasmine continued to pay her salary.

Jasmine's door hurtled open and a young man marched in without knocking. He had a handsome, pouty face with high cheekbones, a wide forehead, and a navy-blue five o'clock shadow.

"Ah, Robert," said Jasmine, half-rising, evidently taken aback.

Robert glared at her, then at Jude. He was wearing baggy pleated trousers, a long-sleeved rayon shirt buttoned at the throat, and pointy-toed basket-weave shoes. Fag shoes, Simon would have called them. His black hair was spiky on top and long in back, and a tiny gold hoop was dangling from one earlobe. Without taking his dark, wounded eyes off Jasmine, he sank uninvited into a chrome-and-leather chair, hands resting on his knees.

They sat in silence, Jude waiting for Jasmine to introduce her. He was young. Could he be her son? Jude had no idea how old Jasmine was or if she even had children. She had the beginnings of that parenthesis people got around their mouths as they approached fifty, which made their chins look hinged like Charlie McCarthy's. But if she'd had a face-lift, this process would have been forestalled. Yet her body was as taut and shapely as a thirty-year-old's.

Robert was furious with Jasmine, his eyebrows meeting in the center in a deep frown. And it was clear that he didn't care for Jude, either. What wasn't clear was why not, since he'd never before laid eyes on her, so far as she knew.

Maybe he was Jasmine's lover. Despite Simon's belief that she had a husband stashed away somewhere, Jude had concluded that Jasmine liked women, having mostly seen her surrounded by devoted female employees. Yet if Jasmine had in fact come on to her that night when Jude dined with her—which she wouldn't have sworn to—Jude had turned her down. She was no threat to Robert. So why was he glaring at her as though she'd opened the oven on his soufflé?

"Do you work in publishing, too?" Jude finally asked him.

"Don't ask me what work I do. All Americans ask that."

"What should I ask instead?"

He sighed. "Why not ask, for example, if I am *sportif*?"

"Okay. Are you sportif, Robert?"

Jasmine smiled.

Robert spat air through loose lips. "I am not obliged to answer such a stupid question."

Jude shrugged. She had merely been trying to stave off homicide. She sat in silence, staring at a yellowed photo of a young man with Jasmine's hooded eyelids that was in an antique silver frame on the bookshelf. Jasmine's friends and colleagues displayed the most intriguing mix of impeccable manners and breathtaking rudeness. She wished she was back in New York playing "Indiana Jones and the Lost Temple of Atlantis" on her computer at work.

Finally, Robert stood up and strode from the room without looking back.

"So who's Robert?" Jude asked.

Jasmine waved her multiringed hand as though shooing an annoying fly. Once Jude had finally summoned the courage to ask her some personal questions, she had discovered that Jasmine never answered them, anyway.

Jasmine resumed her discussion of why nurse novels wouldn't sell in Paris. Jude was getting the impression that her readers regarded life as a cross between a Greek tragedy and a Harlequin romance— all storm and betrayal and suffering. Probably Jude would have, too, if she'd grown up in a country that had been invaded by marauders from every direction throughout recorded history, instead of one founded by madcap dreamers who believed you could pack up your sorrows and hop the next ship for the promised land.

Her eyes kept returning to the photo on Jasmine's desk. The young man looked a lot like Jasmine.

"My brother," she said, noticing that Jude wasn't paying attention to her discourse on the limitations of realism in fiction.

"You look very much alike."

"So I'm told. But he is dead now. Tortured and shot by the Germans. He was a messenger for the Resistance. Fifteen years old. I was ten. I thought I would die, too, because I adored him so much. But I didn't."

Jude looked at her with new interest. This might be the first real thing Jasmine had ever said to her. She seemed embarrassed, exhaling a cloud of cigarette smoke like an octopus spewing ink in a predator's face.

Quickly, Jasmine asked about Anna's poetry anthologies. She had decided to try one for French schoolgirls, feeling they might take themselves more seriously as writers if they received that kind of confirmation at an age before hormones fogged their brains. Jude agreed to organize one but expressed doubt about whether her French was up to the job of dealing with the schools.

"Martine can help you."

Jude nodded cautiously.

"It will give you a chance to get to know her," she said, looking at Jude from beneath her hooded eyelids. "She is a marvelous lover."

"I'm sure she is," muttered Jude, wondering how Jasmine knew this. "But I'm not really interested in a new lover right now."

"What *are* you interested in?" asked Jasmine irritably, a repeatedly thwarted Aphrodite.

"My job. Paris. The French."

"If you wish to understand the French, you must take a French lover. It would expand your vocabulary as well."

Jude laughed. "You make it sound like a self-improvement course."

"It would be, I assure you."

The door opened again, and Martine walked in carrying a shopping bag that was almost dragging the floor. Her shiny, chin-length auburn hair was parted in the middle and layered at the nape of her neck. Her huge dark eyes, like licorice throat lozenges, were ringed with kohl, giving her a bruised urchin look. Beneath her navy-blue silk suit, she wore an ivory silk blouse, which was unbuttoned to reveal a lacy camisole.

It was a Saturday, so Jude was wearing blue jeans, a Big Apple T-shirt, and cowboy boots with silver toe guards. She hadn't expected anyone to be at the office when she stopped by to leave off some memos en route to a hike across Paris. Already weary of the daily fashion parade at the office, whose corridors functioned like a couturier's runway, she cherished her collapse into dishabille on weekends.

"Ah, Martine," said Jasmine. "We were just speaking of you."

Martine nodded to Jude, but her eyes never left Jasmine's.

"Did you know that Martine also writes poetry?" Jasmine asked Jude.

Jude shook her head no.

"Martine, get your last book off my shelf and sign it for Jude."

Martine did so. Then she handed Jude the book, still not looking at her. Flipping it open, Jude read an obscure inscription about secrets between them that awaited revelation.

"*Merci beaucoup,*" she said to Martine, who nodded, still looking at Jasmine.

"So what have you bought?" Jasmine asked her.

"A skirt," she replied in a small voice. "And a blazer. A dress and some boots."

"Very good. But you must try them on for us."

Martine disappeared into the next room.

"She is a very gifted poet," said Jasmine.

"I look forward to reading her book," said Jude, in fact dreading it because all poetry reminded her of Anna.

"They are love poems. To her last lover, who has now left her."

Jasmine gave Jude a look loaded with meaning. But what meaning? She wished Jasmine would just back off and let her pick her own poison. She couldn't love on command.

Martine reappeared in a mauve chiffon skirt, the silk blouse, and the camisole. Watching her, Jude wondered how she'd tried to kill herself. There were no scars on her wrists or rope burns at her throat. Pills probably. Someone as fastidious as Martine wouldn't use anything so messy as a gun or a knife. Jude was impressed by the purity of her response to lost love.

Jasmine was studying Martine's flawless physique. "Yes, lovely. But the blouse—no. Take it off."

Martine unbuttoned the silk shirt and let it waft to the floor like an apple blossom on a spring zephyr. She stood there in the camisole, her shoulders and upper chest goose-bumped, whether from cold or excitement Jude couldn't have said.

"And now the blazer," said Jasmine in a low voice.

Martine picked up the cream-colored cashmere blazer and slipped it on over the camisole.

"No," announced Jasmine. "*Absolument pas*. Not with the camisole. Take it off."

Martine removed the jacket and folded it carefully across the back of a chair. Then she shrugged off the camisole, revealing high, firm breasts with small, stiffening nipples. Putting the jacket back on, she buttoned it, leaving a pale canyon of flesh down the middle of her torso, breasts rising up on either side like rounded mesas.

"Magnificent," murmured Jasmine, eyes locked with Martine's. "But now try the dress."

Martine glided into the next room. While they watched, she let her skirt drop slowly to the floor. Then she bent over to remove the boots from their box, and Jude glimpsed in the grid of shadows cast by the blinds smooth black-silk bikini briefs, a garter belt, and black-stockinged legs in high-heeled pumps.

Martine kicked off her shoes and drew on the boots, which had spike heels and rose up above her knees. After letting the black knit dress fall down over her admirable lingerie, she walked toward Jude and Jasmine, a slit up the front of the ankle-length skirt displaying and then concealing the high black boots and dark-stockinged thighs.

Jude realized that Jasmine was now watching her. Evidently, the next move in this game was up to her, but she didn't know what it was supposed to be. Martine still hadn't looked her way. She continued to gaze at Jasmine. She seemed afraid. Jasmine had been exercising some sort of dressage on her, and on Jude—spurring their desire, then reining it in. Should she leave? Jude wondered. Were Martine and Jasmine lovers? If so, what did Jasmine want Jude's role to be? What did Martine want? She recalled Jasmine's attitude toward the apricot tarts in Frankfurt. Was Martine the dessert du jour that one savored without touching? Jude was a guest wandering in this foreign land. She wanted to do the appropriate thing, but what was it?

"Where did you buy them?" Jude finally asked.

There was a long silence.

"It is not important," murmured Martine, finally looking at Jude, irritated.

Jasmine sighed like a teacher with a slow pupil.

Jude recalled that she was an orphan raised by wolves. Her family coat-of-arms read: "When in doubt, get the hell out." She struggled up from her chrome-and-leather reclining chair.

"I'd better get going," said Jude, pulling on her Levi's jacket. "Miles to go before I sleep and all that."

Jasmine smiled, perhaps challenged by Jude's seeming indifference. Maybe she imagined that Jude was finally learning to play. But all Jude really knew how to do when faced with a situation that smacked of sadism was to flee, as her forebears had. One day, maybe she'd stick around to explore her own capacity for the dark, but at the moment all she wanted was a cheeseburger.

As the Métro clattered toward Porte des Lilas, Jude contemplated the concept of lovemaking as blood sport. Anna and she had approached it as a mystic rite. They had ascended from this vale of tears for hours at a time. The stimulation of the hunt, or spiritual transfiguration—which was its proper goal?

At the far end of the car, Jude heard a man singing an interesting jazz version of "Desperado" in a Georgia accent, accompanied by a guitar and harmonica. Leaning forward, she saw that the ponytailed young man wore a Stetson and cowboy boots. His harmonica was fastened to a frame around his neck so that he could alternate between it and his voice. As he strolled up the aisle collecting change, she handed him some centimes. The car pulled into a station and the door hissed open.

"Have un bon weekend, y'all," he called to the passengers as he stepped onto the platform. Noticing Jude's silver toe guards, he pointed to them, then gave her a thumbs-up signal. Two southern cowboys riding the Paris range. Jude smiled at him as the door slid shut and the car whisked her out of his life, presumably forever.

Getting out at Porte des Lilas, Jude walked west until she came to a Burger King disguised as a bistro. Inside, she ordered a Whopper with cheese, fries, and a Coke, sop to her sudden homesickness. When the man behind the counter handed her the tray, he said, "Bon appetit, madame!"

As she munched her greasy fries under the awning along the pavement, Jude pictured Martine in her camisole, flesh riddled with goose bumps, eyes riveted on Jasmine's. What had that been all about, anyway? Martine had been trying to please Jasmine, who was her boss and maybe her lover. Jude had been trying to keep her job and be a polite guest. But what had Jasmine been doing? She appeared to be teasing Jude—or testing her. Did she want to help Jude and Martine in their grief or merely manipulate them for her own inscrutable purposes? Or was it all a friendly romp, intended to welcome the new kid to the neighborhood? She realized she was bowling out of her league with these complicated women.

Back in Montmartre, Jude went into her neighborhood patisserie to buy herself a reward for the completion of walk number four.

"I would like a tart," she told the man behind the counter in French, rhyming *tarte* with *rat* and clearing her throat in the middle to indicate the *r*. She'd been practicing this alone in her apartment and felt she'd finally mastered it.

"*Une quoi?*" asked the man, looking at her as though she were a litter box that needed cleaning.

"*Une tarte,*" she repeated, drawing back the corners of her mouth as though playing an oboe and exaggerating the gurgle.

"*Ah,*" he said, "*une tarte?*"

To Jude, this sounded identical to what she'd just said. "*Oui, une tarte.*"

"*Mais, bien sûr. Une tarte.*" His *r* was the growl of a puppy at play. "What kind of tart?"

"*Poire,*" she growled back.

"*Poire,*" he corrected.

She had wanted a tart, not a language lesson. "*S'il vous plaît,*" she said, accepting defeat.

Exhausted, Jude dragged herself up the six spiral flights of steps to her apartment. Throwing open the glass doors, she gasped the fresh air, free of exhaust fumes that high up. It was starting to rain. A sullen black cloud was almost obscuring the Eiffel Tower.

As she placed her pear tart on a plate and took a fork from the drawer, Jude decided to watch "*La Classe*" on television. Every evening, a schoolroom of famous French comics did send-ups of everything their fellow citizens held sacred. Jude plopped down on the couch and switched on the TV with the remote control. A comedian dressed as a matador was sitting on a stool, playing a guitar and singing a mournful ballad. The refrain was, "My bull is dead./I killed him this afternoon./Now I'm alone and, oh, so blue."

Another comedian appeared, dressed in the ruffled skirt and busty peasant top of a female flamenco dancer. He began to clack his heels and castinets with dignified restraint, giving the matador smoldering over-the-shoulder glances. Gradually, both sped up, trying to outdo each other, until they were in a frenzy over the dead bull, the matador strumming frantically and the dancer whirling around the stage like a clattering Valkyrie. The teacher and the class were in hysterics.

Nuking the program with her remote control, Jude sat there holding her empty plate and realizing that that afternoon at the office, Jasmine and Martine had spread out an entire smorgasbord of sensual delights to lure her back from the graveside. But she had departed without even sampling the finger foods. She was like a starving dog who snapped at every hand that offered her food. She had been very rude, and she probably owed Jasmine an apology.

Reaching over to the end table, she picked up Martine's book. Its white paper cover bore the title *Le Coeur Sauvage* in dark red letters. Flipping it open, she reread Martine's mystifying inscription: "With the hope of one day exploring the secret passages and chambers between us that remain to be revealed."

Jude decided to invite her to lunch. Martine was beautiful and intelligent. Jude admired her wardrobe and her physique. Although they'd gotten off to a bad start, it sounded as though the interest might still be mutual. They were both in mourning. If they could just get out from under Jasmine's surveillance, maybe they could help each other rejoin the ranks of the living.

As the phone purred, Jude remembered it was Saturday night. If Martine answered, it would mean that she was as alone and lonely as Jude.

"*Allo?*" She sounded drunk or drugged or sleepy.

"Hi. It's Jude. From the office."

"*Oui?*" She sounded deeply uninterested.

"Uh, I wondered if you'd like to have lunch with me tomorrow."

There was a long silence. Jude could hear some voices in the background. But if Martine was entertaining, would she have answered the phone?

"*Pourquoi pas.*"

"Great. When and where?"

She suggested a brasserie called Le Vrai Paris near her apartment south of the Luxembourg Gardens at about one o'clock.

"I'll look forward to it," said Jude.

"*Et moi, aussi. A très bientôt.*"

Her voice had warmed up as the conversation progressed, and by the end she had sounded downright pleased. Jude sat back in her chair, smiling thoughtfully. Lightning had begun to lash the monuments of Paris, and thunder was rumbling in the Bois de Vincennes. God moving furniture, Molly used to say. Jude felt happy for the first time in months. She would cook Martine nice meals and serve them on the table by the window, with the lights of Paris flickering below. She would cheer Martine up, help her feel alive and attractive again. And Martine could do the same for her.

JUDE SAT IN LE VRAI PARIS watching people come and go. Martine was an hour and a half late. Jude had spilled kir on her white jeans, and her hair was kinking as last night's rain evaporated in the hot afternoon sun. She went to the bathroom and struggled hopelessly with her unwanted curls. Then she phoned Martine for the third time. But there was still no answer.

In an upstairs room, accordion renditions of French dance-hall tunes were pouring out the open windows into the street. After each number, people stamped and cheered, making Le Vrai Paris sound like a happening kind of place. But Jude had been there long enough to hear the songs recycle a couple of times and to realize that it was a tape.

Returning to her table, Jude ordered another kir from the burly barman and watched the TV above his head. A matador in Nîmes was plunging his sword into a bull's neck. The snorting bull sank slowly to his knees in the swirling Midi dust. An instant replay in slow motion showed the pass with the muleta that preceded the coup de grâce. Contorting his torso and gesturing with his arms, the commentator critiqued the angle of the matador's shoulder in relation to the horns.

The bull, soaked in blood and coated with flies, was dragged from the arena on a sledge pulled by horses. Then the next bull entered, outraged and defiant, immediately charging the waving red cape. Jude was rooting for the bull. But he was the only one in France not to realize that he didn't have a prayer. The picador leaned over from his horse to plunge his spike between the bull's shoulder blades. He worked the lance up and down like a lover.

Jude realized that not only was her hair a disaster; she'd also been stood up. But why? Paying her bill, she wandered out onto the sidewalk in her stained jeans. An American in a DON'T FOLLOW ME. I'M LOST T-shirt collared Jude to ask the way to Notre Dame, which he pronounced like the American university.

Too distressed to deal with directions, she said, *"Je ne sais pas. Je suis Cherokee."*

He looked at her and crossed the street.

Jude went into a *tabac* on the next block and bought some Marlboro Lights. Leaning in a doorway in the sun, she lit a cigarette and wondered what to do next, taking the pulse of her emotions like a doctor by a deathbed. She didn't want to go back to her empty apartment. She hadn't felt its emptiness until last night, when she had allowed herself to imagine Martine there with her. Her overzealous imagination had deformed the reality of the situation. Martine was evidently like an overcooked meringue—luscious on the surface but hard as nails beneath.

Eventually, Jude noticed half a dozen coral roses thrust through a metal ring that hung from the stone molding beside the door. Above it was a plaque that read: *"Ici est tombé le 22 juillet 1943 Pierre Beaulieu, combattant pour la liberation de la France."* The stone all around the doorway was chipped and pocked. A Resistance fighter had been gunned down where Jude was now standing. She imagined him dropping to his knees, riddled like a Gruyère with bullet holes, pavement and doorway splattered with blood. . . .

Jude stamped out her cigarette. Since her calf muscles were aching badly from yesterday's crosstown trek, she couldn't undertake another. She decided to head home. Maybe stop off at a movie or phone Simon at his house on the Cape.

Wandering across the Seine toward Montmartre, she passed the spot where the grand master of the Knights Templars had been burned at the stake after seven years of torture. She followed the route alongside the river taken by the rubbish carts that had carried Marie Antoinette and Louis XVI to the guillotine. Then she crossed the Place de la Concorde, where the vast crowds had assembled to witness the beheadings.

Strolling along the boulevard past the Madeleine, she arrived at a café with a scarlet awning: L'Élite. Pausing, she studied the customers sitting in bow-backed basket chairs at small, round tables along the pavement. They were surrounded by ancient killing fields. Yet there they sat, laughing and eating and drinking, smoking and flirting. Like Jasmine, they seemed to know how to enjoy life, despite its legacy of horror and its inevitable end.

All of a sudden, Jude understood that she had been drawn to Paris in the first place in order to learn this art. But she'd been fighting it off, like a bat who prefers the dark to the light of day, insisting on doing everything in ways that were already familiar to her. Martine was right to have stood her up today. Jude was the neophyte here. It was up to her to figure out how to fit in. It wasn't necessary that she understand what was going on in order to participate.

As she turned the corner toward l'Opéra, Jude caught a glimpse of the white domes of Sacré Coeur floating above the dance halls and leather shops of Pigalle, shimmering in the afternoon heat like a mirage of the Holy City in a desert.

THE NEXT MORNING, JUDE was awakened from a dreamless sleep by a cavalry of cooing pigeons charging across her skylight, their claws skittering down the glass. Daylight was pouring through her doors. Getting up, she threw them open. Swallows swooped and dipped in the fresh morning air all around her. The pewter rooftops of Paris, washed clean by a rainstorm in the night, were gleaming silver, rows of red-tile chimney flues stretching across them like crenellated ruins. Five women in flowing robes stood behind curly iron grilles at open doors on different floors across the courtyard, conjuring the golden ball of sun in the east like a coven of pagan priestesses.

CHAPTER
17

JUDE WAS LYING NAKED on her living-room carpet in the sunlight streaming through the open doors. Propped up on cushions like a pasha, she was smoking a miniature Dutch cigar and drinking a foamy glass of Michelob. The phone rang, destroying her fantasy that she was on the beach at Cannes, about to be discovered by a major Hollywood director.

It was Jasmine, inviting her to a strip club that night. Jude hesitated. A burlesque show seemed a questionable way for alleged feminists to spend their time. Once in New York with Sandy and Simon, she'd watched the disheartening bumping and grinding of gaunt heroin addicts, and she'd left feeling embarrassed and full of pity.

"You must come," said Jasmine. "It will amuse you."

Since she was Jude's boss and both these sentences sounded like commands, Jude accepted. Besides, her current self-imposed assignment was simply to observe the Parisians at play, like a kitten learning from a cat how to lap milk. Out her doors, she could see two pigeons balancing on either end of a television antenna, carefully seesawing up and down. Even the pigeons here knew how to have fun.

JUDE WAS STANDING on the sidewalk when Jasmine's Citroën pulled up. Jasmine climbed out, resplendent in electric-blue silk that molded her admirable curves. Behind her exited a man with lots of silver hair and piercing umber eyes.

"Jude, allow me to present my husband, Philippe," said Jasmine. "Philippe, this is my remarkable young American editor."

"Enchanted," he said, holding Jude's outstretched hand in both of his. He was wearing a cream-colored double-breasted suit, with a tie and pocket handkerchief in shades of salmon and indigo.

Jude was speechless at the appearance of yet another character from Jasmine's personal soap opera. It was getting as complicated as "The Young and the Restless." Martine and Robert had also just gotten out, both greeting her with all the enthusiasm of a woman discovering a run in her stockings. Martine was wearing a size six Hell's Angels outfit—black leather miniskirt, net stockings and ankle boots with spike heels, and a miniature motorcycle jacket with so many snaps and zippers that a team of assistants would have been required to fasten them. Behind her stood a fair, slight young man with the face of an aging altar boy. His name turned out to be Jean-Claude.

Since Martine had never mentioned their date manqué at Le Vrai Paris, Jude finally asked her one day at the office what had happened. She pursed her lips, shrugged, and said that she had run into a friend. They had stopped for an espresso. Then she found it was too late to meet Jude, so she went to visit someone else. She neither apologized nor suggested a new rendezvous, so Jude let it drop. If this was how things were done in Paris, she was now pledged to accept it without complaint. Though she couldn't help but wonder if Martine had planned to stand her up from the start to teach Jude not to trifle with her. But Jude hadn't been trifling. In fact, she'd been trying not to trifle. But maybe Martine liked trifling and had become alarmed when Jude wanted lunch as well.

Nevertheless, Martine and Jude now comprised an efficient team for dealing with nuns, headmistresses, and teachers regarding their student-poetry anthology. Although as they strolled across town to these meetings, Jude couldn't help but notice that she was the only woman in Paris whose arm Martine didn't take as she walked. She had decided that Martine wasn't avoiding and insulting her in order to provoke *le désir*. She simply didn't like her.

A tuxedoed maître d', whose brilliantined hair was combed straight back off his forehead like a mobster's, escorted them into a room with crimson wallpaper and carpeting. Jasmine alternated them boy-girl in the velvet seats circling the round table. Many others in the room appeared to be Japanese and American businessmen, with and without dates or spouses.

The waiter brought champagne in a silver ice bucket and filled their glasses as they discussed Jude's tan. Evidently, she wasn't the first in Paris to discover the delights of sunbathing on her living-room floor. There was already a ground fog of cigarette smoke in the room, so they passed out Gitanes and lit up all around.

The stage was flanked by statues of two giant female nudes. As the glittery sequined curtain between them rose, a dozen women appeared in Beefeater hats, garter belts and net stockings, black boots, and nothing else. They marched and saluted mechanically to the tune of ''Rule Britannia.''

From the corner of her eye, Jude watched Jasmine, with Philippe on one side and Robert on the other, as respectable-appearing as any fashionable Parisian matron. For all Jude knew, she was one. She looked amused as the women goose-stepped on their lovely long legs. Jude felt something, but it wasn't amusement. For one thing, she wasn't sure she enjoyed seeing other women objectified like this for the delectation of a roomful of horny businessmen.

The Beefeaters exited and the curtain came down. When it lifted again, clouds of orange smoke were rising like mist from the stage floor. A woman in a plumed Athena helmet with narrow gold tubing around her neck and waist performed what looked like a sacred temple dance, her feet planted and knees flexed. Her upraised arms were squared at the elbows, and her torso was swaying and whipping, like a cypress in a hurricane, to jarring, clashing sitar music.

The lights went out and when they came back on, there were four dancers in Athena helmets. Each time the stage darkened and the lights returned, there would be a different number of Athenas lashing and writhing in the swirling mists in their plumed gold helmets. Just as they began to seem interchangeable and eternal—the female essence embodied—the curtain came down.

As it rose again, a bald man in camouflage gear with a huge beer belly marched out. He had rifles, machine guns, and pistols slung all over him. In an Indiana accent, he told a very boring battle story that involved artillery fire and fighter planes, which he imitated with his mouth. Everyone in the audience began to laugh uproariously at all this testosterone run amuck, startled by the contrast to the intoxicating sensuality of the Athenas.

The curtain came crashing down like a guillotine blade on this overweight warrior. A few moments later, it lifted and a woman with a dark ponytail cascading over her shoulders was slithering like a python around a large, red, neon hoop, to the accompaniment of eerie harp music. Her pale body was bathed in swirling rainbow spotlights: long legs, finely muscled arms and shoulders, full, tight breasts, a narrow waist tapering into firm, boyish buttocks. The pulsing lights were making dizzy hallucinogenic patterns across her flesh as she wound in and out around the hoop and slowly splayed her perfect naked limbs in shifting geometric patterns across its disk.

Jude watched, transfixed. This performance was probably politically reprehensible, but it was the most erotic thing she'd ever seen. For the first time since her months of watching Anna decay in her hospital bed, Jude's palms turned clammy. Here was a woman who could teach her how to enjoy life again.

Through the shifting veils of cigarette smoke, Jude spotted Martine's hand caressing Robert's forearm. Her eyes shifted ever so slightly in Jude's direction.

Just as the entire audience was beginning to hyperventilate, the ponytailed woman vanished. And then the other women emerged from backstage, floating one by one across the stage on a conveyor belt. They wore headdresses with tresses of golden coins, and they were striking the poses of flexing Greek athletes.

To the strains of a Chopin funeral march, six of the women strode off the belt and through a poison-green neon tube out front, which was bent into the shape of a large coffin. Forming three couples along the front lip of the stage, they performed stylized love play, never touching, hands molding and caressing the air beside a breast or a buttock, hips slowly swiveling closer and closer but never meeting.

The conveyor belt continued to carry the other posing and preening women across the stage in front of the backdrop. And the neon coffin stood there changing colors, trying to assert its dominance. But it was unable to distract the audience's attention from the magnificent women out front as three of them knelt before the dark pubic triangles of their partners. Each slid an arm between her partner's legs to clasp a buttock and draw her closer. And the lights faded discreetly away.

These young women were not sad sacks like the New York

burlesque queens, Jude reflected. They were temple prostitutes, pet-
ulant goddesses, self-sufficient and aloof and unattainable. Like master
electricians, they themselves were in charge of the currents of desire
sweeping the audience, stepping up the voltage, then pulling the plug.
The lesser mortals in the audience were here to worship their beauty,
which was immortal, even if the bearers of it were not. And like true
goddesses, they were mocking the audience for giving them the homage they demanded, an homage that would never be rewarded with
anything more than amused scorn. This was a form of femininity Jude
knew nothing about, one that must have prevailed when the race
began, in the days when the female body was revered as the source
of all life.

She smiled, at last getting the sobering joke. The women were
now back on stage in their Beefeater hats. The eyes of the woman
with the dark ponytail seemed to meet Jude's for a moment, before
looking right through her. They fell into formation and tottered off-
stage like windup toys to a cacophony of "Stars and Stripes Forever,"
"God Save the Queen," and "The Marseillaise." This was their final
comment on male martiality, in pathetic bumbling contrast to their
own insolent, indolent sensuality.

Jude's group drifted up the sidewalk toward the Champs Elysées.
Jasmine was holding Martine's arm, and Philippe was stroking John-
Claude's nearly beardless cheek as he whispered something in his ear.
Robert ambled alongside Jude in silence, like a tamed bear. They sat
down around a table on the terrace of a restaurant with a front-row
view of the Arc de Triomphe. Philippe ordered more champagne and
a platter of shellfish, which arrived packed in enough crushed ice to
chill a corpse. They employed implements worthy of the Inquisition
to drag the only half-dead sea creatures from their elaborate armor.

As the others discussed the performance, Jude looked back and
forth between Jasmine and Martine. Not only were they elegant and

seductive; they were smart. Jude now understood that Paris was perhaps the last outpost of matriarchy on earth. Everywhere she went— the Luxembourg Gardens, the Tuileries, the facade of the Hôtel de Ville, the Place de la Concorde, l'Opéra—there were statues of women, naked and robed, queens and goddesses, priestesses and saints. She thought about the Provençal courts of love in the twelfth century, where flocks of pages had devoted themselves to the grandes dames *sans merci*, and the Paris salons in the eighteenth and nineteenth centuries, which had destroyed careers and toppled governments. Where else in the world were women both outspokenly female and completely in charge?

Tuning into the conversation, Jude discovered that Robert was accusing the strip club of nationalizing eroticism, domesticating it for consumption by tourists, like the Hawaiian hula.

"And why not?" demanded Jean-Claude, who Jude had learned was a medical doctor just back from a famine relief project in the sub-Sahara. "If others are exotic to us, why should we resent being exotic to them? We are not, after all, the master race."

The point, according to Robert, was that the tourists weren't being exposed to the real thing. Tonight's show was like an innoculation against some deadly local plague. The tourists were being given a minute dose of eroticism in a safe setting by indifferent professionals. Afterward, they could go home to Iowa thinking they'd experienced all that Paris had to offer.

Jude was discouraged to realize that she'd missed the point. But she was still wrapped in a haze of eroticism, and it didn't feel like a minute dose. In fact, she couldn't seem to get rid of the image of that woman with the ponytail splaying her perfect limbs across the neon disk in the swirls of rainbow light.

Martine had been studying Robert speculatively. Finally, she said, "Yet you are not the first to have said this, Robert. Barthes calls such shows 'the theater of fear.' He says we display the evils of the flesh in order to exorcise them. Not for tourists, for ourselves. We wish to convert the female body into a household property/propriety."

Robert looked caught out, struggling with himself over whether it was less cool to have plagiarized from Barthes or to claim never to have read him.

"I believe some of us did not find the performance unmoving," said Jasmine. "Me, for example. And you, Jude. What did you think of it?"

Jude struggled to translate her complicated thoughts into her rudimentary French. She ended up saying only that she had found it magnificent. She realized that she had no personality in French. No wonder Martine always acted so bored by her. She was, and who could blame her?

Philippe observed with a smile that French men were good sports to put up with their peevish female consorts, who demanded deference as their right yet mocked their men's little foibles mercilessly.

Jean-Claude remarked sotto voce that perhaps that was why he saw so many men in wedding bands at Le Trap. Jude gathered Le Trap was a gay bar, and she was beginning to suspect from the way they looked at each other that Philippe and Jean-Claude were lovers.

Jasmine said that unfortunately the cunning little foibles of the male were going to destroy life on this earth, or at least render it unbearable.

With regard to male foibles, they began discussing whether passion and domestic affection were incompatible. They reminded Jude of dragonflies, alighting on a topic for a shimmering moment, then darting off to the next, so inexplicably that she could scarcely keep up, much less join in.

"Within a marriage," Philippe was saying with a wry smile at Jasmine, "lovemaking becomes an expectation and a duty. Once it is no longer a free choice, it ceases by definition to be passion. And you can be sure—"

"So you are saying," interrupted Martine, "that duty is rational and passion—"

"Yet a slave might passionately—" interjected Robert.

The three were now holding forth all at once, none listening to the others. In addition, they were speaking so fast and using so much slang that Jude couldn't follow anyone. So she looked back and forth among them in the din. Philippe was Domestic Affection for Jasmine, but who was Passion? All perhaps. Probably not Jean-Claude, but who knew?

Someone's knee was pressing hers under the table. Whether deliberately or not, she couldn't tell. She glanced at all the faces but uncovered no clues. She had no idea who was what to whom here.

Suddenly, Robert was yelling at Martine that whatever controlled restricted. And whatever restricted was tyrannical. And whatever was tyrannical was fascist. That language itself controlled and restricted and therefore was fascist.

"*Ah non,*" murmured Martine. "To label is to unmask, and to unmask is to alter."

"To label is to limit," insisted Robert, "and to limit is to destroy."

Jude suddenly had the feeling neither cared all that much about labels. They had just picked opposite sides for the pleasure of the clash.

"*Donc,* if language is fascist," replied Martine, blowing smoke in Robert's face, "you, who talk so much and all the time, are fascist, *n'est-ce pas?*"

Robert erupted into hysteria. Jude realized she was witnessing the famous *furia francese,* the French fury, the sudden frenzy that used to possess French warriors on medieval battlefields, terrifying their more laid-back Italian opponents. But Martine merely gazed at him with ennui. She would definitely have flunked Charm Class.

Behind Martine's auburn head loomed the Arc de Triomphe. Thirty years before, the aunts and mothers and grandmothers of Jude's companions at this table, their men having been slaughtered on battlefields to the north, had silently lined this sidewalk to watch the precision rape of their beautiful city. The Nazis had tromped through the Arc de Triomphe with their rifles and jeeps and tanks and horses in a shimmering haze of dust and exhaust fumes. But then, with small daily humiliations, the women of Paris had made the Germans regret that they'd ever left Prussia.

Jean-Claude had somehow managed to capture the floor, regardless of his faint voice. He was summarizing Stendhal's discourse on the different types of love and the different stages of each type. His comments had something or other to do with the relevance or irrelevance of labels in the face of a lived passion.

As Mark Twain once said about Americans and the weather, Parisians talked endlessly about *l'amour*. But did anyone ever do anything about it? Jude wondered. Because it was this relentless intercourse of ideas within their quicksilver minds that seemed to give them pleasure. And after all, only people with a profound aversion to bodily fluids could have invented the bidet.

As though reading Jude's mind, Jasmine explained to her, "Everyone in Paris talks about love, but only two hundred people actually do it."

"The rest of us prefer to watch," said Philippe.

Everyone laughed.

The others decided to go to some private club to continue their discussions. Jude declined because she was exhausted from concentrating so hard to follow the conversation. They offered to drive her home, but she said she'd walk. When Jasmine looked alarmed for her,

Jude promised to take a taxi. But she felt so safe in Paris after New York City that she foolishly went on foot wherever and whenever she pleased. The others embraced her and made kind comments about enjoying the evening.

As she walked down the Champs Elysées toward the granite obelisk at the Place de la Concorde, Jude felt happy. Her apprenticeship was apparently working. The group she'd just left seemed to like her—apart from Martine, who didn't like anyone. And Jude liked them. In fact, Jasmine and she were well on their way to a serious friendship. Her games had sometimes seemed malign to Jude in the beginning, but she now understood that they were the French version of a Maori welcome, intended to help newcomers feel included. And Jude finally did. There was no longer any doubt in her mind that the French were the world's most charming and interesting citizens, from whom she had a great deal to learn.

Jude's senses were wide open from taking in the beauty of the women onstage. And from the sonorous flow of her companions' voices, punctuated by Robert's _furia francese_ like a trumpet solo in a Baroque concerto. From the prickly feeling of champagne bubbles on her tongue, the salty taste of the creatures fresh from the sea, and the swirling scent of tobacco mixed with perfume.

So stimulated did she feel, with the warm night breeze off the Seine ruffling her hair like caressing fingers, that she walked to a women's club in the Marais called Marrakesh, which someone at work had once mentioned. The outside room contained a massive oak bar surrounded with high stools. As she perched on one and sipped a kir royale, she could see an inner room for dancing, which was ringed with low tables and easy chairs. Sinuously bulging marble columns held up the ceiling.

Jude moved from the bar to the dance area and watched the room fill up with women, mostly young and casually dressed, although there were a few fifties-style butches in men's suits and ties and a couple of transvestites in blond wigs, black leather shorts, and garters. There were also a few men lurking in the shadows, watching the women with the glassy eyes of prizefighters who'd just been knocked out but hadn't yet fallen.

Eventually, the dancing began, to music that was a blend of New Age synthesizer and classical guitar, along with what sounded like a team of crickets shoveling coal in the background. It didn't seem to matter if you had a partner, because most dancers were just swaying to the music and watching themselves in the mirrored walls as the strobe lights pulsed.

As Jude began to notice that she had drunk too much, the ponytailed woman from the strip club walked in with several other women. Jude scarcely recognized her with her clothes on, but the ponytail was unmistakable, with large spit curls below her ears, like Hasidic *peisim*. She wore cordovan boots to her knees, tight, faded jeans, and a white T-shirt with some kind of bone carving on a cord around her neck. She and her friends sat down two tables away and ordered drinks. As they lit Marlboros, Jude strained to hear their voices in the breaks between the songs. But all she could catch was a word with a lot of vowel sounds, which appeared to be the ponytailed woman's name: *o-eee-ah*.

After a while, one woman seized Ponytail by the hand and dragged her to the dance floor. The two writhed back and forth in perfect synchronicity, eyes closed, only inches between them. Jude wondered why she knew how to dance so well. Maybe she was a ballet dancer waiting for a break, supporting herself by her job at the club. But she wasn't gaunt enough for ballet.

Jude sat there watching admiringly as women of all sizes and shapes and colorings laughed and talked and danced and flirted. Some-

time soon, once she had completed her novitiate in the convent of
pleasure, she hoped to be able to join them. After several songs,
Ponytail and her group got up and left. Shortly afterward, Jude did,
too.

That night, Jude dreamed about the woman. She was just standing there in her jeans and T-shirt, looking at Jude and saying nothing.
Then she was gone. Jude woke up, bemused not to see her standing
by the bed, so real had she seemed. She looked at the clock. It was
only 3 A.M., so she turned over and went back to sleep.

A few evenings later, as she walked home from work, Jude
decided to celebrate the return of her appetite for life with an early
dinner at a restaurant near the Porte St. Denis, to which her *Guide to
Gay Paree* had given three stars. Apart from the huge fourteenth-
century stone portals from an early town wall that blocked traffic in
the middle of the street, the area was dominated by luggage stores.
A prostitute stood on the corner near the alley where the restaurant
was located.

Inside were only a dozen tables. Grouped around two were several more prostitutes, one dressed in leather. Another wore a feather
boa and a black ribbon around her neck with a crucifix dangling from
it. They were chatting and laughing and eating a lot, apparently stoking
up for a long night. A couple of other women in street clothes sat
with them. One, Jude realized, had long black hair sweeping down
from a ponytail atop her head.

Jude sat down. A pleasant woman in black leather trousers came
over to describe the menu and take her order. As she sipped Sancerre
and tried not to stare at the group in the corner, she wondered
whether her own features were becoming as familiar to Ponytail as
hers were to Jude—the long, narrow nose with a slight hook where
it joined her brow, pale eyes that narrowed when she smiled, high

cheekbones that were flushed even without makeup. Jude kept hearing
that word with all the vowels—*o-eee-ah*.

When the hookers got up to hit the streets, so did the woman.
As she reached the door, Jude heard someone call her Olivia. So at
least that mystery was solved. Before exiting, Olivia turned her head
Jude's way. As their glances met, Jude thought she noticed a flicker
of recognition in the woman's blue-gray eyes. And then she was
gone.

Having lost her appetite at the sight of those eyes, Jude rearranged the food on her plate, hiding a duck leg under a lettuce leaf.
She tried to figure out if Olivia was a prostitute. But the others were
in costume, whereas she was wearing just jeans and a T-shirt. But
maybe that was her costume.

After paying her bill, Jude walked down the alley and turned
into the street. Although she looked around for Olivia or her friends,
she saw no one familiar. For a moment, she considered going back to
the strip club alone, just so she could watch Olivia again. But it was
too early, and Jude wasn't dressed up enough. Besides, she couldn't
see going by herself and being pointed out by the waiters as a lecherous
lesbian, and she didn't know any men to invite as her cover.

In any case, she could feel an obscure longing starting to stir,
and she didn't want to encourage it. She planned to give herself a
break and take life lightly from here on out.

For the next couple of weeks, she read through a stack of English
and American novels and wrote reports for Jasmine. She sent postcards
to two dozen friends in New York. She planned visits to publishers
in London, Amsterdam, and Copenhagen. She organized a new address
book, eliminating many Tennessee and New York City entries and
adding some French ones. She also pruned her large pile of business
cards, many of which she had no memory of receiving, though no
doubt she'd promised letters and lunch dates. Life was like a motel,

and your job was just to change the sheets and get ready for the next guest.

THE MORNING OF HER FLIGHT to London, in the taxi north through Paris toward the *périphérique*, Jude was startled to find herself scrutinizing each woman they passed for a black ponytail. Even though she hadn't seen Olivia since that night at the restaurant, she realized that she had been halfway looking for her whenever she had turned a corner. Not to be able to do this for three days in London seemed suddenly unbearable. As they approached Charles de Gaulle airport, her agitation increased.

At the departure terminal, marchers were circling, wearing signs saying that Air France mechanics were on strike. Relieved, Jude told the driver to take her back to Montmartre. As they retraced their route, Jude took a good, long look at her cacophony of emotions, and she was appalled. Was she becoming infatuated with a woman she'd never even met?

That night, she dreamed again of Olivia standing before her in blue jeans. Slowly, she smiled. Then she said in French, "If you love me, you must tell me so. Do not be afraid, because I love you, too."

Waking up the next morning, Jude recalled the dream. It was the first time she'd ever dreamed in French. What did it mean? Or was it just her solitary brain slipping its gears? It would be absurd to say that she loved a woman she'd seen only three times from across the room. Besides, she was finished with all that nonsense. She didn't want anything heavy anymore—just some good times and some tenderness.

LATE THAT NIGHT, JUDE sat at a corner table in Marrakesh, smoking a Dunhill and nursing a kir. The thrill of spending her evenings watching the Eiffel Tower until its spotlights switched off at midnight was beginning to pale. She wanted someone to watch it with her. It was past time to emerge from her widowhood. So far, she had exchanged *le regard* with three candidates, but none had clicked.

Stubbing out her cigarette, she glanced toward the doorway. And there was Olivia, alone, dressed in black stretch pants and a baggy blue sweater. As she searched the room for her friends, her face fell slightly. She sat down at a table and ordered a drink, which she sipped slowly, trying to make it last.

Once the dance floor was full, Olivia got up and moved to the center, nodding to a couple of women who called her name as she passed. Wrapping her arms around herself, she closed her eyes and swayed to the music like an underwater plant. As the tempo picked up, she ran her palms down her torso and writhed gently to the beat.

Jude considered and dismissed the idea of going out on the floor and dancing beside her. The Hully Gully she had mastered. Her Boogaloo was passable. But this New Age trance dancing escaped her.

After studying the dancers for a long time, though, Jude got up and began to copy their languid movements. Slowly, she wended her way through the swaying, twisting torsos until she reached Olivia.

Dancing beside her, Jude pretended not to notice her. Finally, she allowed herself to glance at Olivia, only to find Olivia watching her with sulky blue eyes. They held each other's gaze for nearly a minute. Then Olivia nodded once, slowly, as though coming to a decision.

They swiveled around to face each other. Eyes locked, they moved back and forth in unison, a pair of mating cobras. Then, with a contemptuous toss of her ponytail, Olivia walked away.

Mortified, Jude kept dancing, not knowing what else to do. Olivia reached across her table for her cigarettes and headed for the door. At the door, she stopped and looked back, right at Jude. For a moment, Jude couldn't breathe. Olivia inclined her head toward the street ever so slightly. Jude smiled, trying to stay calm.

Olivia smiled back. Jude started through the crowd, moving toward the door. Olivia smiled more broadly, turned, and headed for the street. Jude followed, heart pounding like Japanese drums.

Outside, Jude stood alone in the dark street, with Olivia nowhere in sight, feeling ridiculous. But then she spotted her under a streetlight at the corner, looking back for Jude.

As Jude walked toward her, Olivia turned down the cross street. When Jude reached the corner, she turned, too. And there was Olivia, waiting halfway down the block. Jude began to trot to catch up, but Olivia started running, too, ponytail lashing side to side. The full moon was bathing the narrow streets in yellow, and the buildings were casting dark shadows as though at high noon. Olivia darted in and out of the shadows like a ghost.

Running out of breath, Jude slowed down, suspecting that she was making a fool of herself by chasing this young woman through the nighttime streets of Paris. In any case, Olivia had outrun her, and now she didn't see her. She glanced up and down the street several times, but Olivia didn't reappear.

Dejected, Jude walked toward the river to find a taxi back to Montmartre. It was probably just as well.

But there by the Pont Marie stood Olivia, hand resting on the stone parapet, watching for Jude, smiling in the moonlight.

Jude caught up with her. Before she could think what to say, Olivia put an index finger to her lips and shook her head. Then she reached out and stroked Jude's flushed cheek with her fingertips. Jude shuddered. Their lips touched and Olivia's tongue caressed Jude's lower lip.

As Jude gasped, Olivia whirled around and dashed across the

bridge to Ile St. Louis, the silver Seine licking the pilings below. Turning down a tree-lined street, she paused in the doorway of a building with a huge, stone lion head above the lintel. Punching in the night code, she shoved open the heavy maroon door and entered. When Jude reached the door, breathless, it slammed shut in her face.

Bewildered, Jude crossed the street, leaned against the wall above the Seine, and looked up. It was very late, and the entire building was dark. No lights went on anywhere to indicate the location of Olivia's apartment. She began to wonder whether she'd hallucinated the whole thing. A firm grasp on reality had never been her forte. She touched the spot on her lip that Olivia's tongue had caressed. It was still tingling.

The Métro had stopped running, but Jude walked until she found a taxi by the Louvre. The driver, a woman, was wearing a gold silk shirt with lots of Afghan jewelry at her ears, throat, and wrists. She turned to look at Jude in the light from the dashboard. Her skin was olive, eyes and eyebrows dark, teeth a flashing white as she told Jude that the street she'd named didn't exist.

Jude insisted it did.

She snarled that she'd been driving a taxi in Paris for five years and had never heard of it. Therefore, it didn't exist.

"But your singer Dalida lived at the end of it. She committed suicide there."

"This is impossible," she said. "How could Dalida have committed suicide on a street that doesn't exist?"

"Look, I live there myself. I know it exists. Please just look it up in your street guide."

She shrugged in the shadows. "Why should I look it up when I already know it isn't there?"

Jude was beginning to wonder whether she had passed through a black hole when she entered Marrakesh that night and had emerged in a parallel universe. Finally, she persuaded the woman to drive her to Place des Abbesses.

After crossing the square by the Bateau Lavoir, Jude was delighted to discover that her street was still there, dozing in the moonlight. She concluded that her driver was probably accustomed to driving men who gave her large tips just for the pleasure of her profile during the ride. She hadn't wanted to waste her time on a woman, especially one who was bewitched.

JUDE BEGAN TO LIVE FOR THE DARK. Leaving the office at the end of each day, she returned to her apartment, where she bathed, dressed, made herself up, and sat at her glass doors, welcoming the descent of dusk over the city. She passed the time trying to figure out which building among the thousands spread out below her was Olivia's. She could see Notre Dame. Olivia's street was somewhere to the east. Once it was late enough, she went to Marrakesh and sat at her corner table. But for the first two weeks, Olivia failed to arrive.

On the fifteenth night, Jude walked from Marrakesh to Ile St. Louis along the route they had followed in the moonlight. As a half-moon rose over her shoulder, she stood by the wall above the Seine, gazing at Olivia's darkened building. Every few minutes, a *bateau mouche* went by, illuminating her in its spotlights. But she outlasted them all, leaning against the wall until the moon peaked and began its trajectory toward dawn.

Then she hiked back to Montmartre, slept for a few hours, and went to the office, where a lunchtime debate was underway over whether the loss of Alsace-Lorraine during the Franco-Prussian War had incited French enthusiasm for a colonial empire. As she listened in the shifting ribbons of light from the pierced dome overhead, she found herself nodding off, chin on her chest.

When she awoke, she slipped from her chair and out the door. Back in her office, she grabbed the phone directory. But then she realized that she didn't know Olivia's last name. So she dialed the strip club and asked the woman who answered for Olivia's home number, explaining that she was a friend from America. The woman asked if Jude was her friend, why didn't she know her phone number? As Jude sat in silence trying to think of an answer to this trick question, the woman hung up.

Each night for the next week, Jude stood by the wall above the Seine as the moon waned, waiting for Olivia to come home. But she never did. On the seventh night, it finally occurred to her that maybe Olivia stayed at a lover's. Was one of the women she'd seen her with at the bar or the restaurant her lover? For a moment, she was limp with jealousy. Steadying herself with one hand against the rough stone wall, she tried to talk herself out of this, since she'd never even officially met the woman.

Looking down at the water, which was paved with sheets of silver light reflected from the streetlamps, she tried to figure out why she always ended up on the banks of some river—the Holston, the Hudson, now the Seine—obsessed with someone who had vanished.

The next night, she wandered through the alleys around the strip club with a handful of lavender tulips, in the company of several other flower-clutching perverts, searching for the stage entrance. After an hour stationed before a steel door they had decided was the one, they watched it swing open. As they held their collective breath, a white poodle pranced out, lifted his leg, and peed against the wall. His owner, who looked like Peter Lorre, leered at them from the doorway.

Finally, Jude decided to go back to the club as a paying customer so that she could at least see Olivia onstage again. Shopkeepers sometimes called her monsieur because of her jeans and boots and androgynous build and because many French men were themselves androgynous. So Jude went to the hairdresser's and got a spiky punk clip. Experimenting with her eyeliner pencil, she gave herself a fairly convincing five o'clock shadow. She bound her breasts with an elastic bandage. Then she put on a black T-shirt, a black silk blazer, jeans, and her cowboy boots. Just to check, she stopped in at several shops en route to the club. And for once she was pleased when everyone called her monsieur.

As she strode down the street toward the Champs Elysées, she began to swagger. It was restful no longer to be groped by men's eyes and to relax the radar that informed her of who was in her vicinity and whether anything about him suggested potential rapine. As she passed a woman in a miniskirt, she glanced at her legs, then ran her eyes up her torso to her face. The woman's eyes met hers for a moment, then flicked disdainfully away like a tango dancer's chin. Jude grinned. No wonder men didn't want to give up their erotic prerogatives.

The maître d' at the club also called her monsieur as he seated her on a banquette near the stage and brought her a scotch. But when the Beefeaters came out, Olivia wasn't among them. As Jude disconsolately watched the other women strut their stuff, she wondered whether Olivia had gone on holiday. Where would such a gorgeous creature go? Greece, Jude concluded, so that she could cavort with all the other goddesses.

MARTINE AND JUDE WERE SITTING in the conference room reviewing submissions for their anthology. Jude was struggling to say that although the New York City students had sometimes lacked a grasp of English grammar and syntax, their poems had displayed energy and invention. Whereas the French students had so far written poems that were technically perfect but full of images and insights as uninspired as if they'd been selected from a prix fixe menu. She was finding it difficult to be tactful in a language not her own. At some point, she realized that she'd been calling Martine *tu*.

Martine replied that they needed to draw up some guidelines for the teachers to assist them in encouraging their students to depart from the norms. She had a look of distaste on her face, and she was pointedly calling Jude *vous*. Jude realized that no one in all of Paris called her *tu* yet. She was still their resident Other. Yet she was intrigued to have inspired such contempt in Martine. She didn't understand why. Trying to make friends with her had been like trying to cozy up to a barracuda. Writing it off as a lost cause, Jude retreated to *vous* with an apologetic shrug.

The door opened and Jasmine walked in. She sat down at the round table and began questioning them about how many pages the anthology would be and when they expected to have a finished manuscript.

As Jasmine's and Martine's voices droned on and on, Jude found herself picturing Olivia naked beside her on cushions on her living-room carpet, sunbathing in the rays coming through the open door while swallows swooped past outside.

"Jude, can you tell us some more about this?" asked Jasmine.

Jude started. "I'm sorry. I missed the question."

"I was telling Martine about your handbook for the schools," said Jasmine, studying her quizzically.

"Oh, right." She began to describe how the handbook could help local schools set up their own programs and contests.

The door opened again, and Giselle arrived, clutching half a dozen lunchtime baguettes like a bat boy. She was followed by Cecile, Robert, and several others.

While everyone else passed food and poured mineral water, Jasmine turned to Jude and said, "This new short haircut of yours is most attractive."

"Thank you."

"Is something the matter? You do not seem well."

"I'm just tired. I was up late last night."

"Ah," said Jasmine, eying her speculatively, "you have a new friend to keep you awake?"

"No, not really." Keeping secrets was no way to fuel an evolving friendship, but Jude had no wish to tell Jasmine about Olivia or about her return alone to the strip club. Besides, what was there to tell?

"What a pity," said Jasmine with a smile. "But in that case, perhaps you would care to come to my house in Picardy this weekend? You could get some rest. I would provide you with a large curtained bedstead from the seventeenth century. Covered with fresh linen sheets and a fluffy duvet of goose down. I would fill your room with flowers from my garden and feed you pâté and champagne on a tray by your bedside."

As she talked, she was giving Jude *le regard*. Jude felt herself sinking into Jasmine's invitation as though into the goose-down duvet. But she wasn't sure exactly what she was being invited to do. Jasmine made even the most normal everyday activity sound like an episode from the *Kama Sutra*. Although she couldn't have said for sure if that was Jasmine's intent. In any case, she realized that she didn't want to leave Paris and the possibility of finally finding Olivia. All she really wanted out of life anymore was to be lying in Olivia's embrace on Ile St. Louis.

"It sounds marvelous, and I'd love to some other time," Jude replied. "But I'm afraid I'm tied up this weekend."

Jasmine studied her, trying to divine from her face what her engagement might be, but Jude struggled to offer no clues.

After Jasmine departed, Jude excused herself from the lunchtime seminar and returned to her office. Plopping down in her desk chair, she gazed up at the map of Paris spread across her wall. The red meanderings of her routes across Paris were beginning to weave themselves into a tangled web. Picking up the phone, she dialed Simon in New York.

It was early morning there, and Simon sounded bleary when he asked, "So how's New York's most tenacious graveyard lover today?"

"It's no laughing matter, Simon. I've done it again."

"Fallen in love?"

"I think so."

"Bloody hell, Jude, I can't leave you alone for a minute."

"Mock me all you like, Simon, but tell me what to do."

"Relax. Enjoy it. You're in Paris. Tell me about her."

"She has dark hair and blue eyes."

"Surprise, surprise. What does she do for work?"

"She's a dancer."

"Ballet?"

"Not exactly."

"Ballroom?"

"Burlesque."

Simon chuckled. "I see. Rough trade. So you've finally decided to take a walk on the wild side?"

"I didn't decide anything. These matters aren't rational."

"Not for you, that's for sure. Her age?"

"Young."

"Does she love you back, or is it another of your lost causes?"

"I have no idea."

"You haven't asked her?"

"I've never talked to her. I saw her dancing in a strip show. And then I saw her again at a lesbian bar. And she kissed me once on the bridge to Ile St. Louis when I was following her home."

There was a long silence. "Good Lord, Jude," said Simon. "Get a grip."

"I'm trying to. That's why I called you."

"Track her down. Get to know her. Immerse yourself in her annoying little habits. Watch her pick her teeth and chew her nails."

"I can't find her. I'm not even sure I didn't make her up."

"Jude, why don't you ask Jasmine for some time off? Come back to New York and see your friends. I think you must be alone too much over there. This sounds serious."

"Maybe I will, but first I have to find her," she said vaguely. "If she exists."

"Okay, but if you don't find her, don't panic. Call me up. I'll fly right over. Don't brood alone in stoic silence. And remember that there are many people here across the sea who adore and admire you."

After thanking Simon and bidding him good-bye, Jude hung up and left the office, marching directly to Ile St. Louis, determined to stage a showdown. Since it was afternoon, the night code was off at Olivia's building. So she buzzed herself in and crossed the mosaic courtyard. She climbed the iron staircases and walked the hallways on all five floors, studying each door. But she could detect no clue as to which might be Olivia's.

Verging on despair, Jude returned to the street and began to wander across the bridge toward Montmartre. People kept passing her, carrying their baguettes for dinner, waving and stroking them like giant phalluses. Pausing at the spot where Olivia had kissed her, if she had, Jude gazed down into the water as it swirled around the pilings. She wondered if she was losing her mind—or had already lost it.

Glancing back at Olivia's building, Jude saw her coming out the huge maroon door. She was dressed in a short skirt and a tank top, and she was carrying some books. Spinning around, Jude dashed back across the bridge. As Olivia crossed to the Left Bank and wound through the crowded side streets, Jude ran after her, trying to catch up. But Olivia was moving as fast as the shadow of a bird in flight.

Finally, in the doorway of an ancient Sorbonne lecture hall, Olivia paused and turned. Looking right at Jude, she smiled. Then she vanished into the building.

Enchanted finally to see her again, Jude decided that she had to speak with her. She couldn't sleep, and when she did, she dreamed of Olivia. Her clothes were hanging off her, limp as sails in the Sargasso Sea. She couldn't concentrate enough to read manuscripts for work. She couldn't follow the discussions at editorial meetings. Maybe if she could talk with Olivia, the spell would be broken. Maybe she'd tell Jude she was a disgusting pervert. Anything would be better than the past several weeks of living with her absence.

As Jude sat at a café sipping a *crème* and watching the door to the lecture hall, she mapped out their life together. Evidently, Olivia was a student when she wasn't busy driving other people crazy. Jude would support her while she finished school, so she could quit the club. She had seemed so vulnerable up there all alone on the stage in the swirling rainbow spotlights. Jude wanted to protect her. She didn't like the idea of all those revolting businessmen watching her dance naked. Besides, it was dangerous. What if one of them started stalking her?

They could have an apartment in Paris for Olivia and another in New York for Jude. Maybe Olivia would like Tennessee. They could build the cabin overlooking the Smokies that she'd planned with Molly and Anna. Olivia was young, so hopefully she didn't have a lot of baggage like husbands and children. Jude looked forward to being with someone long enough to grow thoroughly bored by her. She'd enjoy watching her hair go gray and her face crease and her perfect breasts sag. They'd take care of each other when they got sick, and Olivia could hold Jude's hand as she died, as Jude had Anna's.

Other students were exiting from the lecture hall, but not Olivia. Jude paid her bill and walked to the doorway. She asked a young man what the course was, and he said Anglo-American Philosophy. So Olivia was apparently a philosopher. She'd have a professor's schedule, and they'd be able to travel in the summers and at Christmas.

Olivia still hadn't emerged. Jude walked into the musty old building and poked her head into the lecture hall. It was empty, apart from some wads of paper on the floor by the lectern. Olivia must have slipped out a side door. Jude was getting irritated. Here she was planning their future, yet Olivia seemed to be evading her. The only way out of this endless nightmare seemed to be to plunge into it ever more deeply. So she returned to Ile St. Louis and stationed herself by the wall in front of Olivia's building. She would stay there for as long as it took to confront her.

For a while, she studied the wrought-iron grilles across all the windows on Olivia's block, wondering whether the bars on French jails were similarly patterned. Like snowflakes, no two designs were the same. Then she started thinking about this stale analogy. Presumably, no one had ever seen every snowflake that ever existed, so how did scientists know that no two were alike? She was willing to bet that some were.

She looked down and discovered a woman with a green Michelin guide standing before her. The woman asked in a French even worse than her own if she knew which building had been Camille Claudel's studio.

"I'm sorry," said Jude. "I don't actually know."

"I think it must be the one with the maroon door," she mused. "She went insane in there after Rodin rejected her."

"No kidding," said Jude uneasily.

After a couple of hours, her feet were hurting. She sank down to the sidewalk and sat with her back against the stone wall, studying the downspout on Olivia's building. It was gilded to resemble fish scales. At the bottom was the fish's head, with round eyes and a gaping mouth through which the rainwater from the roof would pour. Jude wondered why Olivia lived in such a fancy building. Maybe her father was a diplomat who didn't realize how his daughter earned her pocket money when he was on assignment abroad. Or maybe she was an au pair for a wealthy family by day and a goddess by night.

As the sunset faded into dusk, Jude began to feel chilled, so she buttoned the jacket of her cotton suit and turned up the collar. Then she reviewed her entire history with Olivia, from the moment she first saw her in the neon hoop at the strip club until she vanished that afternoon into the Sorbonne lecture hall: the glances they'd exchanged, her dreams, their dance at the Marrakesh, their flight to Ile St. Louis through the moonlight, Olivia's fingertips caressing her cheek on the Pont Marie, her tongue stroking Jude's lip.

At last, Jude unraveled what had happened: Olivia had revealed herself just enough for Jude to become intrigued. Then she had removed herself so that Jude would feel the lack of her. This lack was now generating Jude's crazed desire, just as Martine had insisted during that first lunch at the office.

A woman began to scream through an open window on the top floor of Olivia's building. The hair on the back of Jude's neck bristled.

Someone was being attacked. Could it be Olivia? As the screaming increased in intensity, Jude jumped up, trying desperately to think what the Paris equivalent of 911 might be. She glanced up and down the street for someone who would know what to do, but the sidewalks were empty.

But then the screams modulated into a strangulated tattoo of *oui*'s. "Oui . . . oui . . . oui . . . oui . . ." Like the fifth little piggy who couldn't find her way home. Only *l'amour* this time, Jude realized, not *la mort*. She sank back down on the sidewalk.

"Merde, ça me fait mal . . . ," moaned the woman from on high. *"Plus. Plus. Plus. Oui, plus . . ."*

Jude leaned her head against the wall and closed her eyes while the woman gasped, "In the name of God, don't stop yet, you filthy swine!"

Jude drew a deep breath and tried to think about something else—the number of *bateaux mouches* that must pass that spot every day, for example. As she performed calculations in her head, the woman emitted several high-pitched shrieks, like a buzzard swooping down on a field mouse. Then she fell silent. Jude was pretty sure she'd faked her orgasm. Her own armpits were clammy.

Extending her trousered legs across the sidewalk, Jude studied her high-fashion cowboy boots with the filigreed silver toe guards. What was she doing sprawled on a Parisian sidewalk outside the apartment of an exotic dancer she'd never met? She had finally fallen into the pit. She now understood the fascination for Molly and Sandy and Anna of people who made them suffer. It was the promise of extinguishing your lonely separate self in a power you had defined as greater than your own. It was graveyard love run amok.

Her head began to nod. Finally, her chin fell forward and settled on her chest. As darkness descended, she slept.

When she next opened her eyes, the sky overhead was black,

with a faint golden tint from the city lights. And Olivia was passing beneath the stone lion head and into her building, ponytail swishing. But Jude was so shocked by the sight of her that she couldn't utter a sound.

Crazed with frustration, she continued lying against the wall and tried to figure out what to do next. The night code would be on, so she couldn't get in. Besides, she still didn't know which apartment was Olivia's. She noticed a round object on the sidewalk beside her hand. Reaching out, she touched it gingerly. It was smooth. Examining it with her fingertips, she realized that it was an apple. When she picked it up and studied it in the glow from the streetlight at the corner, she discovered that it was a perfect yellow Delicious apple. She sniffed it. What if it was poisoned like Snow White's? She thought for a moment about the rolling golden balls on her smashed Atalanta flask.

But Olivia must have left it, she realized with a stab of delight. She must have squatted down and placed it gently on the sidewalk right beside Jude's hand. Suddenly overcome with hunger and thirst, she bit into it. The juice ran all over her hand and down her chin.

As she lay there devouring the apple, a light came on behind the sheer curtains over the glass doors of a third-floor apartment facing the river. While Jude watched, the silhouette of a naked woman appeared behind the curtains. Slowly, she began to undulate to unheard music, hands caressing breasts and thighs, ponytail swirling and lashing.

The roaring of ocean breakers filled Jude's head, and a softness fluttered through her veins like the velvet wings of a thousand moths in flight. Tossing the apple core over the wall behind her, Jude wrapped her arms across her chest, gasping and shivering. The light went off and the building plunged back into darkness.

Jude lay motionless against the wall all night long, awake but stunned. A stray cat stopped by to rub up against her, purring. It smelled of spoiled fish. Occasional solitary cars passed by on hissing tires on the Right Bank. The silver Seine slapped the stone banks below like laundry snapping on a line.

As birds began to chirp in the chestnuts along the river, Jude managed to stand up in the rosy dawn and go in search of coffee. Finding a café in the Latin Quarter that was just opening, she went to the ladies' room to wash her face and hands. Looking into the mirror, she studied her own eyes, mahogany like her father's, dim with fatigue and ringed with mauve. This couldn't go on. Soon the police would arrive to cart her off to an asylum, as they had Camille Claudel. Maybe she'd better take Simon's advice and return to New York.

But after drinking a *crème* and eating a *tartine* at a table in the café, she began to feel calmer. So she bought a couple more buttered tartines and returned with them to Ile St. Louis, where she leaned in Olivia's doorway. Eventually, a man with a briefcase emerged, and she ducked through the door before it sucked shut. She climbed the iron staircase to the third floor. Calculating that the window where the silhouette had appeared was in the far-right apartment, Jude rang the bell, palms clammy, heart pounding.

Since no one came, she rang again.

Olivia opened the door on the third ring, wearing a royal purple chenille robe, ponytail undone so that her dark hair hung around her face like a mantilla. *"Oui?"* she said in a sleepy voice.

"I've brought you some breakfast." Jude pointed at the bag of *tartines*. "We need to talk."

"Excuse me, madame, but who are you?"

Shaken, Jude said, "You know who I am, Olivia. My name's Jude."

"No, I do not know who you are." She began to close the door.

"But you've seen me a dozen times," pleaded Jude.

"I am sorry, but you are mistaken."

Jude looked at her helplessly. "Well then, please excuse me, madame." She turned to leave, completely numb in order to stave off an eventual collapse into utter chagrin and despair.

"All right. Yes," she said as Jude started down the hallway. "Now I remember you. What is it that you want?"

Jude turned back around, hopeful, relieved, and angry. "What do *you* want?"

"But I want nothing," she said with a laugh. "I am not the one who is ringing a stranger's doorbell at dawn."

Jude stared at her, beginning to dislike her, afraid that it would show and that Olivia would slam the door in her face. "Then why did you want me to follow you home that night from Marrakesh? Why did you kiss me on the Pont Marie? Why did you leave me that apple last night? Why did you dance for me at your window?"

"I do not know what you are talking about. This is very annoying."

"You're damn right it is!" Jude hurled the *tartines* at her feet and stomped off down the corridor.

"Wait," she called.

Jude stopped, head lowered like a charging bull's, not turning around. It was awful, but at least it was over. She didn't even want to think about the price she would have to pay for the folly of letting herself love another phantom.

"Come back."

Jude hesitated, consulting her family motto: "When in doubt, get the hell out."

"*S'il te plaît,*" she said softly.

This was the first person in Paris to call Jude *tu.* If only she had understood that the pathway to endearment here was paved with anger, she could have saved herself a lot of fake smiles. She returned to

Olivia, who was looking down at the bag of *tartines*. Bending over, Jude picked it up and handed it to her.

"Come in," she said, standing aside.

They went down a narrow hallway to a small kitchen that reeked of stale cat food. Jude sat down at a square wooden table. They exchanged remarks concerning the strength of the coffee and Jude's wish for milk and sugar.

"So what's this all about?" Jude finally asked.

"What is what all about?" Olivia poured coffee and hot milk into two giant cups and placed the tattered *tartines* on a plate.

"Well, your performance last night by the window, for example?"

"It is whatever you care to make of it."

Jude finally understood why so many French men had gone on the Crusades—to get away from French women.

"So it was totally without meaning for you?"

"A brief fantasy between two people is pleasant, is it not?"

Jude looked at her while the words *brief* and *fantasy* sank in. But she was relieved finally to have Olivia take some responsibility for this disaster. "Perhaps," she said. "If both people know it's a fantasy. If not, someone gets hurt."

"People must watch out for their own hearts in these matters, no?"

"In America, when we love someone, we try to watch out for their hearts as well as our own."

For a long moment, Olivia studied Jude, as though she were an exotic pinned butterfly struggling not to succumb to formaldehyde. "So you have come to love me," she said matter-of-factly, as though discussing the price of mangoes in the market.

"Oh, I suppose so. Yes." Jude finally understood the rules of this game: The one who fell in love first lost. She had lost. She'd thought that the goal was to get past the game to the substance. She now realized that the game was all there was. There was nothing beyond. Only a new game with someone else. Paris was one vast Disneyland of Desire.

"But this is madness. You do not even know me."

"If I knew you, I might not even like you." Jude laughed loudly, like the lunatic she had become.

Olivia's eyes widened with alarm. She put her hand on Jude's forearm and scooted closer, apparently intrigued by the danger Jude suddenly represented. Jude smiled at this notion of herself as a barbarian at the gate. Olivia didn't realize that she was dealing with Cherry Ames, rural nurse, helper and healer.

"You know, Olivia," said Jude in a low voice, "you could have made my life much easier if you'd just left me alone."

Olivia blinked, looking baffled. "But why would I wish to make your life easy?"

"I suppose that is awfully unsophisticated of me."

"But now you are being sarcastic, and this is not nice." Standing up, she took Jude's hand and pulled her to her feet. She led her down the hallway and into a bedroom strewn with clothing. Glass doors with sheer curtains looked out on the Seine.

Settling herself against her pillows, she held out her arms so that her robe parted. "Come," she said softly.

Jude stood there looking at Olivia's perfect body in the morning sun, at her shiny, dark hair fanned out across the white pillow. "Shouldn't we get to know each other a bit first?"

"What better way?" asked Olivia, smiling.

Jude reminded herself of her pledge not to insist on always doing things her own way. Olivia was offering her magnificent body, but Jude wanted to chat first about her inner child? With trembling hands, she removed her own clothing as gracefully as possible and then joined

Olivia on the bed, feeling like one of the Seven Dwarfs approaching Snow White.

AS SLIM FINGERS OF SUNSHINE pushed their way through the folds of the curtains across Olivia's glass doors, she gazed into Jude's eyes and moaned and murmured at all the appropriate spots. And she employed her various body parts with an admirable technical efficiency. But Jude quickly understood that her heart and her soul were elsewhere, well protected by her exquisitely arranged flesh. For Olivia, this was just another performance.

Lying there afterward with Olivia's shiny hair swirled across her chest like a swath of new-mown hay, Jude reminded herself that the first time with a new person was sometimes awkward. It took a while to learn someone else's rhythms. Besides, Olivia was young. Jude would enjoy awakening her to the pleasures available through the sense of touch, as Anna had her. There was no rush.

"And now you must go so that I can sleep," Olivia said amiably. "Because I must work late tonight."

Jude looked down into her eyes, a bleary turquoise in the sunlight, with tiny translucent rings of butterscotch around the pupils, just like Molly's. "When can I come back?"

"But this is what you came for, is it not?" She seemed perplexed. "And now you have learned that it is no more remarkable with me than with anyone else."

"Well, I agree that it wasn't that exciting," said Jude. "But never mind. We can work on it."

Olivia propped herself up on one elbow to look at Jude, eyes amused and bemused. "Why would one wish to work on something that is meant to be play?"

"Well, to make it more satisfying for both of us."

"But I am satisfied," she said. "I see that you are not. *Mais ce n'est pas grave.* It is always disappointing, is it not, compared to what one dreams will be possible?''

Jude didn't agree. ''In any case, this isn't what I came for,'' she said, feeling she was swimming out of her depth. ''I came to tell you that I love you.''

''Oh, yes. I forgot. You believe that you love me.''

''No, I know that I love you.'' But as Simon had predicted, the better she knew Olivia, the less lovable she seemed.

''If one loves, one wishes to please the beloved, *n'est-ce pas?*'' Olivia asked, drawing on her skills as a philosophy student.

Jude could see this one coming. She braced herself.

''So my wish is that you will go away now and enjoy your life and remember that you passed a pleasant hour one summer morning on Ile St. Louis with a woman who found you ravishing in every way.''

This was the most charming brush-off Jude had ever heard of. Smiling doggedly, she stood up and began pulling on her underwear. ''I should never have come.''

Olivia pursed her lips and shrugged. *''Ce n'est rien.''*

To you it is nothing, thought Jude as she stepped into her trousers and pulled on her silk T-shirt. To me, it is everything. But that's not your problem.

Olivia got up and pulled on her robe. Jude shrugged on her suit jacket and followed her down the hallway.

''I am sorry if I have disappointed you,'' she murmured as Jude walked past her out the door. ''I meant only to please. But you must understand that you are not the first to have trailed me around Paris like a hungry ghost.''

As Jude passed under the stone lion head above the doorway and out into the street, she reflected that cats at play probably didn't know how their claws felt to mice. She walked out onto the Pont Marie and stared down into the Seine for a long time. She wondered whether to jump. She would not be the first to die for the love of a beautiful dancer—although she might be the first woman. Feminism was truly a wonderful thing. She decided not to jump. It would be just her luck to land in a *bateau mouche* full of Baptist Youth from Tennessee. Besides, Simon would never forgive her for such a lapse into cliché.

She spun around and headed south, dazed like the sole survivor of a plane crash. As she skirted the Luxembourg Gardens, she tried to figure out how to get through the rest of her life now that all pleasure and purpose had gone out of it yet again, like a leaky beach ball. Olivia was very skilled at her craft, tossing out the bait, jerking the line when Jude struck so that the hook would lodge firmly, and then reeling her in. But why? Did she enjoy watching another creature flopping and gasping on dry land, with no idea how to return to the water?

Heading south down the Avenue du Général Leclerc, Jude spotted the entrance to the Catacombs. The labyrinth of ancient stone quarries stretched beneath her feet for nearly two hundred miles. In the eighteenth century, 6 million skeletons from crowded Parisian cemeteries had been transferred down there for storage.

After paying her entry fee, Jude descended the winding stone steps to a dim, damp corridor well below the sewers and the Métro. A message carved into the stone lintel read: "Stop! This is the empire of death." Jude kept going.

The passageway within was lined on either side with bones, stacked so that the ball ends protruded to form a textured wall. At chest height ran a row of skulls, lined up as neatly as coconuts at a greengrocer's. Sometimes a pillar of skulls also ran vertically from ceiling to floor, forming crosses.

Jude strolled for what felt like miles down the shadowy gravel pathway with no one else around, water dripping from the ceiling. Here and there, barred side tunnels headed off into the blackness. This place had been the headquarters of the Resistance during World War II. In Roman times, early Christians had held services down here. Smugglers had stashed contraband and criminals had hidden out from prosecution.

Carved into a stone by a doorway, Jude spotted a verse from Lamartine that Anna had once recited as they crossed Central Park:

> Into the ocean sinks the plaintive wave.
> Onto the winds, the fugitive leaf.
> Dawn fades into evening,
> And man into death.

Just beyond were skeletons from the Innocents Cemetery, where the Huguenots fished out of the Seine had been buried. Jude stopped to contemplate the stained ivory femurs and tibias of her ancient cousins. But there was nothing so unusual about their plight. Every group had its victims and its executioners.

Glancing around to be sure she was unobserved, she climbed a gate and wedged her body between the top bar and the stone ceiling. Dropping to the ground on the other side, she stood there for a moment. Once she set out, she wouldn't be able to find her way back. She'd read about men who had wandered into these tunnels and been found as skeletons centuries later.

Steadying herself with her hands against the damp carved walls of rock, she scrambled in her cowboy boots up the rubble and set out down the side passage. She walked and walked, lighting her way with the tiny flashlight on her key ring, randomly choosing one fork or another at junctures, until she had lost all sense of direction. She remembered reading about a man who had gotten lost down here and stumbled across a room piled high with cat heads and no bodies. The restaurant in the street directly overhead served as its specialty an incomparable rabbit stew.

After what seemed like hours, short of breath and calves aching, she ran headlong into a wall. Feeling all around herself with her hands, she discovered that she was in a more or less round chamber, from which there was no exit except the narrow chute by which she had just arrived.

She cleared away enough stones to make room for herself on the floor. Then she plopped down and tried to figure out what she was doing pitching camp in the empire of death. But why not? Cruelty was the law of the land above her head. Love was the only antidote, yet its pursuit led merely to more pain. Life was a boxed canyon with nowhere left to turn.

Using her pocketbook for a pillow, she stretched out on the floor and wrapped her suit jacket around herself. Surrounded by six million skeletons of people who had already made their final voyage, she tried to imagine what it was going to be like to die. Anna could have told her. But if Anna were still alive, she wouldn't have known, and Jude wouldn't have been lost in the catacombs in the first place.

ANNA'S CHILDREN, HOME from their colleges because things were looking so bad, finally departed. They had been sitting beside Anna's bed in the Roosevelt all evening, wearing jeans and rugby shirts and acting sullen.

Then one of Anna's students arrived with a flute and a music stand to play "Jesu, Joy of Man's Desiring" for Anna. The off-pitch warble filled the room like a robin being tortured. Jude watched Anna struggle to raise her splinted hands to cover her ears. Jude gently maneuvered the student out the door.

In the silence that followed, Jude took one of Anna's hands in hers. Undoing the tape, she unwound the gauze until the splint beneath it fell to the floor. Then she moved to the other side of the bed and did the same thing to the other hand. She watched Anna's fingers as they stirred to life and flexed slightly. She usually undid Anna's hands until a nurse noticed and made her bind them up again. Anna liked to move her fingers, and Jude liked to feel their warmth when she held them and to rub them with lotion, and to clip and file the nails.

She picked up the cup of crushed Popsicle and held out a spoonful to Anna just as Anna smacked her lips to signal that she wanted some The moments of almost uncanny closeness that Jude had begun to experience with her had become more and more frequent, until now they constituted a steady state. By some instinct, Jude knew when and where to scratch her, when she wanted a Popsicle. They had finally achieved that perfect harmony possible for a couple only when one of them is in a coma.

Jude was surprised to hear herself begin to enunciate in a low, even voice a poem Anna used to recite when they walked along through the swirling apple blossoms in Central Park:

> *They are not long, the weeping and the laughter,*
> *Love and desire and hate:*
> *I think they have no portion in us after*
> *We pass the gate.*
> *They are not long, the days of wine and roses.*
> *Out of a misty dream*
> *Our path emerges for a little while, then closes,*
> *Within a dream.*

Afterward, Jude sat very still, timing her breathing to Anna's, as she used to during lovemaking. And in a quiet, matter-of-fact voice, she found herself saying, "All right, I guess it's time now, Anna? Time for you to go. Go ahead. It's all right. I can take care of myself. Jim can take care of himself. Your students can take care of themselves. Your children can take care of themselves. We're all fine. Just go. Don't be afraid. Everything is going to be all right.'' For several minutes, she repeated these phrases, understanding that Anna needed to let go of her now but that she needed Jude's help in order to do so. A sob caught in her throat as she chanted the necessary phrases like a litany.

But then she jumped up abruptly, as though attacked by a swarm of bees. And all of a sudden, she was absolutely furious. She didn't want to be in this dreary hospital room any longer, watching bouquets from Anna's students wilt and shrivel and be replaced, watching the body she had loved rot. She had been here for days. Weeks. Months. Other women her age were out dancing and singing and making love. Damn it, why couldn't Anna just go ahead and die and get it over with?

Striding to the far corner, Jude threw herself down in a lounge chair. She lay back and closed her eyes, breathing unevenly.

She looked around for Molly, but Molly had deserted her years ago. So she jumped on her horse and galloped alone along the beach, salt spray drenching her shirt, hooves pounding beneath her like pistons. She slid off the heaving horse by a dune and watched the turquoise waves arc and tumble, advancing and receding, crashing and hissing, leaving lips of foam flecked with shells like tiny broken teeth.

Jude opened her eyes and watched the white sheet over Anna's chest rise and fall time after time, the bellows that was stoking her flame.

And then she realized that the sheet was still. Getting up, she walked over to the bed. Anna wasn't breathing anymore. Jude reached down and took one of her hands in both her own and stared at her composed yellow face with disbelief.

Finally, she managed to whisper, ''Godspeed, Anna.''

Anna drew a deep, rattling breath, leaning forward, almost sitting up, vacant lapis eyes wide open, seeming to stare at something across the room. Then she exhaled, eyes fluttering shut, and sank back into her pillows.

Jude shuddered violently, as though Anna's soul had just passed right through her own body, the force of its transit carrying her along halfway to the brink of death.

Then Jude felt elation surge up from the pit of her stomach and spread throughout her body. And she was flooded with the sudden conviction that Anna had just cast aside her scab-pocked body like a withered husk and moved on.

Jude stood there holding Anna's hand for a long time as it began to cool and stiffen, unable to make the least effort to comprehend what had been there in her body, which Jude had known so well, that now was absent. And where it had gone.

JUDE TOUCHED THE FLOOR of hewn stone with her fingertips. It was pitch-black. There was no sound except for some water dripping from the ceiling and her own heartbeat pounding in her ears. She was in the empire of death, surrounded by those who knew the answers to these questions. She had come here like a homing pigeon. Once the 6 million skeletons surrounding her had all loved and suffered in the streets above her head. Now they were here below, neatly stacked domes and cylinders of calcium, finally at rest.

Jude realized that the only thing she wanted from life anymore was to leave it. It was a Saturday, and Monday was a holiday, so no one would miss her at work until Tuesday. She tried to figure out whether the ticket takers kept track of their visitors. If one fewer emerged at closing time, would they come looking for her? If so, she needed to be dead already. She had a bottle of aspirin in her pocketbook for menstrual cramps. A sorority sister at Vanderbilt had killed herself with a bottle of Bayer aspirin.

As she planned her death, she began to feel sleepy. Deciding that she wanted to be well rested and wide awake when she made her final journey, she let herself doze for one last time, lulled by the scurrying of rats' feet like soft whispers in the velvet darkness. The dreaded empire of death was actually a peaceful place. It was in the streets up above that pain roamed and horror reigned.

Jude's mother, Molly, Sandy, Anna, and her Tennessee grandparents were planting daylilies all over the ridge where Molly and she had planned to build their cabin. The green river valley below meandered toward the misty mountains. Mockingbirds were calling from the Wildwoods, which were decked out with redbud and dogwood blossoms in shades of pink and crimson and purple and white. Jude dug all afternoon in the steaming soil under a hot spring sun.

When they had finished, the others came over, hands caked with dirt.

Anna, whole and well again, said, "Jude, we are happy here, and we want you to be happy there."

The others nodded.

"How can I be happy apart from all of you?" asked Jude.

"You have to try," said Molly.

"It's too soon for you, Jude," said Sandy with his sweet smile.

"Virginians never kill themselves," said her grandmother.

"Darling," said her mother, "once you can love without needing an object, then you are love. And you will rush to unite with love and will leave behind that strange place, so beautiful but so marred by hate."

"We are always with you, Jude," said her grandfather, gesturing to the others. "A cloud of witnesses watching over you."

One by one, they dissolved, becoming the sunlight playing on the ripples in the river, and the breeze that rustled the blossoms in the Wildwoods, and

*the mist that drifted down the coves and veiled the high mountain peaks and
knobs.*

JUDE COULDN'T REMEMBER where she was. Someplace as dark
and silent as a tomb, except for a steady dripping sound. Then she
remembered that she was supposed to kill herself now with her bottle
of Bayer. But now it suddenly seemed like a really dumb idea.

She sat up. She had a headache. She had no idea whether it was
day or night, or how long she'd slept. She stood up, feeling dizzy and
steadying herself with a hand against the wall. She grabbed her handbag
from the floor. The leather strap had been gnawed through. Clutching
it, she headed down the tunnel in what she thought was the direction
from which she'd come, flashing the light on her key chain now and
then, trying to make the battery last. It seemed unlikely that she'd
find her way back. Probably she'd wander beneath the streets of Paris
until her strength gave out. Then she'd sit down somewhere and await
death by starvation and ravening rats. If she was ever found, no one
would know that it had been a suicide by default.

After what seemed like several hours of doomed, dogged plod-
ding, she was astonished to detect a faint light ahead. Soon she heard
the hollow echoing voice of a French child telling his mother that dead
people were boring.

Reaching the main corridor, she climbed back over the grating,
ignoring some startled German tourists. As she ascended the long,
winding staircase to the street, she was pleased to find herself still
alive. Death would come soon enough. One day, this baffling life of
hers would simply peel away like a bad sunburn.

She walked out the door into the amber dusk. Asking the date
of a barman at a café, she learned she'd been underground for two
days. From the way he looked at her, or rather tried to avoid looking

at her, she realized that she was a fright in her rumpled suit and chalk-caked boots.

Getting off the Métro at Place des Abbesses, she wandered down the shopping street, dazzled like Rip van Winkle by the foodstuffs spilling from the shops—grotesque spiny creatures from the sea, slabs of shimmering neon fish, pungent cheeses in all shapes and shades, pastries oozing fruit or dribbled with chocolate or smothered in whipped cream, chickens swiveling on spits, walls of wine for every occasion, exotic fruits and vegetables from the former colonies, which she squeezed and poked as though she knew what she was doing. Suddenly, she was ravenous.

Back at her apartment, she ran a bath, pouring in some raspberry bubble bath Jasmine had given her that she'd never opened. Shedding her disgusting clothes, she studied herself in the bathroom mirror. Although she admittedly looked better with her clothes on, she wasn't so bad without them. She subsided into the foam.

Dressed in fresh jeans and a T-shirt, she set a place for herself on the table by the glass doors, complete with a single coral rose in a bud vase, a cloth mat and napkin, and a candle in a holder. In the kitchen, she alternated firm white rounds of mozzarella with thick, juicy slices of tomato on a bed of crisp romaine, then sprinkled it all with chopped basil and olive oil. She dismembered the herbed chicken, still warm from the shop spit. And she cut up a crusty demibaguette, putting the pieces in a woven basket. She set all this on a wooden tray, along with a wineglass and a chilled bottle of Sancerre, and carried them to the table.

As she sipped the wine, cold and sharp on her stale tongue, she watched the huge orange sun sink behind the Bois de Boulogne, turning the Eiffel Tower and the Panthéon and the Arc de Triomphe and the Invalides into dark silhouettes on the horizon, fronted by the black arabesques of her wrought-iron railing. Dipping a piece of baguette into the olive oil and the juice from the tomato, she tried to figure out what had come over her two days earlier when she'd been prepared to give up all this splendor in order to die in a stone cell surrounded by rats and bones.

CHAPTER

1 9

O N HER WAY TO WORK the next morning, Jude took her usual
detour across Ile St. Louis. Standing on the sidewalk in front of
Olivia's building, she was surprised to find that everything looked just
as it had for the past several weeks, oblivious to her transfiguration in
the Catacombs—the maroon door with the lion-head lintel, the elaborate wrought-iron grilles at the windows, the gilded fish-scale downspout, the stone wall above the Seine, the relentless *bateaux mouches*
plowing the silver waters, the thrushes singing in the chestnut trees
by the river, the tourists clutching their guidebooks and searching for
Camille Claudel's studio.

Jude allowed her eyes to shift to the third floor. The glass doors
in Olivia's bedroom were slightly parted. The sheer curtains were
stirring in the breeze, fluttering like a ghost. Olivia was probably right

there behind them, asleep in her bed after a late night at the strip club.

Every cell in Jude's body screamed out for another try. The night code would be off by now. She could enter the maroon door and climb the steps, ring Olivia's buzzer. Who knew, maybe Olivia would be pleased to see her.

Using all the strength at her disposal, Jude turned away from the building and forced herself to plod, one step at a time, toward her office.

As she left Olivia behind, dozing in the sunlight like a lazy lioness, she sent her a mental apology. Olivia had engineered a light and charming flirtation, designed to disarm Jude's absurd passion for her in a fashion that would have left Jude's ego intact. If only she could have accepted it in that spirit, both would have gone through the rest of their lives harboring a sweet memory. Instead, Jude had insisted on turning it into *Romeo and Juliet*, crawling into her earthen vault and petitioning Death as her witness. As she trudged up the steps to her office, she realized that she was nothing but an uptight Anglo-Saxon asshole.

Giselle was sitting at her desk as Jude walked past. "*Bonjour*, Jude," she called.

Jude backed up and paused in her doorway. "*Bonjour*, Giselle," she replied. "How are you?"

"Fine, thank you. How was your weekend?"

Jude smiled wryly. "Fine, thank you."

"Did you go away?"

"Sort of," said Jude.

Giselle looked at her quizzically, her copper-colored pre-Raphaelite hair framing her face.

"Not really. I just did some tourist stuff. The Catacombs."

Giselle grimaced. "Not so nice, eh?"

"I kind of liked it," said Jude. "But I wouldn't want to live there."

Giselle laughed.

Jude spent the morning at her desk extracting, adapting, and translating a series of exercises from Anna's workbook designed to help writing students find their own voices. She and Martine had decided to give them to the schools in hopes of stimulating some more original poems. She remembered when she and Anna had invented the exercises. It had been a happy time, love and work merging seamlessly. The sad thing about happiness was that while you were in it, you believed it would last forever, so you appreciated it less than you might if you realized what a rare and precious gift it was.

Jude laid down her pen and leaned forward, resting her forehead on her desk. She had just understood where she had gone wrong with Olivia. She had been captivated by Olivia's physical beauty. She had woven a fantasy around that rather than trying to get past it to the beauty of Olivia's soul. No wonder Olivia had felt insulted and vengeful.

Jude reached out for the phone. Then she remembered that she still didn't know Olivia's last name or number. Grabbing a fresh sheet of paper, she picked up her pen and began a letter of explanation and regret to Olivia. But right in the middle of assuming the blame for everything that had gone on between them, she paused. How could anyone get past Olivia's physical beauty to her spiritual beauty when she wouldn't even sit down and talk to you like a normal person? Besides, Olivia flaunted her wretched body like a baker his cream cakes. Jude ripped up her letter and let the pieces flutter into the trash can like a flock of dying moths.

Realizing that lunch hour was already under way, Jude stood up and walked down the hallway to the conference room. Half a dozen of her coworkers were sitting beneath the shifting ribbons of sunlight, sipping Evian and nibbling roast chicken. Jude nodded to everyone, sat down, ripped off a hunk of baguette, and picked up a chicken leg.

Tuning into the debate du jour, she discovered that it concerned the question of whether the modern world was sexually repressed or sexually obsessed. Cecile's team was maintaining that capitalists had seized control of sexuality via repressive laws and religion in order to divert libido into production. Martine's team was insisting that, to the contrary, contemporary societies provoked preoccupation with sexuality to drug their citizens into submission—like giving alcohol to Native Americans or heroin to ghetto blacks to prevent them from rioting in the streets.

"But at least we are agreed, are we not," inquired Cecile, removing her large red-framed glasses to peer around the table like a NATO commander, "that any discourse on the deployment of sexuality must privilege the issue of power?"

Martine thought for a moment, inspected her teammates, then nodded reluctantly. She was a woman who hated agreement.

Jude had finally figured out that the route to conversational brilliance here was to take an assumption, such as that sex shows were sexy, and contradict it. So, launching her first plunge into the waters of lunchtime controversy, she suggested haltingly that Americans were often more interested in the pleasurable sensations their bodies experienced during lovemaking than in power manipulations.

Everyone looked at her as though she were a kindergarten pupil in a graduate seminar.

"But of course Americans do not understand eroticism," said Martine. "That is why it is impossible to be attracted to them. They are too obvious." She bit off the ball end of a chicken bone and sucked at the marrow. Most of the others nodded agreement.

So she hadn't been attracted to Jude? Or was this just another come-on? Suddenly, Jude was fed up with Martine's bad manners. She had lacked the courage to open herself up to Jude. She had insisted on remaining safe behind her kinky games. She had no idea who Jude really was. Yet just like Martine herself, Jude had earned her spurs in the rodeo of *l'amour*. She had won several purple hearts on the killing fields of love. She had crawled on her belly through the trenches of despair. She had faced down death in the foxholes of failed affection. She had stripped off her armor to parade unafraid on the battlements of passion. She deserved honor and respect from her fellow combatants, not contempt.

Jude felt her own recessive French genes rear up and triumph over Charm Class, yielding a sudden fit of *furia francese*. In her stumbling French, she told her colleagues that most ancient civilizations such as India and China and Persia had an *ars erotica* that instructed people, not in how to dominate each other, but in how to cooperate to achieve mutual pleasure. That these pleasures were carefully classified, not as forbidden or permitted, but in terms of quality, intensity, duration, and spiritual significance. That forcing children, as they themselves had been forced, to confess their sexual desires as "sins" and thus teaching them to despise their bodies, was a recent local disease. That they used their endless boring debates on sex and the sexes as foreplay, like debauchees trying to flog a response from senses blocked by misuse or shame. But that elsewhere in the world people possessed ample erotic energy as a natural endowment, which they could call on as they wished without a need for tiresome gimmicks. That some people approached sex as a normal human appetite, not as a sinister plot designed to deprive them of *la liberté*. That no self-respecting American would want to attract them in any case because they were too weird, and because they ate octopus and tripe. That the world was old and France was young. That the world was large and France was small. That life outside their sacred hexagon was not necessarily as they saw it. That they should stop deconstructing everyone and everything else and deconstruct themselves.

Remorselessly, Jude vented her months of frustration with Martine and Olivia, heaping one generalization atop another, just as she had watched them do all these weeks, until she had constructed a magnificent sand castle in thin air—one that began to crumble as she realized that she'd just lost her job. Normally, someone would have interrupted her diatribe and saved her from such total self-demolition, but they must have been so astonished to hear her speak, and so ferociously at that, that everyone had remained silent.

There was a long pause, during which everyone blinked several times. Then Cecile reached over to offer Jude a Gitane, an invitation to join her platoon. Jude declined it.

Giselle thrust her baguette at Jude like a fencing foil so she could rip off a hunk if she wanted—which she didn't.

Gazing at Jude with new interest, Martine murmured, *"Mais tu as bien parlé."*

But Jude didn't care if it turned Martine on to be treated as contemptuously as she treated everyone else. Drawing on Gary Cooper in *High Noon* for inspiration, she stood up, squared her shoulders, gazed out the window into the midday sun, and marched out the door in her silver-toed cowboy boots.

Upon reaching the street, Jude had no idea what to do next. All she really wanted was to return to Ile St. Louis. And to kneel before Olivia on the pavement and beg for another chance to behave more lightheartedly. Voluntarily giving up a graveyard love while the other person still walked the earth was unheard of. Yet Jude knew that was what she had to do now if she wanted to avoid another weekend in the Catacombs.

She dodged through the ambling crowds until she reached the Luxembourg Gardens, where she strolled along the paths of pale dirt, raked into patterns overnight, past orderly ranks of marigolds, geraniums, and artemesia that stood at attention like troops on parade. Past palms and oleanders and orange trees growing in square green boxes. Past ivy trained to hang in symmetrical swags. She came to a cage containing hundreds of espaliered fruit trees, twisted and bound like heretics on the rack into the shape of minorahs, with white paper bags over their nubile fruits.

Through some lime trees, planted in rows, their tops sheared into rectangles, Jude spotted a bronze lion with a dead ostrich at her feet. And just beyond was an eight-point buck with his doe and fawn, frozen as though by a stun gun while sniffing the morning air.

Jude descended some steps guarded by two lions that had been turned to stone in midstalk. And in the center of a lawn that was clipped as closely as a putting green, poised on a high stone catafalque, stood Artemis, a quiver of arrows on her back and a young stag leaping by her side. She, too, was frozen in midstride in her flowing tunic, so that she had to stand there eternally in the summer sun and winter winds. A dozen queens of France, several resembling transvestites in their elaborate robes and crowns, gazed down at Artemis from the encircling terrace through pitiless stone eyes.

As Jude studied poor captive Artemis, goddess of the wild, a voice inside herself demanded, "What is a wolf child like you doing in this petrified forest ruled by a mob of icy granite drag queens?"

Jude walked quickly to Jasmine's house. Eying the stone gods supporting her balcony on their shoulders, she rang. The Portuguese bonne ushered Jude into the living room, where she perched on an uncomfortable Louis XVI armchair, beneath the dyspeptic gaze of Jasmine's crusader forebears.

When Jasmine finally appeared, wearing a black-satin robe patterned with magenta Art Nouveau lilies, Jude told her she was going back to New York.

"But you have just arrived," Jasmine said with a perplexed laugh. "We have been trying to help you feel welcome here. You do, I hope?"

The bonne carried in a black lacquer tray on which sat a coffeepot and some cups and saucers.

"You've been very kind."

"Then why do you wish to leave?" She set the cups on the saucers.

"I'm not really much use to you, Jasmine. You haven't published any of the books I've recommended."

"*Mais, doucement,* Jude. This will happen. You are learning. Life is long. Do not be so impatient." She carefully pushed the plunger on the coffeepot to force the grounds to the bottom. Then she filled the cups and handed one to Jude.

"And socially I'm as inept as a banjo picker in a string quartet."

"I warned you when you arrived, did I not, that you needed to learn to play?"

"I'm afraid I'm a slow learner."

"Ah." Jasmine nodded and fell silent, studying her long, mauve nails. Looking up, she said, "Simon phoned. He says you have fallen in love with someone rather inappropriate."

"Jesus Christ," snapped Jude. "Who does he think he is—my father?"

"He was very concerned about you."

"He's one to talk," muttered Jude. "His bed is as crowded as Jones Beach on the Fourth of July."

"He was worried that you might try to . . . harm yourself. I tried to phone you all weekend. I admit that I became worried myself.''

Jude said nothing as Jasmine watched her through narrowed eyes.

"This inappropriate someone does not return your love?'' she asked gently.

Jude nodded no.

"But you know that we at the office are all very fond of you?''

"Not anymore,'' said Jude, recalling her lunchtime seizure of *furia francese*.

Jasmine smiled. "Martine phoned just before you arrived. She said everyone was most impressed by what you said at lunch——not that they agree, *naturellement*.''

"*Naturellement pas.*''

"So why not stay? You will soon find another love. Martine, for example.''

Jude gave her a look. "I don't want another love. I want Olivia. But she doesn't want me. So I have to go. If I stayed, it would be a constant battle not to bother her.''

"Why must you be so stubborn in love?'' asked Jasmine. "People come and people go. Only desire remains.''

Jude did her imitation of an insouciant French shrug. "Maybe it's because I'm an Aries. Look, Jasmine, the point is that this just isn't my scene. Love as a martial art doesn't do it for me.''

Jasmine smiled. "Of course you must do as you think best,'' she said. "But I, for one, do not wish to lose you. Our friendship is just beginning. And who knows where it will take us?'' She gazed into Jude's eyes.

"Jasmine, just give it a rest.''

"Well, I can see that you are determined to suffer,'' she said, annoyed at Jude's refusal to carry the beat.

"I have a gift for it. I've done it all my life."

As Jude left, they kissed several times on alternate cheeks, like chickens pecking grain. They assured each other that they would write and phone and meet at book fairs just as before, but Jude wondered whether they really would. Sometimes absence made the heart grow fonder, but often what was out of sight was out of mind.

At the travel agency down the street Jude asked a handsome young man in a navy-blue uniform for a plane ticket to New York.

"But of course, madame," he said with a dazzling smile. "A plane to New York. And when do you wish to go?"

"I can go anytime. When are the flights?" She had offered to stay until Jasmine could find her replacement, but Jasmine said she'd invented the job for Jude and wouldn't be looking for someone else. Martine could complete the poetry project alone.

"Ah, but madame, there are flights from Paris to New York constantly. You have only to decide when you wish to go, and I will give you a ticket. Eh, voilà! You will be in New York City!"

"Oh," said Jude, brightening at the prospect of immediate escape. Soon she'd be on Simon's deck on the Cape, watching the waves pound the sand. She could imagine his hilarity over her haunting by the wraith of Ile St. Louis. They would do what they'd done for each other so often—laugh the pain away. "In that case, I'd like to go tomorrow afternoon."

"So," he said with his charming smile, "madame would like to go from Paris to New York tomorrow afternoon?"

"Yes, exactly. Paris to New York. Tomorrow afternoon." Suddenly, Jude was desperate to be back home, where she could cease to be the Other who had to be seduced and demolished lest she prove the bearer of new ways that might threaten to topple the old.

"Ah, but madame, I am so terribly sorry," he said with a delighted smile. "You cannot go from Paris to New York tomorrow afternoon, because there are no seats available until next Monday."

Jude burst out laughing.

He looked at her, alarmed to be alone in his office with a crackpot. "Something is the matter?"

"I'm almost sure you wouldn't understand."

THE FOLLOWING MONDAY, JUDE looked out the plane window at the massed columns of clouds below, papillae in the gullet of the sky. She reclined in her seat as drinks, meals, headsets, blankets, pillows, and duty-free purchases appeared and disappeared for her seatmate, a Vassar student returning from her junior year in Paris. Out of habit, Jude searched the wispy pillars of cloud for some trace of Molly or her mother, but she saw only a lacy pattern of ice crystals on the plane window.

As the plane plunged through the billowing white canyons, Jude suddenly understood that although those she had loved were largely illusions of her own making, the love that she had felt for them was real. Graveyard love was the love itself, not the specters who inspired it. And it belonged to her. It *was* her. It was the only thing about her that would survive if the plane crashed at that very moment. She was nothing more than a spark who yearned for the flame. And the fact of the yearning was proof of the flame.

As Jude watched her seatmate stand up and head down the aisle toward the toilet, she reflected that if Simon wouldn't give her back her editorial job she could always find work writing lyrics for Barry Manilow. A stewardess paused in the aisle to lean an elbow against the back of the seat in front of Jude. She had a braided twist of dark hair. A gold-and-scarlet scarf at her throat coordinated with her lipstick.

"But you have asked for nothing since we left Paris," she said. "Is there anything at all that I can do for you?" She studied Jude closely with her deep blue eyes.

Jude returned her gaze for a long moment. "Who knows?" she finally replied.

The woman raised one dark crescent eyebrow. *"Et pourquoi pas?"* she murmured, the ghost of a smile playing around the corners of her lips.

ACKNOWLEDGMENTS

I am very grateful to my editor Carole DeSanti, my copy editor Carol Edwards, my publisher Elaine Koster, and my agent Gloria Loomis, for their invaluable assistance on this book. Many thanks also to my daughter Sara Alther, who, as she says, "has been in this writing thing with you from the beginning." To Francoise Gilot, for guided tours of Paris and important insights into the creative process. To Jan Hokenson, for the use of her room with The View in Montmartre. To Carey Kaplan, for her gift for titles and her incisive critiques of more drafts than she probably cares to remember. To Max and Sissy Strauss, for furthering my opera education. To Jody Crosby, Sandra Norton, Andy Senesac, Christine Tissot, Vicky Wilson, and Evan Zimroth, for careful readings and useful suggestions.